MISS MASON'S SECRET BARON

The Troublemakers Trilogy
Book 2

by

Addy Du Lac

ARE YOU SIGNED UP FOR DRAGONBLADE'S BLOG?

You'll get the latest news and information on exclusive giveaways, exclusive excerpts, coming releases, sales, free books, cover reveals and more.

Check out our complete list of authors, too!

No spam, no junk. That's a promise!

Sign Up Here

www.dragonbladepublishing.com

Dearest Reader;

Thank you for your support of a small press. At Dragonblade Publishing, we strive to bring you the highest quality Historical Romance from some of the best authors in the business. Without your support, there is no 'us', so we sincerely hope you adore these stories and find some new favorite authors along the way.

Happy Reading!

CEO, Dragonblade Publishing

Dedication

To my village, thank you for always having my back and loving me through all disappearances and anti-social behaviors.

To Kiri, thanks for the insight.

For Tori, here's your man!

PROLOGUE

Miss Pollitt's School for Young Ladies,
Hertfordshire, 1847

FREEDOM WAS SO close for Regina.

A few hundred feet ahead was her school, an unexpected sanctuary from her mother's expectations and her responsibility as a role model to her little sister. This school meant a chance to be a young girl with her friends. She could see them now, Adelaide and Elodia, standing just outside the school waiting for her to be released from her mother's clutches. But there was no way her mother would allow her daughter out of their carriage without a few warnings and instructions.

"Make sure to behave well," Mrs. Madhavi Mason repeated to Regina as she brushed an errant curl back from her forehead. "Remember you are here to make connections with other daughters of the ton."

"Yes aai," Regina replied.

"You have to behave like they do, or you will not be able to fulfill your role of baroness when the time comes."

That godforsaken role. The noose her parents tied to lift her prospects was, in fact, choking the life out of her. Seventeen and her future already decided. What on earth would she do among a class of people who didn't even believe she had the right to be wealthy let alone entitled? How would she survive it? What would decades of that torture do to her? The prospect of a life in an illustrious golden cage, bereft of hope or kindness, filled her with dread.

"And don't go out in the sun! You are getting darker and darker."

That advice had her struggling not to roll her eyes. "Yes *aai*."

As if the ton would like her better with lighter brown skin. As if it would make her more acceptable in their eyes.

"Don't look at me like that. We made you a good match, but barons don't like girls with dark skin, Regina."

It was always "Regina" with her mother, now. Not her given name, Rajani. Not since her father had struck a deal with a baron and moved their small family from Bombay to England when she was fourteen. From then on she was a baroness in training and a baroness couldn't have a name like Rajani. It was strange the first time she'd been introduced as Regina. Now it was instinctive. Rajani had been left behind in India. Regina was who she would need to be from now on. Regina, for Queen Victoria. The queen regent. The figurehead of the empire devouring her native land state by state.

There was only one place where her name didn't hurt. Elodia and Ada had taken to calling her 'Gigi'. They were the first to give her that name and Regina hadn't objected. It was the only name that fit her at this point. Halfway between Regina and Rajani. Part way between England and India, just as she was.

"Then I hope you match me to a French man aai." She was sick to death of that marriage contract, and she wasn't even engaged yet. Technically. She'd been party to the legal contract since she was thirteen, but the bans had yet to be read. The obsession of her marrying into the nobility had been a constant drumbeat in her life. A beat that was only silenced by the laughter of her friends. For now, she could be herself with Ada and Elodia. She could leave that ominous future where it was for a year or two.

Her mother frowned at her and shook her head, but just as she opened her mouth to say more, her father interjected.

"My dear," he said with his blue eyes twinkling, "I think it's time for Regina to go." He opened the carriage door and ordered the porter to take her trunk down.

"Make sure to practice your dancing," her mother instructed as tears began to flood the dark eyes she'd given to Regina.

"I will." A dull ache pulsed to life in her chest and throat. She wouldn't miss the nagging or the suffocating weight of expectation, but there was nothing like her mother's warmth. For all her mother's ambition, Regina had never doubted her love.

"Stay away from those girls who bully you."

Regina took her hand and smiled thinking of Elodia and Ada. "I told you it's not like before. I have friends now aai. I'm not alone anymore."

"Mājhē badaka," she paused and touched her cheek gently.

Her duckling. She'd been calling her that since before Regina could remember. "I love you too *aai*," she said before leaning in to embrace her, breathing in her scent of cardamom and jasmine. Then she leaned down to touch her mother's feet and felt that gentle hand pass over her head to give her blessing. "I'll write to you and baba."

"Don't forget Lillian. She misses you."

Regina smiled at the thought of her little sister. She was a sweet little sprite who wanted nothing more than to attach herself to Regina at all times. "I will be sure to send her something as well."

"You have the anarsa?"

"Yes aai," she hopped down from the carriage, turning to catch one last glimpse of her mother's tearful face before shutting the carriage door and turning to face her father.

He took one look at her and smiled fondly. "She'll be fine. She just hates having you so far away."

"Whereas you can't wait to see me leave," she replied taking his arm and leaning against his firm shoulder as he walked her to the front entrance.

He was a cheerful man of average height and build, with bright eyes, pale freckled skin, and light brown hair. He was always ready with a cuddle or a kind word for his family, but that kindness carried a spine of steel.

"I know, my *choti rani*," he replied wryly, kissing the thick dark curls that her maid had wrestled into a low bun. "They need protecting from you not the other way around."

He always called her that. *Choti rani*, his 'little queen'. He always joked that he'd known her mother had chosen the correct name for her when he noticed her love of swords. Most girls her age had wanted to be Guinivere caught between a good king and a devoted knight. Regina wanted to be Rudrama Devi, the warrior queen of Kakatiya. Or Rajmata Ahilyabai and Maharani Tarabai, warrior queens of the former Maratha Empire.

"I'm going to take that as a compliment."

"As you should, also I have something for you."

She glanced up at him in excitement as she recalled what she'd asked him for. "You got it?"

"Just yesterday." He replied, handing her a slim twelve-inch-long box.

She let out an undignified squeal as she snatched it out of his hands.

"Shh, you want your mother to get suspicious?" he hissed, glancing over his shoulder at the carriage.

"Don't look at her," she said jerking his arm, "now she knows we are colluding."

He wrinkled his nose at her, and she grinned before kissing his whiskered cheek. "Thank you, *baba*."

"Don't get in trouble with those. If they are confiscated and shown to your mother, I can no longer help you."

"Yes, *baba*." He always allowed her more than her mother did, but only on the condition that it remained a secret. Regina knew from experience that Colonel Mason wasn't prepared to risk his happy marriage for anything or anyone, not even his children.

"This marriage…" he continued.

"Oh lord not you as well," she grumbled. If she never heard another word about this marriage for the rest of her life it would be too soon.

"Regina." The note of steel in his voice was unusual and indicated that she was speaking to her mother's husband, not simply her father. "This marriage is important to both your mother and me. We have a rare opportunity to see our daughter break a barrier we have never managed ourselves. You are fulfilling a dream we never got to. It isn't a game."

"I know, *baba*," she murmured.

Marriage to her father had given her mother a happy life, but even marriage to a white British officer had given little in the way of protection from the cruel remarks of the ton. There would never be perfect protection from that, but people would exercise more caution snubbing the mother of a baroness than the wife of an officer and a gentleman.

"Listen to your mother, she is trying to ensure your success."

Success. Success would mean abandonment to smug cold faces and humiliation. Public regard and private desolation. "Yes, baba," she muttered.

He nodded and kissed her forehead firmly. "Now be a good girl, and if you can't be good—"

"Be careful," she finished.

He grinned broadly, nodding toward the school building, "Off with you."

She nodded and turned away, clutching the box in her hands. Marriage wasn't worth thinking about anymore. For the next six months, she didn't have to think about anything but the world within the confines of the gray brick building looming before her. She caught sight of Elodia and Ada waving enthusiastically at her, as if she could miss the Chinese and African girls in a sea of white English ones. With a smile, she ran towards them until she was caught in a tight embrace full of laughter. This was her sanctuary. No matter what happened, she would always fight to keep this.

"You're here!" Ada said bouncing with excitement.

"I thought she'd never let me leave, it's always a near thing."

"She loves you," Ellie pulled back, rubbing a gloved hand up and down her back briskly.

Regina rolled her eyes, "I know. Honestly, I don't know what I'd do without her. But it's school. Hardly a voyage into terra incognita."

"Gigi," Elodia shook her head with a laugh.

"She'll be fine. My father will coddle her all the way home, and she has my little sister to occupy her." She glanced over her shoulder to check for her parents' carriage and noted it was missing. "I have something for us," she said, turning to face them again.

"What?" Ada asked.

"Let's go to our rooms first."

"What is it, Gigi?" Ellie asked.

She opened the box and showed them three ten-inch hairpins with silver filigreed tops. "Papa had these made for me, for us."

Ada's eyes widened with delight as she ran a finger over one engraved top. "Is that an 'a'?" she asked, peering carefully.

"Our initials are hidden in the pattern."

Ellie reached in and took one out, turning it over in her hands. "Is this…" her voice trailed off as she pulled on the handle, revealing the wickedly sharp blade hidden in the makeshift scabbard.

"Oh, my goodness," Ada breathed out as her eyes widened in excitement.

"Ladies should always have protection," Regina said, echoing a sentiment she'd heard from her father a thousand times. He'd said it when he taught her to shoot, when he'd taken her fencing, and when he'd taught her the basics of wrestling. *With or without a weapon, a lady should never be without protection.*

"They are perfect," Ellie said with a mischievous grin, snapping the blade back into its hiding place.

CHAPTER ONE

Gatwich Place, Mayfair, London
June 1852

S HE WAS TIRED of waiting. This glittering, exclusive event hosted by Lady Trawley was meant to unofficially announce her engagement to her fiancé, The Baron Starkley. It would mark the beginning of the end of her autonomy, the first step into a life of privilege and desolation, and Regina had spent it flanked by her parents, watching couples swirl before her in a lukewarm room choked with the musk of exertion and the sickening sweetness of perfume. The frank stares and stilted smiles followed by almost discreet whispers were more insulting than a pointed finger. Didn't they find the pretense exhausting? She'd almost rather they behaved with an ounce of integrity and spoke up, so she didn't have to strain her ears to hear what they had to say.

She missed Elodia and Ada. They had always been able to lift her spirits even at the worst of times, but after their adventure involving Mr. Thompson, a stolen carriage, a kidnapped driver and a jaunt to Gretna Green, her parents had refused to let her out of their sight. Under her mother's insistence, and to Lillian's delight, her father had returned them to Kent a fortnight before Ada's delayed wedding reception, hosted by Ada's newly recovered brother, Mr. Richard Thornfield. Then Ada had gone on honeymoon with Mr. Thompson.

Regina's mother had even banned contact until a few months ago. Her mother had only allowed the family to be in London because Regina's fiancé was expected back this season. If not for that, she would still be at their estate in Kent practicing her Bharatanatyam and Kathak dancing with her mother and Lillian or fencing and shooting with her father.

So, she was here, trotted out yet again for a social gathering she couldn't participate in to visibly await a man who would finally marry her and bestow a title. She knew she was destined to be a baroness, but the man to do the job was proving to be far more elusive. Her father, currently tapping his fingers restlessly on his arm, had taken the ingenious step of setting up the contract of marriage between her and the title of the Baron Starkley. It was unusual to be sure, but Mrs. Mason wanted a baroness for a daughter and Captain Mason was nothing if not a devoted husband.

That being said, Regina was entirely unsure if the Barony of Starkley wasn't cursed. First there had been Mr. Robert Starkley, the original baron in waiting under contract. He had gone on holiday to Italy and never returned due to an unfortunate run in with a signora or, rather, her husband. Then there had been his brother, Mr. Francis Starkley. He had elected to race a phaeton on the beach and broken his neck when Regina was nineteen.

Now there was Lord Reginald Starkley, cousin to the late Misters Starkley. He had been 'under contract' for at least three years now. Regina had never met Sir Reginald Starkley, but what she'd heard hadn't disposed her kindly towards him. All of them were only too willing to leave her waiting while they used a down payment of her dowry to revitalize their estate and fund their adventures, but none of them would be able to break the contract without reimbursing what they had spent with compounded interest.

Which meant that at some point before she died, one of them was going to have to marry her or forfeit upwards of eighty thousand pounds.

And counting.

She was meant to be Penelope to his Odysseus, Psyche to Eros. The devoted, chaste companion who patiently awaited his return and guarded his interests with an open loving heart. At this point, she felt more like Clytemnestra. The minute Lord Reginald set foot on English soil; she was tempted to strangle him in his bathwater. She wasn't even dreading the prospect of marriage anymore so long as it put an end to the interminable waiting. At least then she'd have something to do, even if it was putting up with a foppish buffoon and his offspring. She'd never be happy stuck among the nobility but at least she'd be certain she was a part of it. At least then she'd have a sure position.

She'd been a future baroness for so long it was starting to become a joke. No one knew how to treat her, and she didn't know how to see herself.

"How are you holding up, choti rani?" her father murmured, resting a hand on her lower back.

"I'm tired," she replied.

"Stand up straight, he could still come," her mother hissed, nudging her in the ribs.

"The guests stopped arriving over an hour ago, aai. If he was going to be here, he would already have come."

"A baroness doesn't slouch."

"When you find one, please be kind enough to let me know. She might appreciate the guidance." Regina replied, earning her a glare.

Her father cleared his throat. A warning that she was on thin ice. She glanced at her mother and noted the grip she had on her white gloved fingers, the downturn of her mouth she struggled to hide behind a mask of aloofness. She was nervous and disappointed. Perhaps embarrassed? Regina hooked her arm through her mother's and gave it a small squeeze. "I'm sorry, aai. I'm tired and it is utterly impossible to take an unpolluted breath in this room."

Mrs. Mason shook her head in response and patted Regina's hand gently, the only signal that she was forgiven. Her mother rarely smiled in London and never smiled when they left the house. The ton had never been kind to her, and Regina knew it had been precisely that treatment which drove every action her mother took when it came to her and her little sister Lillian. No one knew it better than Regina. She'd been subjected to the same behavior.

"Gigi!"

Regina looked up to see Elodia approaching her with a broad grin. Her father, the Viscount Melbroke, was just behind her, wearing his customary polite smile. She reached out her hand to take Elodia's and pulled her closer. "Ellie," she glanced at the viscount and sank into a curtsy. "Good evening, my lord."

"Good evening to you, Miss Mason," he turned to her parents. "Mrs. Mason, Captain."

"Good evening, Lord Melbroke," her father said. "Have you been here long?"

"About an hour. We only just got to this side of the room."

"Mr. Mason, may I steal Gigi for a turn about the room?" Ellie asked, hooking her arm through Regina's.

"Why?" Mrs. Mason asked. There was no teasing in her face or her voice.

"I haven't been able to speak to her for some time. I promise to bring her right back."

"Five minutes," she conceded, her dark eyes narrowing.

Elodia blinked at her twice before looking to Regina for help. Five minutes was hardly enough time for anything.

"Aai, it will take that long to go two steps in a room this crowded."

"Your point?" She stared Regina down, daring her to push the point.

Captain Mason laid a hand on his wife's shoulder, bent low and murmured in her ear. Elodia and Regina watched expectantly as she huffed in annoyance, pursed her mouth against a torrent of objections, and finally, blessedly, let out a sigh, closing her eyes. Regina glanced at the viscount who was staring pointedly at the ground with his eyebrows raised. Was he amused by her mother's clear distrust for anyone who wasn't Captain Mason?

It was true that her mother hadn't fully forgiven Regina for taking off with Ada and Elodia last summer to Gretna Green. She still inexplicably blamed Elodia more harshly than Ada or even Regina for that debacle despite Regina's assurances that it had in fact been as much her idea to go.

Mrs. Mason's dark eyes opened once more and fixed on Regina. "You come right back."

"Yes, aai."

"She's not dancing," she snapped out to Elodia who nodded fanatically.

"Understood." She slipped her arm around Regina's waist and drew her away along the wall of spectators towards the refreshments area. "Your mother is so terrifying."

"Yes, she is."

"What on earth did your father say to her?"

"I have no idea." It was the truth. Her father was a consummate diplomat handling them all deftly with minimum force. Her mother shouted at times and snapped, but Regina couldn't remember having ever heard her father raise his voice in her life.

"It's been so long since I've seen you, how have you been?"

"Well enough. We only just returned from Kent a month ago."

"I'm sorry for that."

Regina shook her head. Elodia and Ada had apologized profusely for landing her in hot water with her parents, as if they had dragged her kicking and screaming into the entire enterprise. "It was in the service of a friend, and I daresay the mission was a successful one."

"That is my thinking as well."

"How have you been?"

Elodia shrugged. "Well enough, I suppose. I've missed you dreadfully. I haven't been on my own in years and I find I have no taste for it."

"Have you not been able to attend assemblies?"

"No, I have. But my experience of them is not exactly favorable without you or Ada there."

"At least they don't stare and point fingers and whisper about you."

"Well, they don't point fingers at least," Elodia replied with a scoff. "In any event, my papa has agreed to help us."

"Us?"

"Yes. He is currently inviting you and your parents to enjoy our box at the theatre when we attend next week."

"Is he really?" Regina's eyes widened in shock. The viscount had always been cordial, but he'd never taken such explicit action to befriend her parents before this.

"It's the perfect plan I thought. I cannot withstand another season without your company, and your mother is anxious about your reputation and surely being seen as an open acquaintance of the Viscount Melbroke cannot be a bad thing."

"Of course it cannot! Ellie, you are a genius!"

Elodia winked at her. "'Like calls to like' as they say. So, you should be at the modiste a good deal more often seeing as I shall be inviting you to tea, dinner, the theatre, and whatever else I can manage."

"How did you get your father to agree to this?"

"I didn't. I think despite his complaints, he's grown used to both of you, and seeing me with friends. Without you I am… quite on my own." She smiled but there was little humor in it. "It's selfish perhaps. Ada is married now, and you will be soon as well. We won't be as inseparable as we once were."

"Oh, Ellie."

"It's alright. It's only that what little time we have, I won't want to be without you both."

"I understand. But I can assure you that no husband would be able to replace a friend such as yourself. And you will have the both of us to help you find the most gentle and loving of husbands, if it is what you wish."

"I don't know that it is possible for me to have the sort of man I would wish. But I should be glad of your company either way." Elodia looked around the room and exhaled. "There is a lovely garden here. Why don't I fetch us some lemonade and meet you out there?"

"That sounds perfect, Ellie."

SHE'S HERE. LEO watched from his post at the fringes of the ballroom as Miss Mason observed the dancers. She was a friend of Adelaide's, he knew, but in his mind, she was primarily the captain's daughter with the terrifying Marathi mother. Both Captain Mason and his wife were present, no doubt keeping a very close watch on their bold daughter.

Leo never forgot a face, especially when it belonged to a nosey woman who had glimpsed more of him than he was comfortable with while he was enjoying a sea bath on his last day at Brighton. He'd just wrapped up a case of missing jewelry and had elected to spend one more day at the seaside before returning to London. While he was pulling on his clothes, he'd spotted the top of a purple bonnet through the grass. Then, when it was clear he'd spotted the pervert, he saw a brown faced girl with wide dark eyes scamper away as the sunlight glinted relentlessly on some metal momentarily blinding him.

He hadn't expected to then see her again at Kings Cross Station when he'd arrived to greet Basil, who was now married to Ada. The glare had been a metal applique of flowers along the inner brim of her bonnet. A small detail, possibly missed with the way she'd styled the rest of her travel costume, but the design had glinted in the same way as she emerged from the train. In that moment, he knew it was her. Considering what he now knew of Ada's friends; however, he couldn't exactly be shocked that she had befriended a girl who stole peeks at innocent men while they were sea bathing. Perhaps it had been because he recognized her instantly last year at Kings Cross via her bonnet. Seeing the glimpse of her face by the ocean hadn't prepared him for the full effect of her when she was standing in front of him with her small hand in his.

Nothing had prepared him for the frankness of her stare. Leo had never been coddled. From the army to Scotland Yard and now as a private investigator, he'd made his way through the world with blood, sweat, tears and intellect. He faced his problems, found a way to manage them, and moved forward. It was inexplicable the effect that a bold stare from a young woman had had on him. The only word that came to mind to describe her was lush. From her plump mouth, bounteous midnight curls and heart shaped face to the full curves of her body. She brought to mind the carvings of women he'd seen on the Hindu temples in Khajuraho, while he'd been stationed in India. But those carvings didn't watch him with open curiosity and interest or have the whistle of a dock worker.

Miss Regina Mason was no doubt a virtuous young woman but there was nothing demure about her. She may have been able to fool the people in the room as she stood between her parents in an elegant and fashionable yellow silk gown, but he'd already seen more of what she was capable of.

"She's a pretty one," a voice came from his left. He glanced in that direction and saw an old woman hovering just inside the doorway. Her silvery hair was piled on top of her head, her face creased with countless lines. Her ice blue eyes were fixed on him with rueful amusement.

"Beg your pardon?" he asked, unsure whether or not he was annoyed yet.

"The girl in yellow. She is the one you are watching is she not?"

She was old but her eyes were sharp. Part of him was annoyed at being caught by this crone gawping at the young woman. He wasn't there to watch Miss Mason, after all. He was there to track down Roger Henry, a thief known for infiltrating houses while pretending to be a servant before making off with jewels. "Thank you for weighing in."

"Are you a guest?"

Now he was annoyed. "Are you the host?" he asked, already knowing the answer.

"I am not."

"Then I don't believe it's any of your concern."

He expected her to huff and call a servant. Instead, she smiled as if amused. "What is your name?"

"What is yours?"

"Mrs. Theodosia Burghley-Harrison," she said.

The reason he was here at this overcrowded event shifted past a guest and caught Leo's eye. *There you are.* "Good."

"I don't have yours."

"I haven't said it." He looked her over once more before strolling away. "Good evening Mrs. Burghley-Harrison," he called over his shoulder. Personally, Leo didn't care if some rich assholes lost a few insured jewels they could easily replace, but Mr. Henry had a nasty habit of assaulting house maids as well and that was something he couldn't stand for. So, when he was hired by Sir Archibald Cox to track him down and get him behind bars, Leo took the job. The pay didn't hurt either.

So far, he'd followed his trail across London, and everything pointed to him striking tonight at Lady Trawley's ball. So, Leo got his hands on a footman's uniform and laid low banking on the assumption that Lady Trawley wouldn't notice another black footman.

He was correct. The woman had looked him dead in his face and called him by some other poor sod's name. It wasn't the first time Leo had masqueraded as a footman, but it was always nice to be reminded that he'd made the right choice opting for the military. His temperament was not made for servitude.

Like a spectre, Henry glided about with one tray of drinks in his hand. No doubt collecting billfolds and necklaces as he went before moving further inside. Henry was cunning and cool headed, but he was greedy. Trying to catch him in the house during an event would only draw attention and spook him. Far better to catch him on his way out. Henry liked to leave before the event was over, before the servants were all needed to clean up the mess of over a hundred aristocrats. He would try to slink out through the back garden if his previous jobs were any indication.

Leo started moving across the stone terrace until he reached what seemed like a refreshments room for exhausted guests. The french doors opened out to the stairs. Quietly Leo slipped down the stone staircase and hid near a row of manicured trees. When Henry came, he would be ready.

A few moments later he heard footsteps coming. He planted his feet and waited, shoulders relaxed and hands ready. Then the footsteps stopped. He heard a woman's voice. It was familiar although he couldn't place its owner. Then he heard Henry. That voice, at least, he'd heard enough to recognize it, and he knew what it could mean for the woman with him. He couldn't stand there and wait for Henry to come to him. It would cost him the tactical advantage but if he hurt that young woman, he wouldn't be able to face himself.

As Henry rounded the corner, he heard a grunt and saw two feet go flying up into the air before a loud dull thud sounded in the night air. The sight that greeted him was a surprise but not overly shocking. Kneeling on Henry's shoulder, pinning one arm on his back was Miss Mason. One of her curls had slipped from her pins and now floated on the night breeze as she pursed her lips and leaned more of her weight onto the thief.

"Miss Mason," Leo called, and she looked up at the sound of his voice, her face brightening with a cheerful smile. Far too cheerful for what she had just done.

"It is Mr. Kingston, isn't it?" she asked.

"It is."

Her eyes swept up and down his body. "Nice uniform. I assume you haven't elected to switch professions, so you must be here on business?"

"Mmm," he nodded at Henry. "You are currently kneeling on it."

"Oh!" she looked down at the man she had pinned to the grass. "I was going to wait until Ellie arrived and have her call for my father."

"Very clever."

"But as you are here, I suppose I'll leave him to you."

"Much obliged." He gestured to her to move. Henry, seeing a chance to escape, tried to stand up. Leo delivered a swift kick to his ribs that sent him tumbling back down. Then he delivered a sharp blow to the back of his head that made him go limp.

"Whenever I try to do that, it never works," Miss Mason said, watching with fascination.

Did she have more than one occasion to knock men out? "I suppose it comes down to practice. You must get the precise spot with the correct amount of force."

"I suppose you're correct."

"You manage well enough without it, however. I didn't expect to see him on the ground when I heard you call out."

"Yes well, he was being impertinent."

"Who taught you to flip men over like that?"

"My father. He believes that a lady should always have a weapon."

"Even when it's her."

"Oh, especially then. I've been out of practice though. Took me two tries to get him over."

"Too busy kidnapping eligible gentlemen?"

"Mr. Thompson was an aberration due to an extreme circumstance. You are quite safe, I promise you."

"I am relieved to hear it." He replied, wondering when exactly he'd become an eligible gentleman in her eyes.

"For my sake or your own?"

Leo chuckled softly shaking his head. She was truly a delight, even if he had to admit she was capable of far more than he'd imagined previously. "You would have had a difficult time of it,

Miss Mason."

Slowly she lifted one eyebrow and tilted her head. "Underestimating your opponent? Not at all up to your usual standard, Mr. Kingston."

She was an adorable mix of earnest and audacious. It was far too intriguing.

"Gigi, your—oh, Mr. Kingston. Good evening," Miss Hawthorne paused halfway down the stairs watching them both before glancing down at the unconscious man on the ground. "Who is that?"

"Business," Miss Mason replied, and Leo chuckled.

"I'll leave you ladies to it." He bent down and rolled Henry onto his back before hoisting him upright and tossing his limp body onto his shoulder. Then he rose to his feet and turned to face the two young ladies watching him.

"Good evening, Miss Mason, Miss Hawthorne,"

"Good evening, Mr. Kingston," Miss Mason said.

"Gigi, your mother has been looking for you."

"Oh lord, has it been too long?"

"No, she and your father are leaving, but they can't find you."

Regina gathered her skirts and rushed up the stairs, back into the refreshment room. Elodia followed suit. "Are they still in the ballroom, Ellie?"

"No, they are in the foyer."

It was impossible not to notice the looks sent her way as she hurried past rows of gossiping socialites.

Bad luck.

At least they'll be gone.

Nothing is truly certain yet.

The snippets of conversation floated past her ears. One pointed look nearly stopped her in her tracks, but Ellie's tug on her arm kept her moving. Was it something she'd done? Had they found out she had been speaking to Mr. Kingston? Were they gossiping about her because she was alone with him?

The shock of seeing him so unexpectedly had wiped every thought of what she should have been doing clear out of her head. Her memory of how handsome he was had not served her at all. His rich brown skin, a few shades lighter than hers, his heart shaped face and high cheekbones. Those full lips that smiled slowly, as if his amusement grew in each passing moment. He was so tall and broad with that rich deep voice.

And his eyes, those hazel brown eyes had sparkled with admiration and amusement and all she could think was how much nicer he was than she'd expected. He could have dismissed her out of hand or scolded her for handling that ruffian in her own way, but instead he'd taken it in his stride and thanked her.

But now a moment of mental distraction had resulted in a scandal that she couldn't explain to her family. No matter what she felt, or didn't feel personally for Lord Reginald, she never wanted to give the English ton another reason to slight her mother or embarrass her father. It was another lesson; the ton would always be looking for a way to remind their family of where they ought to be. Only by doing her part could Regina ensure that her mother never had to bow her head as a matter of course in this country. She just had to remember what was at risk instead of what it felt like to be noticed by a man like Leo Kingston. She could do it. She *would* do it.

She caught sight of her parents and moved through the crowd narrowly dodging elbows and careless hands. It was the blessing and curse of her height. While she certainly wasn't diminutive, she was short enough to move through a crowd by making use of the smallest spaces. Which also meant people didn't see her until it was too late. Her mother was standing perfectly still, her eyes fixed on the floor and her father was beside her, his arms crossed over his torso. Only her knowledge of them had her eyes drifting to where she knew his hidden hand held onto her mother's arm. A private show of solidarity and love for a woman who could never relax enough to smile in society.

When she reached them, her father shifted his weight taking a deep breath and nodding in her direction but the tense expression on his face didn't shift. Her mother exhaled and pursed her lips.

"Aai, whatever you have heard—"

"It is time to leave," she interrupted. "Your baba has called for the carriage."

"I thought we were waiting for Lord Starkley," Regina replied. Then her mother uttered a sentence in Marathi. Three words that were growing harder and harder to hear.

He is dead.

CHAPTER TWO

S OMEONE WAS FOLLOWING him. Leo didn't know who they were, and they clearly had no idea who the fuck he was. When he first noticed them, he was alarmed. He had inevitably rubbed many people the wrong way either by virtue of his work or his race and disposition. Sometimes it was all three, but he made no apologies for any of them. If his calculations were correct, they'd picked him up shortly after he'd left Sir Archibald Cox's residence, reward in hand.

Were they thieves? The pay was substantial enough to warrant it, but it would also require them to know the amount in question. They also would have to know his business with Sir Archibald. Business that he had been very clear about keeping private, lest anyone associate the gentleman with the likes of Leo or become aware that he had been the victim of a criminal.

An inside job then. Perhaps Sir Archibald was thinking twice about having to pay a black man two hundred pounds to do what Scotland Yard hadn't managed. It wouldn't be the first time a former client had tried to double cross him after he'd collected his fee. Normally they waited a few days before trying it knowing he had the capability to link it to them.

Sir Archibald was prejudiced enough, but was he stupid enough? Leo wasn't certain. Could it be a connection to Roger Henry perhaps? It had taken a day or so to find the stolen jewels and connect them to Henry. Were these men connected to the buyers Henry intended to sell the loot to? Angry associates now looking for their pound of flesh where they could find it? Or were they closer to home? Leo had managed to find a connection between Donald Trent and Richard's uncle, Simon Thornfield. The man hadn't tried anything else since that audacious scheme, but perhaps he'd only just realized his part in Richard's escape. Perhaps he'd grown tired of waiting.

Leo was more annoyed than anything. He wanted his supper and his bed. He wanted to get home so his mother could stop worrying. The last thing he needed was two idiots testing his patience after nightfall. As it was, he would need to lose them or risk leading them back to his home. He didn't go out of his way to cause trouble, but life experience had taught him that changing course didn't mean he could avoid it indefinitely. Especially when the trouble had made a point of coming to him. Again.

He cut down a short alley and increased his pace until he cleared the corner. Then he waited for the hurried footsteps of the two jackasses who were now making him late for dinner. Within minutes he heard them, hurried but undecided the cadence swift and yet faltering every few paces. They were searching the alley for him. He pulled his pen knife from his coat pocket and waited, his hand steady on the ivory handle. As soon as the first one came around the corner, he struck. He slammed the heel of his hand into the man's sternum sending him to his knees gasping before delivering a swift kick to his face. Then, dodging a fist, he turned to the next assailant.

He saw the glint of the pistol just in time to grab the man's wrist and twist it behind his back, slamming him face first into the filthy stone wall. The pistol clattered to the ground, and he kicked it away from the man currently heaving, curled up like an infant. He pressed the blade to the neck of the man he had pinned.

"It's rude to follow people without a proper introduction," he said noting the weight of the broadcloth coat the man wore, the smell of lavender soap. Whoever these men were, they weren't exactly working class. Which meant that whoever had hired them was decidedly above them.

"Wait, you don't understand," the man said raising his free hand in supplication. Definitely not a threat.

"No, *you* don't. That's your first problem."

"We mean you no harm."

"Who are 'we' precisely?" he asked.

"John and Patrick Locke."

"Which one are you?" he asked.

"John."

Which made the one crawling to his feet Patrick. Easy enough.

"We are private investigators like yourself."

"I beg to differ."

"I swear we are," he insisted trying to turn around.

Leo tightened his grip on the man's wrist and leaned in, keeping him pinned in place. "You aren't like me. You've been following me since I caught a hackney in Mayfair."

"No, we weren't," Patrick gasped rubbing his chest where Leo knew a bruise was forming.

"Did you even notice I've been leading you in circles on foot for twenty minutes now?"

John sighed in defeat. "Let me reach into my pocket."

"Do you want me to break your arm?"

"Don't," Patrick wheezed holding out a card to Leo.

Leo stared at him for a long moment before lowering his knife and taking the card.

"Why are you following me?" he asked sliding it into his pocket. Reading it now was a fool's errand.

"We only meant to verify your identity."

"My identity? You need a pistol for that?"

"You attacked my colleague."

"You and your colleague have been following me all evening without attempting to disclose yourself or your business."

"I conceded the point. Now will you please release my arm."

He had half a mind to break his arm anyway, but he was

curious. And he already knew he could take both of them without trouble. "Anything funny and you get what you get."

"Understood."

Leo released his hold on John's arm and took a step back, looking him up and down. Honestly it was embarrassing. The man had followed him to a wrong side of town looking like he'd just come from his club. Didn't they know how to blend into their surroundings at all?

"Thank you," he turned around and rubbed his wrist. "Now are you Leopold Kingston, son of William and Naomi Kingston?"

"I am."

He nodded. "Your presence has been requested by our employer. Be at this location on Thursday for tea." He handed Leo a neatly folded envelope. "That's at four—"

"I know what time tea is," Leo said pocketing the envelope and calling card before walking away. He didn't head home directly. No matter what they said, he wouldn't head that way until he was certain he wasn't being followed.

Ten minutes later, with no tail in sight, he turned his path two blocks down to the modest three-bedroom house he shared with his mother. It had been his home his entire life, had passed from father to son for at least three generations in the Kingston family. The outside was stark grey stone, and the sidewalk wasn't perfectly even, but Leo knew that inside would be warm and redolent of whatever meal his mother had pulled together with their cook. Maybe a stew.

She'd never trusted anyone but herself to feed her family. The fact that she had taken a step back to supervising only was a miracle in itself.

He had barely managed to get his key in the lock before the door swung open to reveal his mother, glowering at him. He took a deep breath and smiled. "Good evening, mother."

"So, you still know to come home?"

"I am late tonight. I'm sorry. I was unavoidably detained."

She squinted at him, no doubt weighing whether she was

going to believe him.

"Am I still welcome here, or shall I rely on the kindness of strangers?"

She pursed her lips in annoyance and stepped back allowing him to enter. He tucked his key into his trouser pocket, and shut the door firmly behind him, flipping the deadbolt.

"When was the last time you heard from Richard?"

"A few days ago. I even have an invitation from him to the theatre in a week or so. He's fine."

She huffed but said nothing more. She didn't need to, Leo already knew. *That boy worries me.* It was as if she was half expecting him to go missing again. It was a long-standing joke that she enjoyed Richard more than he or Basil. Leo was her son, but Richard was her baby. He was obnoxiously charming when he wanted to be, all deference, wit and consideration.

"Have you already eaten?" he asked, hoping to distract her from her worries.

"It would serve you right if I had," she snapped with a half-hearted glare.

"Mother." He took her hand as she passed him, halting her progress until she turned to look at him. "I was detained. I knew you were waiting. I wouldn't have delayed without a good reason."

She nodded. "That gentleman kept you?"

"No. Two others. They were tailing me. I couldn't come straight home as I planned."

"Why were they following you?"

"No idea. They asked about father."

She turned to him fully now, suspicion and alarm in her eyes. "What did they want with him?"

"Nothing. It appears they were trying to verify my parentage."

"To what purpose?"

"I do not know. I have an appointment to find out in a few days."

She nodded again and rubbed his arm. "Are you hungry?"

"Starving."

She gave him a small smile. "Come eat then. I told them to keep it for you." She wasn't meeting his eyes now. She was nervous. He shouldn't have said anything until he knew the truth.

Number 12, Mayfair, London

DEAD.

It had been two days since that ball. Two days since she'd realized that her fiancé had again been called to his maker. Regina didn't know how to feel about the fact that she was yet again left twisting in the wind by fate. When she was eighteen it had felt like a stay of execution. When she had turned twenty it had been a deferment. Now, it just felt like a waste of her time.

Whenever this happened, she never knew what to do. This time was no exception. Her parents never knew what to say to her, and she could never quite manage to control her face in their presence. So, she'd elected to stay in her room for the time being.

The door opened and she heard the patter of feet. From her spot at her window, she could see her sister's dark hair before she rounded her bed.

"Tāī," Lillian called out.

"Lilli," Regina replied watching fondly as she trotted up to her. Lillian was a bright-eyed, eight-year-old bundle of joy who never walked when she could run. "What are you up to?" she asked in English. Lillian hadn't been allowed to learn Marathi beyond the honorifics used within their family. Yet another casualty of their mother's mission to conform.

"Are you sad?"

"Why do you ask?"

"Aai and baba said your baron is gone."

"Were you listening at doors again?" she glared at her playfully.

"Is he dead again?"

It should have been a ridiculous question, but the frequency with which she had been asked it only served to encapsulate the farce her life had become. "Yes Lilli, he is dead. Again."

She ran her small brown hand over Regina's arm in an innocent attempt to comfort her. "Are you sad?"

"A little." It wasn't a lie exactly. She was sad for herself mostly, for yet another year wasted. She felt some pity for another life cut short. Mostly what she felt was frustration at the reality that her life was once again on hold.

"Did you like him?"

"I never met him." She'd never managed to meet any of them. She wondered if she would have felt more if she had managed to see their faces at least.

"Who do you have to marry now?"

"His replacement. Whoever he is."

Lillian reached out and wrapped her arms around Regina in an awkward but heartfelt embrace. "Do you want to be a baroness?"

No. "It would give me a good deal more power."

"Like a princess?"

"Yes. And then you would be the sister of a baroness. Someday you will be the aunt of a baron. That will give you a blood tie to the nobility which protects you and aai and baba. Does that make sense?" Lillian didn't need to know the cruel reality of what her marriage would be or bear the weight of her sister's choice.

"Will you live in a castle?"

"I have no idea. Perhaps I should have checked that before I agreed to marry the man." She tickled her and Lillian grinned, squirming away from her fingers.

"I would want to live in a castle," she said taking Regina's hand.

"I'm sure you will, sweetheart."

Footsteps sounded in the hallway and they both looked up to see their mother in the doorway.

"Lilli, your governess is looking for you."

"Yes, aai," she scampered away, shooting a quick look at Regina.

Lillian's presence in London during the season was the result of a month's long campaign involving perfect behavior on Lillian's part and a two-pronged approach from Regina and her father. Her ability to stay in London during the season would depend entirely on her capacity to stay in their mother's good graces.

"Your friend, the wild one, is here with the Viscount."

"Ellie and her father are here?"

She nodded. "Come down at once." She cast a sharp eye over Regina's blue muslin gown before leaving the room with Regina in tow.

"Ellie isn't so wild, aai," Regina said taking her mother's arm as they walked down the stairs. Her mother spared her a sardonic glance but made no reply.

"I believe they mean to invite us to something."

"That is good is it not?"

"It cannot hurt," she said with a shrug. A tepid endorsement if ever there was one.

"Have you heard anything about—"

"No, nothing."

And from that sharp tone, she didn't want to discuss it. So, Regina simply patted her arm and continued down the stairs silently, hoping her trepidation didn't show. Would they consider letting her out of the engagement? After so many years with no result, surely they had grown wary of the entire affair. Not to mention the Barony of Starkley clearly had some sort of curse on it. How else could they explain such an inexplicable run of bad luck?

As they entered the sitting room, Elodia shot to her feet and headed towards Regina with her hands outstretched. "Gigi!"

Regina took her hands and nodded to her father, the viscount, who was watching his daughter with obvious amusement.

"Good afternoon, Miss Mason."

"Good afternoon, my lord."

"My daughter and I have come to issue an invitation to share our box at the opera this Saturday."

"How wonderful." A pointed look passed between her and Ellie. Privacy. "Aai, may Ellie and I take a turn about the garden?"

"Ten minutes, the viscount has more business than us today."

"Yes, aai," she gave them all a quick curtsy before whisking Elodia out of the room and down the main corridor to the back garden.

"It is the latest by Verdi, based off a book written by Alexandre Dumas. So, feel free to cry without any comments from witnesses."

"How very kind of you to take my current emotional state into account."

"I am nothing if not the soul of consideration," Elodia joked. "How are you, truly?"

"A bit annoyed. He is the third one to die before completing his end of the bargain and I'm on to the fourth with no real assurance history will not repeat itself. I can neither move forward nor reverse course. It's all a mess."

"I'm sorry."

"You don't suppose they are doing it on purpose?"

Elodia pursed her lips and shook her head, her eyes sparkling with repressed laughter.

"It's that or the sins of their ancestors are catching up with them." The idea of it being pure happenstance was too ridiculous to contemplate.

"I like the idea of our ancestors protecting you from the progeny of their enemies."

"Mmm."

"What was Mr. Kingston doing at the ball?" Elodia asked.

"Working. He was tracking down the gentleman who was on the ground."

"Who was he, Gigi?"

"I have no idea."

"I forgot how handsome he was," Elodia said wrinkling her nose.

"Oh?" Regina hadn't, that was for damn certain.

"Oh, please, Gigi. I know you are engaged but you can't have missed how attractive he is."

It was true. Leo Kingston was a man worthy of the name. A gentleman of such capability and intelligence with eyes like her father's whiskey and the most beautifully proportioned face Regina had ever seen. A man with a tall frame and powerful body who knew when to be still and how to act. It was impossible not to notice him.

The only man she'd ever met who could compare was perhaps Ada's brother, Mr. Thornfield. But while Mr. Thornfield had always been kind and personable with them, there was a detachment in his very nature which Regina had always found intimidating, as if all the warmth in him was reserved for Ada.

Mr. Kingston was discreet to be sure and poised with the bearing of a warrior prince, but instead of detachment, there was awareness. It made his gaze almost too direct, too focused, but to Regina it made her feel seen. From the first time she met him at King's Cross, Regina had been struck by how different it felt to have his gaze on her. When that slow appreciative smile slipped over his face, lighting his eyes from within, she hadn't felt leered at or objectified. A giddy rush had swept through her, and her heart began to thump strangely in her chest. It wasn't faster but deeper somehow, or louder.

"Gigi?"

She looked at Ellie with wide eyes as she noted the expectant look on her face.

"Were you not listening to me?"

Oh, hell. What had she been saying? "I'm sorry. I haven't been able to concentrate lately." It was dangerous to think of him considering the effect he had on her. It was pointless torture to allow her mind to dwell on the impossible when she did not have the luxury of romance.

"Because of your fiancé?"

She wasn't going to admit to where her mind had drifted. Elodia would never let it go. "Yes, it is an uncomfortable position." She took her hand and turned to Elodia. "I'm sorry, what were you saying?"

Elodia blinked at her silently. "It feels a bit silly now. I was of a mind to distract you but now I wonder if you would rather I listened."

It was always jarring when Elodia was silent and somber. She was usually so animated and charming. With her thoughts going every which way, Regina didn't need her friend observing her that closely.

"There's not much to say really. I'd much rather hear what you were telling me."

"I was saying I'd received a letter from Headmistress Pollitt."

"Oh, how lovely! How is she?" The headmistress of their school had stayed in touch with them long after they had left, always writing to give them encouragement.

"She said she was thinking of retiring as headmistress and passing it along to one of the other teachers."

"That would be the end of an era. How soon would she be leaving?"

"A few years perhaps."

"That is disappointing. I'd rather hoped Lillian would be able to benefit from her supervision when she was old enough for school."

"Well, perhaps she can be there as a family friend. It cannot hurt to be the friend of a baroness."

"I wonder if my mother would let me invite her to my wedding."

"What if I invite her to something first?"

"Would your father object to that?"

"I doubt it. It's not as if she is unknown to him." In honesty, Regina wasn't worried about her mother so much as her mother-in-law. When it came to her wedding, her mother-in-law would be the one determining Regina's role and duties, beginning with her wedding. She could likely dictate it all according to her wishes leaving Regina as a means to an end for the baron and his legacy. The beginning of her erasure into the role she had been marked for.

CHAPTER THREE

Harley House, Mayfair, London

A MAYFAIR ADDRESS typically meant money, so when Leo arrived for his appointment, he'd expected to be shown in through the back door as usual. None of these uppity people wanted to be seen letting in a member of the middle class, let alone a black man through the front like an equal. So, when he'd arrived only to be told to use the front, he wasn't sure what to expect. Was this about his family or was it about a job?

Now he sat in the atrium having had his coat taken by a butler. He wasn't sure what to do with himself, so he observed. The surroundings were not only lavish but old. The style and makeup were Early Georgian, which meant this residence was likely one of the first of its kind there. The furnishings had been updated but the style had not, which meant the age of the house mattered to them more than fashion. These people cared about their history.

His clients tended to find him by reputation. But they also tended to seek him out at his office, not on the street. These people, whoever they were, knew his name, which meant they could have made an office call. Instead, they had gone through the trouble of having him followed. They were either testing his ability or they had no respect for him whatsoever. But if they didn't respect him, then they could have dragged him to meet them. It would have been difficult, but not impossible to bring him in by force. They had the money to hire the manpower. Instead, they left it to him and let him walk in through the front door.

So, they were testing him. To what end? Logic said it would have to be a job, why else bother evaluating his competence? But the questions they had asked, and the information they had was disconcerting to say the least. Why would they bother looking at so much of his family tree to hire him for work?

A young man walked out to meet him with a cheery smile that immediately made Leo more suspicious. "Good afternoon, Mr. Kingston. My aunt is ready for you."

Aunt? "Does she make a habit of keeping people waiting?"

"Not as a rule, no. But she wasn't feeling well this morning." He gestured down the hallway to an open door. "Please follow me."

Leo nodded and walked behind him with his hands loose at his side.

"Who are you?"

"My name is Albert Upton sir."

Albert. The name didn't ring any bells. He would stay only to understand their game. Once he knew it, he would leave. That was the plan. Until he entered the room and saw his host.

He almost didn't recognize her as the presumptuous old bat from the Trawley Ball. She sat in a wheelchair, eyes closed, skin almost grey from exhaustion. Despite the summer heat, she was wrapped in furs and placed in a puddle of sunlight to warm her back. This was a fragile, sickly old woman, not the brazen busybody he'd encountered days ago. Then her eyes snapped open, and they were sharp and clear as day.

No matter the state of her body, her mind was as sound as ever.

"Hello again," she said.

"Still here, I see," he replied. There was no need to stand on ceremony, the woman had likely been school friends with Queen Elizabeth, and her sense of humor seemed as perverse as his.

Her answering smile was almost feral. "Oh, yes. I have unfinished business."

"Is that why you had me followed? For showing up to a ball uninvited?"

"Not quite." She let out a tired breath. "Have a seat, Mr. Kingston."

"Is that an order?"

"A request. I cannot stand just now, and looking up at you hurts my neck. I assure you; I mean you no harm."

Strangely, he believed that. This woman was not well. If his mother were here, she would have glared him into an early grave for inconveniencing an elder. He sat in the chair opposite her and watched her expectantly.

"Tea?" she asked.

"No, thank you."

"It's not poisoned."

"I don't take tea. As a rule." Not since he'd had chai in India. The weak flavorless swill in England couldn't compare. He'd take coffee any day.

"Ah."

"Why am I here?"

"What an interesting question."

"Is it?"

"There are so many ways it can be answered."

"Seeing as you are short on time, and I am short on patience, might I suggest the direct approach." He leaned back in his seat, aiming to give the impression of boredom even though something in her eyes had his teeth on edge.

She chuckled again, genuine amusement crinkling the corners of her eyes. "Very well, I will obey you. What do you know about your father's family?"

"I know he comes from men of learning and women of dignity. They valued hard work."

"All true."

What was her angle here? "Lovely, was that meant to be illuminating?"

"Your name, Leopold. Were you named for him?"

The back of his neck prickled. Was that a good guess on her part or did she know something about his family? So far she knew too much for comfort. "For my great grandfather? Yes."

"What do you know about him?"

"Less than you, I take it."

"You'd be correct. Did you know for example that he was the third son of a baron?"

"A what?"

"You are the great grandson of the twelfth Baron Starkley."

Impossible. "How very curious."

"Isn't it just?"

"Your delivery was sound, but the tale is a bit much for my tastes," he said incredulously.

"Your grandmother was a lady's maid from the West Indies, Antigua if I recall correctly. She was called Matu, but her name was Matilde Kingston."

That caught his attention. His stomach dipped sharply as his mouth went dry. How on earth did she know about Grandmama Matu? Had his grandfather chosen to take his grandmother's last name when they married? Why would he do that? "You've been looking into my family?"

"I've known your family longer than you have, my boy."

"I'm not your fucking 'boy'," he snapped, the thread holding onto his patience, dangerously thin. She likely didn't mean anything by it, he knew that, but it felt too much like other times where his life had been twisted beyond recognition by the whims of someone else. He hated the slippery feeling in his gut, the horrible sensation of unwanted exposure.

Who the fuck did this old woman think she was, looking into his family and having him followed in the middle of the night? What gave her the right? But she was not angered by his response. Instead, a strange, almost wistful look passed over her face.

"Yes, that is true. You are a Cambridge man by way of Eton, yes?"

He gripped the arms of the chair he was sitting in and struggled to get a hold of himself. This was absolutely an ambush, but one couldn't lose control in a fight. The only way to survive was to get back control. "How long have you been looking into me?"

"Long, and not long at all. I've known you since you were born, but I didn't recognize you until the Trawley Ball."

"Explain yourself."

"Nearly a century ago at age fourteen, I was engaged to your great grandfather Leopold Starkley until he threw me over for a former slave from the colonies."

"I can't say I blame him. You're an impudent little busybody." Who was determined to upend his entire life for the sake of her own agenda. What gave her the right? He was angrier than he'd expected, or perhaps he was afraid although he'd rather die than admit that.

"You forgot old. But I earned the right to be all three of those things. I was fourteen when he did it, he and your great grandmother were both of an age, twenty. My father was appeased, and I was married into a branch of the Starkley family when I was old enough."

Burghley-Harrison. Now that his brain was in overdrive, he was remembering why that name was so familiar. Edward Harrison. His former comrade in arms. A vicious, pompous man with more arrogance than courage. Were they actually related then? He'd rather not think about it. How many blows was he meant to withstand in one day?

No. He couldn't take this nonsense seriously.

"Did you watch me out of malice to my grandparents?"

"How boring would I be if that were true? I was young, but I loved your grandfather. I loved him when I married my husband and bore my children. I've loved him my entire life. I loved him more than any grievance I could have felt towards him for following his heart. When his family cast him out for eloping with a former slave, I made sure they knew that I would still be his friend. When his son, your grandfather was born, I was his godmother. When his grandchild needed funding to attend the school of his forefathers, I funded it."

"You funded my father's education?" How much of his life was entangled with this woman?

"Mmm. I made sure you went as well."

"You—"

"With your grades you could have gone into law like my nephew Albert. He's the young man who greeted you. But you chose the military instead."

"You expect me to believe that my family owes their prosperity to you?"

"You owe it to your own effort. I gave one thing, the funding for an education equal to your family which you were entitled to by blood. What you made of the opportunities that education afforded you was your own business."

"Why would you waste your money on the child of a man who abandoned you?"

"He fell in love. When given the choice between abandoning his principles and the woman he loved, or the protection of his family, he chose the wiser of the two. I was angry at first, but he would not have been my Leopold if he had chosen differently. My children are responsible for every ache in my bones, every silver hair on my head, every line on my face, but I would never turn my back on them for doing what was right instead of what was convenient."

He couldn't imagine anyone having that kind of a heart. What sort of woman supported the family of the man who had abandoned her? "He broke his word."

"He never promised me anything. His family pledged him to a child. He wasn't obligated to keep such a promise. The one he made a promise to was Matu, and that word he did not break. He was a man of integrity after all, and he passed that example down all the way to you."

"You knew me at the ball."

"I recognized those eyes. Only Starkley's have those curious brown eyes. That shade is unmistakable."

There had to be a reason she'd done all of this, a reason she was telling him about all of this, and it had nothing to do with the kindness of her heart. He was sure about that. "Why are you telling me this?"

"Because you are the last of that line."

What on God's earth? "I beg your pardon?"

"The last male descendent of the twelfth Baron Starkley is you."

"I thought you said my great grandfather was disinherited."

She shook her head. "He was cut off financially, not disinherited. No doubt they imagined he would abandon your great grandmother and return to the luxurious fold. But he was more stubborn and clever than they thought. Eventually with the first and second son married off and producing their own heirs, they likely expected it was too unlikely for his children to inherit anything."

"Are you telling me I'm a Baron?"

"I am telling you that you have an undisputable claim to that title, should you decide to do so."

"And why would I want to associate myself with a family that would have preferred I had never been born?"

"For the fun of it."

There it was. In the end it was all for her own amusement. As if this wasn't his life she was playing with. "You and I have different ideas of 'fun'."

"Are you telling me the idea of the rejected corner stone receiving the estate they preserved so diligently doesn't tickle you a little."

"Are you so petty?"

"Are you not?"

"Almost." He was, but he'd rather cut out his tongue than admit it to her.

"So, you won't do it?"

"I will not. Even if what you say is true." And he resented her digging around in his family and ruining his peace for the sake of her own amusement. For some ridiculous loyalty to a man who didn't even want her. His great grandfather left his family behind for a reason, what right did she have to drag him back there and expose himself and his family to the ton and their prejudice. No doubt she imagined she was doing him a favor, as part of her ongoing charity work. A last-ditch attempt to save herself from the blood money she inherited from her own forbears by enslaving his.

"If?"

"I have no interest in that life or in participating in a legacy that treated my grandparents like a gangrenous limb to be disposed of. I would rather belong to my namesake Leopold Kingston, not Leopold Starkley."

"A rose by any other name."

She would never understand. There was a tenuous peace that existed for people like him so long as they didn't achieve too much, aspire to too much. He'd learnt that lesson the hard way. Now she'd dropped this in his lap, what the fuck was he meant to do with it? Better to leave it behind. He rose to his feet, sick to his stomach. "I am sorry to have wasted your time seeing as you have so precious little left." It wasn't a kind thing to say, but he wasn't feeling kind.

"Everything I have told you can be verified in any court in this land. My Bertie has a set of documents waiting for you in the hall. Proof for you to verify my claims by whatever means you deem fit."

He and his family had not only survived but thrived in spite of this no doubt cursed barony and its cruel legacy. He would only be borrowing trouble by lowering himself to take it up. "I do not need it. Whether it is true or not my answer is the same. No," he bowed and walked away.

"I did not ask if you wanted it, I simply told you it was there."

He kept moving refusing to glance left or right. He didn't trust his fingers not to snatch those documents. He wanted to return to his life and forget this ridiculous interlude ever happened.

"Mr. Kingston?" He heard Albert call him, but he kept walking. He paused only to snatch his coat from the rack by the door before yanking it open and rushing out into the bright sunlight.

CHAPTER FOUR

Her Majesty's Theatre, Haymarket, London

I T HAD BEEN over a year since Regina had been to the theatre. In the previous year, Ada's trouble had resulted in Regina's season being cut short. After their adventure to Gretna Green, her parents had snatched her back to the country where she was meant to wait until her fiancé returned. They had only returned to London this season in anticipation of her fiancé's arrival, which they now knew wouldn't happen. Not until they knew who the new one would be.

Enjoying an evening with Ellie while their parents grew more closely acquainted opened up so many new possibilities. She didn't know why they hadn't done this before. She knew that Ellie and Ada had managed to spend more time together because their families were less restrictive unlike her parents. She had only ever wanted to be Ellie's friend and hadn't ever truly considered using her father as a connection to better her own standing. But now, she wondered how much of her life over the past years could have been different.

In her excitement, she'd chosen one of the dresses she'd managed to get past her mother. A gown of rich cerulean silk with gota patti of gold and silver in a floral motif along the neckline and in a broad border at the hem of each flounce. It was an indulgence, like her favorite bonnet, something that showed a little more of who she was or perhaps who she wanted to be. Who she hoped she would be after all was said and done.

The excitement she felt had even extended to her mother,

who had forgotten for the first time in her life to check what Regina was wearing before they had arrived at the theatre. Regina had left her cloak on until the last minute when she had been forced to remove it at the theatre in full view of her mother. Her mother's eagle eye had gone directly to the unmistakably Indian design, but before she could speak, the viscount had commented on it in glowing terms.

Regina couldn't be sure it was a victory, but for the moment at least, there wasn't anything to be done about it. If enough positive feedback got to her mother perhaps Regina would be able to wear more of these designs this season. It would be a kind of freedom, even if much of her life was still decided. Tonight, she wouldn't worry about that. Tonight, she would enjoy being able to wear this dress and relish the opera with her friend. Her eyes drifted over the assembly of patrons around them. Some were familiar, but most were not.

She'd been in this theatre once before but never in an area like this. These gilt seats were upholstered in red velvet and this performance was the premier of the latest opera by Guiseppi Verdi.

"What is this one about, Ellie?" she asked.

"Well, I believe it is based on a book by Alexandre Dumas' son, *La Dame aux Camélias*. Have you read it?"

"No."

"It's about a fallen woman, Violetta, who finds love too late."

"Sad but probably realistic."

"Indeed, but the music should be good."

"Thank goodness for those Italian lessons, eh?" Regina joked, nudging Ellie with her elbow.

"If only Ada was here. It would be a perfect evening."

"Indeed. Although she's likely already seen it."

"That is very true, at this point when she returns, we will be able to discuss it with her instead of staring like country bumpkins."

The lights flickered and they turned their attention to the

stage. As Elodia predicted, the music was wonderful, but what struck Regina the most was Violetta's quandary between freedom and love. The idea of being caught between what seemed to serve her best and what her heart cried out for once she'd tasted it. She heard Elodia gasp beside her and turned to her.

"What is it, Ellie?"

"He's here," she whispered, her gloved hands clenched in her lap and her eyes fixed across from their seat one row down. When she saw the object of her focus her own breath caught in her throat. There in the dim light of the torches sat Ada's brother, Mr. Thornfield, and beside him was Mr. Kingston. His gaze was fixed on the stage, his brow furrowed in concentration as he leaned on the arm rest of his chair, one strong hand covering his full mouth. Every time she saw him, she was struck anew by how handsome he was and how attractive every part of him was to her. How much she liked the way he looked at her, the way he appreciated her as she was. Could she find that with the man she was destined to marry? Was it possible that the white man who would no doubt inherit the barony and her along with it would see her as a boon instead of a burden?

On the stage Alfredo's voice rang out reminding the heroine of her opportunity to taste what she'd never experienced before with a person of pure heart and intentions. Violetta's voice faltered as the ache of longing sprang to life and in Regina's own heart a treacherous seed of yearning took root. She forced herself to look down at her hands and then back to the stage. She tried to focus on understanding the Italian instead of recalling every detail of each encounter she'd ever had with Leo Kingston.

"Oh," Elodia murmured, and Regina glanced over in time to see her nod in Mr. Thornfield's direction. He returned the gesture to her and Regina, and she glanced at Mr. Kingston to see those eyes fixed on her. Her heart thudded in her chest at the impact of his stare. He nodded as well before returning his attention to the stage. Could she be disappointed? Did it make sense? He owed her nothing, they'd met only twice before. What had she hoped for?

Her heart was thumping away with her chest. She could feel his gaze on her skin and the tingling in her belly moved lower, forcing her to press her legs together. It was terrifying and exhilarating to have his interest even if it was only polite. It was maddening having her body react in such a way to someone she knew full well she couldn't have. Someone who had no interest in her outside of a passing acquaintance.

The first half ended, and the curtain mercifully closed as the audience broke into scattered applause.

"Oh, they've left," Elodia said.

"What?" Regina's head snapped up to see the empty seat Mr. Kingston had once sat in. She wasn't disappointed. She wasn't. She didn't know the man for the love of Christ. Perhaps it was a mercy. The last thing she needed was more distractions.

Then Elodia stiffened beside her. "Oh, Lord. He's coming over, Gigi."

Regina's head snapped up as her body went cold with shock. "What?"

"Good evening gentlemen," Elodia said with a bright smile. "Papa, you remember Mr. Kingston and of course Mr. Thornfield."

"Of course, good evening, gentlemen," Lord Melbroke said, "Mr. Thornfield you must already be familiar with my guests, but Mr. Kingston allow me to introduce Captain and Mrs. Mason and their eldest daughter, Miss Regina Mason."

"Good evening to you all," he said giving them a smart bow.

"Mr. Kingston, I believe I saw you on the platform that day last year, did I not?" Captain Mason said with a curious head tilt. Her father remembered him? Of course her father remembered him. The man had a mind like a steel trap.

"I believe so, but it was hardly a formal introduction by any means."

"No. More like guerrilla warfare."

Mr. Kingston pressed his lips together as if fighting back a smile. "As you say, sir."

Her father turned to her mother. "Mr. Kingston was instrumental in safeguarding Mr. Thornfield's life, and the former Miss Thornfield's dignity."

"Yes, he was," Mr. Thornfield confirmed.

"He also was the reason my Ellie was returned to me so quickly when she was taken last year," the Viscount added with a nod of admiration.

"It seems more than one person is indebted to you, Mr. Kingston," Regina's mother said.

"That is true, but none are present here. What I did was in the service of a friend."

"How gallant of you." Her expression seemed almost convinced, but Regina knew better than to read anything more into it.

"Do you enjoy the opera, Mr. Kingston?" Regina asked, hoping her voice sounded as steady as she imagined, even though her stomach was a mess of nerves.

"I do in general, Miss Mason. How do you find this one?"

"Intriguing. I'm not one for romance in general but this one isn't terrible." It was better to be honest. Her parents would certainly know the truth.

"A young woman who isn't a fan of romantic tales, how very peculiar." Mr. Thornfield said with clear amusement.

She smiled. Yes it would seem odd to him, but Regina had never been interested in hurting herself for the sake of curiosity. Romance would have no place in the life she was going to live and she had no interest in tasting it even vicariously. "I'm a peculiar sort of female."

"You're in good company tonight. My companion here is less than enthused himself." He cast a frustrated glance at Mr. Kingston.

"Oh? What fault do you find with it?" she asked. Was he a kindred spirit?

"Is the subject matter too shocking?" Elodia chimed in.

Mr. Kingston shot an annoyed look at his friend before chuckling and shaking his head. Regina's breath caught in her throat. That laugh. She was losing her mind. "Well, I confess I much prefer comedies myself," he replied.

"How peculiar of you," Regina teased, and he crinkled his nose in mock protest.

"Perhaps, but I've dealt with enough tragedy in my line of work. When I pay to be entertained, I prefer a happy ending."

"Whereas I live for drama as an escape from mundane leisure." Richard joked.

"You do not believe that art should hold a mirror up to the world, Mr. Kingston?" The Viscount asked.

"I have no objection to it in principle, but for myself I'd much rather laugh than cry."

"Especially in public," Ellie teased, and Mr. Thornfield snickered before wagging his finger and squinting at the ceiling in consideration.

"You make a fine point, Miss Hawthorne. Imagine spending all that time on your toilette only to ruin your hard work with a rogue opera."

"Oh, the tragedy," she lamented with a grin.

"The futility."

"Oh dear, are you in danger of a public emotional exhibition, Mr. Kingston?" Regina asked, wondering how Elodia was able to speak so easily with Mr. Thornfield, a man she was clearly in love with.

Mr. Kingston chuckled and shook his head, "Not tonight, Miss Mason. I believe it is time to return to our seats to further witness the tragic futility."

"Such is always the way. I shall bid you all good evening then," Mr. Thornfield said before bowing and leaving their box.

Mr. Kingston followed suit, meeting her eyes for a moment before he left and Regina returned the gesture, watching greedily as he strolled away with his friend. Even his walk was attractive. What on earth was this? Could it be mere attraction? Was it that powerful?

"He's a cheerful fellow," Captain Mason commented.

"Who, Thornfield? He is rather, but don't let it fool you," Lord Melbroke replied.

"What do you mean by that, papa?" Elodia asked.

"Only that he's not as straightforward as he likes to appear."

It was true. Ada's brother wielded his charm in a way that was calculated without being harmful. She didn't hold it against him, she had to do the same in her own way far too often. She imagined Mr. Kingston's humility was another way to play to the crowd in order to avoid too much scrutiny. How else could his refusal to accept credit for his actions the year before be explained? "Few people are," Regina replied without thinking as she watched him and Mr. Kingston retake their seats.

"Oh?" Captain Mason asked.

Regina glanced over to see four pairs of eyes staring at her; three inquisitive and one knowing and wary. "I only meant that it is the price of engaging in society, is it not? We none of us can be truly who we are all the time."

"I suppose that is true enough," her father replied.

"Indeed," Mrs. Mason said watching Regina with cool consideration. "Mr. Kingston is quite the hero."

Regina met her stare evenly but said nothing. She knew. Somehow her mother knew who her mind had begun drifting towards. If her voice wavered it would seal the coffin.

"He is a good sort," Elodia said. "Very clever and discreet."

"A military man as well by his account," Lord Melbroke added.

"Oh? Which battalion?" Captain Mason asked, his interest piqued.

"I didn't get that far with the introduction. Perhaps I can invite him to dinner next week and you can have the opportunity to ask."

"Very good." Her father nodded with his typical cheerful grin.

Regina turned to face the stage and forced herself to keep her eyes on the performances she was lucky to witness, and not on the man across from their box. And if she felt the weight of his stare, she told herself she was imagining it.

SHE WAS STUNNING tonight, and it was getting even more difficult not to notice it. Verdi's latest work was rapidly losing his interest in lieu of the young woman seated above him in the theatre with her friends and family He didn't know if it was the full moon or the doomed romance of the opera, but Leo would swear he had sensed her before he saw her. Which was utter madness. More than likely the torchlight had glinted off the golden accents on her dress and caught his attention.

Now he couldn't stop staring. She of course was entirely focused on the stage, her expression composed, her posture poised but not rigid. She looked like a damned princess in that blue and gold silk, with all that shining hair piled on top of her head in curls and twists, that lush body with its smooth deep brown skin curving in and out. He felt like a lecher or at the very least an impudent peasant coveting what he had no business wanting.

Except he wasn't a peasant according to that old woman. He was a baron. Or a prospective one at least.

A reality he was barely willing to acknowledge let alone accept. He didn't like knowing that some old white woman funded his education. He didn't like knowing that his grandfather's family were the sort of people who were so racist they would cut him off for marrying outside of his race and below his station. He was everything they hated everything they would have fought to prevent and yet here he was poised to get everything if he chose to take it.

He could vie for Miss Mason's hand then as black as he was. It wouldn't matter with a title behind him.

"Something the matter?" Richard murmured.

Yes. "No."

"Have the Mason's offended you in some way?"

"No," he glanced at his friend and recognized the amusement on his face. "What?"

"You tell me."

"I was merely admiring Miss Mason. She is a credit to her parents."

"Indeed, quite lovely. It's no small wonder she is engaged already."

Disappointment curdled in his stomach. Engaged? "What?"

"She's been engaged for some years now. It's why she is rarely out in society. She's been waiting for the man to come marry her."

"That is ludicrous. Why waste her time when he could be marrying the girl?"

"Perhaps they are unwilling to settle down just yet, or perhaps he objects to the prospect of marrying her."

"If they find it so disagreeable, why don't they just call it off?"

"There is a good deal of money at stake as I understand it."

"Of course." Money. He could never hope to keep her in the kind of luxury she'd been raised in, not without taking the title. Leo had not benefited from the same level of prosperity her father had enjoyed in the military. He'd had some luck to be sure and had managed to save enough to open his business after gaining more experience with London at Scotland Yard. Careful stock investments by Basil had produced a healthy enough return that Leo could pick his clients with more scrutiny, but nothing to bedeck anyone in silk and gold.

The comfort he was able to maintain for himself and his mother had always been a source of pride and satisfaction for him, but Miss Regina Mason would require more. She deserved more. He couldn't provide it without changing himself entirely and that wasn't something he was prepared to do for anyone, let alone a chit he'd met three times regardless of how charming and gorgeous she was.

So, he contented himself with watching her and imagining what it would be like to sit next to her in a theatre like this one, to court her openly, to hold her hand at will, to investigate the hidden depths of those glittering dark eyes and know that she was his.

CHAPTER FIVE

*S*TILL *LOOKING ABOVE your station, eh Leo?* Edward Harrison thought as he watched his former brother in arms with amusement from his seat in the theatre. He thought he'd cured the jumped-up darkie of setting his sights too high when he'd had him drummed out of the army.

Kingston had always been a good soldier, disciplined, loyal and strong as an ox. But he had a sanctimonious strain that made him think he was better than he was. Made him think he had a right to lecture others on morality or integrity just because they sought entertainment with native whores. As if any of them had minded. His blood still boiled when he remembered the way he'd spoken to him about comporting himself like a British Officer. A representative of their country.

Their country.

As if it would ever belong to the likes of Kingston. It was his people's lot to build it, not own it or represent it. How could a black man represent England? How could Kingston dare to compete with his betters for promotions or think he had the right to pull rank on them?

So, Harrison had taken it upon himself to remind Kingston of the reality of his position. It had been almost too easy in retrospect, to get him out of the army. A rumor here, a murmur in a free ear there, or money in an idle hand and Kingston was gone. In the end the white Englishman would always prevail, because the truth was unmistakable. They were meant to lead, to rule, to win.

Harrison had only one reason for returning to England. It wasn't his mother and her interminable winging or homesickness after being away for months at a time after years in the army. No, he was here to claim the birthright he was entitled to by law and by blood. Fate had placed him too far down the line of inheritance, but that was no real barrier to an enterprising gentleman such as himself. The barony should be his and so it would be. If the gold bedecked harem girl that Kingston was currently ogling came with it, then he would take her too.

For a time.

She was temptation itself with that flowing hair, the dark eyes of an odalisque, and the body of a cosseted whore. The exotic females of the orient were more fun than their frigid English counterparts, but he had no intention of allowing her to contaminate his family line, no matter how alluring she was.

No, he would enjoy her for as long as she held interest, and then she would meet with an unfortunate accident just like all the others who stood between him and what he deserved. Then he'd marry a proper Englishwoman and get an heir off her.

But first he'd have to wed her, bed her, and pocket the rest of her enormous dowry.

CHAPTER SIX

Regents Park, London

MORNING RIDES WITH her father were one of the small joys Regina held dear. It was something her mother's anxiety hadn't yet forced her to give up. Having a military father meant most of their quality time was spent shooting or fencing or riding. His self-defense lessons had saved her at least once some nights ago at the Trawley Ball. Her father's presence, however, gave her the look of a paternally inclined daughter rather than an untamed Indian native racing across a civilized English park.

"What did you think of Mr. Kingston, choti rani?" he asked.

"I think he's been a very good friend to Mr. Thornfield."

He smiled, "That seemed a rather prepared response."

"It was a rather leading question."

He shook his head ruefully and glanced up at the sky as he was wont to do. Jokingly praying for patience. "You did seem rather taken with him."

"Because I participated in a conversation?" What on earth was she meant to do, sit there like a statue and stare into the void?

"Your mother said you were staring at him."

"I was looking at him when he spoke." Not quite the truth, she'd had difficulty looking away from him regardless of who was speaking but she'd die before she admitted it. No matter how skeptical her parents were.

"So she was lying?"

"No but she can blow non-issues out of proportion, you've seen it yourself." Again not quite true but close enough. The last thing she needed was to be banned from any social interaction at all. She'd only just managed to get a full taste of it over the past week.

"Your mother can tend towards being overly cautious, but I would draw the line at hysterics."

"You are ruining our father-daughter time with this line of questioning."

"Regina…"

One word was all it took. She sighed and turned her head to face him. "Mr. Kingston is an interesting, admirable, and amiable gentleman."

"A gentleman?"

"By nature, and education, yes."

"What do you know of his education?"

Damn. Her mother wasn't the only one who knew how to lay traps. "I know that Mr. Thornfield attended Eton and Cambridge and was schoolmates with Mr. Thompson and Mr. Kingston. It is how they became acquainted. It is true he has a profession, a trade if you will, but I defy you to find his equal among the ton irrespective of birth and race. But it doesn't mean I have forgotten myself entirely."

"That is good to hear," his tone was noncommittal but even that was part of the trap.

"Yes. You can report back to aai that I am not in danger ruining years of preparation."

"I was not trying to interrogate you."

"No, you were engaging in reconnaissance."

He sighed heavily and she mentally scored a point for herself. "It is an immense opportunity, choti rani."

"I am aware of the fact."

"Good morning, Captain! Miss Mason," a dark haired, middle-aged woman with a small dog and two maids in tow called out to them.

Regina tried to place her. She was only familiar in the most basic sense, as in she looked like every other chubby dark-haired woman in England from the abundance of sausage curls, bows and lace, to the forced smile and milky complexion they seemed to prize.

"Mrs. Harrison-Cox, isn't it?" Captain Mason greeted her, tipping his hat. "Good morning."

"Yes, it is." She smiled and Regina had the distinct impression of watching a snake bare its fangs. "I imagine you have both received our good news."

Regina glanced at her father who shook his head in confusion.

"We have not been so fortunate," Regina replied with a practiced smile.

"My Edward is to be the new Baron Starkley, and as such our families are to be united."

Oh God. Had that come already? Sweat bloomed on her glove covered palms and her stomach flipped over.

"Oh, my felicitations," Captain Mason replied when Regina found her mouth glued shut.

"Indeed," she turned her eyes on Regina. "I mean to visit your home soon to check on your progress, young lady, before my Edward arrives."

The outrageousness of the statement shocked words out of her. "My progress?"

"Indeed, I see you are keeping more rarified company such as viscounts which is good. Smart to get acquainted with the sphere you are moving into beforehand, but there are things only one such as I can teach you."

That hadn't taken long at all. The utter temerity of the woman. "Of course."

"You are infamous already. When the term 'noble savage' was coined, I don't believe anyone expected it to be a literal social aspiration."

Her father bristled visibly. "Madam—"

"Oh, I mean no offense, Captain," She interrupted, all wide-eyed innocence and good intentions. "And rest assured while I do not relish the idea of an exotic daughter-in-law, we must all make the best of things, it is the British way after all."

She knew how to play that role at the very least. She'd been surrounded by women like this her whole life. "Yes, we must," Regina replied evenly, breathing carefully through her nose to stave off the sudden nausea. The idea of such a creature existing so close to her for the majority of her life however, was sickening.

"Well good day to you, Captain. I shall see you very soon." She nodded and bustled away, leaving the day somewhat darker than it had been a few moments ago.

They rode along in silence for a few minutes while Regina came to terms with the reality of her new mother-in-law. It was a good deal of information to digest before breakfast. Her time was ostensibly up, and the woman who raised her fiancé was the most obnoxious, racist *bitch* of a woman.

"Perhaps we should head back," her father said frowning after Mrs. Harrison and her dog.

"You go ahead, baba."

"I am so sorry you had to hear that."

"Her sentiments are offensive but not novel. Please, baba, give me a few moments more."

For a moment as he sat quietly, she was afraid he wouldn't agree. If her father had made one thing clear to Regina it was that he wouldn't sleep alone just to satisfy a whim of hers. His first priority was always his wife, and Madhavi Mason wouldn't appreciate her daughter being left alone in public for five minutes let alone the twenty it would take for her father to get home and send back a chaperone. Then he let out a sigh and shook his head. "Shall I send back a groom for you?"

"If you wish, baba."

"Rani," he reached out to touch her shoulder, but she couldn't let him. She didn't want him to know how upset she was.

"I'm alright. I just need a moment to myself." A moment to catch her breath.

He nodded and set off at a leisurely pace. She watched him

until he was out of view and then dismounted her Arabian mare, Kali. She didn't trust herself to keep riding when her emotions had her fingers curling into fists around the reins. It had been a long time coming, but she was beginning to understand that very little could have prepared her for the reality of the life she was about to enter. If she was lucky her husband would not be on close terms with the woman who sired him. If she was very lucky, he would be the sort of man that was easy to get around.

She strolled along the path, the reins in her hand until she reached a park bench. She sat there still, watching absently as Kali nibbled on the grass. She'd spent so long imagining her married life, and while she'd known better than to expect a loving husband or a supportive mother-in-law, she didn't know what it would feel like to know that the people with the closest control of her life would be so cold and intolerant.

It didn't lessen her resolve, but she'd be lying if she said it hadn't set her back on her heels. She would always be that 'noble savage' to them. She wondered if perhaps she should have adhered more closely to her mother's advice instead of clawing at every ounce of freedom she could.

Would it have made a difference? Would she have been able to conform enough to satisfy Mrs. Harrison and those who thought like her? She had lost so much in the name of assimilation and appeasement. To be judged as wanting at first sight without so much as a test was infuriating and demoralizing. But perhaps it was a path. It was always a mistake to underestimate one's enemies and if anything, they would always be counted on to underestimate her. They never understood those like her as well as she had been forced to understand them for her own sake.

There would be little dignity or peace if any, but perhaps if she bided her time and played a long strategy she would be able to win a victory for herself. It could be through her children, or by simply surviving him. As long as she secured an heir quickly, the likelihood of her being subjected to her future husband would be slim.

"Miss Mason?"

Her head snapped up to see Leo Kingston watching her carefully, the morning sun framing him in its lemony light. "Mr. Kingston."

"Are you well?"

Regina didn't know what to do with her face. How long had he been standing there?

"I am, thank you." Why was he here? Why did he look so fresh and perfect while everything inside her was ragged and sickly.

"You are here alone?" He glanced at Kali, running one ungloved hand over her chestnut hide with easy familiarity. She was trying to remember if she'd ever seen him wearing gloves.

"Not for long. My father is sending a groom to escort me. I asked him for more time this morning."

"I didn't mean to intrude on your privacy. You looked...disturbed."

"I had an encounter with the mother of my new fiancé. Supposedly." She probably shouldn't have told him that, but for some reason she couldn't keep it in. It could have been the fact that he was interested, when so many others had only thought to offer congratulations, or the fact that something about his presence seemed to settle her spirit even as he sent her nerves haywire. Or perhaps it was that she needed him to know why she couldn't give into whatever mysterious force had compelled him to stop and talk to her instead of nodding his head at her and walking on.

"An encounter that required solitude after," he filled in.

"Yes." Should she ask him to sit? It would be the polite thing to do, but if she was seen sitting with a gentleman without a chaperone... she would never be allowed to leave the house again.

"I heard from Mr. Thornfield that you were engaged. Normally I would congratulate you, but I'm not sure that is appropriate now."

Neither was she. "Indeed."

"Are you…" he paused for a moment and pressed his lips together. "Are you being forced?"

What would he do if she said yes? Part of her was curious whether he would whisk her away, if he would confront her parents on her behalf. Would he take issue enough to do something about it? She'd never been a damsel before, had never wanted to be one. But the idea of someone coming to her defense, especially if that someone was Leo Kingston was appealing if nothing else.

She wasn't curious enough to lie, however. The truth was as desolate as her future. When she answered her smile felt as fragile as her composure. "Not exactly. The contract was made without my consent, but I am not exactly opposed."

"Contract?" He frowned in confusion or perhaps distaste.

"Yes. It is not a typical engagement. It is enforced with a contract set up with the title not any one person, and it has been solidified by an exchange of funds, so it isn't easily broken."

"The contract is with the title?"

"Yes. Until the owner of the title marries me the contract is not fulfilled. And if he reneges on the contract, he will owe my father quite a bit of money."

Mr. Kingston blinked rapidly and raised his eyebrows. "That was very cleverly done on his part."

"Yes, a bit too clever. It was meant to prevent them from wasting my time and subjecting me to disgrace if they changed their minds. Instead, it has left me trapped."

"Is that why you dislike romances?"

The clarity of his insight was startling. Her hands fisted in her lap. "I can't allow myself to think about things like that." Although her mind and heart had been dangerously close one too many times of late. Like now. What right did he have to appear like a prince in disguise full of chivalry and concern? The sight of him made her sick with longing.

"That is very practical."

She smiled and nodded. Practical. She didn't think a first-born daughter had any choice but to be practical. Did choosing duty matter when it was already inescapable?

"I imagine there are considerable advantages at stake for you to acquiesce so resolutely to something you are dreading." Anyone else would have left by now, but he stayed standing there beside her horse stroking its neck with gentle surety. When her eyes began lingering on his hand, when she found herself growing envious of a four-legged animal, she turned her gaze to the gravel on the ground beneath her leather boots.

"My father is a good and honorable man who married outside of his race. He loves my mother dearly but while he is rich, he has no title and no connections to the nobility. Nothing to truly shield her from the ton."

His head tilted and she could almost see the cogs turning in his mind. "Until you."

"Yes. With one act I can give her the protection he cannot. Her and my sister."

"I didn't know you had a sister."

"Well, you wouldn't. She's very young."

He stared at her for a long, somber moment. She wondered what he was thinking. Was he judging her? Judging her parents? "You must love her very much." His voice was the softest she had ever heard it. The notes of it fell on her ears like a caress. Like an embrace.

"She is the light of my life." That was one truth she could admit without any difficulty at all. When the compassion in his eyes made hers sting, she turned her gaze to the grass, the people walking past, the sky. Anything but him. Whenever she thought of her sweet little sister, of that impish light leaving her black-brown eyes due to the racist impertinence of some blonde, blue-eyed brat, she wanted to wage war. There was no way she would allow that to happen. No matter what, her sister would be secure in herself. She would keep her name, her culture. She would never have to hide the truth of herself from the world.

"Were you christened Regina, or were you called something else?"

Her head snapped up in surprise a gasp catching in her throat. Where on earth had that come from? The question was impertinent to be sure especially for the level of acquaintance they shared, but that wasn't the reason her body felt like she'd fallen into a frozen pond. It was the question itself. There wasn't a person in her acquaintance who had ever doubted her name. Not even Elodia or Ada. "What made you ask that?"

His head tilted again in consideration before he continued, neatly picking apart one of the best kept secrets of her life. "Mr. Thornfield has a name only his sister uses and vice versa a name only their mother called them. It is one of the many ways they stay connected to her and that part of their heritage."

Had she known that? She'd never heard Ada refer to her brother as anything other than Richard. Unless he was referring to…"You mean when she calls him 'gēgē'? Is that his name?"

"No that is an honorific I believe. It means 'older brother'. When he calls her mèimei that is also an honorific. It is essentially, 'little sister'."

"Oh," How on earth did he know that?

"Outside of that, if you were to visit their home there would be little to show their continued connection to their mother's heritage. But in your case your mother still speaks her native tongue, and I know you understand it. The embellishments on your dress last night and that bonnet you wore the first time we met, I've only seen once before when I was stationed in Jaipur. Not to mention your jewelry," he gestured to her jhumkas and she nearly reached up to touch them. "And that black beaded marriage necklace your mother wears. Forgive me but 'Regina' doesn't seem to match the rest of you."

He even knew the significance of her mother's mangal sutra? Any other day she would likely have found his observations thrilling, but today, it filled her with a terrifying longing that left her aching with loneliness. She had made a mistake encouraging this. She needed to get as far away from him as possible before this feeling grew even sharper, and made her desire even harder to deny. "You have been making quite the study of me, Mr. Kingston."

His head jerked backwards as he caught the change in her tone. "I apologize if I have over stepped."

He hadn't, not really, but the power of her anguish was frightening. She needed the protection of formality if she was going to stay the course as she absolutely had to. "Not at all. But I suppose it is to be expected from someone like you."

"Like me?" He blinked at her in bewilderment, but there was the beginning of umbrage in his eyes. Good. She needed him to be polite and distant before she did something unforgivable.

"Someone who likes to observe others from a distance," she clarified with a polite smile.

He shifted his stance and dropped Kali's reins, gathering his irritation no doubt until he could understand why she was picking a fight. "You've been making a study of me yourself."

"I'm a woman. I survive by studies," she replied.

"And what exactly have you noticed."

She fixed her gaze on him, her hands folded tightly in her lap. It was a gamble, but she would bet anything he wouldn't enjoy her attention at all. "You don't like to be noticed, or rather you dislike too much attention. Perhaps you associate it with danger because of your profession. Or disappointment from your personal life."

He swallowed and she knew she had pinned him neatly. "Disappointment?" he repeated.

"I find it strange indeed that a man of your capabilities with your loyalty and cleverness managed to go unnoticed in the military."

"Perhaps you aren't well enough acquainted with the world, Miss Mason," he replied evenly, but there was a new defensiveness in his tone he couldn't fully hide.

Good.

"Or perhaps you were far too outstanding and attracted the jealousy of others as a result. Which is why you left both the army and Scotland Yard and decided to be your own master, so to speak."

He stared at her for a long moment then his eyes flicked up to the horizon. "There is only one thing I dislike more than attention, Miss Mason."

"Being wrong?"

"Being late. Your servant has arrived to escort you, and I cannot miss my appointment." He gave her a curt smile and a bow. "Good day to you."

"Good day." She watched him walk away, striding past Thomas, one of their stable hands who was nearly jogging up the path to meet her. That was a little too easy. She was almost disappointed. "Coward," she murmured, but she couldn't say who it was more for, herself or him.

LEO WOULD DENY to his grave that he had run away from Regina Mason because he'd lost his nerve.

He had an appointment, it just happened to be with his mother.

And he wasn't running.

He'd walked briskly for about two miles without looking back over his shoulder.

Because he was late.

It had nothing to do with the chill of discomfort that made his pores rise when Miss Mason fixed those resolute shimmering eyes on him and declared that he didn't like being seen.

The girl was correct in her assessment of him, of course, which made it even more disconcerting. He had elected to leave the army because his prospects there had been unpromising regardless of his efforts. Scotland Yard had somehow been worse. He was more used to being underestimated than anything else and as a result had learned to use it to his advantage. He knew what people saw when they looked at him, or at least he generally did until Mrs. Theodosia Burghley-Harrison and her investigation into him, and now Miss Mason. That was twice now he had been read like a book by virtual strangers and he didn't like it.

Even now, half an hour later his heart was still racing in his chest from that little encounter. Or the walk. Somehow between the Trawley Ball and this morning, he'd forgotten that Regina was nothing if not a strategist. So, when he'd seen her sitting on a bench next to her horse in the park, looking despondent, he'd decided to cheer her up. Or at least that had been his original intention before his curiosity had gotten the better of him.

He didn't know how that young woman had managed to turn that conversation on him so deftly. A part of him, the part that didn't have cold sweat running down its back, was impressed. The part that always stayed an observer like she had said and knew that he shouldn't have stayed to speak to her in the first place, let alone ask those questions. Did he have a right to the answers? Would they change anything about the reality of who she was and what he had decided he would have to offer?

No.

Why did it matter to him that she was choosing a marriage that would most certainly make her miserable to complete the circle of protection her father had started? She had said it so calmly, her voice was so steady without a trace of self-pity. He knew the realities of what it meant to have a bad husband, he'd seen too many broken women with no recourse. From the look in her eyes, she understood what she was doing and the cost. He never imagined seeing someone like Regina Mason, a girl gently bred and most likely sheltered, look that future in the eye and plant her feet instead of scrambling to escape.

He'd always heard stories of saints and martyrs walking into flames or lion's dens with nothing but their faith to guard and comfort them. Miss Mason was no saint, nor would she consider herself a martyr, but it was unquestionable that the path she walked would strip her of what little shielding she had in order to provide it for her family. He knew adult men who couldn't and wouldn't make that choice, and yet she had managed it with grace.

Perhaps it was because he'd never seen that level of bravery or self-possession in a young woman of two and twenty. She was young to be sure but perhaps not as sheltered as he had previously imagined. She was much more than stunning and unconventional. She was a guardian, a protector, someone who faced a frightening and uncertain future with determination instead of resignation. He didn't know how she had time to pay attention to him while she was dealing with so much herself but the fact that she had made him…twitchy.

Mostly because he hadn't noticed her noticing him, much like he hadn't noticed Mrs. Theodosia Burghley-Harrison. Only with her he'd assumed she was watching him out of distrust, not recognition. He hadn't contacted her since that tea she'd requested his presence for, and she had kept her distance, seemingly leaving the decision in his hands. It had cooled the worst of his ire at her for stirring up his life for her own revenge on people who were long dead and buried. For that at the very least he was grateful. He had decided then and there to leave it in the past and pretend as if the encounter had never occurred, but every time he saw Regina Mason the possibility became too intriguing.

He walked up the stairs to his home and once inside, removed his shoes, replacing them with house slippers.

"Mother, I'm back," he called out and was met with dead silence. Was she not home? He glanced at the rack as he hung up his coat. Hers was still there, so why didn't she answer? He walked into the dining room and saw her sitting at the table with a stack of documents in front of her. In the dim sunlight he saw his grandfather's name and in a second he understood what had happened. That meddlesome old harpy had sent her little parcel of confusion to his home.

"What is this?" his mother asked, her voice unnervingly calm.

Leo stared at the documents, wondering if he could get away with feigning ignorance. His instinct when cornered was to find the quickest route out, through guile or force. He couldn't attack his mother, so guile it was. "You tell me."

"This was delivered here about an hour ago by courier. Don't try your games with me on this, Leopold." She tapped one tapered fingernail sharply on the stack of papers. "Answer my question. Now."

"It appears my great grandfather was the son of a baron."

Her eyebrow came up, which meant the ice was getting thinner by the moment. "I can read. What does this mean?"

"According to the meddlesome old woman who produced this information, I am now the heir to the Barony of Starkley. Apparently, all the cousins ahead of me died from excess or stupidity."

A moment's pause and then. "That night you were followed; this is what it was about?"

Damn. He had foolishly hoped she wouldn't put that together so quickly. "Yes."

"And you have known this since you had that meeting?"

"Erm…" How had he fallen into this level of hot water so quickly? Were all the women in London conspiring to thwart him?

"And you elected to keep it to yourself because…?"

"Because I have no intention of taking up that title." The minute the words left his mouth he knew they were the wrong thing to say.

His mother rose slowly, drawing herself up to her full height, her eyes wide and flashing with temper. "I don't give a damn about the title. You were followed home by two men in the dead of night. Did you think I'd forgotten that fact?"

Damn. She had been worried. Of course she had been worried. "I'm sorry."

It was too late for him to apologize. His mother was well and truly vexed, and when Naomi Kingston was vexed, there was nothing to do but wait out the storm.

She leaned forward, bracing her hands on the wooden table. "You couldn't even let me know it had been resolved and that your safety wasn't at risk?"

"I'm sorry."

"And then you have the audacity to behave as though it doesn't affect me?"

Not for the first time in his life, he wished his father was still alive to help him smooth things over. Not that the man would have been helpful in this particular moment. The bastard would have stood to the side fighting to hide his amusement behind his hand, waiting for him to hang himself fully before offering any assistance.

It was what he had done when he had announced to them his intention to join the army. He was concerned to be sure and after he'd expressed as much to Leo. But in the moment, when his mother had made her displeasure abundantly clear he had merely watched with that sparkle in his eye, his lips pressed firmly together, his arms folded.

Much like Richard. The similarities between Richard and his father had never been so apparent to Leo before this. Perhaps it was why she favored him so much. It was no doubt what had drawn Leo to him when he was at Eton, homesick and nervous. No one was coming to help him with this current mess, however. This one he'd have to smooth over all on his own from beginning to end.

"Mother," he walked towards her, and she held up one imperious hand.

"Don't call me that." She straightened and shook her head.

"Mama…"

"Who is 'mama'?" she looked over her shoulder theatrically. "Where is your mother, young man? Clearly, *I* am not your mother." She fixed a glare on him with an ire that instinctively had him backing up a few steps. "I must be one of your business associates, yes? One of your contacts. Don't bother telling me anything, I must be some person you let in off the bloody street!"

With that she stalked away, gliding up the stairs and leaving the resonant crack of a slammed door ringing in the uncomfortable silence behind her.

Wonderful. Yet another unneeded upheaval he could thank Mrs. Burghley-Harrison for.

CHAPTER SEVEN

Number 12 Mayfair, London

THE SUMMONS TO join her parents in the parlor came as Regina finished her morning toilette. That could only mean one thing: guests. She opted for green silk and golden studs at her earlobes before heading downstairs. The sight that greeted her as she neared the staircase gave her pause. There, near the top of the stairs, sat her little sister peering down at the parlor door. The sight of her little body curled up near the banister, her skinny arms wrapped around her legs was harrowing. It reminded her too much of how she and Elodia had first met Ada.

"Lilli, I thought you were picking flowers with aai. What are you doing here?"

"She had to go," she replied, her little voice soft and tremulous.

Regina crouched down beside her, stroking a hand over Lilli's thick braided hair. "What happened, darling?"

"People came," she said.

That didn't explain much. Lillian was isolated to be sure, with not much in the way of friends or family members her age. She was a bit shy of strangers, but certainly not so much as to hide away at the sight of guests.

"Well, you don't need to stay here, dearest. Come down with me."

Lilli shook her head and turned her face into Regina's chest. "The lady was not nice. And the man has funny eyes," she mumbled.

"Funny eyes?" What on earth did that mean? Who was there?

She hugged Lillian tightly and kissed her hair. "Go find your governess, sweetheart. I'll come pick flowers with you later."

"Do you promise?"

"I do. We'll make fairy crowns as well."

"Really?" her eyes lit up.

"Really," Regina tweaked her little nose, and watched her spring to her feet and run down the hall to the nursery, whatever uncertainty Lilli had felt a moment ago already forgotten. She would do anything to make sure she kept that innocence, that ease of mind for as long as possible.

Regina stood and continued down the staircase, bracing herself for whatever was waiting for her. As quietly as possible, she drew closer to the salon where they typically received guests and listened to the conversation taking place inside. If she was meant to interact with the enemy, then she wanted to do so with as much information as possible.

"What a quaint home you have, Mrs. Mason, and how comfortable you have made it."

Ugh. That woman. Mrs. Harrison.

"Thank you, ma'am."

"Such interesting little details everywhere." A pause. "Is this an English biscuit?"

"Is it not to your taste? I'm sure we can find a different kind for you, Mrs. Harrison."

"Could you? I have a very delicate disposition."

A pause. "Of course."

Regina frowned and glanced at the wall separating her from the room. The biscuits were made by their cook, a very round and very Irish woman who was always a faint shade of pink and loved to sing and curse in equal measure. Was her mother truly going to change out the biscuits?

Regina waited, the heavy footfalls indicated her father was approaching. When he rounded the corner, she saw him holding the plate in his hand. He pulled her further down the corridor before letting out a deep sigh.

"Baba?"

"She wants to speak with you alone. If you can manage to stay civil with her, I will buy you any pistol of your choosing, personalized to your liking."

"To use on her?" she asked glaring at the door. She was only half serious.

"If needed," he replied flatly.

Her head snapped towards him in shock. "Baba! That was a jest."

"Was it? I was serious." He handed her the plate of biscuits, rearranged the stack slightly and nodded. "Off you go. Don't leave your mother alone with her."

"Won't she know these are the same biscuits?"

He shook his head and rolled his eyes. "They are shortbread Regina, there's nothing special about them." Then he gave her a cheeky grin. "If you weren't my beloved daughter, I'd bet you twenty pounds she doesn't notice."

Regina shook her head and walked towards the room with the questionable confectionary in her hand.

"Is that Miss Mason? Come here girl and let us have a proper look at you."

Regina stepped forward and fashioned a smile, dipping into a deep curtsy. "Hello, Mrs. Harrison, and my Lord Starkley."

"Ah, my lovely bride to be. I have been anticipating meeting you for some time. Now at last we are here."

He was very typical of an Englishman. An elegant figure, light brown hair and a pointy face. But his eyes... one glance explained what her sister meant by 'funny'. Those blue eyes were like glass, brilliant but flat, almost dead. His wide smile was unsettling when paired with them. This was her future husband. The only thing exceptional about him was his unconvincing facsimile of an expression.

Regina stood up and set the plate down on the table. "I am very glad to meet you as well, my lord. I've brought you both some fresh biscuits from the cook. They are lavender shortbread I believe."

Mrs. Harrison turned to her mother. "Thank you, Mrs. Mason. I will call you when we are finished here."

Regina's mother stood and walked past her, shooting her a pointed glare as she left.

Apparently, neither of her parents were fans of her future mother-in-law.

Wonderful.

She walked over and took her mother's place on the settee, folding her hands in her lap, her back straight. So, this wasn't an interview, it was an ambush.

"How delightful," he commented, his gaze filled with rapacious glee. "I knew you would be lovely, but never could I have dreamt up a woman of such grace and refinement."

Did he even know how to smile like a normal human? It was chilling, how he couldn't manage to let it reach his eyes. "You flatter me, my lord."

"Not at all. With such virtues it hardly matters what you look like. All flowers have their own beauty after all."

Was that meant to be flattering? "I am so pleased to hear you will not be breaking the engagement, my lord. I have been waiting for this for a long time."

"We both have, but I mean to make it worth your while as my baroness."

She smiled in lieu of reply. It was always safe to smile with men like him. God, there had to be *something* there. Some sign of a human soul. A hint of kindness. She looked deep into his eyes and saw nothing but lust and greed. It was exactly what she had feared in her husband. That he would see her as nothing but a fiefdom to be plundered and conquered.

"Well, your deportment is adequate, and your complexion is even although the color is common. A figure like yours will do well for children I suppose," Mrs. Harrison said at last, casting another critical eye to Regina's figure.

Regina watched her silently, imagining the kind of pistol she wanted.

"Of course, mother," Mr. Harrison agreed, watching her with an entirely different sort of interest despite their audience.

"You will need to restock the family line, you know. If you fail in your duty, it all ends in your hands. Your father may have been willing to let your mother off, but my Edward and I certainly will not."

Something modern of course, the latest from America ideally. Perhaps Mr. Colt had a new iteration of his Dragoon. "I have every intention of fulfilling my obligations."

"Yes, your kind shouldn't have much difficulty with it based on what my Edward tells me about your fellow natives."

"I hear you were educated here at least?" Mr. Harrison began.

Could it be white metal? Was that even possible? "Yes, at Miss Pollitt's," Regina replied.

"A reasonable institution, if a bit common for a baroness." Mrs. Harrison sniffed before sighing.

"It was good enough for the daughter of a viscount," Regina noted.

"Don't interrupt me, girl." The older woman snapped and Regina bit down on the inside of her cheek to keep from saying anything else. "Your father has neatly tied our hands with this alliance like only the son of a tradesman could, but you will not be allowed to embarrass us any further. I shall leave a list of things with your mother that I expect you to be practiced in."

"A list?" she repeated, unable to believe her ears.

"You must and *will* be perfect. My Edward must find nothing else wanting," she said, patting her son's knee adoringly. The gloating obeisance was almost obscene coming from her.

Regina glanced at 'her Edward' who was wearing a smug expression and decided in that moment she wanted the grip of her new pistol decorated in a mandala of mother of pearl.

"Do you understand me, girl?" Mrs. Harrison snapped. "Good God, don't tell me you haven't fully mastered English."

"I understand you, Mrs. Harrison. You didn't want me to interrupt you, I wasn't sure you were finished speaking."

Maybe she could get her father to give her a pair of them. Would that be pushing her luck?

"Mmm," The woman rose to her feet, tugging sharply on the bodice of her dress. "I'm glad we understand each other."

Mr. Harrison stood as well with a satisfied expression. "Well then, I say we post the bans and arrange for the party. I have a list of family we would need to invite."

"Of course, my lord," Regina replied easily. It was almost over. She would have her two pistols. One per annoying guest.

Regina stood and watched them leave, keeping her hands clasped and her teeth clenched against a torrent of words.

So that was her mother-in-law. Every single fear viciously confirmed in the stark light of day. There had been too many insults paid to her to count to say nothing of those levied at her parents. To imply that her father had 'let her mother off' by not risking her life and insisting on a son, and that her mother was a failure as a result.

No, it wasn't an implication, the bitch had stated it outright.

If the mother had so little compunction about openly insulting her to her face before she was married, what would she be like once she was her son's legal property?

Even Ada had managed to garner more respect from the Viscountess Sterling, and she had not been exactly welcoming after Ada's scandalous elopement with Basil. Of course at least half of that good luck was due to Basil's insistence, if Ada was to be believed. Regina couldn't dare hope for the same support or consideration from her husband when this was the woman who had raised him.

She sank back down onto the settee, as her future took on an even grimmer cast. What would be the worst-case scenario now? Her future husband seeing her as an object would be demeaning, but she knew how to cope with that well enough. Could he be violent? If he was, what would her recourse be then? Would there be a way to appease him or at the very least manipulate him into not harming her? What if he forbade her from helping her mother and sister? What if all of this was for nothing?

"Regina?" Her father entered the room with her mother close behind.

"Is she gone?" she asked.

"Yes, priya," her mother said sitting beside her. "I am proud you held your tongue."

Regina nodded but didn't dare to meet her eyes or speak.

"She is a horrible woman," her father commented, throwing himself into a chair.

"We knew that already."

"Madhavi," there was a tinge of impatience in her father's voice. "We knew she wouldn't be ideal, but that piece of baggage is disgusting."

"Perhaps if she can make her fiancé fall in love with her, then he can get rid of the mother." Her mother leaned her head against her knuckle and sighed deeply.

If. Perhaps. A fool's hope meant to comfort her.

"Choti rani, tomorrow we go to the gun shop."

Her mother sat up, her head swinging back and forth between the two of them in shock. "The what? Why are you getting her one of those things?"

He gave her a grave look. "If her charms don't work, then at least her aim will be true."

Thornfield House, Mayfair, London

WITH HIS MOTHER baying for his blood, Leo opted to drop in on Richard. His mother worried about him more often lately, and the consistency of it made him wonder if there was perhaps more to it than a mother hen clucking after her chick.

Richard's parents had been dead for some time, leaving him

to finish raising himself and his young sister far from any family that might have wished them well. Indeed, with family like his Uncle Simon, Richard had little need for enemies. He'd never mentioned his abduction the year before, but Leo knew it had left a mark. It was nothing obvious of course, Richard was nothing if not an actor.

It was small things that only Leo or his mother would have noticed. A slight pallor in his complexion. An unease in crowded outdoor spaces. Before Richard was always out and about, now he was more than likely found at home unless he'd received an invitation. And with Ada married away on her honeymoon with Basil, Richard was more isolated than ever, and his uncle still wasn't fully dealt with. So Leo tried to find time to check on Richard, even if it was reporting on his uncle, which more often than not was the same report. Or going to see a play he knew he wouldn't enjoy.

The fact that his mother was still cross with him was as good of an excuse as any to have dinner with his old friend and make sure he wasn't left too much on his own. Not that it was a great sacrifice. Richard's cook was prodigiously blessed. One thing he could always count on with the Thornfield's cook was a well-seasoned, perfectly cooked meal. Now he sat with him in the parlor in front of the fire lazily swirling brandy in one hand.

"Not that I'm opposed to the company, but to what do I owe this visit?" Richard asked, breaking the companionable silence.

"You make it sound as though I only come to see you on business." Leo would never let Richard know he was there because he was worried about his mental state.

"Did I? You've tended to be busier of late. When I see you it's either in passing or with an update about my uncle."

"We went to the opera only the other day." Leo glanced at his friend, and saw his eyes were closed, his head leaning back against the back rest.

"By my invitation," Richard replied wryly.

"Oh, fine. My mother is cross with me." It was a reason even if it wasn't the only one, and he wasn't above using his own temporary humiliation as a way to lift his friend's spirits.

He smirked. "What did you do?"

"Why do you assume I did something?"

"Because your mother is a perfect angel."

Typical. Richard never found an older woman he wouldn't charm or champion. It was a standard practice established in his youth. The most frustrating thing was the way those women met his good-natured flattery with blushes and encouragement. "I beg to differ."

"Your begging is your problem."

Leo rolled his eyes. In his concern for Richard he'd forgotten one key detail; the man was infuriating whenever he was in high spirits. He loved nothing better than teasing those around him to distraction. At least he was still talking. "I had a bit of a run in with some people that made me late for dinner some nights ago. When I received some clarity about the reason for the delay, I didn't inform her promptly."

Richard's eyes opened and he turned his head to pin Leo with an annoyed glare. "Only you answer questions in a way that produces more. It is exhausting. If you don't want to answer, you could have simply said as much."

"After I received payment from a client, I realized I was being tailed. When I confronted them, they seemed only interested in my identity and informing me of an appointment with their employer. As a result, I was late to dinner."

"And after the appointment you didn't feel the need to tell your mother she had no reason to worry."

"Yes."

"So, I was correct?"

Leo glared at him in response. Richard was so charming and entertaining that it was easy to forget how fucking insufferable he was when he was smug. The only thing worse than his smugness was how good natured he was about the resulting ill humor he instilled in his victims.

"If I may, what was the appointment about?"

"I am apparently the heir to a barony," Leo replied.

Richard's eyebrows shot up before a slow smile crept its way across his face until his eyes were all but glinting with silent laughter.

"Don't grin at me you bastard," Leo grumbled.

"How very interesting."

"If you don't fix your face I'm leaving."

"I'm sorry. I just…" he sighed and made a concerted effort not to let his obvious humor show. Somehow it made it worse. "I can imagine how delighted you were when you found out you were related to some rich white asshole."

"I'd never been more insulted in my life."

Richard's resulting chuckle grew into a belly laugh that had him wiping the corners of his eyes.

"It's not funny, Thornfield."

"Oh, come now. It is at least moderately amusing."

He rolled his eyes, but wry amusement tugged at the corner of his mouth. If the tables were turned, he would have been equally amused. He was man enough to admit that.

"Which relative inflicted this white man's burden on you?"

"My great grandfather, apparently. This according to the old bat who fucking hunted me down to tell me."

"Hunted? So, she sent people to track you down. Oh, this is getting even more interesting."

"Mrs. Theodosia Burghley-Harrison, may she rest in peace soon."

"Well, that's not sporting Leo."

"And then she sent proof to my mother because I wouldn't take it."

Richard nodded. "I like this woman."

"You can have her. She's obnoxious, pushy, rude and older than the fucking wheel."

"She sounds delightful."

"Now I can't go home because my mother found out this

nonsense before I could tell her."

"Mmm…" Richard sat in silence, absently swirling the port in his glass for some time. "Are you truly not going to accept the title?"

"Why would I?"

"You mean beyond the obvious perfect revenge of inheriting the thing they tried to deny you due to their own stupidity?"

It was disturbing how similar that woman was to Richard. "You sound like her."

"I like her more and more, but back to your question. This would be an unprecedented opportunity for you."

"Which is more trouble than it is worth."

"How so?"

"Why must I change who I am for some property and money? I have made a good life for myself. My father and grandfather made that possible, not those worthless shits. Why should I trade their legacy for a title? What makes a title worth more than their effort?"

Richard stared at him for a moment, his expression strangely serious. "I have an answer, but I can already see you won't like it."

"You mean the power and prestige?"

"For one thing."

"You're right, I won't like it."

Richard nodded, the ghost of a smile reforming on his face. "More brandy?"

"No, I must go home at some point. If she is going to throw things at me, I need to be quick on my feet."

"Understood. Take the carriage."

"I don't—"

"For my sake, if not for your own comfort."

He swallowed back the refusal on his tongue. It had never occurred to him that Richard's unspoken fear now extended to him as well. It was also stupid to turn down a free ride when the alternative was to pay for one or walk clear across London.

"Thank you. I'm not cross with you."

"Of course you aren't. I'm a delight."

"Right."

Leo watching his friend carefully. No matter his mental state, Richard never gave up that easily, unless it was part of a plan. The fact that he was sitting there so calmly with that pleasant expression on his face was reason enough to have the hairs on the back of Leo's neck at attention. If he pushed, Richard would cave, but did he have the energy to deal with the consequences?

Probably not. He stood and began to leave, when Richard's voice came again.

"Incidentally, which barony are you due to inherit? In theory, of course."

"Starkley. The Barony of Starkley," he replied.

Richard blinked and then a slow smirk spread across his face again. The one that meant he knew something and wasn't going to share.

"Something of note there?"

"Not yet," he replied with a smile. "Give your mother my regards, will you?"

Leo nodded and walked away wondering if he was imagining the low chuckle that he heard behind him.

ALTHOUGH HE COULD have managed well enough on his own, Leo had to admit it was much nicer to ride in Richard's state-of-the-art carriage. Even if it gave him much too much time to dwell on Regina Mason and what she'd looked like in that dress at the opera. The truth was as unconventional as she was, she was also everything a woman should be in his estimation; brave and sensible, ambitious but caring, loyal and cunning. He hadn't even touched on the rest of her, those wide, heavily lashed dark eyes, that lush but firm figure, all abundant curves wrapped in the smoothest dark brown skin. Her black curls were no doubt softer than they looked even when piled in an elaborate coiffure with a halo of candlelight.

That crisp practical nature wrapped in such a feast for the senses made his head spin. It was the only explanation he had for why he'd asked so many personal questions of a young woman whom he barely knew. She had been right to reproach him, but he hadn't been prepared for how cold those dark eyes could go. He'd been too curious, digging too much for information that he wasn't entitled to. He wanted to pick at the mystery of Regina Mason until he knew everything. So much of her was trapped within the role she'd accepted for herself. A role that fit her even if it left her squeezed into an unnatural shape.

He knew that if she had the chance, she would be just as sensual and giving as her plush mouth, as eager as her curious mind, as sweet as her smile. The idea of all that staying trapped in a life of survival was torturous to him, but it wasn't his place to stand with her. Even if he had taken the silver spoon fate had handed him. She was promised to someone else. No not promised, precontracted with no way out unless she betrayed her family.

Either way it wasn't his problem. She likely didn't see him as anything but a fascinating if impertinent character, especially considering their encounter at the park. Could he dare imagine she saw him as a gentleman? Did it matter?

The carriage came to a stop and the driver thumped on the roof. He was home. Better to stay here with the life he understood, he thought as he stepped down from the carriage and walked up the stairs to his front door.

The house was dark when he entered, save for a candle at the top of the staircase. His mother hadn't stayed awake to greet him, but she had left that faint light to guide him. It was better than nothing.

He hung up his coat and removed his shoes before walking up the stairs as carefully as he could. If she was asleep, he didn't want to wake her.

"How is my baby?" Her voice came as he neared the top of the stairs. He fought back a smile as he reached the corridor and glanced up to see his mother standing in the shadows, a thick shawl wrapped around her shoulders.

That question was growing more and more frequent in their house, but at least this time he was certain of his answer. "He is as he always was. He sends his regards."

"Mmm… he worries me."

He nodded. "He took your side of things, if you are interested."

"Was there another side to take?" she asked before turning to return to her bedroom.

So, she was going to play it that way. He stepped forward and snatched hold of her wrist, pulling her into a tight embrace that she didn't return.

"Mother."

She smacked his back. "Let go of me."

His hold tightened and she let out a sigh. Nothing would do but complete capitulation. Thankfully he had a good amount of experience in the area. "I'm sorry. It was selfish and thoughtless not to tell you the minute I knew the truth. I did not mean to make you worry and I am so very sorry you found out about something so important the way you did. It won't happen again."

A humming silence replaced his voice for a moment, and he wondered if he had truly made her angry enough to hold a grudge.

"Fine," she finally said.

Success. "I hope you can forgive my momentary lapse in consideration for you and your feelings."

"I'll consider it," she grumbled, but he knew he'd been forgiven.

He rubbed her back and rocked her from side to side. She was prickly but there was nothing like her love for him, even when it put them at odds.

"What are you going to do about that title?"

"Nothing. I don't want it." He drew back from rubbing her shoulders.

"You really mean to give it up?"

"It was never mine. I don't need it, and while I have a feeling you and your baby boy are of a mind on that topic as well, I'd rather not discuss it."

Her lips pursed together, and she shook her head before letting out a breath. Annoyance shone in her eyes. "I am too tired to argue with you tonight."

He doubted it but he appreciated the effort. "Thank you," he said, kissing her forehead.

"But this isn't over."

He closed his eyes. A reprieve, but a needed one. "Take the candle," he said.

"I left it for you."

"And I'm here now. Take it with you."

With a dull headache brewing behind his eyes the last thing he needed was more light.

WHILE IT WAS certainly true that Regina wasn't exactly looking forward to her wedding, there were certain benefits to having nightmarish in-laws. Like the new pistol she and her father were on their way to purchase. She had been waiting for two days before her father announced at breakfast that today was the day. She sat across from him in their carriage, in her favorite blue silk calling dress, fingers tapping restlessly against her wrist. Captain Mason was watching her in amusement.

"What?" she asked.

"You are unusually animated today."

"I'm excited about my new pistol."

"The pistol or the prospect of using it on your mother-in-law?"

She opened her mouth to contradict it, but he tilted his head and raised his eyebrows.

"Are you going to deny it?"

"Both can be true," she said.

"What a blood thirsty little wench you are," he said with a chuckle, as the carriage came to a stop. "I believe we are here."

The door opened and her father jumped down before offering her his hand.

"You are certain aai approved of this?" she asked, taking his hand and disembarking onto the sidewalk.

"Yes, rani. Even she can see the necessity of this."

"Small mercies. Maybe we can practice fencing more after this."

"That is a fine point, darling. Let's walk before we run."

She wrinkled her nose at him then looked up at the wood and glass door in front of her. She didn't register the crowds of people milling to and fro. All she saw was the sign above the door.

Wilson and Sons, purveyors of fine handcrafted firearms.

Wonderful. She could almost smell the gun oil. She'd never been inside such a place. Her father had taught her to shoot, but he'd previously drawn a line at allowing his young daughter to accompany him to purchase those firearms, no matter how much she had wheedled him.

With an excited little giggle, she took the arm her father offered her before following him into the shop. It was a strange smell—gun powder, linseed oil and polish. The inside of the shop was busy but not oppressively crowded. A curved staircase led to the upper floor, but Regina didn't notice many clients going up the stairs.

Her father led her to the wall under the staircase. "Stay here for a moment, choti rani. I'll be right back."

"You won't be long, will you?" she asked.

"I won't. I promise. I need five or ten minutes and I'll be back. Just stay here." He dropped a kiss on her forehead and hurried away up the stairs. She didn't relish the prospect of going up those stairs in her full skirts any more than she enjoyed being left in a room full of men. True her father was close at hand, and very few had noticed her at all. The ones who had also noted her father and gave him nods of acknowledgement. Perhaps they knew him or at least knew his reputation. He wouldn't have left her there if he didn't believe it was safe.

Her eyes wandered over the wooden paneled walls, catching glimpses of the glass case where some of the ready-to-purchase pistols were displayed. Older pistols were in display frames on the dark green walls.

"Mr. Kingston, your pistol." A clerk said and a chill went straight through Regina.

Kingston?

Was he here? She watched the clerk walk past her with a box until he stopped in front of none other than Leo Kingston. As always he was neat, his clothing well-chosen and well put together, if not quite fashionable. He wore his customary brown broadcloth coat, she could see a flash of the cravat around his neck. It was the same coat he wore when he'd met her at the park. Suddenly she couldn't help but think of how she had attacked him the last time they had spoken. She hadn't anticipated seeing him again so soon and the idea of it was both thrilling and terrifying.

Mr. Kingston nodded towards the counter and the young man placed the gun down on the glass surface. He pulled it towards him with those long-fingered hands and opened the case with a deft flick of his wrist.

She watched in awe filled fascination as he inspected the weapon carefully, a frown of concentration creasing his brow. Every single inch of him spoke of mastery over his body, of confidence and efficiency.

"Bullets?"

"Just here, sir," the clerk set down a carton.

Mr. Kingston opened it, his full lips moving silently as he counted the bullets in the container. Satisfied with the purchase, he closed the box and nodded.

"Twenty-five pounds I believe you said," Mr. Kingston said

pulling his bill fold out of his coat pocket.

"Thirty, sir."

Mr. Kingston paused, billfold in hand, and those eyes fixed on the clerk with a steady weight that had even Regina squirming. What was happening? Was the clerk lying about the price? Mr. Kingston's eyes swept up and down the young man as he took a step back despite the safety of the counter.

Resolute, calm and sharper than a winter wind. He was magnificent. "Is it indeed?" His voice was soft but there was an unmistakable threat there.

The clerk's eyes shifted away from Mr. Kingston to land on Regina who continued to stare, wondering if he had the gall to see his farce through. "I could be mistaken," the clerk confessed.

"You could be," Mr. Kingston replied. "You could, of course, check the order book to make sure." Then he smiled, reminding Regina of a snarling tiger. "If you were of a mind to be sure, that is…"

"Such a loyal customer as yourself, Mr. Kingston, let us call it twenty."

"Let's not," he replied, laying down a few pound notes.

Regina craned her neck to see the amount, now fully invested. *Twenty-five.* She couldn't help the smile that curved her mouth. He was marvelous. He glanced around the store as he put away his billfold and she quickly turned her eyes away, pulling at her gloves. Had he seen her? Would he ignore her? Did she want him to ignore her? What if he was cross with her and took this as an opportunity to scold her as she had done to him?

"Miss Mason."

She turned to face him hoping she appeared calm and unaffected. "Mr. Kingston, are you shopping for a new pistol?"

"Picking it up actually."

"Ah." *Think Regina. Think!* "Which do you favor?"

"Colt's Navy Pistol, and yourself?"

Of course he would think of asking that. "I enjoy his Dragoon."

He nodded and Regina again found herself unsure of where to take the conversation. He didn't seem cross at all. Should she apologize for earlier? Did he even care? Perhaps it was vanity to think she had wounded a grown man like him.

"Would I be mistaken in assuming you are here with your father?"

"No, I am here with my father." She glanced around for him but could not locate him. "We are looking at the particulars for my new pistol."

"Are you indeed?" His head tilted as he watched her with that frank admiration she still hadn't grown used to.

"Yes, we struck a bargain involving my new mother-in-law and one of those fine instruments, but I'm currently in negotiations for a pair."

His eyes widened comically. "I'm almost afraid to ask."

"Afraid, you?" She could think of nothing more ridiculous than him being afraid of a question. Unless of course it was coming his way. "It is a possibility, I suppose."

He smiled softly but it wasn't the same. He looked down at the package in his hands, and for a horrible moment she wondered if she had done irreparable damage. It was what she wanted in the moment, but faced with him now, the idea of having harmed him was intolerable.

"Miss Mason, I believe I offended you the last time we spoke," he said finally, looking back at her.

She didn't know what to say to that. It wasn't so much that she had been offended. Rather that she had felt herself slipping even further into that wildly inconvenient feeling which surfaced every time he was near.

"If so, I apologize."

"You didn't offend me. I was in an irritable mood and reacted badly. I apologize."

"Not a word of it. What little I do know... you are a rare person indeed."

She couldn't look at him. "Thank you." She almost left it

there but the idea of him believing she was annoyed or angry with him was uncomfortable even if convenient. "I was only disconcerted by your question and the accuracy of your reasoning after such a short acquaintance."

"Ah, likewise," he replied.

"It is good of you to acknowledge it. You ran away quickly enough, didn't you?"

His head was shaking before she even finished her statement. "I did not run away."

"Yes, you walked. Swiftly."

He looked as though he wanted to argue but instead shook his head and looked away from her with a wry smile.

So they were friends again. It gave her the courage to admit what she wanted to ignore. "What you asked me before, about my name. No one has ever asked me that."

"Was I correct?"

That would be his concern. She nodded. "Yes."

"I… although I risk your ire, I only wanted to say that I am sorry for the necessity of your actions. Being extraordinary under duress is exhausting."

She swallowed past the sudden tightness in her throat as her heart fell further under his spell. "It is."

"Regina, who are—oh, it is Mr. Kingston again," her father's face went from wary curiosity to delight. "Good day to you, sir," he said holding out his hand.

Mr. Kingston blinked as if in surprise and shook his hand firmly, "Good day, Captain Mason."

"My Gigi and I are shopping for a new pistol." He slipped his arm around her shoulders, pulling her into a warm hug.

"So, she said." Mr. Kingston nodded in her direction.

"She is a crack shot you know," her father bragged, pointing to her.

"I did not." Mr. Kingston glanced down at her, "But somehow I am not surprised by that fact."

"Are you purchasing one yourself?"

"Yes."

"You know, Lord Melbroke mentioned that you were in the army?"

Mr. Kingston seemed to hesitate before he responded. "I was, yes."

"I take it you were stationed overseas, yes?"

He shifted from one foot to the other. "Yes, I served in the Thirty nineth Foot."

"My old squadron!" Her father announced with excitement, missing his discomfort.

"So it would seem."

"But I've never seen you at the Oriental Club."

"No, no you wouldn't have. I'm not a member."

Not a member of the Oriental Club? Even Regina knew that was strange. It would have been such a social boon that would have undoubtedly helped his business to grow.

"It is for men like us who served in India. I'm sure you have your own connections but, if you have need of a sponsor, I would happily serve as one on your behalf."

"That is very kind of you, sir," Mr. Kingston replied, although Regina would have wagered any amount of money that the last thing he wanted was to join the club. Had he been rejected? What on earth could have happened to make him avoid such a place?

"Not at all. And while we are discussing invitations, Lord Melbroke is having a soiree soon. I believe you should expect an invitation."

Mr. Kingston frowned in confusion. "I have no idea why he would have me as a guest at his table."

"Nonsense, 'one good turn,' Mr. Kingston. I believe he sees you as a good person to have close by. I cannot say I disagree."

"Especially after what you did for Miss Hawthorne and Mrs. Thompson," Regina added.

Mr. Kingston shook his head, already rejecting the idea. "I cannot help but feel my involvement in that entire enterprise has become mythologized."

"If you feel strongly about it, you can always take it up with the Viscount," Regina replied, and he glared at her.

"Thank you, Miss Mason."

She tried not to smirk, but her mouth got away from her.

"Not sporting at all, Gigi," her father said. "Sir, we will leave you to the rest of your day. I imagine we will see each other again very soon."

"Indeed. Good day Captain, Miss Mason."

Regina curtsied, stealing a glance at him as he walked out the door.

"What a capital fellow."

"He is very good." Although his discomfort with praise bordered on compulsive. He had admitted she was correct in her assessment of him in the park. Had he truly been targeted for excelling to the point that he actively disliked praise of any kind?

"He is indeed. Now, do you know what you want yet, choti rani?"

Unfortunately for Regina, she knew exactly what she wanted, but she also knew what was possible. There was no point in conflating the two, even if she allowed her eyes to wander. She would never have the husband she wanted but at the very least she'd have a gun of her choosing. "Yes, baba."

CHAPTER EIGHT

Melbroke House, London
One week later

SURE ENOUGH, AS Captain Mason had predicted, an invitation arrived from the Viscount Melbroke inviting Leo to dinner. It was ludicrous. He had no business accepting such an invitation to dine with a lord at a formal dinner but to decline the invitation would have been the height of disrespect. Or so his mother insisted. She was still annoyed about his refusal to consider accepting the title, so he decided to give her this one victory. He was presently in a hired carriage on his way to dinner.

Left alone with his thoughts, he was once again second guessing the wisdom of this idea. He would probably stick out like a sore thumb among those guests. What if word got around that he was dining with aristocrats? He'd never be able to show his face in The Yard again. He shifted uncomfortably in his seat rolling his shoulders under his dress coat. It fit well enough, but it was just a touch too snug. It was a fine dark broadcloth and had been cut to perfection two years ago. Possibly three. Apparently, his shoulders had gained at least two inches in that time.

He did like the waistcoat, however. It was one of a pair of silk waistcoats he'd allowed Richard to gift him. Like the suit, he rarely had any occasion to wear it. His choice for this evening was a floral brocade in shifting shades of dark coffee brown and deep violet. Neither was au courant, and he had no idea if his choices were appropriate, but they would have to pass muster. The Lord only knew he wouldn't have to use them for long.

He had nothing against earned appreciation but there was absolutely no reason for a viscount to invite him to dinner, no matter what he'd done for his only child. When he was younger, he would have enjoyed the attention and the glory. He would have demanded it as his due. Now Leo knew the cost of too much attention, the dark side of too many eyes focused on him. Not all were friendly or encouraging. Some saw it as cause for envy or umbrage, and others saw it as anathema and acted accordingly to redress balance.

It had taken two knocks to learn the lesson, first in the army and then at Scotland Yard, but by God he had learned it. But being singled out like this for nothing more than doing his job was making him itch. He just wanted the whole evening to be over and done with so he could return to his life. The carriage came to a stop and Leo opened the door hopping down onto the cobblestoned streets of St. James.

Melbroke House, the London residence of the Viscount Melbroke, was a free-standing residence of unrelieved pale grey stone from the walls to the columns bracketing the door to the steps leading up to the deep green door. It was one of the rare detached private residences only owned by the oldest noble families of the ton. The ones who had multiple residences long before the terraced residences became so popular over a hundred years before.

What the fuck was he doing here? *Madness.*

He shook his head once to clear it, paid the driver and strode up to the front door. He knocked briskly before he could talk himself out of it. Moments later the door opened, and Leo came face to face with a butler as stone faced as a gargoyle.

"Good evening, sir."

Well, that was a good beginning. "I am—"

"Is that you, Kingston?" the viscount's voice came from over the gargoyle's shoulder, and Leo glanced up to see the older man and his daughter, Miss Hawthorne, walking towards him with a friendly smile. The Viscount Melbroke and his daughter cut noble figures, him tall, fit and handsome in black and white and her small, dark and elegant, in her pink silk dress. "Thank you, Varis."

"Very good, my lord," Varis nodded and walked away.

"Good evening, my lord, Miss Hawthorne," Leo said giving them both a bow.

The Viscount walked up to him and shook his hand firmly. "Good evening to you. I am pleased you were able to attend this evening."

"Far be it for me to turn down the invitation of a viscount."

"Nonsense, an enterprising young man as yourself, I am gratified you could make the time."

"You are too kind, my lord."

"Papa, I will take Mr. Kingston in to the rest of our guests," Miss Hawthorne suggested, taking his arm.

"Ah." This was going to be the longest night of his life.

"Very good, Ellie," the Viscount said, "I'll let cook know we are ready."

"Other guests?" Leo murmured to her once her father was out of earshot. She snickered in reply shooting him a sidelong glance.

"Oh, yes. It is a full table tonight, but I made sure you were familiar with most of our guests. There were a few family members father insisted upon, but never fear, Mr. Kingston, I will make the introductions."

"I can't imagine who I would know within your father's social circle."

"Can you not?" she asked, with a cheeky sparkle in her eye that reminded him alarmingly of Richard. Once they reached the drawing room he understood why.

Assembled there were none other than Basil's parents, the Viscount and Viscountess Sterling who were conversing with Captain Mason and his wife. Miss Mason sat beside an older woman in a pool of firelight in a gown that shifted from the deepest burnt orange to crimson, chatting politely with a gentleman Leo didn't recognize from behind. Was that called shot silk? Richard would know the answer. He'd thought the blue dress she'd worn at the opera was a sight to behold, this one was even more exquisite, with a golden motif embroidered into the hem of each flounce of her skirt and along the neckline of her bodice.

She was so gorgeous it hurt. Her hair curled softly around her face teasing the curves of her shoulders and brushing the golden bell-shaped earrings at her earlobes. His fingers itched to touch her, to see if her hair was as silky as he imagined. If her full mouth was as soft as it looked. Would she taste as sweet as her smile? Who was that idiot she was speaking to? A horrible thought occurred to him. Was that her fiancé? Had he already arrived? A hard knot formed in his stomach at the sight of them together.

She seemed happy enough and he knew he should be happy for her. She had been terrified of him turning out to be a brute. He was happy for her sake, but Jesus he didn't know if he had it in him to watch her smile at her fiancé all evening. Then the man turned his head slightly and Leo squinted. No, he recognized that young man.

The blonde curls, the cheery smile.

That was the Harridan's great nephew. The solicitor. Albert, was it?

"Is everything alright, Mr. Kingston?" Miss Hawthorne asked.

He turned to her, catching his face in a mirror. When had he begun frowning? He smiled at her and nodded. "Yes, thank you."

"Ah, Kingston, you're here." Was that Richard? Leo looked to his left and saw him sitting near the fire with none other than Mrs. Theodosia Burghley-Harrison. The Harridan. The current bane of his existence. And that backstabbing, insufferable little fucker was smirking. "Come join us."

"Mr. Kingston," Captain Mason stood to greet him, and Leo strode forward and took the escape offered in the gentleman's outstretched hand.

"Captain Mason, good evening. Mrs. Mason, resplendent as always."

She didn't quite smile at him, but her face had softened a bit then as she gave her customary greeting of a slow deliberate nod. He decided to take that as a win. Then he turned to the Viscount and Viscountess Sterling.

"Good evening, my lord, my lady," he bowed to both of them, feeling a bit like a marionette.

"Good evening to you. I am afraid I am not acquainted with you, sir," the Viscount Sterling said glancing from his wife to their hostess who was still holding his arm.

"No, although the name seems strangely familiar."

Miss Hawthorne spoke up, fulfilling her end of the bargain. "My lord, my lady, allow me to introduce our guardian angel, Mr. Leo Kingston, formerly of Scotland Yard."

"What an epitaph," Lord Sterling commented, his expression saying he wasn't any more certain Leo should be here than any of the other non-white members of the party.

"He has more than earned it, I assure you," Miss Hawthorne continued, "he was the agent of justice behind the trouble Mr. Thornfield experienced last year, to say nothing of my and the new Mrs. Thompson's rescue."

"My goodness, yes!" Lady Sterling's eyes lit up. "I read it in the paper, about Ada's rescue and the subsequent uncovering of some sort of crime ring, wasn't it?"

"Human smuggling. Scotland Yard sorted out the most of it, my lady." Once he'd practically gift-wrapped the culprits for them.

"You were named in the issue if I recall. And your offices in Pimlico, was it?" she continued.

Leo blinked in shock. Christ, the woman had a memory. "Just the one office, but yes."

"How delightful. I never imagined I would be able to shake the hand of the man who saved my daughter-in-law," she said, with something like genuine appreciation in her eyes.

"It is entirely unnecessary, my lady. Mr. Thornfield is a long-time friend; I could hardly stand aside."

"But the speed of it," the woman marveled to the other guests. "No sooner had the girls been taken than they had been found, the scoundrels rounded up, and the girls safely returned to their families."

"I'm sure it didn't feel that way for you however, Miss Hawthorne," Mrs. Mason said in her accented English. Leo tried not to gape at the sound of her voice. It was always a rare thing when she graced others with it.

"You are correct, but I am sensible of and grateful for the efforts Mr. Kingston made on my and Ada's behalf."

"Oh, course you are, dear," Lady Sterling said, smiling at her.

"Hello again, Mr. Kingston," Albert, the curly haired smiler said, walking over to shake his hand.

"Good afternoon, sir."

"You know Mr. Kingston, Bertie?" Miss Hawthorne asked with a curious frown.

"Yes, we met the other day," he glanced at Leo, choosing his words carefully, "a service to Aunt Theo."

Aunt Theo, was it? "Yes, I remember, how are you?" Leo replied.

"Well enough, this is my mother, Mrs. Upton with Miss Mason."

Leo nodded in her direction, and she smiled returning the gesture.

"Good evening, ma'am."

"Did you see Aunt Theo there with Mr. Thornfield?"

"He saw me, Bertie," came her sharp voice, "Galant he may be, but his curtsy still needs some work."

"I could say the same of you, Mrs. Burghley-Harrison," he replied with a benign smile.

"Oh, they *are* acquainted," Miss Hawthorne joked patting his arm. "I'll leave you to it then."

"Indeed," but he walked over to where the old crone sat with a fur blanket on her lap and a shawl around her shoulders. "Thornfield," he nodded to Richard who returned the gesture with his customary no good grin.

"Kingston. This delightful woman has been regaling me with her exploits."

"I'm sure she has," he replied, determined to remain civil. He had stopped himself from storming over to her residence more than once after she pulled that stunt with the folio sent to his home. His mother had raised him to be a gentleman and no matter what, he had no intention of making a further spectacle of himself here.

"We are making plans to elope," Richard said winking at her.

"You'd have to, she doesn't have three weeks to waste on bans." Leo replied.

Richard looked at him, eyes wide and mouth wider in fake outrage, shaking his head slowly. "Shocking." he scolded. "I can't believe you called her a harpy."

"I called her worse than that," he replied, and the woman had the nerve to smirk at him.

"You won't abandon me to this cruel gentleman, will you?" she turned pleading eyes to Richard.

"Never, my queen," he vowed extravagantly, taking her wrinkled hand in his. "I shall stay close to you all through the evening."

"You'd better," she said squeezing his hand. Then she turned her attention back to Leo.

"What are you even doing here?" Leo asked.

"Ah, you've been introduced to my godmother," Lord Melbroke said, walking up to them.

"Godmother?" Leo glanced between the two of them. How was it possible that she was a part of this family?

"Indeed." She wiggled her eyebrows at him, and he pursed his mouth against a sneer. She was the height of entitlement and audacity. If she wasn't so bloody nosey, he would have been able to appreciate it.

"How many godchildren do you have exactly?" Leo asked.

"When you are as old as I am you have several, of all ages. If you get a move on, I can squeeze in one more before the veil descends."

"As if I'd let you near any of my children." The words were out before he could stop them. A low cough reminded him that his host was still standing there. "My apologies my lord."

Lord Melbroke pressed his lips together and shook his head. Was he amused?

"You'd need to get a wife first," Richard commented.

"Shouldn't be too difficult for a man like him," Lord Melbroke said. "Dinner is ready, shall I take you in, Aunt?"

"No Cuddy, you've been replaced by this strapping young man here," a gnarled hand patted Richard's shoulder fondly and he smiled down at her with genuine appreciation before standing behind her.

"Can you handle her?" Lord Melbroke asked.

"I shall endeavor to withstand her brilliance with all my might," Richard somberly replied. The Viscount's eyebrows shot up at his theatrics and Leo rolled his eyes. "Come along, my lady," Richard said, wheeling her slowly and carefully around the furniture. "We shall plan our nuptials over dinner."

Chuckles scattered throughout the room at his declaration. His charge shook her head ruefully but there was a new tinge of pink in her cheeks that was almost adorable. *Almost.*

"Rapscallion," she mumbled as she shook her head.

LEO HUNG BEHIND, waiting as they all stood and ushered themselves in to dinner. Lord Melbroke taking his daughter, Lord Sterling taking his wife, Richard wheeling his unlikely future bride, Captain Mason and his wife, and Albert with his mother.

"I think that leaves you with me," Miss Mason said softly. He turned to her and his breath caught in his throat. She was even more beautiful up close.

"Yes, I believe so."

"Good evening," she added with a smile.

"Good evening." He felt like a fumbling idiot.

She stood there staring at him for a moment, before pressing her lips against a smile. "If you offer me your arm, you can lead me in to dinner."

"Oh, my apologies," he said, sticking out his elbow. She didn't laugh, but he knew she wanted to. Instead, she tucked her small hand into the crook of his elbow and nodded towards the door through which the rest of their party had passed.

His heart was pounding in his chest as he walked with her by his side, that light touch triggering a cascade of tingles across his skin. It was ridiculous that a young woman would have such a visceral effect on him. When they entered the dining room, he saw there were only two places left directly opposite each other.

"I believe you are seated beside me, Mr. Kingston," Miss Hawthorne said, and he blinked in incomprehension before nodding in want of a response. He took the empty seat beside her and glanced around the table wondering if he was going to be moved before food was served. Regina took her place beside Lady Sterling directly opposite him. So, he could spend the night trying to avoid staring straight ahead at the person who had most of his concentration.

He glanced at Mrs. Mason and found her eyes fixed on him; absent what little warmth she had previously exhibited. As if she knew where his thoughts were drifting.

Then he caught a look between Miss Hawthorne and Richard. Had that meddlesome little bastard done this on purpose? Had she? Were they in cahoots together? Somehow he'd fallen into a trap. He didn't know how or what the trap was quite yet, but if there was one thing he knew, it was when he was in the middle of an ambush.

REGINA COULDN'T HELP her eyes drifting to Mr. Kingston. He was impossibly handsome in his formalwear tonight, tall, broad shouldered. But there was an edge to his voice and a tension in his body the more people spoke to him. She wanted to reach out and hold his hand, to let him know that he wasn't alone in his unease. That he was amongst friends in this room.

He kept glaring at Mr. Thornfield, who was blissfully ignorant of his friend's ire. Or perhaps he was aware but refused to acknowledge it. Instead, he focused his attention almost exclusively on Mrs. Burghley-Harrison, hanging on her every word, tending to her every need, making sure she was comfortable.

Mr. Thornfield was a charmer, there was no doubt about it, but there was a gentle quality to his expression and his voice which was mostly absent at any other time. It was obvious, at least to Regina, that his affection for her wasn't feigned to antagonize his friend. It was genuine and beautiful to watch.

"What do you get up to when you aren't seducing the decrepit?" Mrs. Burghley-Harrison asked him as the fish course of trout in a lemon, butter and white wine sauce was served.

"Well, I refute 'decrepit', but currently I am finalizing my sister's homes," Mr. Thornfield replied.

"Homes?" Captain Mason asked.

"Yes, it's a sort of wedding gift for her and her husband."

"Where do they live now?" Mrs. Mason asked.

"They are on their honeymoon at present in France I believe," Lady Sterling chimed in, and Mr. Thornfield nodded in agreement.

"Who did she marry?" Albert's mother, Mrs. Upton asked.

"Mr. Basil Thompson, Lord and Lady Sterling's son." Elodia replied.

The woman turned to Richard with wide eyes. "Ah! Congratulations, a very good match indeed."

"Yes, if an unexpected one." Mr. Thornfield's smile was small but somehow, to Regina, it was the truest one of his she'd seen all night.

"Man proposes and God disposes," Lord Sterling commented. He didn't seem too upset over the fact, but he wasn't as pleased as Mr. Thornfield or indeed his wife.

"I believe that is called providence," Regina's mother said.

"Indeed," Lady Sterling agreed. "His will is always wisest and best."

"Speaking of, Miss Mason, I hear congratulations are in order for you?" Mrs. Upton said as the fish course was cleared to make way for the meat course. Regina stared at her in surprise, wondering how the topic had suddenly swung in her direction.

She glanced at Mr. Kingston, wondering what he was thinking behind that perfect mask of a face. He continued eating his wine braised lamb seasoned with garlic and rosemary, but Regina had the distinct impression he was listening to every word that was said. "Oh?"

"Yes, your wedding. I hear it is finally to take place."

Regina smiled, but she didn't trust herself to speak. When had it become common knowledge that her marriage was imminent? How many people had Mrs. Harrison told?

"Yes," her mother replied for her.

"Six years, wasn't it?" Mrs. Upton asked.

Eight, but who was counting?

Lady Sterling smiled at her. "You must be very excited, my dear. I commend you on your patience."

"It's not as though she could drag the boy back by his ear." Mrs. Burghley-Harrison commented.

"That was the next plan," her father joked.

Regina maintained her smile but in her lap her hands clenched her napkin.

"Are we to learn the name of this lucky fellow?" Mr. Upton asked.

She looked up when the question was met with ringing silence. Eleven pairs of eyes were on her. "I'm sorry, I thought it was common knowledge. Starkley, the Baron Starkley."

"So, you are the young woman," Mrs. Burghley-Harrison mused with a strange smile.

"I beg your pardon?" Was it possible she hadn't known?

"Now I will tell you something you don't know. Your fiancé is my great nephew."

Everyone but Regina and her parents turned to Albert who shook his head almost violently. "Not me. My cousin Edward."

"Yes, that's right," Mrs. Burghley-Harrison said.

Regina stared at her in disbelief. The coincidence was incredible but also comforting. This crochety old woman was one person Regina wouldn't mind inheriting with her marriage. With her as the matriarch perhaps Regina would be able to keep some autonomy.

"It's a small circle, Mr. Kingston," Lord Melbroke said, "these kinds of coincidences can be rather common I'm afraid."

Regina glanced up at Mr. Kingston who was staring at her visibly stunned, saying nothing. Even the viscount had noticed apparently. She couldn't understand what he was thinking. Was he upset? He'd known she was engaged, after all, why would this name mean so much to him?

Mrs. Burghley-Harrison continued speaking, "His mother was prattling on about her *dear Edward* inheriting the title, and she mentioned a marriage contract, but she hadn't been more forthcoming. I had a mind to miss the wedding altogether. I can't stand that woman, but now I know you are the chosen one. I think I shall stick around a little longer."

"You are very kind, ma'am," Regina said, trying to ignore Mr. Kingston's intense stare.

"Not at all, my dear. At my age, kindness is a waste of time. Patience and tact are for you young bloods."

She glanced at Mr. Kingston again wondering what on earth he could be thinking. His face had gone slack at the announcement, as if he were in shock but now he was simply staring at his plate.

"So, Miss Mason's betrothed is Mr….?" Mr. Thornfield asked.

"Edward Harrison," her father replied, his tone betraying none of his true feelings.

That got Mr. Kingston's attention again, but his expression

seemed to have shifted even more. He was disturbed by the idea of Mr. Harrison as her fiancé.

"You look as though you are acquainted with my nephew, Mr. Kingston." Mrs. Burghley-Harrison seemed almost smug, as if she knew something she wouldn't tell anyone else.

His head shot up and he blinked rapidly before nodding. "Yes, ma'am, we both served in India."

"What is he like?" Elodia asked.

"He was a lieutenant last I heard," he replied, not meeting anyone's eyes.

"Ah, how dashing. I do love a man in uniform."

"Easy, Euphemia," the Viscount Sterling joked, and more laughter ensued as she swatted the air dismissively.

The conversation continued with the guests joking but Regina couldn't take her eyes off Mr. Kingston, or her mind off his words. They had been polite enough and non-committal, but Regina couldn't help noticing he hadn't answered the question, which only meant one thing, he didn't like him, and he didn't want to offend anyone.

If a man like Leo Kingston didn't like her fiancé it only confirmed what she had already suspected; he was a brute. A hard cold knot formed in her stomach at the realization. There was no way to wiggle out of the reality of her circumstances. What on earth had that man done? Was he only racist and selfish or was he also violent and cruel? The first two were bad enough but expected. It was something she at least knew how to navigate. But what would her life look like if he was violent? If he intended to harm her? How was she meant to survive? What would it mean for her family?

"I will host a small gathering soon to welcome you and your parents to our branch of the family, my dear."

"That is very kind of you," Mrs. Mason replied.

"Nonsense, as the matriarch it is my duty to ensure such things go as they should."

Mr. Kingston fixed a look on the elderly woman that struck

Regina as almost unreasonably hostile, but it was the woman's response that caught her attention. She smirked defiantly and toasted him with her wine glass while Mr. Thornfield coughed lightly into his fist and seemed almost amused. What on earth was going on between those three?

She couldn't imagine what Mr. Thornfield could find amusing, or what Mrs. Burghley-Harrison could have to be smug about, but one thing was undeniable, whatever it was, it involved her, and Mr. Kingston was not remotely amused.

"HOW LONG HAVE you known?" Leo growled under his breath at Richard as they watched Miss Hawthorne play the piano. Leo wasted no time pulling Richard aside after dinner, lingering near a wall covered in cream and gold silk.

"What? That you are technically Regina Mason's fiancé?" Richard murmured, keeping his eyes fixed on their hostess as she exhibited her mastery of the instrument before her.

"Yes."

"Guess."

The whole fucking time. The asshole had probably known since he'd asked him the question over a week ago. He shouldn't have started this discussion now. He should have waited until they were in the carriage... or a boxing ring. As it was, he couldn't help but be keenly aware of the curious eyes glancing in their direction. "How did you know who her fiancé was?"

Richard gave him a slightly pitying look. "I think you know the answer to that."

Leo closed his eyes momentarily as the obvious answer made itself known. Ada. Of course. She was best friends with the girl, of course he would fucking know. "Unbelievable, and you didn't think to mention this earlier."

"It didn't seem to be a particularly salient point until the opera," Richard replied, clapping along with the other guests as Miss Hawthorne finished her piece.

"The opera?"

"Yes. That was when I first began to suspect you had an interest in the young lady."

"You don't have enough to do. That's the problem."

"Not really. I'm lobbying parliament, overseeing the renovations of two properties to say nothing of my own family business. I just found it so very interesting that the same peculiar run of bad luck that put off her marriage was what delivered a title to you."

"I hate it when you are smug," Leo grumbled as Miss Mason took her friend's place at the piano and began to play.

"I know. It is a flaw but to be fair to myself it is only one of a rather short list."

"I beg to differ."

"When will you tell her?" he asked after a moment.

"What?" Leo glanced at him.

"That you are taking the title." Richard stared at him as if the answer was obvious.

"I'm not taking the title," Leo replied. Nothing good could possibly come of him putting himself in the ring for that. Miss Mason had enough to deal with. If he came forward and took her as his wife the scandal would be unimaginable. The ton could just about handle the reality of an Indian baroness, how intolerable would it be to have an African baron thrown into the mix?

"Are you some special type of jackass?" Richard asked, something like true annoyance alighting in his eyes.

"I don't even know if Miss Mason would have me as her husband." Leo replied. It was the height of vanity to assume she would even be interested in him as an alternative.

"She'll take you over that idiot. I assure you."

"That's not the point. She wouldn't want me any more than him." He would only be another fiancé she was forced to make do with. She wanted social advancement, not more trouble by marrying a man that the ton would never accept any more than they would her. Harrison was a monster, but he was white. There would be no denying his worthiness on that basis alone.

"So, what are you going to do?"

Unless…

She smiled softly as she played, a goddess of fire and earth. What if she did care for him? What if he wasn't the only one trapped in this torturous situation? What if she was his wife and he was her husband? There would always be those against them but if they had each other…

She glanced up and caught his eye and, at that moment his heart began thumping madly. What if he didn't have to sneak glances at her anymore? What if that brave, loyal, passionate loving, beautiful young woman could accept him? If she wanted him, if she loved him. Wouldn't that be different?

"I… I need to know if she would be interested in being my wife first."

"I think she is," Richard replied.

"You don't know that, and until I do, I am not altering my life beyond recognition."

Richard rolled his eyes and shook his head before joining the rest in applause as Regina finished her piece and stood up from the piano. She smiled at her audience, and her eyes lingered once again on him. What did it mean?

CHAPTER NINE

Harley House, Mayfair London
Two Days later

AUNT THEO, AS she now insisted upon being called by Regina, was the only redeeming factor in her pending nuptials. She was a sharp-tongued old woman to be sure, with a peculiar sense of humor, but for all her acerbic wit, there was true kindness that Regina had found to be rare among the ton.

The congratulatory tea party she'd elected to throw was meant to show members of the ton that Regina had her backing as a prospective baroness and as the newest member of the family. So far it seemed to have done the trick. An enormous tea service had been set up in the sitting room with tables and chairs put out on the stone terrace spilling out into the back garden allowing the guests to enjoy the beautiful sunshine and scent of flowers. She'd even hired a string quartet and set them up on the terrace.

It was so wonderful. Regina could almost ignore the fact that her mother-in-law was present. Her fiancé had elected to skip this event, deeming a tea party with 'a flock of hens' to be beneath him. Regina's mother had decided that between her father, her mother-in-law and Aunt Theo, Regina would be appropriately chaperoned and hemmed in. Regina would have agreed except for one detail.

Mr. Kingston was here.

She wasn't sure why he was in attendance. He didn't have any social cache to lend her. He wasn't related to the family. In fact, he was barely civil with most of them. He hadn't even drunk any tea. He'd paid his respects and walked out into the garden. That had been two hours ago and all she could think about was him. Less than ten minutes in the room and her thoughts had been consumed entirely by his presence. The only thing keeping her anchored in the room was Elodia's arm in hers. She had never been so grateful for her friend's presence in her life.

"How are you doing, my dear?" Aunt Theo asked her quietly.

Regina turned towards her with wide eyes. "I am well, aunt."

"We were asking you if you had hammered out any details on your upcoming wedding." Elodia reiterated, watching her carefully.

"It will be upon you faster than you can blink," Lady Sterling commented.

"What color dress would you like to have, Gigi?" Elodia asked.

"I…" She couldn't think of an answer. She'd been trying not to think about her upcoming wedding all things told.

"White of course," Mrs. Harrison interjected, walking into the room and selecting a few sandwiches before seating herself in a chair.

Aunt Theo rolled her eyes. "Alyssia, the girl may not want white."

"What color are wedding dresses in India, Miss Mason?" Lady Sterling asked.

"It depends on the region," Regina began, "but—"

"She's not partaking in some heathen practice. This is a Christian wedding in England," Mrs. Harrison interjected. "Her gown will be white in keeping with tradition."

"It's hardly a long standing tradition," Elodia commented.

"If it is good enough for the queen then it will be good enough for the Baroness Starkley."

"I have no objection to a white gown," Regina said, wanting only for the dreaded topic to come to an end. "I haven't really thought about it much."

"I find that very hard to believe," Mrs. Harrison scoffed.

"Hard to believe a girl hasn't thought about her wedding?" Elodia asked pointedly.

"That this one hasn't thought about her wedding considering the machinations of her parents."

Regina's hands fisted in her lap as she fought not to roll her eyes. There was no reason to argue the point when it was for the most part true. It was the implication of avarice on her parents' part that she objected to the most. Elodia's warm hand closed around Regina's fist in a quiet show of support.

"When it comes to machinations, we are all guilty of that in some way are we not?" Lady Sterling said with a nervous laugh. "What parent doesn't aim to provide the best life possible for their children?"

What parent indeed? Even if that life came at an increasingly high cost.

"Have the banns been posted, Mrs. Harrison?" Elodia asked.

"Oh, yes. Everything is well in hand. In a short month for good or ill, Miss Mason will be the Baroness Starkley."

A month.

Thirty days.

Thirty days and she would be given away to that man for good. In the eyes of the law, she would cease to exist, and he would have complete control of her body and her fate. It was the terrifying truth she'd been struggling against her entire life and now it was right before her. God she could hardly breathe. She ripped her hand from Elodia's and rose to her feet.

"Are you well, Miss Mason?" Aunt Theo asked.

"Yes, I…" Regina took a breath and pressed her hand to her stomach, in a desperate bid to quell the queasiness. "I only need some air. I think I will take the time to peruse the beautiful grounds you have here."

"Of course, dear girl. Go on."

"Shall I come with you, Gigi?" Elodia asked, concern etched on her face.

"No, thank you, Ellie. I just need a moment alone."

"Stay near," Lady Sterling instructed and with a nod, Regina quit the room, making her way down the stairs and onto the grounds with slow steady steps. The further away she got, the easier it was for her to breathe. She headed towards the small pond on the grounds. If she had chosen a green dress, she would have sat down and put her feet in the water. As it was… she closed her eyes as a cool breeze drifted over the water and tilted her head back.

"Miss Mason."

She froze. Her eyes flew wide open as she turned to see none other than Leo Kingston holding his jacket in his hand, his shirtsleeves rolled up to reveal his muscled forearms, watching her a few feet down from where she stood. *Oh blast.*

HE FELT A little guilty interrupting her peaceful moment. She had been in her own world when she approached the lake, her face drawn and anxious. No doubt the preparations were wearing on her. It had taken ten minutes in that room to know that he wouldn't be able to stand there and pretend like she wasn't going to spend the rest of her life with a monster. Not with his chest tight with unresolved emotions he would likely never get a chance to express.

He'd needed time to clear his mind and think about how on earth he could go about finding out what he needed to know without compromising her. Then she'd appeared like a frazzled vision stomping through the grass in a turquoise blue dress as if summoned by his thoughts.

But now she was looking at him with those wide doe eyes and he couldn't think what to do.

"Hello again," she said with a tight smile.

"We seem to keep meeting."

"Yes, it's almost suspicious."

It could seem that way. Of course, he knew the only reason he was here was by the machinations of The Harridan. "Is it?"

"Almost." She smiled, before looking around her. "I was seeking a moment for myself."

"I didn't mean to intrude."

"It's alright, I..." she paused and looked down, her small brown hands knotting together before she met his eyes again. "I wouldn't mind your company."

He should have turned her down. He should have made an excuse and left her where she stood. "We will walk then."

She smiled again, but this time it seemed more natural. "Yes."

He waited for her to come to him and then he fell into step beside her as they made their way around the outer edge of the garden.

"So, you managed to escape your mother for a day, eh?" he commented.

"Yes, your Mrs. Burghley-Harrison proved to be an effective chaperone from her perspective."

He shook his head in annoyance at the mention of that woman. *His* Mrs. Burghley-Harrison indeed. He glanced at Regina and saw the corners of her mouth twitching. *Cheeky little brat.*

He still found Mrs. Burghley-Harrison meddlesome and presumptuous, but he couldn't deny the old bat was growing on him. Like mold. Whether he enjoyed her methods or not, the plain fact was that the opportunity he now had to be with Regina was only possible because of her meddling. Now that he knew there was a chance to be with her, he couldn't help but be grateful for the knowledge. If he could thank her for this moment alone with Regina, he was willing to name a child after her and all. "How curious."

"Mother finds her just strict enough to be trusted with my behavior."

"How are your parents?" he asked. It was the done thing, wasn't it? Social politesse demanded an inquiry into the family health before anything of substance could be addressed. Her father was too excitable by half, but he was a good sort.

"In good health," she replied.

"And your sister?" he asked suddenly remembering she had a younger sibling.

"Eager to be a flower girl."

He wondered if the next question was too personal to ask. "And how are you?"

She sighed deeply, her eyes fixed on the path ahead of her. "Eager for it to be over with one way or another."

He loved watching her. Especially when she was thinking. "That makes sense."

"My fiancé, Mr. Harrison…"

"Yes."

She glanced up at him. "You do not like him, do you?"

No. "What makes you say that?"

She raised one, skeptical eyebrow. "The expression on your face when he was mentioned at that dinner implied he was well known but not well liked."

"There are those who enjoy his company well enough." There were always men who would enjoy the company of a man like Harrison. He was charming and outgoing with an edge of cruelty that made it easy for him to command the obedience of some and the admiration of others. If one possessed no scruples whatsoever.

"But not you."

"You are asking very pointed questions today." The politesse she seemed to desire earlier was dispensed with entirely.

She nodded, turning her attention back to the path ahead. "True. Then I will offer you a trade. If you satisfy me on this point, then I will return the favor."

"A dangerous premise. You don't strike me as easily satisfied." Not at all what he should have said, even if it was true.

Her mouth twisted against a smile but she didn't meet his eyes. Clever girl. "We are well matched then."

They would be. Well matched. And he would have made sure to leave her satisfied if she was his. But she wasn't. He needed to remember that. There was a life she needed even if she didn't want it for herself, and he couldn't compromise it for his own selfish ends. "As you wish."

"So, my fiancé?"

"I do not like him," He admitted following her example and looking straight ahead.

"Is he a brute?"

"He is capable of being charming enough when it suits him."

"So, he is insincere?"

She missed nothing. "Among other things. He has regrettable tendencies when it comes to women, especially women who look like you. I expressed my distaste for his behavior more than once, and he did not appreciate it."

"What happened?"

"Sabotage." The memory still burned in his stomach. "He didn't like that I was outperforming him, so he made a few choice comments to sympathetic superiors to produce the desired effect. Neutralize the competition."

"Is that why you left the army?"

"Yes and no. He was more annoying than anything, it was the fact that it worked. I'd served longer than him, my record was exemplary. They could not deny it. But one word from the 'correct sort' and none of it mattered."

"So, you joined Scotland Yard."

"Yes. And Private Harrison became a Lieutenant. He has a talent for acquiring things he doesn't deserve."

"Mmm, like the barony?"

"And you." The words left his mouth before he could stop them. It was becoming a worrisome habit, this inability for him to keep his rogue thoughts to himself.

Her head whipped around to face him, her big brown eyes wide with surprise. "Me?"

For the first time since he'd met her, she seemed to be at a loss for words. If it had been anyone else, any other girl of two and twenty, she would have blushed or at least looked away. Not his Regina. True to her nature, she held his gaze, searching for an answer he wasn't quite ready to reveal, and yet he couldn't take back what he'd already said.

"You are far too good for him and deserve more than what that jackass can give you."

She scoffed. "If only the world operated on that criteria. Who is to say what anyone deserves? Who's to say what I deserve?"

There was no point in pretending to be neutral now. "Me."

She gave him a sidelong glance and rolled her eyes, but a smile lingered at the corner of her mouth. "Forgive me, but you are hardly qualified to make such an assertion after a month's acquaintance."

"I'm a fast learner."

"Mmm," she hummed doubtfully but the smile dallying with her mouth grew wider. "I appreciate the sentiment." She paused and grabbed his wrist to stop him. "I am sorry about what happened to you in the Army."

"It wasn't unique to the army," he replied shaking his head. "People get jealous all the time. It just so happened that it's easier to step on others when you're white and rich."

"Is that why you don't like compliments?"

"I don't mind compliments."

"You mind when they are from white people. Especially when they are titled. I thought you were about to come out of your skin when Viscountess Sterling sang your praises."

"I—" he nearly denied it but it seemed pointless. "Yes. I don't like that much attention because it always brings trouble. You never know who is watching and scheming. You think you're among friends until suddenly you're not."

"They aren't all like that. Mr. Thompson isn't like that."

"Good old Basil. No he's not, but he is very much the exception instead of the rule. I don't trust in what I can't see."

"You must think I'm borrowing trouble by marrying a baron."

"I think you're incredibly brave. Possibly braver than I am."

"I don't believe that," she said. "You're correct of course that it's dangerous to be seen. The higher you climb the more visible you are. I simply don't have the option of running away. If I could, I'd be far less impressive to you."

"Is it worth that much to you?" he asked. He didn't judge her but he couldn't help but wonder about her family. Didn't they understand what they were forcing her to do? Didn't they care about subjecting her to this?

"I suppose it is your turn to ask the questions." She let out a sigh and the sweet smile on her face turned caustic. It almost made him regret the inquiry. "But that is the wrong question. We cannot escape the realities of this world. In my case, the price of being Marathi *and* a member of the ton. My mother has been paying that price most of her life. You notice she barely speaks in public."

"I did notice that."

"Her accent isn't as pronounced as it was, but she is so self-conscious about her accent, whether she is pronouncing things properly. She was lambasted by the good people of England. People doubted her place regardless of how much my father doted on her. Even though father's family was not titled, they were respectable and landowning. She wasn't supposed to be his wife according to them, and even if she was, she wasn't supposed to be *here*. Speaking around people outside the family is rare for her.

"She knows there is no way for her to hide what she is any more than I can, but she wants to protect me from the worst of the whispers. She has no cache to draw from outside of my father, no status here outside of him, so her goal is to align me as much with him as possible. Remove any trace of her influence. I want to alleviate some of her suffering if I can. Give her the protection of my status as well. So no, Mr. Kingston, the title doesn't mean that much to me, but my mother and sister are worth everything and anything to me."

"Will you tell me your name?" The first time he'd asked, she hadn't been willing to share it, and he'd thought of little else since. Now, with the sun shining, and a gentle breeze blowing a dark curl against her skin, he needed to know more than ever.

She came to a stop, and he wondered if he had asked one question too many. When she answered there was a faint sheen of tears in her eyes. "Rajani. My name before my engagement was Rajani."

Rajani. Yes, the name suited her. A dark queen. A warrior and a protector. He had never wanted to kiss anyone so much in his life. He couldn't look away from her eyes, her mouth, the curve of her cheek, the smooth mounds of her breasts.

He wanted to feel those breasts in his hands. He wanted that cheek against his, her breath on his skin. He wanted to unmask the mystery behind those fathomless eyes.

He wanted to hold her hand.

A whisper of wind sent tendrils of fragrance wafting towards him. Sandalwood and something else. Not roses or jasmine, not orange blossom or violets. Not lilies. What was that? There was no one else in the world who smelt like her.

No one else like her.

A cool drop of something landed on his shoulder and he looked up just in time for another to land on his face.

"I think we should—" He began but the skies opened and within seconds they were caught in a downpour.

"Oh damn." He heard her curse and laughed.

There had to be shelter nearby. A gazebo or something. "There's—"

A soft, strong hand closed around his and suddenly he was running with her towards an enormous willow tree.

IT WASN'T A perfect solution. The raindrops would still find them, but it gave them a few more moments together. Moments Regina was only too eager to sustain, regardless of the outcome.

"Your name—am I correct in thinking it is related to the Goddess Kali?" he asked, swiping at his damp clothes trying to dislodge as much water as possible.

"Yes." How on earth did he know these things?

"Why are you looking at me like that, Miss Mason," he asked with a grin.

"I'm only surprised that you would know about that." He kept surprising her at every turn.

"I have always been observant."

He would have needed to be more than observant to have the details he did. He would need to be curious with a memory like an elephant's. "What else have you observed?"

He leaned against the tree and folded his arms across his chest. "That you play the game well. They all see you as demure and biddable but in truth you are clever and calculating."

Calculating? His expression implied that he didn't see it as a flaw. "I can't tell if that is a compliment or not."

"An observation," he replied.

"You are full of those." Did he know what he looked like, leaning against the tree with his folded arms making his shoulders look bigger and his waist smaller. His eyes sparkled with amusement and interest. "I would return the scrutiny, but I wouldn't want you to run away again."

He chuckled and shook his head. "I didn't run."

"Very true. You walked. Briskly."

He chuckled. "I am not afraid of you. What have you made out about my character, Miss Mason?"

"You are discreet and brave. Loyal and clever, caring and respectful."

His eyebrows went up. "Quite the paragon."

"Indeed."

He winced playfully. "But no title."

"True. But I would rather have you for a husband."

He inhaled sharply and her words echoed in her head. Oh lord... had she really said that to him? To *him*. She turned away from him, not trusting herself to keep looking in his eyes and stay in control of her mouth.

"Would you permit one more impertinent question?" His voice came from behind her sending chills up her spine.

"Yes," she whispered.

"Was it your parent's idea to change your name or your fiancé's?"

She looked down at her hands. "My mother's."

She heard footsteps in the grass and suddenly he was standing beside her. "I'm pleased to meet you, Rajani."

"You haven't met her yet. No one has, really."

"Perhaps not, but I should like to."

The ache in her chest was unbearable. As much as she knew there was no future with him by her own admission, she couldn't defend against the desire to choose herself just once, to choose him even if she couldn't keep him. She only wanted one kiss, to know what it would feel like to be kissed by a man who cared for her and wanted to know her as she was instead of what she was forced to be. A man who understood the difference.

Before she could counsel herself against the impulse, she turned to him and took a step closer until she could smell him despite the rain. Fresh and deep like rosemary, amber and aged wood. Close enough to see the golden flecks in his dark amber eyes. If he moved away, she would stop, she told herself. If he tried to stop her, she would leave and never bother him again. She was greedy and selfish to try to take such a thing but if he was willing... her gaze fell to his mouth. It was only a kiss. One thing she could take with her, that she could trust him to give.

She placed her hands on his firm shoulders. She could feel the heat of his body under her hands and against her, chasing away the chill of the rain. She went up on her toes, shut her eyes and pressed her mouth to his lower lip. She half expected him to stiffen, for his lips to tighten in rejection. Instead, they softened and moved against her, pressing back. He was kissing her. She moved one hand to his neck, hoping to pull him closer, hoping he would let her have this much at least for one more moment.

He exhaled forcefully and then his mouth moved to capture her bottom lip. It happened so fast she didn't know how to respond. His broad hard hands gripped her upper back, drawing her closer. The pressure of his chest against her aching breasts shocked a moan from her throat as his lips and tongue worked in tandem sucking at her lips, stroking at her mouth. She didn't know the inside of her mouth was so sensitive, or that kissing could elicit such a reaction all throughout her body. Her heart was pounding. She couldn't seem to catch her breath, and she felt dizzy as if she had spun in circles without a fixed point to focus on. But there was exhilaration as well and an awareness that this man's mouth was the only one she would ever want to kiss. That his touch was the only one that could satisfy or comfort her.

She kissed him back, trying to imitate what he was doing. He tasted like coffee, dark and rich. Only he would taste like coffee at a tea party. Her tongue caught his, and she heard him groan. His arm slid around her waist pulling her flush against him until her feet were off the ground and his other hand slid up her back to curve around her neck, holding her in place as he kissed her deeper. She moaned and tightened her grip on his shoulder, tilting her head, opening wider for him, offering him more, desperate for him to take anything and everything. She wanted to stay here with him in this makeshift cocoon of rain and willow branches.

Was this what Ada had found with Mr. Thompson? What her mother had with her father? Was this what she was giving up? Her eyes burned and her grip tightened.

No, don't. Not yet, she thought. Stay here. Stay with Leo and his big hands, strong arms and soft mouth. If she kissed him hard enough, would she feel it for the rest of her life? Would she feel his mouth even when she was forced to lie with her husband?

Her husband.

A loud crack of thunder startled her back into awareness. Summoning every ounce of strength she possessed, she pushed away from him, relief and despair flooding her as she felt him release her. She stumbled backward, her chest heaving as the chill in the air seemed to settle in her bones.

She was another man's wife, or as close to being that as she had ever been. She was at a tea party. There were people around; people who would gossip and drag her name through the mud and her mother's as well. What would happen to Lilli? She looked at Leo. What would they do to him? What if he had to pay the price for her egotism?

"Oh, God," she whispered. What on earth had she done?

"Regina?" He took a step towards her but stopped when her hand came up to halt him.

She shook her head, unable to say the words. Unable to tell him to stay away from her while her body still ached for him and her heart was crumbling to dust in her chest.

She shouldn't have done it. It was still raining. She couldn't stay here with him. If he touched her again, she didn't know if she could pull away a second time. Ignoring his calls, she turned and ran out into the storm, hoping that the cold water and exertion would chase away the feel of his hands on her body. Within moments she was soaked to the skin, but she kept running and when she couldn't run anymore, she walked. If he came after her, she would be lost. If she stopped, she would turn back.

How had she allowed herself to get that far? When had her hunger to be known and seen grown so far out of her control? How had she fallen so quickly? She knew she would seem out of her senses to others, but it was the only defense she had now. She needed to get back to safety, to where the eyes of others could propel her forward regardless of temptation.

Dimly, she heard the sound of her name and looked up to see her father running to her with an umbrella over his head.

"Regina what the devil happened to you?" He slipped an arm

around her shoulder and ushered her into the house where the remaining members of the party were watching her with concern or blatant interest.

"Goodness, girl, what were you thinking?" Aunt Theo asked.

"I…" she could barely speak, "I was walking."

"I thought you had a headache," Elodia said.

"It doesn't matter now; you need to get her dry or she'll catch a cold." Lady Sterling said, her face set in concern.

"I want to go home," she said, wrapping her arms around herself, pleading at her father with her eyes.

"Regina," he laid his hands on her shoulders.

"Please, baba, take me home." He stared at her for a long moment before nodding brusquely.

CHAPTER TEN

L EO WAITED UNTIL the rain stopped before he returned to the house. It was a solid two hours spent leaning against the tree, but he stayed there. When she'd run away, he'd nearly followed her, but then he'd noticed the tremor in his hands. Best to stay put. If he saw her again, he didn't know what he would do. He hadn't intended to let it go as far as it had. Had been willing to let her have her kiss and then keep his hands to himself. Then she had pulled him closer and before he knew it, he was kissing her like a man possessed.

Until the day he died he'd never forget the feel of her in his arms, her mouth innocent but hungry, her body lush and eager. He had always suspected that there was more she kept hidden, but he hadn't expected it to sweep through him like a wildfire, leaving him aching and shaken. There was so much passion and energy she kept hidden under that pragmatism. All for the sake of an alliance she didn't even want. She was so beautiful and clever, fiery and brave, an utter waste on a sniveling little cretin like Harrison.

She knew that. He'd been looking for a sign that she wanted him, and the argument could have been made that he had received one. But there was another nipping at the edges of his mind. A woman like Regina never capitulated. Even her determination to marry Harrison was a chess move, a calculation with an immense cost but the potential for a meaningful gain.

What if this was another stratagem, seemingly offering everything with one hand while safeguarding one thing for herself? One last chance to be Rajani before she locked half of herself away forever behind a mask fashioned by England.

He wouldn't fault her for it, even if it was true. What he needed to know was what the fuck it meant. He knew what he felt for her. There was no point in pretending the exhilarating hell in his chest was anything other than love, or something very near it. But Regina Mason was anything but an open book. Did she feel something for him, or was he simply a more pleasant option for her fiancé? Was a chance to be her hero enough for him to take that title? Did she even need saving? Was that more wishful thinking?

He'd had one question before their meeting and now he was left with several more. What few answers he'd gleaned offered no clarity whatsoever.

SHE COULDN'T MEET her father's eyes in the interminable carriage ride back to their home, no matter how hard he stared at her. She didn't know what he knew or suspected and she could barely bring herself to speak let alone explain why she'd chosen to walk in the rain rather than seek shelter. She would never breathe to a soul what she had done. That fantasy, that eyes closed wish had somehow manifested itself into being on a rainy summer day in Mayfair. *Leo.* He couldn't be Mr. Kingston any longer. Not after that kiss. She had kissed Leo Kingston. In broad daylight. In the moment, it had felt like liberation, the keenest pleasure she had even known. For those brief minutes she'd allowed herself to feel everything that she was capable of and the power of it was devastating.

She would never have imagined how hard it would be to walk away from him. Even now she could still feel the pressure of his mouth, taste his coffee, smell his scent. For one moment, under a willow tree in the rain, she'd lived her life without apology and kissed a man among men. It was a memory to keep close to her heart, to remind herself in the years to come that she was a woman instead of a machine. Years that now seemed endless with the memory of his body against her still so vivid. She couldn't bring herself to wish that remembrance away. A desolation was taking up residence in her heart with a swiftness that stole her breath.

This was the horrible secret her mother meant to keep. It was why she's insisted she learned to dance but never let her participate at balls. Why she limited her social outings and watched the media she consumed like a hawk. Knowledge was a terrible thing to one who couldn't act on it. This little rebellion was going to torture her with awareness she was never meant to have until she went numb, or mad. Whichever came first.

The carriage came to a halt outside their home and Regina let her father out first before she followed. She only needed to get back to her room. If she could avoid her mother that long, she would have enough time to wrestle her senses back into submission.

But as she came through the door, her mother was standing there like she knew something had happened. "Regina."

Regina. Why was it so strange to hear that name? Leo had only said her name once and now hearing anything else grated. "Aai?"

"What on earth happened to you?" She walked up to her and took one of her hands in hers. "Your dress."

"It's nothing," Regina muttered pulling her hand back. There was a pressure within her threatening to shatter her into raged pieces or crush her heart into dust. She couldn't look at her. There was too much fighting to escape and nowhere for her to hide.

"Did this happen on the way back?" she asked.

"It did not," came her father's terse reply.

"Not at the tea party. In front of her new relations?"

"She claims she got caught in the rain."

"I did," her voice sounded weak, even to her. What had she done to herself?

"You could have found shelter instead of wondering around like a lunatic."

"Aai, please."

"You didn't look as though you had gotten caught in the rain." Captain Mason said, watching her hard. "You looked like something had driven you out into it. Like you were running away from something."

She shook her head and sank down into a chair. She felt weak, ill, like every ounce of her strength was being spent holding up this crumbling facade. "I wasn't feeling well. I just went for a walk and the rain caught me. There was nothing strange about it. This is England."

"Baronesses do not wander around in the elements. What are people going to say?"

"I'm sorry, aai," she leaned forward pressing her forehead to her clasped hands. She was unraveling, she could feel it. Years of swallowing everything back had poisoned her past the point of no return. How was she supposed to bear knowing what true passion felt like, of what it was to be desired by a man for who she was body and soul?

"This is because of the influence of that Elodia girl. The wild one," her mother continued, standing over her fiddling with Regina's hair, trying to lift her head to see her face.

"This has nothing to do with Ellie."

"Miss Hawthorne was inside with the rest of us, as dry as tinder," her father said, sitting down heavily on the couch with a heavy sigh.

"Then it is your fault," her mother turned an accusatory eye at her father.

"Me?" He looked at her almost offended.

"I told you to watch her. You spoil her too much, letting her do too much with the fencing—"

"Spending time with my daughter is not spoiling her, Madhavi—"

"—and sending her to that school—"

"—That school is a fine institution and allowed her to befriend the daughter of a viscount."

"Yes, and that viscount's daughter took Regina all the way to Gretna Green—"

"—for the sake of a friend who is now happily married to the son of a viscount—"

"—And where is Regina now? Soaking wet in our living room after she shamed herself in front of her future in laws. I said it time and again, a young girl needs to be home with her family. Now she is rebelling at every turn with that bonnet and those dresses, running around in the rain like a peasant exposing herself to gossip and ridicule. What is her fiancé to think?"

It was the closest they'd come to arguing in front of her. The most they'd ever disagreed in her life, and it was her fault. She had given into her weakness and already it was tearing her family apart.

She glanced up at her father and saw him watching her mother with visible frustration, his jaw tight and his chest rising and falling rapidly. Then he shook his head and looked away. "She needs to go change." He turned to Regina. "Go upstairs."

Regina nodded silently and rose to her feet hobbling her way to the door. Her hands were shaking. She was freezing. It was summer, why was she so cold? Her entire body ached as if her bones themselves were exhausted with the weight of her.

"Change?" her mother snapped, "Yes, she does. Into a grateful and respectful daughter!"

"Grateful?" That word shocked her out of her stupor.

"Yes! After all the efforts your father and I have made on your behalf to prepare you for this opportunity."

Her father stood and took a step forward. "Madhavi."

"No, it's the limit now." Her mother rounded on her, her

eyes flashing. "Do you think it has been easy? All we have done for you, and you can't even bring yourself to *sit still*."

"For me?" She knew she needed to keep quiet, but the words kept slipping out unbidden.

"We left India and came to this godforsaken country for you. We invested thousands if not millions of pounds into you so that when the time came you could soar into the brightest future, and you don't even have the intelligence to be sensible of the fact."

Her brain was filling with steam like an overheated machine as it struggled to comprehend the words coming out of her mother's mouth. For her? *Her?*

"Look at her face! I don't know what I did to deserve a daughter like you."

This isn't for me. She couldn't imagine how that narrative had taken hold. For her! As if she wanted to be married to that monster. As if she had wanted or asked for any of this.

"Yes! This is for you. It is all for you and you are not only wasting it, you are turning it into a spectacle!"

"This isn't for me!" someone screamed. She didn't feel the words leave her but the rawness in her voice revealed their source. Her body was out of control, vibrating with an incandescent rage forcing its way past her skin anyway it could.

Desperate screaming.

Ragged breath.

Furious tears.

"This isn't for me! You didn't take me from my home *for me.* You didn't take away my name *for me.* This is for you! We are here because when I was *thirteen* baba gave me away to a baron and that man wanted me to be as tamed as possible. I agreed to this for you. So baba could breathe a little easier and not feel like he failed you. So you could hold your head a bit higher when you face those white women in the ton. So you could sing again. So you could finally, *finally* smile as you used to."

She caught her father's eyes and saw them wide, blood shot and glistening with tears. At any other time, it would have shocked her into silence. But it was too late now. The words kept leaking out of her like filth from a festering wound. "I did this for Lillian so she wouldn't have to hide herself like I did when her time comes. So she can have a chance at a life that belongs to her. I'm willing to do it for you, for her, for all of you. I am willing to be the sacrifice that gives you the protection baba could not, because I love you. Because I respect you. Because I understand a small amount of what you put up with. But don't get confused, aai. Marrying a man who doesn't respect me enough to want to know me, who only sees me as something to possess and plunder is not for *me*. It was *never* for me!"

Her mother was silent, staring at her as if she was a stranger or a monster. A changeling who'd replaced her obedient child with a hysterical termagant. The words she'd spoken drifted back into her mind like poisonous petals on the wind. Every word she strangled into a thought, every resentment she'd attempted to fashion into something else while she forced herself into the mold of Regina.

But this rage didn't only belong to Rajani or Regina. The work had been left undone rendering her some twisted bastardization of the two. She couldn't stay in that room a moment longer, raw and exposed as she was with all those terrible words hanging in the air between them. Turning on her heel, she stumbled into the foyer, half nauseated and half numb, and made her way up the stairs. A movement as she neared the top caught her eyes and she turned to see Lillian crouched by the banister with wide frightened eyes in a tear-stained face.

Damn. She had surely heard everything. The romantic illusion of castles and princes was shattered. "Lili," Regina croaked out, and the little phantom scrambled away without a word. She stood frozen, watching her run away, and the regret washed over her. What the hell had happened to her? What had she done? Never before had she felt like more of a failure.

Night had already fallen by the time Leo trudged into the home he shared with his mother. He had walked from Mayfair to Pimlico. He walked up the stairs, physically exhausted but his mind still reeling from the events earlier that day. He didn't know what to do with the information he had. At the top of the stairs, he saw a light in the salon. She was still awake.

For a moment he wondered if he should simply take himself to bed. He wasn't sure he could withstand a debate with his mother. Then there was a creak in a floorboard, and she was in the doorway.

"Mother."

"You look exhausted," Naomi commented, watching him with worried eyes. He nodded and followed her into the room, seating himself on the couch and rubbing his face roughly with his hands.

"I have a question to ask you."

"Go ahead, son."

"It's about the title."

"The one you refuse to accept?" she asked with some ire.

He couldn't help the smile her tone triggered. "The very same. Certain things have happened since, and I find myself wanting to change my position."

"Yes." She moved over to sit beside him, taking his hand in hers.

"But doing that will create upheaval for us. The adjustment to a new way of living among those people. It will make us a target of gossip and even spite."

"It is also a tremendous opportunity, one that you are more than equal to."

"But the cost of it." He rubbed his free hand roughly over his face. "The expectation to say nothing of the responsibility placed on us, on me."

He was afraid. At the end it was as simple as that. Because he did want it. He liked being important. He wanted power and prestige and all the rest of it. But he was sick of people coming for him because of his accomplishments. Staying low had served him well in the past, over-achieving had not. What price would he have to pay, would his family have to pay for his vanity?

"Why are you considering changing your mind then?"

Regina. Rajani. Her tear-filled eyes filled his mind. The desire and fear. She had been pushed into the spotlight against her will and had risen to the occasion despite her antipathy for the circumstances and her personal wishes. She had to be terrified, but she wasn't flinching or turning away as he was. If she was up to it, surely he could be as well. He could at least be as brave as a twenty-two-year-old woman facing down a lifetime of mistreatment. "There is a young woman—"

"If she will not take you as you are, then she is not worth it."

"I—" he laughed and shook his head. The fist around his heart loosening slightly. "I know that much, mother. Her family has tied her hand to a title and estate. I have felt something for her for some time, knowing that there was no way I could force her into choosing me over them. That would be the choice for her."

"But?"

"But I didn't know she was tied to *this* barony."

"And she is worth it to you?"

"She is… she is extraordinary. You would love her. She is so brave and clever and loyal. Filial. She knows her mind and stands her ground. She is everything a young woman should be."

"Is she pretty?"

An image of Regina appeared from earlier that day flecked with rainwater. Her wide, flashing, coffee-colored, eyes, supple brown skin and black hair full of soft curls. Her warmth and isolation, her passion and resolution. "She is exquisite."

"When did you decide to ask for her?"

Tonight. "That's the point. I haven't decided. I want to know what she feels for me before I take that step. But once I have, there will be no going back for any of us."

"Do you want my blessing?"

"I want to know how you feel about being the mother and grandmother of a baron. I want to know if you would be uncomfortable in that life."

She slipped an arm behind him to rub his back and tightened her grip on his hand. "I would not be. I've wanted to box your ears ever since you told me you refused that title. Of all the things to be pig headed about. But I understood your reasoning. If you are now telling me that you are willing to take on a role that would suit you down to your bones, for the sake of a woman who is your match, then I am ready to stand behind you."

"Beside me," he corrected.

She smiled sadly and slipped her arm around his waist, hugging him close, her eyes shining with love. "No, son. That place will be for your wife. I stood beside your father, and I stood beside you as you grew into the man you are. That is enough."

His eyes were burning at the idea of leaving her behind. "Mother—"

She shook her head, and he fell silent. "It is time. It is time you took what is yours. I hope she is eager for your sake. You will make them see what you are, what you always have been, and I will stand behind you."

"Close behind. We will still need you. I will need you."

She released his hand and rested a warm firm palm on his cheek. "My brave beautiful son. I'm not going to disappear, I promise you. But…"

"What?"

She looked away for a moment a frown creasing her brow. "Is she the only reason?"

"What do you mean mother?" He removed her hand from his face and held it loosely.

"I do understand your reasoning for not taking it, but I worry that she will not be enough. You love her and that is good but you cannot do this for her sake alone."

"I have no need of it otherwise."

"It is about more than what you need now. It is about taking what you are owed because you are owed it."

"I know that."

"You need to find a reason to take it for yourself, for your own sake. Otherwise any inevitable problems will only stir up resentment between the two of you. Marriage is hard enough without the added pressure you will both face."

He nodded but didn't reply. He didn't agree but he didn't want to argue with her about it. He had discernment, he would never blame Regina for the actions of someone else and if he continued thinking along those lines, he wasn't certain he'd be able to do what he needed to do.

It would all be well. He would take the title, marry Regina and do whatever it took to help her attain her goal.

CHAPTER ELEVEN

Number 12, Mayfair London
Two days later

THERE WAS A desperate need within her to keep moving. As the clock ticked down closer to her engagement ball, the idea of sitting and waiting for the inevitable was excruciating. So, she pulled on the loose linen gown she used to practice while they were in the London house and went out into the garden. She'd imagined that facing the reality of her choice would give her strength and clarity, and perhaps it had.

What she hadn't prepared for was the desolation which had set in her spirit. Bharatanatyam in her mind was linked to prayer, a full body meditation that allowed her to inspire herself to be more than she believed she could be. But there was no point in asking for the removal of obstacles. All she could hope for was the strength to endure without losing her purpose or herself in the wilderness she had chosen.

She chose a veneration to Durga, the feminine divine, focusing her energy into all her faces and forms, her strength, her softness, her brutality. To be all things to all beings as the occasion called for it with a firm center. She would dance until the goddess gave her strength. Until the endless void in her chest was filled with something, anything.

Warmth filled her limbs as she began. Counting out the beat in her mind moving her body through the forms. There was a deep satisfaction in feeling the stretch of her muscles as her limbs obeyed her dictates. Moving from Dandapaksha to Parvathy

Hasta, balancing on one knee as she knelt on the ground or standing on one foot with the other folded onto her knee. Moving into a deep lunge with her hands positioned to hold her mighty spear.

Her muscles were on fire now, her lungs pushing oxygen into her body, forcing it to keep moving in a desperate attempt to keep her moving. But her strength was fading, and that emptiness was still there, that feeling that somehow despite all her efforts she would be left with nothing but regret in a lonely cage. Like an exotic bird. There was no doubt in her mind that he saw her as an unusual creature he'd inherited. Pretty only because it was controlled. The fear kept swelling in her belly and she didn't have a way to stop it.

"Regina." She looked up to see her father watching her. His arms were folded, leaning against the gazebo. Had he been there long? She hadn't seen him or her mother since her outburst the day before. She straightened her legs and walked towards him.

"Baba."

"It's time for you to get ready."

Already? She looked around her taking in the twilight shadows. She didn't know how long she'd spent dancing. Hours certainly. All to no avail. She was tired, dripping with sweat but without peace.

"Yes, baba." She sat down and untied her ghungroos before slinging them over her shoulder and following him back to the house.

"How are you?" he asked. It wasn't the first time he had spoken to her since her outburst, but it was the first time he had inquired about her.

"I am as well as I can be. Are you angry with me?" she asked.

"Angry about what?" He frowned at her in confusion.

"About what I said."

He sighed and shook his head. "Not angry, no. Your mother is upset but I can't tell with whom." He walked in silence for a moment. "Do you feel that we failed you? That I failed you?"

It was a difficult question to answer. How could she explain that she had known that for all their love for her, they would contract her out in a marriage without her consent or even her input for the sake of social advancement. She had chosen to see herself as the extension of her father's love for her mother and sister. His red tasseled spear. But there had also been times when she had resented not being afforded any protection at all. "I know that you love me, baba, that you love all of us."

"Thank you, rani, but that's not what I asked."

"Do you believe that you failed me?"

"Not sporting at all, turning my question back on me."

"I'm not trying to be unfair, baba. I'm trying to understand the question."

He nodded but stopped walking. "I suppose I never allowed myself to think too much about what you were feeling. We had our own bond, and I imagined it was enough. I tried to spend time with you outside of everything else, you know, with the fencing and the shooting. But now I wonder if I was trying to make up for things. I'd taken your chance to have a season like every other girl your age, to find love in your own time. I deprived you of your name, your culture and interests in the name of giving you something more valuable. But I never asked who it was more valuable for.

"You were always spirited and mischievous, but you never fought back against the engagement, not really. You seemed to accept things. So, perhaps it was more convenient to let myself believe you didn't have those feelings because you didn't speak of them."

"I didn't want to hurt you or make you worry."

"Yes, but I didn't want to hurt you either. And I have. We both have. It is no secret that I wanted you to marry the baron to protect your mother and sister, and you understood that well. But you are also my daughter. You also deserved that protection and consideration. Convenience isn't a good enough excuse for denying you. You didn't say anything that wasn't true, even if we didn't enjoy hearing it."

"I meant what I said. I understand the reasons and I am willing to marry him, even if I am not delighted by the prospect."

"I can't help but notice you still haven't answered my question."

Damn. "No, baba, I don't believe that you failed us. You did your best for us, but you are only one man after all. You would never have been able to protect all of us from everything."

"Do you think I should have protected you more than your mother, because you are our child?"

"Sometimes. But I also know that there was no correct answer, not really. There still isn't. That is why I want to help you, even if it is like this."

He smiled at her, but she could tell he was less than convinced. "Go on and get ready, choti rani."

She nodded and walked away wondering if she would ever be able to repair what she'd damaged.

IT'S WORTH IT *for them. It will be worth it for them.*

That was the mantra Regina had been repeating in her mind from the moment she arrived at Harley House, the London residence of Aunt Theo. She was dressed in a sumptuous gown of orchid purple silk, trimmed at the sleeves and bodice with blonde lace and pearls and blue silk irises. Her hair was curled and fashioned into a fashionable coiffure, decorated with blue irises to match her dress.

The party was a sincere effort from Aunt Theo, and the old dear had rallied enough to host it with Mr. Upton wheeling her about the room. Regina was grateful for her kindness. She was. But after one hour with her fiancé she was ready to run screaming into the night. He was such a slimy piece of work. Her parents had stayed near her at first, but in no time his mother had taken her away, which left Regina on her own.

Elodia had been there as well but after Mr. Harrison had all but threatened her, she had maintained her distance. Even her hot-tempered friend had understood that standing her ground then could lead to reprisals for Regina after. Again Regina was grateful for her discretion, but she had never felt more isolated in her whole life.

Now she stood beside her husband to be, again at the edges of the ballroom, smiling at the well wishers and wishing passionately that she was anywhere else.

Or that the rapture would come and snatch her away.

Or that a fire would break out.

Anything.

He didn't dance with her, although he'd taken to the dance floor at least three times before this. After Elodia he'd elected to stick to her like a gloating, maddening barnacle.

"You seem unusually quiet tonight, my dear," Mr. Harrison said. Regina forced herself to smile.

I'm not your 'dear'. "Do I?"

"Is there something amiss?" It would have been a sincere question if he had bothered to look at her when he asked it.

"How could there be?" she asked, tightening her grip on her wrist.

He watched her for a moment, annoyance warring with his practiced civility. "You tell me."

"I am fine."

"I thought an English upbringing would have cured you of that strain of dishonesty."

"I don't know why you would think that." The English in particular wielded their dishonesty as a matter of national pride in the name of politeness.

He slid his arm behind her and squeezed her waist hard. "I see I have some conquering to do still."

It was ridiculous to pick a fight with him. What was the point of it? What would she gain? "I am sorry. Perhaps I am a little tired. I danced a little too long tonight before coming here."

"Did you indeed?"

"I did. I am a little short tempered but not because of anything you have done tonight."

He smiled but said nothing, the coldness in his eyes turning to fascination. "Interesting."

"What is?"

"You think you have us all fooled, don't you? You are good at playing the virtuous lady, but I know your kind and I am up to the task of you. I've agreed to this marriage partly in consideration of the years you spent waiting. You are a rare and exotic jewel, a point of uniqueness among the homogenous. That pleases me. But if needed, I can and will replace you. Don't forget Miss Mason, I am the prize in this scenario, not you. It would be in your best interests to keep me happy. Understood?"

She swallowed past the sickly lump in her throat, her gaze dropping to his shoulder, anywhere but the wasteland of his eyes. "Yes, sir."

He extended a long finger and traced her jawline before hooking it under her chin and lifting her face up for his perusal. She clenched her teeth and tried not to shudder in revulsion at his touch. It would only give him more satisfaction. "Good girl." He released her chin and flicked a curl laying on her shoulder.

She pressed her lips together and turned towards the dance floor, tightening her grip on her own fingers as her eyes burned. He was a nightmare of a man, but he was her husband, or he soon would be. Her throat tightened and ached. *Not yet. Not here.* She took a deep breath and focused on her hands, her feet, the glow of the candles in the candelabra, anything but how close she was to tears or the man beside her. She couldn't fight against the inevitable, but she would be damned if she showed an ounce of weakness for his benefit or theirs.

"Darling, darling," Mrs. Harrison called out.

"It seems your mother needs you," Regina said.

"So she does. Excuse me, dear," he turned towards Regina, "I trust I can leave you here without incident."

She stared at him in mutinous silence. Wondering how long he would wait for an answer before leaving. It took a full minute but, in the end, he sneered and walked away leaving her alone in the ballroom for the first time in her life.

Dear. She already hated that word.

He wanted submission, and it would be easy enough to fake. She would find a way around him, as she'd found ways around every member of the ton who wished her ill.

"Miss Mason." She heard Leo's voice over her shoulder and her heart seized in her chest, flashing throughout her body like a shock of cold. She turned and, yes, it was him. Clean and neat as usual, in the same suit he'd worn to dinner weeks before. Handsome as sin and just as forbidden. It was like a dream, or a twisted nightmare. She couldn't tell.

"Mr. Kingston." It came out as a gasp. Her hand curled into a fist over her stomach where a swarm of butterflies had taken up residence.

"I need to speak with you."

"I…" she glanced around the room frantically looking for Mr. Harrison. "My fiancé is here."

"Yes, I'm aware. That is what I wish to speak to you about."

"Where is he?"

"He's in the other room. Come with me." His hand closed over her wrist lightly.

"What?" She gave her head a hard shake. He couldn't be serious about that request. This wasn't the time or the place "I cannot speak with you here, people will gossip."

"A dance then?"

"That would be worse!" she replied, before lowering her voice at the curious looks sent her way.

"One dance and I promise I will leave you be."

"My parent's…"

"Your Aunt Theo is detaining them."

Aunt Theo? Was she party to this? Did she know? Regina didn't know what weakness had seized her, but the next time he tugged at her wrist she followed him. It could have been his eyes or the idea of him being her first dance as well as her first kiss, but she nodded and allowed him to lead her to the dance floor. Too late she realized it was a waltz.

"Rajani," he said, and she shivered, barely maintaining her footing.

"Don't call me that. I can't be that person anymore. I am Regina, or Miss Mason." She could barely meet his eyes as it was. He was too close, too warm and hard and everything a man's body should be.

"Miss Mason then, since we are back to honorifics, I take it you still mean to go ahead with your wedding."

"Of course. I must." It was torture being this close to him, having his arms around her waist. He still smelled like wood and amber and rosemary. It took every ounce of concentration to prevent her from pressing her greedy body a little closer so she could feel his one last time.

"And that kiss, what was that? A dalliance?"

"It was an… indiscretion. I didn't mean to do it." And she could not altogether claim to be sorry for it, even if the consequences were proving to be more than she could bear.

"An indiscretion." He seemed to be weighing the word in his mouth while those eyes pierced her soul searching for the answer she was terrified to give. There was an intensity in them she had never seen before.

She had to be honest with him. She couldn't have him standing in the corner, always testing her willpower, always reminding her of what she was giving up. "I treated you unfairly, I can admit that. I was reckless and you deserve more than I can offer you."

"And what if you could offer it?"

She blinked up at him. What the hell was he talking about? "I… I cannot."

"But if you could?"

She couldn't make her mouth say the words even as her heart was shouting confirmation. "There is no point to answering that question."

"I need to know." The dance came to an end but when she tried to pull her hand away his grip tightened. Would he not let her leave? What was he going to do?

"Please," she whispered, and he released her. But in the next moment, before she could walk back to her station against the wall, he pulled her further away to a sparsely populated enclave, his body standing between her and the guests. She had never seen him look this... earnest before. This intense. She should have been afraid, she should have been outraged at his refusal to adhere to her wishes but instead she found herself... intrigued.

"Did you mean what you said?" he asked. "That you would rather be my wife than his baroness?"

Oh God, her eyes were burning again. She had the answers on the tip of her tongue, but she had already failed her family once before. She couldn't do it again. She had to stand strong even if every ounce of her wanted to hold onto him and never let go. Why was he torturing her? "Why are you doing this to me? I told you that in confidence. Why would you ask me such a thing here of all places? No, I don't want to marry him, is that what you want me to say?"

"I'm not asking that. I am asking if I would be your choice if you could make it."

"I did make it," she snapped, hoping a show of anger would give her a way out. "I chose their happiness over my own."

"What does that mean? Did you kiss me because it was me or because I wasn't him?"

She glanced around the room noting the curious looks from even more guests. "Keep your voice down for God's sake, people are watching."

"Would someone who isn't him be enough?" he asked.

She dropped her head and closed her eyes. "Please, don't do this to me." The sight of his desperate face was *painful*.

"Regina, we are ready. Where is that girl?" Mrs. Harrison called.

Terror filled her at the sound of her mother-in-law's voice. God, if they found her with him… she couldn't even think about it. "They are asking for me."

"You need to answer me first," his hands fell lightly on her bare shoulders holding her in place as securely as bars of iron. His touch… she couldn't stay there. She had to leave but she didn't have the strength to pull away.

"Please, have mercy." She didn't want to cry here, not with all these people standing witness gawking and whispering.

"Just tell me."

"Miss Mason," she heard her fiancé call her name and she looked over in a panic to see him and her parents walking over to her and Leo. She met their eyes, and her breath caught in her throat. It was a nightmare; she had to get away.

"What are you doing?" her mother asked.

"It's all right." Leo assured her.

"I am begging you to stop this," Regina twisted away from him and started away, but he followed her, his firm grip on her shoulders effectively blocking her escape.

His hand rested against her cheek. "Look at me."

Her eyes shifted to his. The tenderness in his expression wrenched her heart but it was the intensity of his gaze that held her attention. He wasn't paying any mind to anyone but her and her answer. "Please, just this once don't think of anyone else, just answer me. If you truly had the choice would you choose to be with me? Yes or no."

Her mouth stayed shut. Yes or no. It was the choice of a lifetime, a choice no one else had ever given her.

"Yes or no, Regina."

"Yes," the answer tumbled out of her mouth on a breath just as a hand closed roughly around her wrist.

His eyes widened slightly at her response, his hold on her shoulders tightened in defiance of the person trying to pull her away. "Say it again."

"I say, Kingston, it's one thing to steal a dance but this is another thing altogether," Harrison said.

She felt someone tugging on her wrist, but she couldn't look away from Leo. It felt like she had been hypnotized. She could hear the voices around him but with his gaze on her, she couldn't turn away. Then the strangest thing happened. With her life's work falling apart around her, and all the eyes of London on her, the fear began to recede. As if his certainty was leeching into her through his hands. He knew something. He wasn't asking for his own edification.

Her answer was the key to something, something that could change her life forever.

"Say it again, Regina."

"Take your hands off her," Harrison insisted.

"Yes," her voice was stronger this time, and she saw in his face that he heard her.

"Yes what?" Harrison asked.

Leo nodded and let out a relieved breath. "Alright."

"Remove your hand you impudent little peasant."

"No," Leo replied, shifting to stand beside Regina, his eyes still fixed on hers his hand curling around hers strong and sure.

Oh God. What had she done? What was happening? Why wasn't he trying to take her away?

"What did you say?" Harrison asked in disbelief.

"I said no. I don't believe I will." He turned his head to look at her fiancé for the first time since he had arrived. There was something different in him. It felt as though he was an entirely different person. Everyone was assembling around them now, her parents, Elodia and the viscount, Aunt Theo. Her future mother-in-law. She wanted nothing more than to run away but Leo…His back was straighter, his shoulders set. There was an air of resolution that seemed new.

"If you are so eager to breed some mongrels of your own you are welcome to whichever poor sighted, dim-witted bitch who will have you, but *that* is mine." Harrison insisted, pointing in her direction.

"That?" she said, fresh outrage filling her chest. Her free hand curled into a fist. He was too much.

"'That' is in fact a 'she' and no, *she* is not."

She turned to him again. He wasn't moving an inch. "Leo what are you doing?"

Mr. Harrison stalked up to him and Leo lifted his chin in response, his gaze steady and steely as if he was facing down a wild dog. "You will remove your hand and leave this house this instant, or I will have you removed forcibly."

"You can try but you will be disappointed with the results, Edward."

"Ed—" he glanced at Regina in outrage then back at Leo. "Who do you think you are to call me by my born name?"

"I am Miss Mason's fiancé," he said, adjusting his grip on her hand. "But you can call me the Baron Starkley."

CHAPTER TWELVE

ONLY REGINA'S HAND in his gave Leo the will to put up with the absolute mayhem he unleashed with those words.

"Thank the lord for that. I thought it would never happen," Aunt Theodosia said loudly, and he fought the urge to roll his eyes. She was outrageous, but he supposed he was in good company because what he had just done broke every single rule there was, and he was likely going to break more before he was finished.

"What did you just say?" Harrison asked, his face slack with disbelief.

Leo couldn't blame him. He could hardly believe he was doing it himself, but Regina Mason wanted him, so there was no way he wouldn't stand his ground. Even if he felt like a fox facing down hounds. He had never felt so endangered in his entire life and he absolutely hated it.

"I believe you heard me."

"Have you lost what little mind you have?" Harrison asked.

"Regina, what is going on, what is he saying?" her mother asked in Marathi, watching them with a mixture of concern and outrage. Captain Mason was harder to read.

Harrison's mother was less so. Without even an attempt at civility she sneered at him. "That Barony is one of the oldest in the country. The day it passes to one of your ilk is the day herds of swine take flight."

"Then there will be pork in the treetops come morning," he replied even as his stomach clenched in warning.

"Leo, what is going on?" Regina asked and the older woman rounded on her, her beady little eyes fixed on their joint hands.

"And you, are you so simple that you believe this twaddle? Or are you too much of a wanton to care about what is fit and right?"

"Don't speak to her that way," he started to take a step forward, but Regina squeezed his hand drawing his attention.

"Is it true?" She was only looking at him, tears in her eyes. Terrified of believing what he was saying. Or perhaps terrified it wasn't real. Either way, she only wanted to know his response. She was here with him, trusting him even though she didn't understand.

He nodded and then her mother walked up and yanked her hand out of his.

"We are leaving." She said brusquely in her native tongue, pulling Regina along with her.

"Aai, wait,"

"No, enough. We are leaving now." Mrs. Mason insisted, sending one glare at him over her shoulder.

Regina tried to unlock the almighty grip her mother had on her but when her father took her other arm she gave up, sending him a desperate parting glance.

"Regina." Her name tumbled off his lips as she was pulled further away, all his attention focused on her dark pleading eyes.

"Yes, do leave," Mrs. Harrison called after them. "They had no business being here in the first place. I can't imagine what that previous Baron was thinking opening a door to those savages."

"She is clearly a better judge of character than you, Alyssia," Aunt Theo said as her nephew Albert wheeled her closer. "She took one look at your lack luster progeny and knew something had to be wrong."

"You are raving, old woman," Mrs. Harrison continued.

"Perhaps, but his claim is something I can prove." Aunt Theo nodded at him, a new light in her eyes. Was that pride? Was that meddlesome little harpy proud? Why did it matter to him so much?

Edward and his mother stared at her in disbelief. "That is impossible."

"I think you mean improbable," Aunt Theo replied sparing them a glance before looking Leo up and down with a smirk. "Well done you."

Her audacious approval in the face of their outrage shocked a chuckle out of him. The tightness in his chest was easing a little now. He wasn't actually alone in this.

"You knew about this? About him?" Harrison growled.

"I knew before he did."

"I'm going to kill you for this, you meddling old bitch."

"This near the grave?" She shook her head and gave her nephew a pitying look. "You'd be doing me a service."

He took a menacing step forward and Leo moved between them. She was a 'meddling old bitch' to be sure but she was also a fragile old woman and there was no way he would let him put a hand on her.

"Easy," he warned.

"And you. If you think I am going to stand for this, you had better think again. I don't care what so-called evidence you have."

"I don't think the rumor mill will be enough to fix this one for you, Edward."

He smiled. "You think that piece of paper you have will stop me? I take what's mine, Kingston, one way or another."

"That would be impressive if anyone wanted what you have," Leo replied. "The title is mine by law."

"For now. That title has belonged to others as well."

Something in Edward's eyes had the hair on the back of Leo's neck standing up. A coolness that went past the typical disdain he'd seen in the eyes of those who deemed themselves his betters. Edward spat at his feet, turned on his heel and stalked away, his mother following closely behind.

Those words made Leo wonder if the rumored curse associated with the barony had an all too human genesis. He'd worried about others harming Regina because of his coming forward, but now it seemed the trouble was closer to home than he'd originally thought.

CHAPTER THIRTEEN

I**T WAS IMPOSSIBLE**. Utterly impossible. He'd been so close. So fucking close to having everything and that fucking *bitch* of an aunt had the all-out gall to ruin it. All for the sake of *him*.

"I cannot imagine what that woman was thinking." His mother prattled on. "The presumption of it all. To hand over what was meant for her own family to that peasant."

Yes. That peasant. How had he missed Kingston? How long had he known of his pedigree? Had Kingston sat there the whole time waiting to snatch the barony away publicly? Had he done it just to humiliate him? Was it payback for the army? Kingston's insolent face surfaced in his mind and Harrison's hands curled into fists. He wanted to smash it to pieces. How dare he lay claim to what was his?

He thought of Miss Mason, as she called herself. Little miss harlot more like. The way she'd looked at Kingston as if he were her savior when all she'd managed for him was ill-concealed contempt. As if Kingston were a better man than him. No doubt she'd already spread her legs for him. So eager to give away what belonged to *him*. They were all the same. Sneaky, conniving, greedy dishonest beasts.

"Edward," his mother stomped her foot on the floor of the carriage and his eyes flicked up to meet her impatient ones. He watched her for a moment, annoyance flowing through him. She was so loud and shrill, too proud and stupid, making plans for his title as if the bitch had any claim to it. How on earth had she given birth to him? How long before he could be rid of her and her nagging voice? He watched the fear leak into her face, as if she'd guessed where his thoughts had turned.

"Mother," he said.

"What are we going to do about that boy taking what belongs to us?"

"You mean if they can substantiate his claim?" he clarified.

"Don't be ridiculous, there is no way that boy is the Baron of Starkley."

So stupid. It was obviously not only possible, but highly likely. That old crone wasn't a fool like his mother who never questioned why he hadn't received his summons to parliament yet. She didn't move without all her ducks in a row and neither did Kingston. He was common, lustful and greedy like all his kind, but he wasn't an idiot. If she had been pushing him to come forward, then she had to be dead certain of whatever evidence she had.

Which could only mean one thing. It was true.

"He could be," Harrison muttered.

"But it should be yours, son."

"Yes, it should." He replied easily. And it would. He'd had it in his hands once and he would have it again. And he wouldn't even have to marry that bitch to get the money either. All he had to do was bide his time, let them marry, finalize that fucking stupid contract. Then he would clean house. He didn't have the title yet, but he was still next in line. And he was still a white man in England. No one would believe a jumped up darkie over him.

At that thought, the worst of the rage left him. He took a deep breath as the ringing in his ears faded away.

"What are you going to do about it then?"

"I wouldn't worry about it, mother. The other barons met an irregular fate."

"Goodness, that is true. Life is so unpredictable."

"Mmm, accidents will happen," he commented.

He would make sure of it.

CHAPTER FOURTEEN

Number 12, Mayfair, London
Later that night

"THERE'S SOMEONE HERE to see you, Miss."

Regina turned to her maid, from her vigil at her bedroom window. "Who is it?" she asked, a dangerous hope taking root in her chest.

"Kingston, a Mr. Kingston. He's in the garden."

Leo. Regina didn't remember rising to her feet. She didn't think about the fact that she was dressed in only a thin linen nightgown and her dressing gown. All she knew was one moment she was seated and the next she was sneaking down the stairway careful to avoid the fourth and twelfth stairs because they creaked. She'd spent the last few hours trying to make sense of what had happened earlier that night. She was somehow engaged to Leo. He was the new Baron of Starkley? Had fate somehow managed to deliver her the perfect solution to her troubles?

Her parents hadn't known what to do or say once they were in the carriage, and Regina had been no better. Outside of a declaration that they were leaving for the country estate the next day, her mother had not spoken since. Regina had opened her mouth to argue but one look from her father had stayed her tongue. This wasn't the time to argue. The contract was still in place as far as they knew. If Leo was the new baron, all would be resolved sooner or later.

All she could think about was Leo and his bright eyes. The

surety in his expression when he staked his claim to her in front of half the ton. She hadn't been able to look away from him in that moment, thrilled and terrified in equal measure. He had seemed like a prince from a fairytale; Lord Krishna come to life to save her from an unworthy husband. His face had been carved in rock as he faced down Mr. Harrison, but his touch on her arm was firm and perfectly gentle.

She never imagined it would feel so good to belong to someone. It had always seemed demeaning to be reduced to a possession. But with Leo, it was clear he saw it as a right to defend and protect, a right to act on her behalf. When her mother had dragged her away, Regina hadn't known what he would do or when she would feel his hand in hers again. When she would hear his voice. With the look on her mother's face, she was half sure she wouldn't be able to leave her house for a month. But he had known that. Beautiful, brilliant Leo had found a way to come to her.

The balmy air greeted her as she slipped out the door to the garden, pressing her body along the wall until she cleared her parents' window to the line of trees. A hand came out from the garden gate and clutched at her wrist. She turned, heart pounding to see Leo watching her with uncertain eyes. He was still dressed from the ball, even though his cravat was loosened, and his jacket was now missing. His shirt sleeves were rolled up in deference to the warm summer night.

Without a second thought, she launched herself into his arms, and he caught her firmly against him, sweeping her feet off the ground. She buried her face in his shoulder breathing his smell of rosemary, wood and amber and wrapped her arms around his neck. His embrace around her unconfined waist was strong and tight pressing her barely clothed body flush with his. She pulled back slightly to meet his eyes and then his mouth was on hers, hot, languid and overwhelming. This time he didn't leave it for her to take the lead. His mouth moved over hers with certainty, one hand anchoring her head in place to take what she offered freely. He tasted of port, his mouth as smooth and soft as she remembered.

But this was different because this wasn't a stolen kiss. She didn't have to wonder if he was indulging her curiosity or flattering her interest. He had sought her out, held her hand and publicly announced that she was his. He wanted her. He saw her as she was and wanted her just as much as she had always wanted him. She tore her mouth away from his with a gasp, and he turned his attention to her cheek and jaw as her exhilarated heart raced in her chest.

His breath wafted over her skin as he sighed, his face pressed to her unbound hair. "Regina," he murmured, and she shivered as the rumble of his voice moved through her body. Then his mouth pressed against her neck, and she shivered again as he lay a necklace of kisses from one shoulder across her throat to the next. Strength leeched from her limbs and her body turned to water, a soft whimper escaping her. Her head fell backwards, eager for more of his tender ministrations.

"Leo," she pressed her cheek to his, hoping her heart rate would slow to something less alarming.

"I'm here." He was here. He was here for her.

"Is it true?" she whispered.

He pulled back and allowed her to slide down the front of his body until her feet finally touched the ground. "Is what true, sweetheart?" he asked, cuddling her against him.

"Is it you? Are you the baron?"

"Yes, it's true."

"Are you sure you want this?" she asked, lifting her head to meet his gaze. Now that he was here, she kept wondering if this was something he would truly want. She knew his aversion to attention. How could he hope to have the life he wanted if he did this?

"What do you mean?" He frowned down at her, his hand passing gently over her hair.

"I mean you hate the idea of having a title. The visibility. You won't be able to stay safe anymore."

He smiled. "I suppose you'll have to protect me," he replied.

"So you are really going to marry me?" It was probably a silly question considering all that had happened before, but it fell out of her mouth, borne of a lifetime of being left behind.

He smiled softly and brushed the back of his fingers over her cheek in a tender caress. "Are you going to have me?"

Tears stung her eyes, and she buried her face in his chest, her fingers curling into his shirt. The relief she felt as she squeezed his strong body to hers was excruciating. He cuddled her close, his hand stroking over her hair. "I feel like I'm dreaming again."

"Did you dream of this often?" he asked.

"I hated it. I never allowed myself to hope for anything like this, but then I saw you and I couldn't get you out of my mind. It broke my heart thinking of you."

"It's no dream, sweetheart."

"My parents are taking my sister and I back to the country estate tomorrow."

He hummed in response. "I had a feeling they would move quickly."

"What are we going to do?" She wanted to keep her face there in his chest for the rest of the night. She didn't want to have to think about anything, plan anything, strategize anything else for at least a month. Her champion was here. He would handle everything. He would have a plan, a way forward.

"What do you mean?"

"I don't want to go with them," she confessed.

He shook his head. "Go."

Maybe she didn't want him to handle everything. "But—"

"It won't matter either way. By law and based on the terms of the agreement they drew up I am your fiancé and believe me I have every intention of executing that contract to the fullest extent of my ability at the earliest opportunity."

A shiver ran through her at those words and her nipples tightened. Yes. She wouldn't have to endure the disrespectful pawing of that ingrate. Leo would be her husband, and she would have his body, his touch and his kisses for the rest of her life. A knowing smile curved his mouth as if he could feel her reaction through her night gown. Her wedding day couldn't come fast enough. Maybe he was right. Fighting now didn't make any sense when the end result would be the same. "Do you promise?" she asked.

"I guarantee it. Go with your family and wait for me. When I have all the legalities in order on my end, I will come for you."

Staring into his face, wrapped in his arms and scent, she was struck by a sudden anxious thought. She'd waited before and all her previous fiancés had died before they could make her their wife. Was this too good to be true? Could she trust that it had always been the divine plan to deliver Leo to her, or was fate cruel enough to snatch him away as well? Mr. Harrison was still in the line of succession. If Leo died before he married her, she didn't think she could bear having to go to anyone else. Everything inside her tightened painfully. Until she had his ring on her finger, and she was in his bed, she wouldn't be able to breathe easily.

"I have to go now."

"Kiss me first," she begged. It had been at least ten minutes and already it was too long ago.

"Don't you think you've had enough kissing for one night?"

It was wanton to be sure, but she didn't care. She wanted as much of him as she could manage before she had to leave. "Kiss me first and then leave."

His head dipped and his lips parted hers, pulling and caressing them, his tongue stroking into her mouth with slow deliberation. His hands swept over her back and waist molding her to him so she could feel him hard and eager against her aching body. She wrapped her arms around his waist with a moan and kissed him back praying for her desire to turn the fear in her heart into something else. After all, this wasn't goodbye. This was only the first of many nights she would spend in his arms.

He drew away too soon and her eyes drifted open to meet his. There was a hunger there that matched her own. Soon she promised herself, soon she would know all of what that meant, and he would be the one to teach it to her. "Wait for me," he whispered.

She nodded once and when his arms fell away, leaving her too exposed to the sudden chill in the air, she followed suit, wrapping her arms around herself and taking a step back. She wouldn't cry, she told herself. He needed a partner, not a child to comfort. If she meant to be his wife and his equal, then she would show him her strength now.

With burning eyes, she turned and walked back towards the house, refusing to look back.

TWO DAYS. IT took two days for his name to be registered and the title to be officially transferred to him. It was a little alarming how fast it had gone. Apparently, The Crown had been only one step behind Aunt Theo which only spoke to the level of efficiency the woman operated at. At the conclusion of that bit of business, Basil, newly back from his honeymoon in France, had insisted upon taking him and Richard out for drinks at his club.

The stares were unnerving, but Leo imagined he'd need to get even more used to those from now on. Just as he needed to get used to the new signet ring on his finger.

"I can't get over you being a Baron," Basil mused shaking his head.

"Shut up, Basil."

"God truly is a comedian," Richard replied.

"And to think we nearly extended the honeymoon again. I would have missed all of this."

"You're welcome." Richard saluted him with his glass.

"You had your hand in this as well, Thornfield?" The man

was a bloody menace.

"Don't bother yourself with that, you have your own things to be getting on with."

"Oh?" He was almost afraid to ask.

"Oh yes, a new wardrobe for starters," he said his eyes sweeping down Leo's clothing.

"Very true and you'll have to pick your clubs," Basil added.

"Clubs?" Did he actually have to join one of those ridiculous things?

"Oh yes, very important for hobnobbing, and we know how much you enjoy that," Richard wiggled his eyebrows at him and Leo shook his head in annoyance.

"He's a champion hobnobber," Basil agreed snickering into his glass of brandy.

"I can't imagine why I'm friends with either of you."

"You don't have to be now." Richard replied, with a sigh. "You're officially a son of the nobility, man. Title and all."

Leo shuddered. "Yes, so it would seem."

"You could be rubbing shoulders with my parents in no time," Basil suggested and Leo groaned in response.

They weren't the worst people he'd met but Basil's mother had been too much even before Leo became a Baron. The idea of her fawning over him now the title was officially his was exhausting.

"Your mother would love nothing better. She's been a fan of Leo for some time now," Richard wiggled his eyebrows.

Basil, bless him, winced. "That could have been my fault. My brother was trying to act as though nothing serious had happened to Ada and Miss Hawthrone when they were taken and I got angry."

"Thanks for that Bas," Leo said, raising a glass to him in a mocking toast.

"All joking aside," Richard said, "I do have the name of an excellent tailor. He'd be only too happy to receive your custom."

"I suppose I should get something before I leave to go for

Regina," he mused. Her parents wouldn't take kindly to his presence at all considering what had happened the last time they met. He would need to present himself as the undoubted heir, capable of providing all the stability and prestige she needed. Many things would be different as they took on their titles.

He didn't really enjoy being around people, it was true enough, but he couldn't hope to enjoy the anonymity he'd had before. At least he wouldn't be alone in that. His Rajani. His devika.

"Yes, you are engaged to Miss Regina Mason. Did you know that when you agreed to take the title?" Basil asked.

Leo looked at him in confusion. "What do you mean, Bas? She is the only reason I bothered with this nonsense to begin with."

Basil stared at him for a moment. "I don't even know what to say to that."

"He was half in love with her nearly a month ago." Richard added.

"That was fast work."

"Our Leopold is a man of action."

"She's a wonderful woman, brave and kind and beautiful." He remembered how she had looked the night he came forward. How beautiful her skin had been against those rich hues. How she had clung to him after, giving him her trust even when he knew she didn't agree with his suggestions. It hadn't taken long for her to win him over at all. The silence at the table caught his attention and he looked up to see his two friends staring at him. Bastards. "She's considerate of others as well which is a damn sight more than I can say for you lot."

"Mmm, I suppose all that is true." Basil commented, but he didn't look convinced.

"Some of us are made of sterner stuff, Bas." Richard commented with a diabolical twinkle in his eye. Leo grinned. Basil would never live down the story of his break neck courtship of Richard's sister.

"Don't." Basil gave him a warning glare.

"It's true, not every man can be kidnapped by their prospective bride," Leo added.

"You absolute little shit."

Leo snickered. "How was the honeymoon with the little abductor, Bas?"

Basil continued glaring at Richard, but nothing could prevent the light in his eyes at the mention of his marriage to Richard's sister. "It was wonderful. You should consider France for your honeymoon, Leo."

"I shall." He'd always wanted to travel more, and he couldn't think of a better reason.

Basil turned his attention to Richard. "And then I suppose it'll be you next, eh, Richard?"

Richard gave them both a flat stare. "I beg your pardon."

"You'll be the last one standing once Leo here surrenders to his well-chosen fate." He saluted Leo with his glass and Leo returned the gesture.

Turnabout was fair play after all. "Very true. You should put Miss Hawthorne out of her misery."

"You noticed that as well?"

All the mirth in Richard's face evaporated. "What the fuck are you two blathering on about?"

"Melbroke's beloved daughter, Ada's best friend, Miss Hawthorne. She is sweet on you."

He scoffed. "She is nothing of the kind."

Was Richard truly ignorant of her obvious interest in him? "She stares at you half the evening and smiles at you for the rest of it."

"She is an only child who sees me as an older brother, nothing more."

"Ada doesn't look at you like that" Basil replied and Leo choked back a laugh.

"You certainly seem to have a preference for her company," Leo added.

"She is an intelligent and charming young woman," Richard said with a nonchalant shrug.

It was a truly novel experience watching someone as sharp and intelligent as Richard ignore so many obvious signals. "Interesting descriptors."

"Oh? And which would you choose?"

Basil blinked at him in disbelief. "Imposing? Forceful?"

"Violent?" Leo suggested, thinking of the way she and Ada had perforated the late Mr. Trent with their knives disguised as hairpins.

Richard shrugged. "If you are afraid of her just say that."

"She's fucking terrifying."

"All three of those girls would have given any sane man pause at one point or another. Ada is more stubborn and doggedly determined than a bulldog and Miss Mason's brain borders on Machiavellian to say nothing of the fact that she is an alarmingly effective liar. But that didn't stop either of you from seeing their finer points."

Leo glanced at Basil whose eyebrows were high on his forehead. There was something going on with respect to Miss Hawthorne, he was almost certain of it. But he was equally certain that his brilliant and perceptive friend was entirely ignorant of it. Somehow.

"You make a fine point, Richard." Basil glanced pointedly at Leo.

"Indeed, but it rather proves *our* point, wouldn't you say?" Leo asked.

Richard closed his eyes and let out a deep sigh, his mouth tightening in annoyance. "You are both being very tiresome," he mumbled.

"Kingston!" Harrison called out stalking up to their table.

"Fucking hell," Basil mumbled leaning back in his chair, and Richard looked to the ceiling and mumbled something under his breath.

"Harrison," Leo replied easily. He couldn't pretend he was

surprised to see him here or that he would wait until now to make a scene. He probably thought that with all the white men around he was perfectly safe in attacking a peer of the realm in public.

"I thought the custom was to refer to you by your title now that you are a Baron," Richard said with obnoxious wide-eyed innocence.

Leo tried not to smile; he really did. The man was more likely than not a murderer, but it was a relief not to have to face the attacks alone for once.

"I'll be damned if I ever call him that," Harrison hissed.

"Well, that's between you and the vicar," Basil replied.

"It's not enough that you stole my title and my fiancée, now I must suffer you at my club as well?"

"You should be grateful. I hear suffering is good for the soul," Leo said, while making a mental note to avoid this club at all costs.

"You insolent—"

"In any event, one cannot steal a title. The plain fact is that you were a bit presumptuous in laying claim to it and Miss Mason before the due diligence was conducted by the Crown."

"Don't—"

"That is not my fault or my problem."

"For now. I fixed you once, Kingston. I'll fix you again. No one takes what is mine, especially not a jumped up little—"

A footman walked up to them, a concerned look on his face. "Excuse me gentlemen, is there a problem?"

"Not yet," Leo replied, watching Harrison steadily. He didn't want to fight him, not really, but on the other hand he hadn't gotten into a fight with Basil and Richard since their school days and he was more than willing to take a trip down memory lane.

"I believe *Mr.* Harrison was just leaving." Basil's tone was cool and sharp as a winter wind. Good old Basil. He wasn't a scrapper but he was fast enough to dodge a blow and strong enough to land a solid one.

With one last murderous glare at the three of them Harrison left. The attendant nodded to Basil and walked away.

"I don't think I like your club, Bas," Leo said after a moment. Basil scoffed and Richard shook his head, still glaring in the direction where Harrison went.

"I didn't even know he was a member here." Basil drank his port.

"He may not be," Leo replied, but he would probably check before applying for membership at any clubs, and he would definitely look into the deaths of his cousins. He knew all too well what that look in a man's eye meant. Only one thing could have put that level of coldness in Harrison's eyes.

"I think I've had enough of my fellow men tonight, gentlemen. I shall bid you good night," Richard said, rising to his feet. "Leo," he reached into his trouser pocket and pulled out a business card, sliding it across the table to Leo. "My tailor. You'll need new clothes and fast."

"Are you free tomorrow?"

"I am now."

REGINA PACED IN her room, anticipation crackling around her like a lightning storm. Soon Leo would come to her to complete their wedding, putting an end to years of waiting. She didn't mind it so much now, because the knowledge that she would have him as her husband was worth anything, everything. She kept imagining what it would be like when he arrived. Would he move slowly? Would he walk right up to her and kiss her like he had that night? Even though she was a bit nervous about the experience she knew he would be perfect. Why waste time?

She glanced down at the dressing gown she wore over her nightgown. It was easily the most scandalous thing she owned. The nightgown that is, if it could be called that. Her skin showed right through the thin green silk. She needed something to do, something to occupy her thoughts other than the memory of his touch, or his voice in her ear.

Wait for me.

Should she be sitting patiently? Should she open the window? It was a bit stuffy in the room. She stood and crossed over to the window, lifting the latch to allow the summer breeze in. It sent tendrils of her hair tickling her skin reminding her of how he'd brushed the back of his fingers over her cheek. Again, she forced herself to take a deep calming breath, attempting to wrestle her rebellious blood into some sense of calm.

Footsteps sounded down the hallway, and her heart leapt in her chest. *Oh God, he's here. He's come at last.* What was this sudden anxiety? She'd been anticipating this very moment all day and now when she heard him, she felt awkward. Shy? The idea of facing him with so little on was daunting. He would understand. She would stay here, and he would come to her, take her in his arms and ease every ounce of worry from her as he'd done many times before.

The door flew open with a crack like thunder, nearly sending Regina out of her skin before she spun around to see Edward Harrison standing in the doorway of her bedroom. An enraged flush covered his face, his hair stood on end and his eyes gleamed with malicious intent.

Regina's stomach lurched and her entire body went cold as she stared at him in terrified incomprehension. How was he here? Where was Leo?

"You—" her weak voice cracked. "You cannot be here." She pulled her dressing gown closed with numb hands.

"You've led me on a merry chase, my dear, but no longer."

"My husband is downst—" she gasped as her eyes caught sight of the blood on his face. What had he done?

"Your husband as you call him is with the rest of the Starkley's, and you are coming with me."

"No," she shook her head frozen in place as Harrison drew

closer. *Dead? Leo is dead?* No, no it wasn't possible. *Run.*

"Get over here!"

"No, I'm not going with you. I'm already married, you can't take me." Why couldn't she move? *You have to run.* She couldn't push away from the window, sheer panic keeping her where she was. *Get away from the wall.*

His hard hands closed over her wrist and her eyes stung with tears. "You mean your unconsummated marriage? I think that can be easily resolved."

He jerked her forward and she tried to work his fingers loose with her free hand, digging her bare feet into the carpet, fighting for breath. But her tears blurred her vision, and her sweaty hands couldn't gain purchase on his. She struggled, but her limbs seemed like lead, weighed down with the terror of what was happening. There was no escape, not for her.

"You caused me so much trouble humiliating me in front of everyone, running off with him at a moment's notice. Don't think I didn't see how quickly you were ready to accept him." He caught sight of her open robe, his eyes drifting over her barely concealed body. "Well, well, well," he murmured. He paused and took her in, a lascivious smirk spreading across his hateful mouth. She felt sick. This wasn't meant for him; she would never have given this to him.

"You're nothing but a little slut, aren't you?"

"Let go of me!"

"It seems there are some benefits to being your husband."

She couldn't break his hold, couldn't remember how to get away from him, couldn't force enough air in her lungs, couldn't get her body to obey. He was dragging her to the bed now with his cruel hands. She hated the way she was pleading, desperate for mercy, a chance to break free. He picked her up and threw her onto the bed and—

REGINA SAT UP gasping for air, her body drenched with sweat, her hair sticking to her clammy skin. Her throat was raw with tears or screams, she couldn't tell. Her stomach was cramping, sickening nausea working its way up to her throat, chilling her blood. Clutching her throat, she stumbled over to the window, pushing it open into the storm raging beyond it.

The wind was harsh, the rain like cool pebbles. She stuck her face out as far as it would go, letting it wet her face and neck. She wanted to go out and stand still in the middle of all that ferocious energy. Allow that heavenly water to cleanse her of Harrison's imaginary touch, of his offensive gaze.

That was the third nightmare she'd had since she left Leo in the garden. They were all different but with a similar theme. In every one, she was waiting for Leo in a moonlit garden, in the study, or in her bedroom but instead of him, Harrison arrived to take her away. In all of them, Leo was dead before she could marry him and consummate their union, leaving her, per contract, to Harrison's ravages. She could never run fast enough or far enough from him. She was never able to hide or fight him off.

She was always left shaken and sickened with an ever-growing fear that this was somehow prophetic. That the joy and relief she now felt wouldn't last and that Leo would pay the price for her greed. Slowly she sank to the floor, leaning against the wall and wrapping her arms around her legs. During the day there was enough to do, but at night she couldn't stop her mind from succumbing to her worst fears. The idea of having to marry that man after knowing Leo was almost as excruciating as a world without Leo.

The door to her room opened and she looked up to see her mother in the doorway. She was bathed in moonlight, the dark thick curls she'd given to her daughters loosely braided over one shoulder.

"Regina?"

"Aai." She pressed her trembling lips together. She couldn't get up, but she wouldn't cry.

"I heard shouting, why is that window open?" She walked

towards her and closed the window firmly before crouching down before Regina. "Are you ill?"

Regina shook her head. Her mother ran her hand over her damp hair, gathering it up and away from her neck in one gentle pass. It had been so long since she had done that. So long since a touch from her was meant to comfort instead of adjust or fix.

"You are soaking wet. You need to change out of this." She helped her to her feet and set her down on the chaise at the foot of her bed before moving over to the chest of drawers and pulling out a fresh nightgown.

"Did you have a nightmare?"

Regina nodded.

"I had those too before I married your baba." Regina looked at her in shock. "It wasn't a love match between us. It was arranged much like yours was. But while your contract was struck when you were thirteen, I was married."

"You married baba at thirteen?"

"Well, fifteen. Girls married young in India, and officers were encouraged to form alliances with wealthy or aristocratic families. He was twenty then, and even more uncomfortable with the idea than I was. We were not in love. We were strangers, and I had already seen what the British were capable of, as young as I was. I was terrified of what my life would be."

"I didn't know that. I thought you and baba were in love."

"No. That came later. Years later."

"I can't believe baba willingly married a fifteen-year-old girl."

"I wouldn't say he was willing, but he was concerned about what another soldier would do if he elected not to marry me. There were many British officers who thought nothing of marrying girls that young and molding them to their will. Some of them preferred it. The girls didn't speak English, the officers rarely spoke Hindi, so even if they wanted to speak to them they couldn't. Those unions produced children, but the girls who survived to adulthood, I don't know how happy they were. Your baba, the first thing he did was get me an English tutor, and himself a Marathi one.

"He didn't want to be with me in that way until I could communicate with him fully. No matter the comments or criticisms from others, your father always prioritized my wellbeing and defended me. He gave me respect and kindness not because he loved or truly cared for me but because he was a good person. The first time he slept beside me I was twenty. We did not consummate our marriage until I was twenty-two."

"Seven years later?"

"He wanted us to know each other, and he maintained that if I wanted to leave, he would have the marriage annulled without objection. It wasn't until those years had passed and I saw him acting in accordance with his words that I began to trust him. That was when I understood the sort of man I had married."

"Why are you telling me this?"

"When your baba told me he was considering a marriage alliance with a baron for you if he could manage it, I imagined he would be more like your baba, a man of principle, gentleness and integrity, so I agreed. Perhaps your first fiancé was like that. The terms of the agreement were arranged to allay my fears of what he could do. It was intended to protect you from shame or humiliation."

"I know that, aai."

"I know I have not been what you would have wanted. I know I forced you to present yourself in a way that would be most appealing to your British husband without thinking of how it would make you feel. But I truly believed this match to be for your own benefit, perhaps willfully so. I believed you would make a fantastic Baroness. I never thought to use you for my own gain, Rajani, and I never wanted you to be a sacrifice. I would never have agreed to that."

Her name. She'd said her name for the first time in years. "Aai..."

"I wanted the best for you always, but I could have done a better job of showing it. Of telling you my thoughts instead of trusting you would understand my intentions. I could have listened to you." She touched her face, tears shining in her eyes. "Malā māpha kara priyē."

"Aai." She hadn't expected an apology, but the effect of it was visceral. She hadn't realized how much she wanted her mother to acknowledge what had happened, how much she had lost for them. She did realize how much she had missed her mother. The tears Regina had been fighting back flooded forward. Her mother reached out and pulled her close, laying her head on her shoulder, stroking her arm and her hair, rocking her back and forth like she was a small child. Her mother almost always smelled of a combination of herself and Regina's father. Regina breathed her in. Pine and musk, jasmine and cloves.

"Mājhē badaka."

It had taken years, but she was finally her mother's little duckling again.

CHAPTER FIFTEEN

One week later

H E WAS NERVOUS. He was enough of a man to admit that to himself. It wasn't that he had never been forced to prove himself to people who didn't believe in him or have faith in him. He'd done that too many times to count. But it had always been as himself, as Leo Kingston. This new avatar of the Baron Starkley was as unfamiliar and uncomfortable as his new boots. He wasn't sure how he was going to convince Regina's parents to entrust him with her future when he was still coming to terms with it.

Richard had been an absolute menace taking him in hand and having him re measured by his tailor. With the amount of times he was stuck with pins he'd nearly asked the tailor if he had mistakenly imagined Leo was there for bloodletting instead of new clothes. The mount of fabrics and shades draped over him felt entirely unnecessary.

Yesterday the tailor had delivered no less than a dozen new waistcoats all in different shades and patterns of brocade silk, twenty snow white linen shirts and cravats, two pairs of gloves lined with cashmere, four jackets and ten pairs of trousers with more to be delivered to the country house within the month. Evening wear, day wear, hunting wear, a wedding suit, more bloody shoes and boots and two coats. All had been altered from readymade options to save time. Everything fit perfectly. He didn't even know how Richard had managed it.

Richard's sister, Ada, had whisked his mother off to the modiste for lord knew how many new dresses and undergarments, although his mother seemed far more pleased with the results. She sat beside him in a dark green velvet travel gown, her hair wrapped in a silk turban. Naomi Kingston didn't wear bonnets.

He and his mother had spent the night at their new country estate in Cheshire, Starkley Manor. He didn't know what they thought a manor was but the damn thing looked more like a castle than anything else. In the morning, he'd decided to travel the short distance to Staffordshire to pay his respects to Regina's parents, taking all his paperwork with him.

His mother, the dear woman that she was, had insisted on coming with him but he was almost certain she was regretting that choice now.

"Stop shaking your leg," Naomi complained for the third time, and he placed a hand on his knee, squeezing slightly to remind himself.

"Sorry."

"I haven't seen you this anxious in a good long time," she commented, watching him in amusement.

"Well, I've never had in-laws before."

"If what you've told me is reliable then the likelihood of her parents denying you her hand is negligible."

"Yes, but I still want them to like me."

"Ah."

"They are important to her, mother. Which means they are important to me as well."

She nodded but the smirk lingered.

"You think I'm being ridiculous don't you?"

"Not at all. Although it is very amusing to witness."

"Do you like your new earrings?" he asked in an attempt to change the subject.

"Oh yes. I think I was always made to wear jewels."

"Oh?"

"Yes, but nothing so insipid as diamonds."

He laughed at that and shook his head, turning his head to

look out the window at the rolling green hills.

Perhaps it was bit undignified, a man of his years rushing to see a young woman of two and twenty, but he didn't care. He was desperate to see her. He had reassured her as best he could that night in her parents' garden, but he had been dreading the prospect of staying away from her for that long. On one hand it was silly. He'd spent longer than a week away from her since meeting her, there was no reason for this intolerable impatience. But on the other hand, now that he knew she felt the same, he wanted the rest of their courtship to continue. She was his wife, or very soon would be. He wanted days strolling in the garden and nights in bed. He wanted to drink her in unapologetically and kiss her until they were both out of breath.

The carriage finally came to a stop, and he took a deep breath before the driver opened the door, letting him and his mother out. It was a sweet little estate, certainly larger than anything Leo would have been able to manage before this, with a garden in the front. Ducks floated in the reflector pond that stretched the length of the driveway, and ivy covered the face of the house, with windows winking through the verdant sheet.

He took his mother's arm and led her to the weathered front door. Before he could knock it opened revealing an Indian butler. Of course he would be. Of course, Captain Mason would have thought to bring as much of his wife's homeland back with him.

"Good afternoon sir,"

"Good afternoon, I am Lord Starkley, I am here for Captain Mason and his wife."

The man blinked as if processing the information, he had just received, then took a step back to allow Leo and his mother to enter. The first thing Leo noticed was the white mandalas painted on the lacquered floors in sprawling detailed flourishes. There was no confusing how rich the Masons were, but this house felt like a home, much like Richard's home in Cheshire. The butler took Leo's hat and gloves, along with his mother's travel cape before leading them both to the salon.

It was only while he was sitting there waiting for them to enter that he considered that perhaps he should have written ahead to inform them of his arrival. He hated unannounced guests. Even if they had to be expecting his arrival considering the nature of their connection, it still had to be annoying for him to arrive without warning. His only thoughts had been of Regina, and making sure they understood he was serious about marrying her and joining their families together.

These people were Regina's family, and they would be his as well. It was essential that he not make things any harder for her than they likely already had been after the ball. Now he was wondering if he hadn't done the opposite.

"Mr. Kingston," Leo rose to his feet as Regina's mother strode in with her husband. "Good evening,"

"Good evening," he greeted them. "Allow me to introduce my mother, Mrs. Naomi Kingston."

"Good evening to you," Mrs. Mason said, meeting his mother's eyes evenly.

"It is Lord Starkley, actually," his mother corrected, calmly. "His excellency, the Baron Starkley to be precise."

"Quite right, good evening my Lord Starkley," the captain replied with a short bow.

"Has that been proven?" Mrs. Mason asked, still watching him carefully.

"Maddie," Captain Mason hissed softly. She shot him an unrepentant side glance in response.

"You think my son is a liar?" Leo knew that tone well enough to wonder if he should have left her at home and faced the Mason's alone.

"I can't say. I don't know your son at all." Mrs. Mason replied evenly.

"She is right to ask, mother," Leo said softly, glancing at her. He shook his head imperceptibly and she pursed her mouth and looked away, acquiescing for the moment. He turned back to his future mother-in-law. "Yes, Mrs. Mason. It has been verified and registered with The Crown through all the proper channels. I would not put Miss Mason at risk if I wasn't certain."

"Why did you wait to come forward?" Captain Mason asked.

"I didn't know myself until a month ago."

Mrs. Mason's eyes lit up with realization. "That old woman, Mrs. Burghley-Harrison."

"Yes, she knew my grandfather. It's through him that the claim is passed. He was the third son of my paternal great grandfather."

"Why then, is your name Kingston?" Captain Mason asked.

"My grandfather took my grandmother's name when they married. His family had cut him off, so he chose to carry on her family name instead of keeping his own."

Captain Mason nodded. "So your name is Leopold Starkley in fact."

"No, it is Kingston." Leo had been clear about that from the beginning, even in front of that lawyer sent on behalf of the crown.

Mrs. Mason frowned. "But—"

"They didn't want him or his family. The title is one thing, but I have no interest in carrying on that family name. My grandfather chose Kingston, my choice is to honor that choice by continuing *his* legacy."

Mrs. Mason almost smiled at that and for the first time Leo saw some of the cheeky humor he loved so much in Regina. "Very well, Kingston it is."

"Yes, however I'm afraid this doesn't answer my wife's question. You found out over a month ago, why would you wait this long before coming forward?"

"Because I didn't want the title, I still don't if I'm honest. But I developed very strong feelings for Miss Mason, and I didn't want her to have to choose between her duty to you and her fear. I needed to know her feelings before I acted. She is very loyal and very determined, so it was difficult to get her to be candid."

"Yes, she is," her mother mumbled.

"Only two of many reasons I find her to be so special."

"Your estate, Starkley Manor is nearby, is it not?" Captain Mason said.

"Yes, it is still being set up, otherwise I would invite you all there. I only wanted to make myself and my intention known to you as soon as possible."

"You will stay," Mrs. Mason said with a nod.

Leo blinked, staring at the woman. "I—"

"You and your mother will stay here for the time being."

His mother nodded with a clap. "I agree entirely, we must get acquainted eventually. Better sooner than later."

"I wasn't intending to force extensive hospitality onto you ma'am," Leo said, keenly aware of the thin ice he remained on with Regina's mother.

She seemed annoyed by his protestations but then turned her attention to his mother, who was smiling. "Your room, would you prefer it to be east facing or south?"

"East for Leo, south for me,"

"Thank you."

Captain Mason watched his wife leave with a small smile before turning his attention back to Leo. "Believe it or not, that was a good sign."

In time he would understand how her mind worked. Until then, he would err on the side of caution.

"Where is Miss Mason?" his mother asked with a bright smile. "I have heard such a glowing report of her I am eager to make her acquaintance."

"Ah she will be in the garden now," Captain Mason replied, but his eyes were on Leo.

"Oh," Leo's hands curled into the couch cushion, his eyes flicking to the door. How long should he wait before excusing himself?

"Go, boy," his mother grumbled, shaking her head in annoyance.

"Excuse me," He rose to his feet and walked out into the

corridor until he was out of sight then he started jogging. There was a brief moment where he wondered how on earth he would be able to find her considering he had never been to this estate before. But then he saw the open french doors opening out onto a verdant landscape and his Regina dancing in the grass surrounded by flowers.

It was a scene that could have been out of any Indian folk tale. A beautiful maiden moving with grace and power in a garden fragrant with lilies and jasmine, her skin glistening in the golden light of the evening and her lush curves wrapped in a simple, white muslin saree. Her long dark curls woven in a braid now loosened from her exertions, her only adornment the joy in her eyes and the satisfaction on her face. She danced to a rhythm only she could hear, the skill and discipline belayed by the seemingly effortless flow from one movement to another.

He'd never seen her dance before, couldn't imagine what it would look like. Her movements weren't as polished as the courtesans he'd witnessed in Bombay, who had studied the art for most of their lives, but there was a charm to the intensity with which Regina moved, as if she was using the exercise to work through some emotion.

He almost left her there. Somehow it didn't seem like the sort of thing he should have been witnessing. As beautiful as she was and as fascinating as it was to watch her dance he couldn't help but feel as though he was intruding on something private. Something that only meant for her and no one else. There were so few things she she'd been allowed to have for herself so far, and in the years to come there would be less. Even their marriage, as happy as it would make both of them, served a dual purpose. Perhaps he should leave her to her dancing and allow her the privacy she was clearly seeking.

Entranced as he was, he didn't realize she had caught sight of him until she stopped moving. He almost regretted allowing himself to be seen. She was a sight to behold when she abandoned herself to her dance. Then a smile to rival the setting sun spread across her face, setting his heart thumping and she was running towards him, hair flying, and one arm flung out towards him in anticipation of embracing him. One moment more and she was in his arms, warm from the sun and slightly damp with sweat, embracing him tightly.

His baroness. He tightened his hold on her and picked her up, spinning her in a dizzying exuberant circle. Her laughter in his ear filled his heart to bursting, and the weight of her body against him soft and strong and full of life settled something deep inside. The fear he'd glimpsed in her eyes had left him unmoored and Harrison's threats had rubbed him raw even though he hadn't wanted to admit it to anyone. But he was here now, his face buried in her hair, and his heart was racing in time with hers. He squeezed her waist tighter because he could, and she drew her head back, took his face in her hands and kissed him in that open, earnest and almost reckless way she had. He could taste spices and ginger on her tongue, and sighed into her mouth as tears stung his eyes unexpectedly. She felt like home. All his life he'd wanted a place to belong, and he'd found it in her arms.

"Who is that?" a small voice asked, and he turned his head to see a doll of a little girl watching him with interest and a level of suspicion inversely correlated with her age.

Penwood Hall, Staffordshire

REGINA COULDN'T HELP the laugh that bubbled up from her chest at Lillian's expression. She had been so caught up in the sight of Leo standing in her parents' garden that she'd forgotten every ounce of propriety which dictated she walk not run and certainly not kiss her fiancé in full sight of God and man. In that moment she hadn't cared, but not watching her little sister she wondered if perhaps she should have exercised a little more caution in her response. Leo however had little compunction about interacting with her sister. He shifted to face Lillian, his arms falling away from Regina's waist.

"Am I correct in guessing that you are Miss Lillian Mason, the second young mistress of this fine estate?"

"You are."

"Apologies for not greeting you earlier Miss Lillian. My name is Leopold Kingston, I am your sister's fiancé."

Her dark eyes went wide and she shifted them to Regina. "He is your baron?" she whispered loudly.

"I am indeed, Miss Mason. I am pleased to make your acquaintance." He gave her a deep bow which was entirely ridiculous considering her age and social status compared to his own but accompanied by her sister's less than confidant curtsy, it struck Regina as adorable.

"I am pleased to meet you my lord," she replied before glancing at Regina for confirmation. She heard the unspoken question. *Is he the nice one?* She smiled and nodded.

"Ah Leo," Regina looked up to see a statuesque woman with the same burnished skin as Leo, approach them. Her strong build was robed in forest green velvet and her hair was wrapped in a patterned silk turban.

"Mother." He shifted and held out his hand to her as she drew closer. She took his hand, but her dark brown eyes were fixed on Regina. "This is Miss Mason, my betrothed."

Then he spoke to her. "Regina, this is Naomi Kingston, my mother."

Regina began to sink into a curtsy, but those slender dark fingers cradled her chin, lifting her face to the light, those dark eyes drifted over her face with steady perusal. It occurred to Regina that if she was going to meet Leo's mother she would have preferred to be dressed for dinner, instead of sweaty and disheveled. But then she smiled, in that slow deliberate way that Leo often did and nodded before saying one word.

"Beautiful."

NAOMI KINGSTON WAS a terrifying woman, but she was also one of the warmest people Regina had ever met. She had no idea what Leo's father was like or how much he favored him but what she knew for a fact was the calm and regality of the mother had been distilled in the son. Both of them had the uncanny ability to remain utterly still while they took in every detail of stimuli in the room.

From the moment she had declared Regina 'beautiful', Naomi, as she insisted on being called, was never far from her, listening attentively whenever she spoke or encouraging her to voice her opinion. Regina had thrown on her blue dress that she'd worn to the theatre for dinner and added more curls around her face. She even dabbed a few drops of her lotus perfume to her neck. Now that she was to marry Leo, she wanted to be at her most beautiful. His slack jawed expression when she came down the stairs was all the validation she'd needed.

After dinner, while the rest of the party had moved to the sitting room, Regina took a moment to make chai the way her mother had taught her with spices and tea leaves from Ceylon, boiled first in water then milk and sweetened with honey. Leo's eyes had lit up when the aroma reached his nostrils as she served the steaming beverage to them all.

It was interesting the little things Regina was learning about him. He had always been sure to avoid tea, even at tea parties, but the minute he saw a steaming cup of masala chai, he couldn't take the gilded glass cup fast enough. Naomi had hummed in appreciation at her first sip, closing her eyes to breathe in the aroma before declaring she'd never be able to drink English tea again. Now, she sat beside Naomi, arm hooked with hers listening attentively to her mother while she discussed posting the bans.

In a way Regina was grateful for her future mother-in-law's

attention. It kept Regina from staring at Leo for too long. It was always difficult to look away from him but tonight, dressed as he was for dinner, his broad muscled shoulders highlighted in a deep blue jacket and a bronze brocade waistcoat pulling every shade of light brown from his eyes she was more distracted than usual. Every time he caught her gaze his soft mouth curved slightly as if he knew where her thoughts were straying.

"Regina," her mother said, and she met her eyes.

"Yes aai."

"I was asking if you had a wedding date in mind."

"Not one in particular." The sooner the better. The only wedding she was interested in was the kind that made her his wife.

"Well that is good, the betrothal need not be too long I think," Naomi said.

"Agreed," Leo said, giving her a wink.

"Two or three months should do it." Her mother said and Regina felt all the blood in her veins go cold.

Two or three bloody months? "What?" she asked.

"A two-month betrothal period."

"Why must we wait two months?" she asked.

"It is hardly an unusual amount of time," Naomi replied.

"I've been engaged to him in one way or another for over five years." Panic was clawing at her throat. Two months?

Her mother raised an eyebrow. "And two more months will not be a hardship."

Anything could happen in two months. One of her fiancé's had died within two months of accepting the title. "But we only need the bans posted for three weeks to marry."

"Regina." Her mother's tone was a warning, but Regina didn't care.

"I don't want to wait."

"People will gossip if you marry too quickly," Her mother pointed out.

"People will gossip regardless, aai."

"So why make it more of a spectacle? It is better to move at a slow and steady pace, it will give us time to plan a lovely wedding worthy of your new rank and send out the invitations to the families of the ton."

"No." She could bend on anything else but not this.

"Regina, it is marriage it cannot be rushed."

"It didn't take us two months to marry," Her father commented, and her mother glared at him.

"You keep a tight lip this whole time and now you say this?" She turned to Leo's mother, looking for an ally. "Mrs. Kingston surely you agree."

Regina looked to her new mother-in-law who was watching the exchange with a measured expression that closely mirrored her son. Naomi leaned forward and sighed. "I can see both your points. Eight years is a long march down the aisle, but on the other hand this is something entirely new. The unique legacy you are both creating deserves due consideration especially at the beginning."

"Precisely."

Regina turned to her father. "I cannot wait that long, baba. I cannot."

"I apologize Mrs. Kingston, she is not normally this disruptive I promise you," her mother murmured.

Naomi shrugged. "She is eager, I can't help but take that as a compliment."

Her mother turned to Leo. "My lord, you agree with me do you not?"

Regina looked at Leo who was watching her with a steady gaze and a contemplative expression. "I don't think we will come to a conclusion tonight," he said carefully. "Let us post the bans this Sunday, as we are agreed there is no time to waste for that and discuss the rest further. Either way we have three weeks at least."

Not exactly the ringing endorsement she wanted but he hadn't agreed with her mother either.

"How very diplomatic." Captain Mason said, hiding his smile behind his teacup.

Her eyes were burning and the dress which had made her feel so beautiful at the beginning of the evening was now suffocating her. She rose to her feet refusing to look any of the occupants in the eye. "Excuse me," she murmured and left the room.

SHE WASN'T HAPPY with him; Leo knew that well enough. The fear he'd glimpsed in her face the night he'd come forward was there now and somehow he was to blame. Which was how he found himself wandering in the garden instead of sleeping in the very comfortable bed awaiting him upstairs.

Like his mother, he understood both arguments and knew better than to wade into such a sensitive subject. The man in him wasn't about to argue against a shorter courtship so he could make love to Regina sooner. The feel and taste of her, the soft sounds she made when she let herself go in his arms haunted him day and night. Yes he certainly wanted to get his hands on her as soon as possible. But on the other hand, if he was going to take up this title and the whole point was to earn Regina more influence among the nobility with their new status, then they could not be hasty and haphazard in their wedding preparations.

They would have to learn the game before they could conquer and lead it.

Frankly, he was surprised that his little general hadn't come up with the idea herself let alone disagreed with it. If anything, she had seemed ill at the idea, panic sprouting in her beautiful eyes.

Like a specter from his imagination, she appeared in the moonlight. For a moment he wondered if he was imagining her, as she walked out onto the lawn clad in only her nightgown. He shouldn't have kept staring. Conceptually she was no less covered than any other time he'd seen her, or when he'd visited her in London after the ball, or earlier in the day when she was wearing her saree to dance. But in London she'd worn her wrapper.

Now there was nothing between her dark soft skin and the gentle summer breeze save for the thin lawn of her night gown and the dark tumble of curls that flowed over her shoulders and down her back. Watching her with that knowledge before he was her husband made him feel reckless.

"Regina?"

She turned her head and smiled softly. Nothing as exuberant as all the other times. He wondered if something had changed for her. "Hello," she said turning her face up to the night breeze. "I love night here."

"It is a beautiful place. I thought you'd gone to bed," he said wondering if he should walk over to her or stay where he was a good ten feet away. He wasn't sure what he would do if she was close enough for him to touch.

"I can't sleep."

"Me neither. What is keeping you awake?"

"You," she replied.

"How ungentlemanly of me." It was meant to make her laugh or cut the tension between them. Somehow neutralize the odd energy swirling around. Instead, she stared at him with that peculiar expression, as if she were trying to decide what she wanted to say to him.

A breeze blew again sweeping a lock of her hair swept across her neck, tugging on her night gown until he could make out the curve of her hip, the swell of her full breasts, her slightly rounded stomach. "You were upset earlier."

"I was," she agreed.

"Would you tell me why? I know you don't want to wait months to marry, and I am not opposed to a quick wedding. But there is a wisdom to taking our time and approaching such a crucial event with caution."

She walked towards him, and with some alarm he noticed the

faint sheen in her eyes. Was she crying? "I've spent my whole life trying not to feel too much. Not to want too much. I always had to remember what I was meant to be, who I was meant for, what I couldn't have. Then I met you and you were… you were bad for that."

"Likewise."

She smiled and bit her lip but it didn't reach her eyes. "You are my fourth fiancé did you know that?"

"I did."

"And you are the first one I want. The first one that makes me feel excited at the prospect of being a wife. The only one. I can't help but wonder if my previous intendeds were swept away by divine providence or if I am cursed to lose you as well."

Was she afraid? "I am not an easy man to kill."

That smile came again, but the tears were filling her eyes. "If I lose you I don't think I could bear it. It was different before, when I didn't know what this felt like. I can't shut myself off again, I can't go back to that."

"I can't either."

"I keep having nightmares, horrible dreams where I'm waiting for you, and *he* comes for me instead and I can't get away."

The tears spilled over her cheeks and his heart splintered. "Sweetheart—"

"—Sometimes he just drags me away, other times he hurts me. Sometimes I wake up before the worst of it."

"That is not going to happen."

"I have been waiting for most of my life and I can't do it again. I don't need a large wedding, I just need one that makes me your wife and turns that nightmare into an impossibility."

"Regina, it's just a dream. I am right here, and I promise you that I won't allow anything to happen to me. I won't risk you in any way."

"You cannot promise that."

He wanted to argue but there was a truth to her words he couldn't argue against. Of course he couldn't make any promises.

He had no more control over whether he lived or died than his predecessors did.

"Have you gone any further into the garden as yet?" she asked suddenly.

"No, not yet."

Wordlessly she took his hand and led him further across the lawn, past the short stone wall and onto a stone path past hedges and rows of trees. It felt like she was pulling him towards some unknown destiny. Like he'd wandered off the path set before him and handed over the direction of his life to this earthen goddess with warm, soft hands. This small creature who drew him inexorably forward to some alien yet powerful end.

"Where are we going?" he asked, just as the scent of jasmine caught his attention. "Regina?"

"The night garden."

"What?"

She glanced over her shoulder at him and smiled. This one held less sadness, but it made him more nervous. There was an energy in her he couldn't quite place and it was as intriguing as it was unsettling. Everything within him urged caution while he couldn't help but seek the unknown. Couldn't help but wonder if perhaps it would suit him better. In the moonlight he could just make out the small white flowers dotting the verdant walls of the enclosure. A place of secrets only revealed by moon shine and starlight.

She turned to him, her hand still in his, her eyes shining with a thousand emotions. "If I asked you to make love to me tonight, would you."

His body flushed from head to toe. His throat clamped shut as his mind processed her words. Of all the things he'd expected her to say, that hadn't even entered his mind. "We shouldn't," he croaked out.

"I know." She took a step forward and he swallowed hard to lubricate his arid throat. "I know it's unfair to ask. You are a man of integrity—"

"It would be disrespectful to your parents,"

"I know—"

"The banns haven't even been posted."

She stepped forward again and slid her hands over his arms. His shirtsleeves were a poor defense against her touch. "I know."

He didn't stop her from moving even closer, pressing her face against his chest, settling every unbound curve of her body against his as her arms came around his waist. There was something unsettled inside her, a tension and a terror that he knew he couldn't shake. Her nightmare was understandable considering her past, but it was hardly a premonition. He understood that perfectly well. So why was a sense of foreboding wrapping itself around his heart tendril by tendril like an ominous fragrance.

Harrison came to mind, his hate filled eyes and contemptible sneer. His murderous capability.

He pressed his lips to her hair line breathing it in. "Tell me, love."

"I need you to take me now,"

His hands clenched convulsively in her nightgown. "Rajani."

"What if something happens to you and I end up having to go to him anyway?"

"It won't, darling."

"You don't know that. I can't bear the thought of anyone else's hands on me. I don't want anyone else to touch me. I need to know that it will only ever be you."

"It will be me, it is me," he said sliding his hands over her bare arms, down to her waist.

"I can't bear waiting. It would only be this one time. I just need to know that I am yours, that no matter what happens you are the first and the only. I'll wait the two months if you give me this one thing."

"That is one hell of a bargain Regina,"

"Please Leo. Just this once so I can sleep without those nightmares. I promise I won't ask it again."

The plea in her eyes was breaking him. The desire to give in and remove that desperate look from her face, to see her smile again. As requests went, it was hardly an extraordinary one. Making love to her to ease her concerns and sate his desire would be no hardship. She would be eager and sweet under him, warm and wet around him, lush and sensual. But he couldn't let go of the fact that everything in his upbringing railed against her request.

As a gentleman it was his duty to safeguard her honor instead of using her vulnerability to indulge himself. Even if they did make love tonight it wouldn't actually fix what she was afraid of unless she told everyone the truth. What if someone saw them come here? How on earth would he explain himself to her father? How could he persuade her parents to trust him again if he ravished her in their garden the first night he stayed at their house?

But how could he walk away from her when she had that look in her eyes? He knew what it was to always have to choose the smart thing, the safe, sure thing. The correct thing. To give into her would barely be one of those. If word leaked out the whispers would begin of the base born baron and his hot-blooded wife, both undeserving of their title. Neither capable of carrying out their office. Giving in would make them all correct. Did it matter? Perhaps he should speak to her parents about dissolving the contract and striking a new one that didn't tie her to the barony. He could persuade her mother to have a modest wedding in three weeks.

Somehow he imagined that none of those things would dissolve her nightmares or remove the fear in her eyes. Explaining would only make her feel more alone than she already did, that he wasn't on her side. Her fingers curled into his shirt and the appeal in her eyes gave way to shame before she looked away from him. Her hands pulled away from him and she wrung her fingers together leaving his stomach rapidly cooling from the absence of her touch.

"I'm sorry," she murmured. "I shouldn't have asked. You are correct, I will wait." She started to walk away but he gripped her arms, unable to allow her to leave.

He could let her go. She would go back to her room, and he would at the very least be able to look her father in the eyes tomorrow. He would make it up to her later and reassure her in other ways. But his throat was tight with regret, and he couldn't help but feel that he was failing her. She had turned to him, confided in him and made one request and he'd turned her away. How many times had she allowed herself to ask for help? How many times had she allowed herself to lean on someone else and seek comfort?

Marrying him should have given her more protection, more freedom than any other man of his station. Already the expectations of nameless masses who cared nothing for her and her dread were winning against her and he was helping them. Was that how their marriage would be between them from now on?

She stole a timid glance up at him. "Leo?" He hated her uncertainty, hated that it was his doing. He was her husband, and he didn't even have the courage for this. Already this stupid title had begun to change him, had forced him to consider gossip over her well-being. She tried to pull away and his grip tightened. No, more. His Regina was here, and she needed him.

His hands would have trembled if they weren't holding on to her. There would be no going back once he kissed her. The moment his mouth touched hers he wouldn't be able to stop until she got what she wanted, until they were both satisfied. He shifted one hand to her tear-stained cheek and the other to her waist drawing her closer. Her midnight eyes widened as she realized his intent.

Then, with his heart pounding in his chest, he lowered his head and caught her full mouth with his. She sucked in a sharp breath and then melted into him her fingers curling into his shirt over his arms. His hand moved from her cheek as her mouth opened eagerly under his and sank into the dark silken curls of her hair.

There would be so many times in their life and their marriage when they would have to defer to societal expectations. Even if it would make facing her parents awkward in the morning Leo was dead certain about one thing: he would regret turning her away in this moment far more than making love to her. Whatever came before or would come in the morning, she would come first *now*.

CHAPTER SIXTEEN

S HE HAD BEEN wondering how she would manage when she
returned to her room that night, how she would face weeks
or months of uncertainty. Leo's hesitation had sapped whatever
little confidence she'd summoned to make such an extraordinary
request. Perhaps she could avoid sleeping all together, or sneak
into her little sister's room. The garden had originally been a last
resort to calm her mind in hopes that the idea of a two-month
engagement wouldn't trigger more nightmares.

But then something kindled in his eyes, and he was kissing
her exactly how she'd needed him to.

With intent.

With hunger.

She wanted to be claimed so her mind would finally rest. So
the only thing she could focus on was the truth of what it was like
to lie with him. What it would be like to be not only a wife but
his wife. She wanted to connect something to marriage other
than the feeling of being left behind and waiting for her fate to be
determined by someone else.

She went up onto her toes and wrapped her arms around his
waist spreading her fingers over the hard expanse of his back. He
kissed her deeper than ever before pressing her back, his strong
hands caressing her neck, his arms wrapping around her waist
and crushing her against his body. His mouth wandered over her
cheek and down her neck, his tongue darting out to taste her skin

sending shivers of sensation skittering over her skin. His hand swept over the length of her back to close around her bottom and she moaned against his mouth.

He moved them backward until her back was against a hard surface, but she couldn't be bothered to check what it was. Not when his body was pinning hers against it. It was delicious to be trapped by him, surrounded by his scent as his lips left a lusty trail over every patch of skin he could find on her neck and shoulders. She was aching from the onslaught of sensations, especially in her breasts and between her legs.

She squeezed her thighs together, desperate for pressure to ease the ache there as something hard pressed against her stomach. He picked her up and her legs parted as her arms wrapped around his shoulder, her thighs bracketing his lean hips. Then he pressed that hard thick ridge between her legs where she was most tender. She tore her mouth away with a gasp and her body almost went limp with pleasure.

"Leo."

He groaned and lifted his head from her skin easing away from her slightly. "Alright?"

She whimpered as the pressure lessened leaving her needy and desperate. "More," she pleaded pulling his head closer. He followed her lead kissing her deeply grinding his hips against hers, swallowing the moans she released into his mouth. He lowered them until he was kneeling on the grass, resting her on his lap. His hands closed around her shoulders, and he pulled back.

"Regina   "

"Rajani," she said. That name sounded wrong here, now. "Call me Rajani."

He smiled and brushed the back of his fingers over her cheek. "Rajani," he repeated.

Yes, that was much better. She leaned forward and kissed him tugging at his suspenders, running her hands under the collar of his shirt, desperate to feel his hot smooth skin. His fingers tugged at her nightgown, pulling the neckline until it slid off her shoulder and down her arm. His mouth followed closely raining kisses over every inch of skin. He cupped her breast, and her head fell back against whatever was behind her. How did everything feel so good?

She tried to pull at his shirt but every time his fingers brushed over her nipples she lost track of what she was meant to be doing. Her body was so restless and greedy for his touch, for him to keep rubbing himself against that one point between her legs that needed him most. She heard the breathless moans escaping her lips, and they would have been embarrassing if his rumbling groans weren't there to answer. The pleasure in her body began to build and coalesce in her center with a suddenness that was almost alarming. She clutched at his shoulders, unable to do anything as it burst within her, leaving her weak and dizzy.

His hand left her breast just as hers came up to press it into her soft flesh. She drew back to ask why he stopped then she felt his fingers on her bare leg, moving up to her thigh, pulling her nightgown higher. She stiffened in surprise and her legs twitched, tightening around his hips. He met her eyes, his gaze like molten honey.

"Alright?" he asked, his voice a husky grumble. She nodded vigorously, unsure if she could manage to speak just then. She'd touched her leg before, but it had never felt like this.

"Was that it?" she asked.

"It can be. We don't have to go further than this, we can stop now."

The idea of him taking his hands off her was enough to have her eyes stinging. She shook her head and touched his face. "Don't stop, please."

He nodded and pressed his face against her throat, sucking at the sensitive skin as his fingertips drew gentle circles up her inner thighs, closer and closer to where all the nerves in her body were awakening to fever pitch once again.

"Leo."

"More?"

"Yes, God yes," she gasped "What are you doing?"

"I'm getting you ready for me," he whispered against her skin.

"Why?"

"You're so wet devika."

She shivered at that name, and her core fluttered around his finger.

"You like that name?"

She nodded.

"Good, you're wet now, but you are too tight. If I take you now I'll hurt you."

Her eyes squeezed shut as she pressed her forehead to his, gasping against his face. He slid a second finger inside her and the stretch had her hissing in a breath. "Alright baby?"

"Yes."

"Can you take one more for me?" he murmured, and she clenched again, crying out as he moved his fingers in and out, curling them to drag along the sensitive walls of her core. She couldn't catch her breath any more than she could keep her hips from jerking against his hand. His thumb brushed against that swollen nubbin at her center, and she cried out before burying her face against his shoulder. The pleasure was almost too sharp, too intense, but with every gentle brush of his thumb the stretch of her body around his fingers lessened and the tension in her core was building again. Soon she was rocking her hips against his hand, kissing him hard, gripping the back of his head with one hand, and clutching his arm with the other.

Every time that feeling came it was sharper, bigger, more overwhelming than before, leaving her breathless and tingling all over.

She pulled at his shirt with weak fingers until he had mercy on her and pulled it off himself and gathered her close, crushing her breasts to his chest. He lifted her slightly with one arm and reached between them to ease himself into her soaked tingling center. She watched his eyes slam shut with a frown as he slid inside her slowly, stretching her past the point of comfort. There was a pinch sharp enough to distract her from the pleasurable echoes in her blood.

It was almost too much. She could barely breathe, wishing he would stop moving for a moment.

"Devika, are you well?"

"It hurts."

"Try to relax sweeting," his hand swept up and down her back, trailing over her shoulders, pressing soft gentle kisses to her neck. Gradually the discomfort subsided, and she felt herself relax in his arms. Which was when he slid deeper stealing her breath away. "Better?" he asked his voice tense. She nodded even as her eyes stayed shut.

Slowly he withdrew from her and with one flex of his hips drove himself back inside. She gasped at the feeling. It wasn't quite as uncomfortable as it had been before, but it didn't feel nearly as good as what he'd done with his hands.

She rocked her hips against him and his pelvis brushed against hers rubbing that sensitive cluster of nerves at the apex of her thighs. She gasped softly, her core clenching down in response and heard him groan. She moved her hips again and his hand closed around one, as his eyes fluttered closed, a frown creasing his brow.

"Is that alright?" she asked.

"It's perfect, you're perfect." He leaned more into her, guiding her movements until they were moving as one. His thrusts went deeper, faster as he gasped and groaned against her skin whispering words of praise, telling her how good she felt, how well she moved, how much he wanted her. In his arms, surrounded by his strength, his care and his passion she truly felt like the goddess he called her. She kissed his temple, pulled him closer, nuzzling his cheek, listening to his tributary moans, reveling in her ability to please him.

She was so caught up in him that her release nearly caught her by surprise. His grip on her body tightened and his rhythm picked up lighting a spark that had her arching against his, her head falling back limply against that tree and her fingertips digging into his shoulders. Her hips churned against his, seeking that ecstatic pinnacle once more and she felt his hand reach between them to touch her and send her over the edge into blinding light. She stiffened against him, crying out into the night, his grip on her hip and her waist almost bruising in its strength as he emptied himself inside her.

It was the strangest feeling, and as the pleasurable remnants of her release faded away she was struck by the weight of his hard body, the heat of his breath as he panted against her skin, the texture of his tightly coiled hair under her fingers. She relaxed against him, relief flooding her chest until tears sprung to her eyes. She was his now, nothing could change that. She closed her burning eyes and let out a sigh.

"Rajani?"

She felt him shift and when she opened her eyes he was watching her.

"Are you alright?" he asked, reaching up to brush his fingertips over her cheek. She nodded, nuzzling into his palm. He leaned in and kissed her softly, pulling her into him, sliding one hand behind her neck. After that explosion of passion this was exactly what she needed. It was a simple thing, sweet and tender, full of promise and devotion. When he pulled away her heart was beating strangely, full to bursting and overwhelmed.

He shifted them sliding from her body and setting her on the grass beside him. He tucked himself back within his trousers and buttoned it shut before adjusting her nightgown, pulling the collar up over her shoulder and tugging on the ribbon to adjust it. Then he sat down on the grass and pulled her against his side, cuddling her close, and stroking her hair.

"Thank you," she sighed.

"My pleasure, devika. You're certain I didn't hurt you?" he asked, and she shook her head.

"It was wonderful."

So, this was what it was to make love to a man. She wondered what would have been different if it were someone else. Would she have been as content to be pinned against a tree as she had been? Would she have found as much delight in the act?

One thing was for certain, she would never have tried to persuade them to ravish her in the garden. Or had she ravished him? What were the conditions that determined ravishment? She bit her lip against a giggle, and he lifted his head.

"I beg your pardon madame, but what exactly are you sniggering at?" he asked, humor waring with halfhearted offence in his bleary eyes.

"I was only wondering, when I relayed this who should I say ravished whom?"

"Who exactly would you be relaying this particular escapade to?"

"Well… no one in the immediate future."

"I'll thank you for that, although to answer your question, I suppose I could be the ravishee this time. It would be in keeping with your general approach of staging ambushes."

"I beg your pardon."

"It is given," he replied.

"Why would you say I ambushed you? You make me sound like some kind of deviant."

"You kissed me first."

"Well, that was different."

It was perfect, the cool night breeze, her warm strong hero, and the scent of jasmine in the air lulling her to sleep. "We can't stay here," he murmured.

She could have stayed there wrapped in his strong arms the rest of the night, the rest of her life. "A few more moments please," she murmured. She felt him press a kiss to her forehead and then she didn't know anything more.

THE NEXT MORNING Leo woke up uncommonly relaxed. For a moment he'd imagined that the night he'd spent with Regina had been a torrid dream, but the ache in his loins and her scent on his clothes soon corrected that idea. He'd been a baron for less than a fortnight but somehow he'd managed to deflower his bride no less than three weeks *before* their wedding. It would have to be three weeks at this point, there was no way around that. He wasn't looking forward to that conversation either.

True it had been her idea, but he would have been lying if he had said he hadn't wanted to. He didn't know how he was going to face her father as it was, let alone her mother. He wasn't sure he'd be able to meet Regina's eye without giving away the reality of what they had done the night before. He could imagine her using the fact that they had already made love as a reason to have the wedding as soon as possible.

Perhaps if he hurried down to breakfast he would be able to avoid being in a room with her until they had a chance to get on the same page. With that goal in mind, he washed and dressed quickly before jogging down the stairs. And concerns he'd had about finding the breakfast room were put to rest the moment he came down the stairs, but another soon took its place.

"Lord Starkley."

Leo froze and peeked around the railing to see his host waiting for him in riding clothes. "Captain Mason, good morning."

"I trust you slept well."

"I did, yes."

"Are you going out for a ride?" Leo asked hoping the answer was 'yes'.

"No, I'm just back. I always begin the day with a ride when we're here at Penwood."

"Ah," *Damn.*

"Will you join us for breakfast?"

He opened his mouth to say he didn't typically take breakfast but in the end he decided it didn't matter. "Of course." He followed him down the corridor into a bright room with dark wood paneling and sunshine yellow walls where his mother and Mrs. Mason were already breaking their fast.

"Oh, good morning mother I see you are here as well." He crossed over to her and kissed her head.

She smiled. "Oh yes, Mrs. Mason was kind enough to show me the gardens this morning."

"Oh, very good."

"I'm surprised you were down so late my lord, being a military man, yourself." Mrs. Mason commented.

Leo cleared his throat and poured himself a cup of coffee. "I haven't slept that well in a long time."

"You were a little restless last night, son."

"Was I?" He choked back the bitter liquid and scalded his tongue.

"I heard you return to your room late."

"Was it not to your liking?" Mrs. Mason asked.

"Not at all Mrs. Mason, it was very comfortable. I have difficulty sleeping in unfamiliar places under the best circumstances and I was restless. Too much energy." Was he sweating?

"Well, with all the excitement of the past week, it is understandable,"

"Yes, but once I managed to drift off I was dead to the world until around half an hour ago."

"Speaking of the excitement, what say you to a September wedding?" she asked.

He could see his plan for a quick breakfast drifting out the door. "I think your daughter will not like that one bit."

"She is an impatient girl," she grumbled shaking her head.

"There is something to be said for a degree of restraint." Not that he had any room to talk about such things.

"Are we discussing the wedding?" Regina asked, entering the room in a pale blue muslin gown.

"Yes, your fiancé was about to agree with me," Mrs. Mason replied with a smug expression.

Regina frowned and looked at him. "Leo?"

The look of confused betrayal was enough to bring him to his knees. There was no way he could deny her anything when she could use her face to such devastating effect. He held out his hand to her and she came to him without another word, taking it in hers. "Well, I see two approaches to achieve the same end. You are concerned about whether a wedding after a three-week engagement would be too rushed, but this engagement has been going on for years. And while a grand wedding may be expected by some, a simple, wedding could be appreciated as well considering how convoluted the engagement has been."

"Simple meaning secretive," Mrs. Mason said, and he shook his head.

"Private. A small ceremony with friends and family instead of a hundred strangers who are only there to gawk and judge."

"It is an idea Madhavi." Captain Mason mused, watching his wife with an amused expression. It was clear she was struggling with the idea.

"It would be simpler to plan aai," Regina suggested.

"And give them a chance to reintroduce themselves to society before the season ends," Naomi added.

"Please aai."

Mrs. Mason let out a heavy sigh. "I will consider it."

Regina squealed in delight and clapped her hands. "I'll take it." She turned to him with a dazzling smile "How handy you are, I believe I'll keep you."

"Well thank the lord for that," he replied. "Shall I fix your plate for you?"

"Oh," she looked away with a bashful smile, "thank you."

He set his coffee cup down. "What would you like, devika?"

"Eggs and ham please." She replied.

"Nothing else?"

"No."

He set about gathering her food selections then set her plate before her.

"Are you not eating?" she asked.

"I don't take breakfast."

"Lord Starkley," Captain Mason's voice came from the other end of the room and Leo looked up to see the older gentleman watching him with a strange expression.

"Yes sir?"

"When you are finished with breakfast I should like a word with you."

"Oh, Leo never eats breakfast." Naomi and Regina replied at the same time. They looked at each other then laughed. It would have been adorable, if not for the queasy feeling in his stomach.

"Even better. I would speak with you alone." He turned and left the room. Leo blinked at the empty doorway. What on earth was that about? He glanced at Mrs. Mason who was also observing him closely as she was wont to do. Did they know? Was that man going to shoot him?

"What is that about?" Regina asked softly.

"Not a clue," he replied before following her father out the door. He saw the captain waiting at the back door leading out to the garden and a sinking feeling took up residence in his stomach.

Clasping his unsteady hands behind his back he walked up to him.

"You wanted to see me sir?"

He turned to him and smiled. "Yes, do you hunt?"

"I...um," Fucking hell. "Generally speaking yes." Leo followed him out onto the veranda and down the stairs.

He nodded. "No taste for it or no opportunity?"

"Either or both to be honest," Leo replied, wondering where the man was going with this.

"Mmmmm." He fell silent until they reached a bank of roses before turning to him with a stone face. "Soldier to soldier I have a question for you, and I require honesty."

"Understood."

"How far do I need to move up this wedding?"

A bead of sweat rolled down Leo's spine. "I... I don't—"

He tilted his head forward a glint of steel in those blue eyes.

"You know what I'm asking."

"Ah."

"I saw you both walking in the garden last night after dinner," he said, and Leo's stomach lurched dramatically. "But more importantly I saw the look on your face when she entered the room. I know that look and what it means."

"Sir—"

The captain held up a hand to silence him and Leo closed his dry mouth. "My daughter is happier than I've seen her in years, and you seem determined to not only marry her but serve her as well, so I have no need to call you out. But I need a frank answer from you sir. I won't have her name besmirched."

"We should not require a special license if that is your concern." Leo replied.

"But?"

"But if we are not walking down the aisle in three weeks' time, I will be the second man your daughter kidnaps to Gretna Green."

Captain Mason seemed to fight back a laugh at that, coughing into his fist. He nodded. "Understood." Then he patted his shoulder and walked away whistling, leaving Leo to catch his breath. He seemed affable, but there was one thing Leo was absolutely certain of; Regina's father was the most terrifying man he'd ever met.

REGINA WAS MEANT to be writing a letter. She had been trying to write it for the past hour, but all she could think about was how handsome Leo had been at dinner. How deftly he managed to manage her mother and walking the fine line between addressing her concerns and making sure Regina got what she wanted. A born diplomat, even her father had said so. He would be a wonderful statesman when the time came.

As a lover… Regina set down her pen and took a deep calming breath. She had promised him that after last night she would be content to wait until their wedding night to resume any and all intimacies. But that was before she understood what those intimacies would feel like. Now she was regretting her promise. After such an introduction she wanted a second taste but if she knew him, he would never agree to it. He'd barely agreed the night before.

"What are you doing?" Lillian asked.

Regina jumped in her chair and spun around to see her sister sitting on the floor beside her in her typical white cotton dress. "I am writing to Ellie and Ada, inviting them to my wedding."

Lillian nodded and fiddled with the end of her long braid. "He looks like a prince." She commented.

"Why do you say that?" Regina asked, pleased at least that Lilian hadn't decided Leo had 'funny eyes'.

"Because he's handsome I think. Isn't he handsome?" Lilian glanced up at her for confirmation.

"He is a beautiful man," Regina agreed. No doubt he would be even more stunning without clothes. She had managed to touch his bare skin which had been delicious enough, but there was a decent amount of curiosity still left about what his body looked like.

"—And he seems nice." Lillian finished and to Regina's mortification she realized she hadn't heard half of what she'd said. "I think aai and baba like him."

Their father was certainly warmer towards Leo than Mr. Harrison but Regina had never seen him around her other fiancés to know if that meant anything more.

"Do you like him better than the others?" Lillian asked.

"I do," Regina said.

"You were sad before weren't you? I heard what you told baba and aai, about marrying to protect us. I don't want you to do that. I want you to be happy. Will you be happy with him?"

"I will dearest. Lord Starkley is precisely the sort of man I always dreamed I would marry."

"When will you marry him?" she asked.

"In three weeks', time Miss Lillian, one month at the very most," Leo said, entering the room. Regina turned in her chair as Lillian's little head shot up in his direction. It seemed everyone was sneaking up on her this morning.

"How did you manage that?" she asked. Her mother had been open to the idea but there had not been anything decided definitively.

"I told you I would speak to your parents. Your father has agreed to those terms, and he will finish persuading your mother," he said, taking her hand in his before his beautiful eyes roamed over her letter.

"Sending out invitations already?" He asked.

"Only to Ada and Ellie."

"That's good. We'll need to set up an invitation list as soon as possible. If we want your mother to plan a wedding in three weeks, then we must give her the tools."

"Agreed. I," she paused and pressed her lips together. It had been something she was afraid to ask for before, but now there was a real chance. "I wish to invite my former headmistress if possible."

"Are you looking for my permission?" he asked with a frown.

"I thought I should get your opinion. It is your wedding as well."

"Devika, my only requirement for this wedding is you and our immediate families, all of whom are here. Speaking to preference, I should like if Basil and Richard were there."

"Well, we should also invite Aunt Theodosia, and her nephew, Albert I believe it was."

"As you wish, devika," he replied, dropping a kiss on her forehead.

"May I be a flower girl?" Lillian asked.

He turned to give her a considering look before nodding decisively. "I can't imagine a better one so add that to my list of requirements, Miss Mason."

"Yes, my lord."

Lillian jumped up and grabbed his free hand. "I'm learning to play scales on the piano, do you want to hear?"

Leo blinked at her and then smiled. "Of course, little one, bring me to your piano."

As he was dragged through the door by her sister, Regina saw him give a small bow to someone out of view.

Then she heard the tinkle of ankle bells and saw her mother enter with a bemused smile on her face.

"Aai."

"He fits in well I see," she said in Marathi. Regina grinned.

"She received his permission to be a flower girl, so he is her favorite person now."

"She is not the only one getting her way through him," she replied giving her daughter a pointed look.

"Mother, I know it is not your wish. But the longer I have to wait the more uneasy I feel. I just want it finished so I can know that I am his wife, and I can finally live my life. So, we can all move forward. Isn't that better?"

"I suppose. Although my task has now become even more difficult."

"Keep it small. Flowers, food and a priest. The guest list will follow in that vein, only the closest friends and family. People who have supported me and us."

"Regina."

"It's not like before aai, that circle includes influential members of the ton. Two viscounts and a viscountess unless I'm mistaken. We do not need half of England to attend, and I do not want them to. We will show that despite our newly elevated status, we are still in our hearts the same people. That our focus is on each other."

"I suppose love matches are always popular. I heard him call you 'devika'."

"Yes." Regina stood and took her mother's hand leading her

over to the chaise to sit. "Did you know he speaks Marathi?"

"What?" Her mother blinked in shock.

"He knows so much about me, about our culture, he's not only unashamed of me he celebrates it. We won't have to hide anymore mother,"

She nodded and patted her cheek. "That is good."

"It is better."

She smiled, tears flooding her eyes. "It does me well to see you so happy."

Regina leaned her head against her mother's shoulder and closed her eyes. Never had she imagined this kind of bliss would be hers. "Do you know, when he revealed himself in that ballroom, I thought he was like Lord Krishna in those stories you told me, coming to save me from marriage to that horrible Mr. Harrison and his mother."

Madhavi laughed, "He is certainly an improvement, in several respects. But you have one thing wrong,"

"Oh?"

"Mmm, that one isn't Krishna, he is Ram."

"What?" Regina lifted her head to look at her mother. "What do you mean mother?"

"King Rama. The king who must subvert his wishes for the benefit of those under his care." She flicked her under her chin while Regina stared in shock, her mind trying to digest what her mother had just said. "As far as he was your choice, he is a fitting one at the very least."

Her mother had named her Rajani, a common epithet for the Goddess Durga, but at her mother's proclamation of Leo being more like Lord Ram, a shiver had passed through Regina. Lord Ram's ending with his beloved Sita had not been a good one. Did that bode ill for her and Leo? Was Ravana still waiting in the wings? She hadn't dreamt about Edward Harrison the previous night but that didn't mean he was no longer a threat to them.

"You think Leo has trapped himself?"

"Not exactly, but he is used to having more control over his life and choices. Titles come with privileges this is obvious, but there are also iron rules. He knows this conceptually, but when he begins to notice the new chains he will not like it. You will have to help him, my duckling, just as Sita did. Both of you must find a path together."

It was an idea she had never considered before but the more she thought of it the more apt it appeared. Sita and Ram carving their path as one in the unknown of the forest, against all odds. Yes, she could see. "Of course I will help him aai."

CHAPTER SEVENTEEN

Two weeks later

REGINA'S REACTION TO the arrival of Elodia, Ada and Headmistress Pollitt was perhaps not the most dignified thing, especially in the advent of her becoming a baroness. But when she'd heard their voices she had dashed down the stairs and swept them all into a tight embrace heedless of the amused looks sent her way by the other present guests.

"My goodness, what an embrace!" Headmistress Pollitt exclaimed with a laugh before pulling back and rubbing Regina's arms. "Look at you." She shook her head and touched Regina's hair. "You look very pleased with yourself."

Regina laughed. "How was the journey?"

"Oh fine," Elodia replied with a wave of her hand. "Papa let me come with Ada and Mr. Thompson, I think he's sick of me."

"It was very easy, and such lovely countryside. Your family home is like a wonderland Regina."

"I will tell my mother, she will be happy with those remarks." Regina hooked arms with the older woman and led them to a sitting room with lemonade and glasses set out with sandwiches and biscuits. "I am so pleased you were able to come headmistress."

"Nonsense my dear, how could I turn down an invitation from a future baroness? Especially when she was one of my favorite students."

"I always knew we were your favorites, even if we caused more trouble than we were worth."

"Oh, I don't know about all that." The headmistress sat down on the sofa and removed her gloves. "You all seemed to finish any nonsense that came your way. And I believe you all can safely call me by my name now."

"That seems wildly disrespectful. Why can't I simply call you Headmistress Pollitt?" Elodia remarked claiming a side chair and stretching out her legs before her.

"Well for one thing my tenure at Miss Pollitt's will be over within the year."

"What?" Regina seated herself next to the headmistress while Ada flopped down into the love seat.

"And secondly, my last name is Walsh."

"I don't understand," Ada frowned and tilted her head.

"My family is Irish. In order to teach at such a place and be promoted I couldn't make such things public. The founder, a Mrs. Burghley-Harrison agreed so long as I used the name of the school."

"Aunt Theodosia founded Mrs. Pollitt's?" Regina asked in shock.

Miss Walsh blinked and smiled. "I believe that is her name, yes."

"When?" Elodia asked leaning forward with wide eyes.

"Oh, decades ago. She hired me for her grandson I believe, and after that she said she wanted to bring me into that school and eventually make me the Headmistress."

"That woman is ubiquitous." Regina murmured, wondering what Leo would think if he heard about this as well.

"How do you girls know her?" Miss Walsh asked, glancing between Elodia and Regina.

"She is my father's god mother." Elodia replied.

Miss Walsh's eyebrows shot up. "Is she indeed?"

"And she was instrumental in securing the title for Leo, my fiancé." Regina added. "She is the reason I didn't have to marry Mr. Harrison, or any man like him."

"Yes, you all mentioned him in your letter. A private detective was he?"

"Oh, he was all sort of things a soldier, a police officer and then a detective before now becoming a baron," Ada commented.

"My goodness," Miss Walsh looked between them with growing amazement.

"He's tall, clever," Regina ticked off the list on her fingers.

"Handsome as anything," Elodia added.

"And very discreet," Ada finished.

"We met him when we were trying to find Ada's brother with Mr. Thompson when he was kidnapped," Regina said.

Miss Walsh turned to Ada. "My goodness yes, Ada, what a trial that must have been."

"All is well that ends well, and it got me Basil for which I could not be more grateful."

"I am pleased you both found such agreeable husbands. Especially you Regina, I was always worried about you."

"I was worried myself, but Leo was a turn no one saw coming. Apparently his grandfather parted ways with his father the baron over an elopement with a woman from the colonies and never looked back. He even took her name so no one would associate him with his birth family, so two generations went down without any mention of Leo and his family."

Miss Walsh nodded along. "But Mrs. Burghley-Harrison."

"Who is as old and wily as the day is long found him and sort of bullied him into taking his place as the baron."

"I'm sure you had something to do with it my dear." Miss Walsh teased.

"A very little." Regina grinned.

"Well, I must say you have been busy,"

"It certainly hasn't been dull," Ada replied.

"So what is your full name headmistress," Elodia asked, "If we cannot call you Mrs. Walsh,"

She laughed. "It's Miss, not 'Mrs.,' Miss Hawthorne. Miss Isolde Walsh."

"Well we are very pleased to meet you Miss Isolde Walsh." Elodia said.

"It is a very romantic name isn't it?" Regina commented. The thing was plucked straight out of Arthurian legend.

"I'm a very romantic person," Miss Walsh joked.

"I will have to take your word for it," Ada replied glancing at Elodia who chuckled.

"Will you be looking to marry now that you are retiring?" Regina wondered out loud.

She looked at her in askance. "I think my marrying days are well behind me my dear."

"But you are not so ancient," Elodia remarked, and Regina couldn't help but agree.

Miss Walsh had always been pretty. No amount of plain clothing or utilitarian hair styling could hide the brilliance of her complexion or the lovely velvety brown color of her almond shaped eyes. Her curling hair was thick and deep brown. Her figure was a bit more robust than Regina remembered but it was still pleasing. All in all, she would make a fine bride for any gentleman on her physical merits alone.

"Thank you very much for that Miss Hawthorne."

"Oh, let us dispense with formalities, shall we?" Ada complained.

"What I mean, Isolde is that you are rather pretty with a fine figure and sense of humor."

"I am also comfortably working class and well into my thirties. No one is looking to march me down an aisle any time soon when there are younger and richer options around."

Elodia sniffed haughtily and smoothed her skirts. "I beg to differ."

"My dears, it is about more than looks and disposition. The plain fact is that men of substance want or need children, and at my age it is a risk. For the man it is an investment of time and money that has a lower chance of a yield and for the woman it is quite literally life and death most particularly as we get older."

"I hadn't considered that." Elodia replied with a serious frown. "I have to admit my interest in you marrying is mostly selfish. I will be on the marriage mart on my own next year."

"Still a little bully," she replied shaking her head ruefully.

"Elodia Hawthorne, are you misbehaving?" They turned to see the Viscount Melbroke approaching with a suspicious glare aimed at his daughter.

Elodia turned to him, her mouth falling open in outrage. "How rude papa! I am the very model of refinement and correct behavior."

He raised a dubious eyebrow as he dropped a hand on her shoulder, giving it an affectionate squeeze. "I have a grey hair or two that would beg to differ. Hello Miss Mason, Mrs. Thompson, and—" His eyes fell on Miss Walsh as Regina was now determined to think of her and he blinked for a moment before frowning slightly. "I'm sorry I don't believe we have met."

"Papa, this is Headmistress Pollitt," Elodia replied, "Although she won't be called that much longer."

"Is it?" It was clear he still didn't recognize her, but he bowed in greeting, nonetheless. "Good day to you ma'am."

"And you my lord," she nodded curtly, and realization flashed across his face.

"That did it," he muttered, and Miss Walsh chuckled softly.

"Had you forgotten me?"

"No, I simply didn't remember you looking like this. But that nod I remembered."

"Ah,"

"Good day to you ma'am," he greeted her with a nod.

"And you, my lord."

The Viscount's reaction could be forgiven. In her avatar of Headmistress Pollitt, Miss Walsh always had her dark hair pulled back tightly in defiance of fashion or aesthetics and wore the same collection of blue dresses to the point that it was assumed to be a uniform of the school. Her expression had always been strictly composed, rarely showing much favoritism or emotion.

Now with the slight curls around her face, the small golden earbobs and the white cotton gown dotted with pale yellow flowers she was nearly unrecognizable. She wondered about the woman she had seen as a confident and now could call a dear friend. The idea of her spending her life alone because she had spent most of her youth working and enriching the lives of children seemed horribly unfair.

"Have you only just arrived Papa?" Elodia asked, curling her hand around his.

"Yes, more or less." His blue eyes fixed on Regina. "I believe your mother is ready for you in the garden Miss Mason. I have been sent by Mrs. Mason and Lord Starkley's mother to fetch you all for the festivities."

"Thank you, my lord."

He nodded once more, his blue eyes lingering once more on Miss Walsh before turning and walking out of the room. Elodia stood and skipped over to him, taking his arm.

"What does she look like Papa?" she teased, and he glared at her.

"Never you mind," He grumbled, and she giggled.

Regina rose with Ada and Miss Walsh, following them out to the garden where her mother had been organizing with Leo's mother for the haldi ceremony. It had been truly heartwarming to see them working together and bonding over the pending nuptials of their children.

"What festivities Regina?" Miss Walsh asked, "I thought the wedding was tomorrow."

"It is of course, but in India our wedding festivities last for days. We didn't do all of them, but this one was non-negotiable."

"How exciting," Ada exclaimed, "Oh Gigi I can just imagine how happy you are. I would have given anything for my mother to share some of the wedding customs of home. Richard did his best for me, but it wasn't the same."

"It is nothing grand, especially on such short notice, but honestly I never thought we would have the chance to do anything like this. I never imagined many things would be possible before Leo."

"I respect what you said about marriage for yourself, Miss Walsh, especially when it comes to the dangers of childbirth," Regina mused, "but I cannot imagine you would dismiss marriage out of hand altogether."

"Isolde, Regina, please."

Regina rolled her eyes in exasperation. "Oh very well, Isolde."

"Why not? I have a good deal of savings from my salary, I shall make investments and support myself. Perhaps your husband could assist me there Ada."

"Of course," Ada agreed readily.

"Well what about companionship?" Regina asked.

"When it comes to companionship, I have my friends, and you girls if you don't mind me being a nuisance."

"That you could never be," Regina assured her taking her free arm.

"Excellent then I shan't be wanting at all. You know, you ladies are a credit to me and to yourselves. We have seen an uptick in enrollment lately at Miss Pollitt's."

"Have you really?" Ada asked.

"Oh yes. Two students of reasonably modest backgrounds by social standards at the very least marrying into a noble family on one hand and then you becoming a baroness. It's all very good for our reputation as a school that produces young ladies of not only substance, but accomplishment. Certainly good enough for even the most discerning of tastes."

Regina had never considered the effect of her marriage on her old alma mater. It was an unexpected pleasure to know that she'd have such a positive influence on the place which had allowed her to forge bonds with three of the dearest people in her life.

"Oh my goodness," Ada declared as they reached the garden, and Regina couldn't help but smile.

The fruit of her mother's labor was a sight to behold indeed. When her mother had told her they would perform haldi, Regina had expected a small affair with her three friends, in her room. Clearly her mother had something grander in mind.

The entire area including tables and chairs had been decorated with flowers in every shade of yellow from sunshine yellow to deep burnished gold interspersed with small brass, lit deyas. The gazebo where she danced had been draped in pale yellow gauze and nearly two dozen garlands of marigolds. On a platform two gurus sat, one with a tabla and the other with a sitar. Lillian darted back and forth in a yellow dress between the gentlemen assembled, bestowing marigold boutonnieres. Her mother, clad in a mustard yellow silk gown stood in the center casting one last discerning eye on the preparations.

"I am delivering them to you, Mrs. Mason," Elodia's father said, and she turned to him before smiling and walking over to them giving him a nod of dismissal. At some point she had reverted from a terrified immigrant back to the Marathi woman who had named her first born daughter for her favorite goddess and told her stories about Hanuman, Ganesha and Lakshmi while she oiled her hair.

"Aai," Regina gasped out with tears in her eyes.

"Do you like it?"

"Like it?!" She released her hold on Isolde and hugged her mother tightly around her neck. Her mother laughed merrily, hugging her back for a moment before pulling away slightly.

"Surprised?"

"When did you do this? I finished all the prep last night this wasn't part of it."

"You weren't the only one working on preparations. What is the point of having servants if they cannot be used for this?"

"How on earth did you get your hands on these marigolds?"

"Magic," she replied with a wink.

"Where did you find the musicians?"

"Oh them, they've been here since your fiancé passed last year. Seemed to make more sense to keep them here just in case instead of sending them back to India."

"Aai," her eyes were burning.

"Hush now. Your guests are watching, what will they say."

LEO FOLLOWED THE directions of his mother-in-law allowing her to sit him down on a cushion beside his future wife who was dressed in a yellow cotton dress, grinning like she had received all her birthday gifts at once. He had been given strict instructions to wear no waistcoat or jacket, which seemed strange to him until he saw what Regina was wearing. The onlookers were a combination of friends and family; Basil, Ada and Richard, Miss Hawthorne and her father, Miss Walsh who was apparently Regina's former headmistress.

He wasn't sure what to expect from the proceedings. He'd never actually participated in a proper Indian wedding before. He caught Regina's and she wiggled her eyebrows at him.

"Hello," she said.

"Hello to you," he replied.

When her mother approached with a bowl of bright yellow paste the last thing he expected her to do was begin smearing it on Regina's face. Leo glanced at her askance but noted the almost blissful expression on Regina's face.

"What on earth is that?" Leo asked.

"You don't know?" Regina teased peering at him with one eye as her mother smeared it lovingly on her cheeks and bare feet.

Little brat. He glared at her playfully, "No, devika I don't."

"This concoction gives the ceremony its name. It is haldi."

"What's in it?" Richard asked, watching with amused interest. "I can smell sandalwood, lemons and is that rose?"

"Yes, and tumeric, curd, rose water, milk, mustard oil, almond powder," Regina's mother replied.

"What is it meant to do exactly?" Leo asked as she approached him. He was still a bit leery, but he nodded his consent and tried not to think about the fact that he was sitting half dressed in a garden allowing a woman to smear goop on his face with witnesses.

"It brightens your skin, and it wards off evil intentions."

"Evil intentions, eh?" A mischievous glint lit Richard's eyes. "How much of it did you prepare?"

"Thornfield," Leo warned, shooting him a look before shutting his eyes as the cold mixture was gently applied to his forehead. The last thing he needed was for Regina to begin to worry.

"I did it for my wedding,"

"Did it work?" One eye popped open at the sound of Captain Mason's voice.

"I'd say it worked a treat," he replied.

A happy marriage, happy healthy children, an advantageous marriage? Yes, that seemed like someone up there liked Captain Mason.

"Mrs. Kingston," Mrs. Mason reached for Leo's mother. "You can put more for both of them," she said handing her the bowl. Leo watched as his mother applied the paste to Regina's forehead and nose before doing the same to him. One by one the guests took turns smearing them with the haldi paste while Leo tried to stay as still as possible.

"This feels very strange," he murmured as Captain Mason applied paste to his hands.

"Yes it does." The older man agreed.

He glanced at Regina again after their guests had finished and fought back a laugh at the sight of her. "You look like you've gone face first into a vat of mustard," he said, and she laughed merrily.

"But it smells much better than mustard."

"I will agree with you there." It wasn't a smell he'd ever encountered before this, but it wasn't altogether unpleasant, even if it was strange to have people rubbing paste on his skin while he sat there like a child. "So, what now, am I meant to wear this the whole time?" Leo asked.

"Yes, however the unmarried guests can get some as well, to

bring them luck in finding their future spouses." Mrs. Mason said, turning to Miss Hawthorne and Richard.

That was alright then, at least he and Regina weren't the only ones. "And once we are all coated?" Leo asked as Ada smeared haldi paste on her brother and her friend.

"We enjoy the repast," she replied, washing off her hands.

Leo stood and helped Regina up before leading her to sit at one of the tables. He hadn't been barefoot in a garden in an age, and it still felt odd, even if no one else seemed to notice. But he had to admit there was something touching and comforting in having close friends and family take turns participating in a task meant to protect them from harm, and it was liberating to feel the grass between his toes and the sun on his face.

Elodia was now chasing Richard determined to cover him with the haldi paste, while Ada attempted to trap him in place. Miss Walsh had settled into a quiet conversation with Viscount Melbroke, but she kept being distracted by Elodia's antics. The viscount was a tricky gentleman to pin down. Friendly and polite, endlessly permissive with his daughter, but somehow he retained an air of distance. Leo got the impression of a man who was very good at tolerance so long as it didn't upend too much in his life. He wasn't certain if the man would prove to be an ally long term, but even he had to admit it was good to have him here for the sake of appearances if nothing else.

All that was before he got to Regina, who was in her element, with a light in her eyes he'd never really seen before. If this brought her that kind of joy, he was willing to do much more, regardless of how strange it seemed. Captain Mason and his wife were near Regina, the older woman carefully feeding her daughter with her hands. The unique beautiful sounds of the sitar floating through the garden and the birds seemed to match its song. The dishes brought out were a delightful mix of desserts and snacks full of flavor and spices.

Was this what he could look forward to? He could already imagine it, Regina dancing while the musicians played for her, her little sister playing with their children. Her mother doting on her grandchildren and bringing out delicious dishes for them to enjoy barefooted on the grass. A safe haven among the general intolerance of the ton. It was a beautiful image, full of love and laughter.

"How are you enjoying it?" His mother asked sitting beside him.

"It's an interesting experience."

"That is for certain."

"Thank you for helping to persuade her parents."

"Not at all. Have you thought about what I said?"

"Yes." And he still didn't agree with her.

"And?"

He nodded towards Regina who was now playing with her sister. "Do you see how happy she is? If I can make that happen every day of her life it will be worth everything. I don't need another reason."

She sighed and shook her head, opening her mouth to argue but Leo noticed a servant approached them with a silver tray, and Leo watched him draw closer until he could see the letter on it.

"For you my lord," he said with a short bow.

Leo nodded and took it, ripping open the seal to read the contents. His stomach churned as he read the results of his inquiry at The War Office as to Harrison's tenure in the army. Contrary to what had been supposed, Harrison had left the army only two years after Leo under dubious circumstances. He had been allowed to retain his rank under the agreement that he resigned his post immediately. That had been at least two or three years before. Where had he been? Had he stayed on with the East India Company? How long had he been back in Europe or at least England since he'd discovered he was the heir?

"What's that Leo?" his mother asked.

"Nothing much, just an answer to a question I'd been asking." He slipped the letter into his pocket. Captain Mason's gaze was fixed on his trouser pocket, however. Had he recognized the seal on the envelope? If he asked, Leo wouldn't lie but he hoped the gentleman had the sense to wait.

There was no point in mentioning anything now. He still didn't have an idea of what was at risk or what it all meant.

CHAPTER EIGHTEEN

THE MORNING OF Regina's wedding dawned bright with a clear blue sky. She expected to be wrecked with nerves. She expected some level of excitement on the day itself. Instead from the moment her maids greeted her all the way throughout the process of getting dressed she only found an extreme calm.

Now she stood in front of her mirror in her dress. It was a traditional design in ivory and gold banarasi silk, but a unique border patterned in red, and gold graced the wide off shoulder neckline, the edges of her sleeves and the hem of each flounce. Instead of a typical English coiffure, she had opted for a traditional Marathi style of a long braid folded up onto the back of her head and anchored with golden hair pins. Instead of orange blossom flower crowns made popular by Queen Victoria, Regina had opted to decorate her hair with jasmine and red tea roses.

She was everything she had hoped to look like as a bride so why didn't she feel more? There was something in her heart. Some strange pulsing sensation was locked away behind her ribs unable to break through. It didn't feel real somehow, even though she was staring at herself in the mirror in her dress. The guests were at the chapel, everything was ready, but she couldn't process what she was looking at.

That this was her wedding dress.

That she would have a wedding that celebrated both parts of her identity.

The door opened and she turned to see her mother enter holding three flat rosewood boxes and a chest carried by a footman.

"Mother,"

She paused, staring at her daughter before smiling. "You look beautiful my darling," she said in Marathi.

"I have these for you," her mother gestured to the boxes the footman was placing on her bed. "These are some pieces we had made for you in India before we left." Regina waited until the man left before walking over to the bed. In the first box Regina saw bell-shaped jhumkas, with pearls and dark jade and a guttapusalu necklace with intricate clusters of pearls and gold beads. In the second there was a kasumala with a coin necklace as a choker and a long necklace with images of Lakshmi glinting between small diamond lotuses. In the chest she saw golden bangles of the most exquisite craftmanship with mango mala and peacock motifs.

She guided Regina over to the third box. "This one is for today; it was part of my wedding jewelry when I married your baba." When she lifted the lid, Regina let out a gasp, her eyes going wide. Within, nested against the dark velvet was a magnificent golden temple necklace nearly 30 inches in length and matching earrings with the image of Durga painstakingly crafted in gold embellished with clusters of pearl and ruby drops.

"Aai, you cannot give all of this to me."

"Nonsense you need your own pieces to give to your daughters, don't you? And this temple jewelry was meant for you, from mother to daughter."

"But what about Lillian?" Regina asked as her mother lifted the necklace from the box and fastened it around her neck.

"I have enough for her when the time comes. Do you like them?"

"They are exquisite. I never expected all of this."

"Don't say that darling," she frowned at her, "you should expect to receive things from your mother."

"I didn't mean it like that. I meant that I never imagined you had all of this."

Madhavi shook her head and stroked Regina's cheek. "It was never about what I had. When we came here, I understood that what I was would not be welcome here. It was the way I believed it had to be for you as well in order to be accepted and safe. But now I think perhaps I was wrong to take so much from you. So, these things are for you, to give you back something from home." She wiped the tears from Regina's cheeks and turned her to face the mirror again. At the sight of her mother's necklace, her mother standing behind her holding her shoulders, smiling at her with tears in her eyes, her throat tightened as her heart filled to bursting.

There it was.

"Thank you aai."

She shook her head. "It is time to go down now, are you ready?"

Regina nodded and turned to face her before crouching down to touch her mother's feet, seeking her blessing for the last time before she became a wife. The touch of Madhavi's hand came seconds later, sweeping over her hair lightly before raising her to her feet.

"My blessing on you, my daughter. May your marriage last a hundred years, may your happiness never be extinguished, may your lap never be empty, may all your wishes be granted."

LEO NEVER IMAGINED he would be so nervous on his wedding day. Had Basil felt like he was about to come out of his skin? He couldn't account for it. It wasn't so much that he was anxious about Regina, he was only too eager to be her husband. The guest list had been kept mercifully limited due to time constraints. The only people outside of their immediate circle were

Basil's parents and Aunt Theo as he was now wont to call her along with her ever-present nephew. She had made fast friends with his mother based on her role in pestering him into his title.

The chapel itself had been beautifully decorated with evergreen garlands, red and white flowers of all kinds and red and gold brocade ribbon. The sun was shining brightly but a cool breeze kept the heat at bay.

He was fighting to keep his hands still. He wanted her here, so he knew everything was well. He needed to set his eyes on her. It had taken weeks, but her anxiety had finally caught up with him. Every time he closed his eyes he imagined some ridiculous scenario involving Harrison kidnapping her or some harm coming to her because he wasn't there.

Abruptly the choir began singing and the doors opened to reveal Regina and her father. At the sight of her the tension in his shoulders evaporated like morning mist. She was just there with her father. Everything was alright.

So far. He couldn't think about that, not with her standing here finally. She wore a gown of ivory silk, pleated and tucked to hug her soft curves before billowing out in flounces. And the light streamed in behind her as if she were some kind of apparition. As she drew closer the light of the sun was replaced by her incandescent smile. He saw the blood red roses in her hair, the tiara of jasmine flowers anchoring her lace veil.

The temple jewelry she wore around her neck and at her ears was at once shocking and yet entirely fitting of the young woman who was soon to be his baroness. Only she would wear an image of her Hindu gods in a Christian church. Her hand when her father laid it in his was warm and soft. The unfettered excitement in her face brought a smile to his, and when she squeezed his hand and turned to face the priest the last of the nausea in his stomach was gone.

The vicar began the service, welcoming the congregation and directing any who had cause for them not to marry to speak. He glanced at Regina and she wiggled her eyebrows at him. He fought back a laugh and shook his head. He couldn't imagine what the onlookers were thinking, watching them giggle like children. Then the vicar warned them about entering into the sacrament of marriage hastily. He raised his eyebrows at her pointedly and she pursed her lips, looking away from him. Then he heard his name called.

"Leopold Hamish Kingston, wilt thou have this woman to thy wedded wife, to live together after God's ordinance in the holy estate of Matrimony? Wilt thou love her, comfort her honor and keep her in sickness and in health; and, forsaking all others, keep thee only unto her, so long as ye both shall live?"

"I will."

"Rajani Elizabeth Mason, wilt thou have this man to thy wedded husband, to live together after Gods ordinance in the holy estate of Matrimony? Wilt thou obey him, and serve him, love, honor, and keep him in sickness and in health; and, forsaking all others, keep thee only unto him, so long as ye both shall live?"

"I will."

"Who giveth this woman to be married to this man?"

"I do," Captain Mason replied.

The Vicar looked Leo in his eye, "Take your bride by her right hand," he said, "and make your vows,"

Leo smiled at Regina, "I Leopold, take thee Rajani to be my wedded wife, to have and to hold from this day forward, for better for worse, for richer for poorer, in sickness and in health, to love and to cherish, till death us do part, according to God's holy ordinance; and thereto I plight thee my troth."

She smiled, a sheen of happy tears in her eyes as she recited her vows to him. The vicar asked for the rings. Leo watched Regina's eyes go wide when she noticed the extra item on the pillow beside his ring. The thirty-inch, three strand necklace, strung with black and gold beads ending with two golden balls as the pendant had been given to Leo by Captain Mason. The older man had presented it to Leo as an alternate to the ring he'd purchased in London.

When he fastened it around her neck, the love in her eyes left him breathless. Never had Leo been more grateful for taking another person's advice.

By the time the vicar was ready to pronounce them husband and wife, Regina was positively beaming, bouncing lightly on her toes, brimming with excitement and his chest was full to bursting. He'd known how eager she was to marry him, how anxious she was to be married, but her giddy anticipation was infectious. All his life he'd wanted a place to belong, and he'd found it here with her. His little goddess. His warrior. His wife. He gripped her hands fighting back a laugh, barely able to look at her with the happy tears burning his eyes.

The pronouncement came and Regina bounced towards him, pressing her lips to his with an adorable giggle that finally had his laughter breaking free. His grandfather had made him a Baron but the young woman clinging to his neck with her lips pressed to his had him feeing like the King of England himself.

CHAPTER NINETEEN

Starkley Manor, Cheshire

S HE WAS MARRIED. Finally, after years of waiting and fretting and praying it was done. The contract had been executed and she was free. But the best part, the thing thrilling her the most ever since the priest had said 'man and wife', was that her husband was Leo. Some gods had intervened and given her mother a baroness for a daughter and Regina a prince of a man like Leo Kingston as a husband.

She had spent every day since the moment she found out about her marriage with an ever-present tension in her mind and heart. A low thrumming dread and sadness about what was taken from her, what more she would be forced to give up. Would she ever get her life back? Would she be altered beyond all recognition before it was over? The first person who had ever seemed to understand what she had been forced to give up beyond dancing and time with friends, was Leo. She still remembered the way he'd looked at her when he asked her what her real name was, the near wonder and sympathy she saw in his eyes.

And now she was waiting in her room for him to arrive so she could make love to her husband without worrying about what people would think or if anyone would see. A man who loved chai, spoke her language, called her by her birth name and looked at her as if she was a wonder. A man who was not only curious about who she was but prioritized what she wanted. A man who kissed her greedily but touched her gently. The freedom she felt knowing that she could finally be who she wanted to be with someone who wanted the same thing for her had a strange energy crackling under her skin.

She couldn't sit and wait as her mother had told her to do. She had to move. There was nothing to fear, no anxiety over the unknown. She already knew what making love with him would be like. Now she wanted to know how it would feel to do that with no clothes on.

The door opened and she turned to see him closing it behind him. He only wore his shirtsleeves and trousers but already she was impatient. At least he'd left his boots elsewhere. He paused to look at her, and when she realized he wasn't moving her eyes met his. Was he nervous? Was that possible?

She smiled at him, and he returned it in that slow admiring way she'd fallen in love with months ago. This was her husband, and she couldn't stay away from him a moment longer. A giddy laugh bubbling in her throat, she ran across the room and leapt into his arms. He caught her easily, chuckling as she pressed kisses all over his stubbled jaw. He caught her mouth with his, smiling against her lips as he walked them over to the bed. Regina wrapped her legs around his waist gripping his shoulders as his hands slid down her waist to close purposefully around her bottom.

She sighed sliding one hand up the back of his neck to the short curls of his hair. He placed her on the bed, and she set about removing his shirt immediately. His mouth moved over her cheek down her neck. Her fingers fumbled as a shiver of sensation slid through her. She could never have believed her neck was so sensitive before Leo, before she'd known what it was like to have his mouth and tongue on her skin. Finally gaining purchase on his shirt she dragged it up over his head pulling away just long enough to let the fabric pass before feasting her eyes on his bare chest. His skin was so smooth and warm, dusted with what she imagined was the perfect amount of chest hair.

Not that she had anything to compare it to. Lord knew the man she'd caught sight of last year didn't count.

She pressed her mouth to the skin over his heart, feeling the muscle thud against her lips, then moved up to kiss his shoulder and neck while he yanked his hands free from his shirt and buried them in her loose hair. He nuzzled her temple, allowing her time to explore while his fingers massaged her scalp. Her hands slid around his waist and up his back, feeling the firm muscles moving under his perfect skin, drawing him closer to her.

"Rajani," he murmured against her skin, and she shivered, closing her eyes against the wave of emotion. She couldn't get used to hearing him call her that. He drew her head back, and she caught sight of the focused desire on his face before he took her mouth, his tongue sliding past her lips, stroking inside her mouth. She didn't notice that his hands had drifted under her nightgown until she felt the rough texture of his thumbs slide up the sensitive skin of her inner thighs.

She gasped breaking away from his mouth, her legs tensing against his hips as a rush of wetness flooded her center. His mouth drifted to her neck again, sucking her skin softly then releasing it before moving further down to do it again, melting every bone in her body.

"Leo," his name drifted past her gasping lips as she squirmed closer. He hummed against her, the gentle vibration and rush of air summoning his name again.

"What is it, love?"

She didn't remember closing her eyes, but the darkness was replaced with the dim firelit room as her eyelids lifted. Had she asked him something? Her mind felt flooded with dandelion fluff. She couldn't keep one thought in her head save one: she wanted to feel all of him against her. Now. "I cannot believe you came to me on our wedding night with clothes on," she grumbled while she fumbled with the buttons on his trousers. His snicker started off low before escalating into a full belly laugh.

"It's not funny." And how was it possible that these things were so impossible to unfasten? Buttons were buttons were they not? Honestly.

"Forgive me, devika," he said between chuckles. She wanted to stay annoyed, but it was impossible with him calling her his 'little goddess'. "I won't do it again,"

"Which one?"

"The clothes." His hands rested lightly on her shoulders just over the ties of her night gown and she looked up at him as awareness settled over her. "Speaking of." With one deft tug he unraveled them, and the soft, thin silk fell away leaving her bare to her waist. It was so different this time with more light. There had been protection from unwanted eyes in the garden with only starlight and moonlight, and while Regina hadn't wanted to hide from Leo's perusal, the lack of light would have made it difficult.

Now, in their bedroom, the fire gave more than enough light to leave nothing to the imagination. She hadn't been prepared for the intimacy, or how it would feel to be bared to him and his judgement.

His eyes darkened as they roved eagerly over her exposed flesh, his fingertips following close behind leaving trails of golden sensation over her neck, shoulders and breasts. She wanted to keep watching him; to keep seeing the desire she elicited in him, but his touch drifted over her nipples as he cupped the full, heavy weight of her breast and her eyes fluttered closed.

She had missed that feeling. The way he made that molten sensitivity pool between her thighs with a brush of his hands, an exhale from his full mouth. She forced her heavy eyes open and reached for the buttons on his trousers again, determined this time to unfasten them so she could finally see what she had taken inside her weeks before. She wanted to stamp herself on him the way she felt branded by his kiss that first time in the rain.

He caught one of her hands in his and pressed a kiss to the back of it. "Why are you so impatient?" he asked.

"I'm not... I just want to see you."

He watched her for a long moment, and she wondered if the prickle of guilt she felt meant she was lying. She did want to see him.

"We have time devika,"

"I know but—"

"I let you have your way before did I not?" he asked. She looked away at that. She didn't like that phrasing at all. It made her sound like a greedy task master. "Trust me now and give me my time."

His hand cupped her cheek, his thumb brushing tenderly over her skin. It was true. As romantic as their tryst in the garden had been, there were so many things she barely remembered. Was it because she had been too impatient and anxious? They were man and wife now by law and by God's holy ordinance according to the vicar. Why shouldn't she allow herself to enjoy her wedding night? She met his eyes, noted the patience and fondness there, and concern. He was worried. She nodded, conceding the point and he smiled.

"Lie down," he commanded, leaning forward to press her backwards onto the feather mattress. She reached for him but again he caught her hand in his, this time kissing her palm before laying a trail of adoration up her arm. Flat on her back she watched in delirious fascination as his mouth moved down her body with deliciously slow intent, drawing the most unreasonable noises from her. A low groan when he paused to tease her nipples into furled attention. A shivering gasp when he scraped his teeth along her ribs. He buried his face in her stomach, breathing in before suckling his way down the curved expanse until her nightgown paused his voyage right above her pelvis.

She watched with anticipation as he stared at her bunched-up night gown, the crumpled silk the only barrier between him and her wet aching center. His hands lingered on her thighs causing them to clench, as weak as they were. He lifted her leg onto his shoulder and with those golden eyes on hers, kissed her ankle. Her breath grew slow and labored as she watched him move his way down the inside of her leg, lingering at the back of her knee when a flick of his tongue had her gasping and arching her back.

Then he was moving again, his mouth on the inside of her

trembling thigh, his hand on the outside holding it steady on his strong shoulder. If he was going to do the same on her other leg she would combust on the spot. He moved higher and higher, her breath coming harder until she was panting, her hands clenched in the linen, her gaze fixed on that hypnotic mouth.

Was he going to stop before he reached her mound? Did she want him to? As sensitive as she felt down there she was desperate for any pressure to ease the ache, but could she bear it? A gasp flew from her lips as he pressed his face just there, over her nightgown breathing her in with a groan that rumbled through her.

"Oh God." The words tumbled out unheeded and her thighs clenched again until she realized where they were. *His poor head.* She gasped and tried to sit up, reaching for him. "I'm sorry."

His answering smile had her mouth going dry. "Don't apologize," he said as his hand clenched in the material at her hips and with one jerk pulled it past her hips, before pulling it down her legs. He shifted them together until her nightgown was floating behind him to land on the floor and then he returned them to their places on either side of his hips. His hand slid up the top of her thighs to the curve of her hip, before one palm rested on the curls covering her sex.

"Leo," she panted, "what—"

"Stay there devika," he growled. "Don't move." Then he bent his head, his fingers parting her folds and pressed his mouth directly to her wet pulsing center.

It was almost a warning, but it wasn't enough to prepare her for her body's reaction to what had to be his tongue dragging across her intimate flesh, or his lips suckling on the throbbing nub of flesh that set her aflame. The sensation was indescribable, like molten waves of pure pleasure cascading over every nerve in her flesh, building with every caress of his tongue, every pull of his soft lips on her throbbing, weeping flesh. Her thighs tightened on his ears again but before she could gasp out an apology his free hand had tightened on her leg, as if wanting her to draw him closer to her.

He slid two fingers inside her and curled them up to press against the front wall of her core and she arched her back against a fresh, stronger current of desire. She churned her hips against his mouth riding his fingers, fisting the sheets near her head, as she called out in ecstasy or desperation as tension escalated at an alarming rate. His answering groan rumbled through her and a supernova of rapture swept through her with overwhelming force, leaving her a shivering, incoherent mess.

Then he was moving over her wrapping her legs around his waist. His arm wrapped around her waist, and he picked her up, moving her further up the bed, and following until he was stretched out above her. His trousers were gone now, she could feel the bare skin of his firm bottom against her calves. She was almost annoyed that she didn't get a chance to see the rest of him, but then she felt his iron length at her entrance and a smile floated onto her face. In two thrusts he was sheathed inside her, thick, deep and warm, his firm lower stomach pressed flush with hers.

Her hands settled on his shoulders as she luxuriated in being filled by him once more. At last. As if he was finally back where he was always supposed to be. After a few moments she realized he wasn't moving. Opening her eyes, she was graced with the sight of him, framed by the firelight, some sleek, dark god of love his eyes burning with love and desire. This was her husband. Every nightmare she'd feared had been avoided. Reaching up she touched his face in wonder, and he nuzzled into her palm.

"What's wrong?" she asked, and he shook his head.

"I was going to ask if you were alright," he said. "It's only you second time doing this after all."

She smiled. "I'm well enough. But if you would be so kind husband, I think you could make it even better."

He snickered and shook his head. "You are such a brat," he murmured before leaning down to kiss her, but his hips began to move and soon he was moving within her in a steady powerful rhythm that left her gasping while she tried to match him stroke for relentless stroke. She moved her hands down his chest, over his sides to grab his back and pull him closer. She loved the way his muscles shifted under her hands as he braced above her. Loved how powerful his body was and how effectively he used it to please her. That wonderful tension was building between her legs again, but slowly. Too slowly.

She moved one hand down his back until it curved around a hard curve of muscle. On his next thrust she pulled him closer, and she felt his gasp against her mouth as she moaned. He was so much deeper inside her now, more so than she ever could have thought possible. He lifted his head to catch her eyes, still moving at that tantalizing but intense, his eyes searching hers.

"Devika," he murmured, his voice rough with desire.

"More, Leo, please," she pleaded. He shifted his arms under her back, and one hand closed around the back of her neck while the other gripped her waist. She lost her grip on his backside which wasn't ideal, but then his pace quickened, and all she could do was hold onto his shoulders and kiss him back desperately between moans. His hold on her body gave him the perfect brace to plunge himself deep and hard like she wanted. His arm around her waist tilted her back just enough that he was hitting that ideal spot within her while his pelvis rubbed against her pressing perfectly against that button of needy flesh that ached for pressure.

She let her head fall back against the bed moaning deliriously, as her body began the climb to rapture, tightening around him. His hand on the back of her neck tightened as he pressed suckling kisses to her throat groaning into her skin. The air in her lungs was thin and hot, the ache inside her was so much bigger, so much stronger than ever before until it burst into a sudden crescendo of light. She arched desperately into his body, her fingertips digging into his shoulders in a desperate bid for security.

His grip on her body tightened almost painfully, as he stroked into her harder, calling out against her shoulder as he shuddered. A high thin whimper like a cat filtered through the haze of gold in her mind as she returned to herself, slowly relaxing under him into the mattress.

Was that her? Was she making that noise? She heard a muffled whisper *yes, Christ yes,* and she smiled, leaning her cheek against his temple. She was a sweaty and perfectly undignified mess; she could already feel the ache in her thighs setting in from her hold on the shivering man above her. Her man.

CHAPTER TWENTY

July, Starkley House, London

"GOOD MORNING," HE heard her murmur as his body began to notice the sheets, the warmth and the smell of his wife that permeated his entire life. Was he on his back? What was his hand on? He gave an experimental squeeze. Firm but supple, smooth to the touch. He cracked one eye open, and he winced at the glare of sunlight. He turned his head away and was greeted once again by the sight of Regina in the morning. Specifically, Regina in the morning after a full night of lovemaking.

Her head was propped up on one hand, the smooth linen sheets draped over her shapely form half obscuring her naked body. All those dark soft curls tumbled around her shoulders onto the pillow. Her mangal sutra as she called it, was ever present around her neck, resting against her dark bare breast.

"Good morning devika," he murmured. She smiled and swept her hand over his chest, down to his stomach. It hadn't taken long for her to get used to touching him openly. He had to admit he loved how boldly she went about it, unapologetically laying claim to his body the way he had done to hers. "How long have you been awake?"

"About half an hour."

"You've been watching me for half an hour?"

"More or less. But it's hardly a record for me. I've watched you for longer than that."

He grinned, "That is true enough. It is after all how we met."

"What are you talking about we met at the train station,"

"Not that time. Before."

"Before when?" she lifted her head to stare at his profile. His eyes snapped open as if he suddenly remembered something.

"Ah," he glanced at her and then chuckled. "I suppose I should tell you."

"Did we meet before?"

"In a manner of speaking. I'm almost certain it was you. Did you go to the seaside last year with your family before you decided to kidnap Basil to Gretna Green?"

"Yes, how did—"

"Did you have a habit of walking on the slopes near the beach?"

"What does that have to do with anything?" a sinking feeling took root in her stomach as one particular evening came to mind.

"Oh I think you know devika," he replied. "Honestly, it's poor form to sneak up on a man in the altogether without so much as an introduction."

She gasped, her eyes wide with horror. He watched her waiting to see if she would deny it. "That is not—" she couldn't get the word out.

"Not what? Not possible?"

"That was you?"

She was so adorable caught between confusion and mortification. "Did you see another naked man at the seaside?" he asked.

She buried her face between his body and the bed. "I did not mean to see you in that state." Her muffled voice emerged.

"So you say, but if I didn't catch you I'm sure you would have invited your friends to have a gander at my expense."

Her head came up, her face the picture of outrage. "That is not fair, I would never! I didn't even mean to see you as it was."

"But you didn't think to look away." He pressed.

"I was in shock. How long have you known?"

"Since I saw you at the train station."

"Oh lord." She buried her face in her hands. "How did you even recognize me from that distance?"

"Your bonnet, the purple one. Not many women who look like you have bonnets that glint in the sunlight."

She shook her head, watching him as if she'd never seen him before. "You really are an investigator aren't you?"

He chuckled, "What was your first clue?"

"I cannot believe you knew this whole time and never thought to say anything."

"Didn't seen the gentlemanly thing to do,"

"You must have thought me the wickedest creature,"

He chuckled, "Curious, certainly, and too bold by half, but never wicked."

"Mother always says I'm too forward."

She was perfect. Every moment in her presence only served to confirm how lucky he was to have her beside him in any capacity let alone like this. "You're a lusty one for sure, but I think I can keep up with you well enough. I like you just as you are devika,"

She smiled and pressed her face into his chest, breathing him in. "I like you as well,"

"I'm glad to hear it." He murmured, giving her a slight affectionate squeeze.

"We have an engagement tonight," she said and the warm delight in his chest evaporated.

"Already? We've only just gotten to London."

"Yes, but we are here with a purpose after all. It's nothing extreme, but Mr. Thompson is back in town with Ada. We've been connected to his mother, now it's time to be seen with him. To make sure people understand that the Baron and Baroness Starkley have very close ties to the Viscountess and Viscount Sterling."

"You make it sound like a military engagement."

"It is a war to be sure. And we are going to win it."

"I retired from the army,"

"Don't be such a brat, it's hardly for a long period of time. The season is still in full swing for a couple weeks before people return to the country for hunting. At that point we can pull back a little more. Spend some time overseas for our honeymoon."

Of course his Regina already had a strategy in place. He shouldn't have been surprised, she had after all, been preparing for this her entire life. But now there was no way for him to deal with Harrison in secrecy and adhere to her wishes as well. She couldn't know the truth of his agreement to return to London. "You have it all planned out I see."

"That my dear husband is my job."

"Mmm." He swept his hand down her back, over her lush bottom. "And mine is to obey?"

She gave him a coy look before walking her fingers down his bare chest. "Your input would be appreciated and duly considered of course. We are meant to be doing this together after all. You aren't going to be annoying about this are you?"

He laughed. "I wouldn't dare devika."

IT HAD BEEN a long time since Leo had been to Scotland Yard. Ever since the debacle with Trent, it had been difficult for him to trust the police the way he had before. He couldn't vouch for every officer there but there were at least some he knew he could count on. A handful who were honest even if they weren't always agreeable to what he wanted. As he drew closer, he knocked on the ceiling signaling for the driver to stop. The last thing he needed was to roll up in front of the building in a carriage with a bloody sigil on the front.

He disembarked from the vehicle and turned to the driver. "Wait here Simmons,"

"Very good my lord."

My Lord. It still sounded incorrect. He didn't need them hearing that nonsense either. He made his way down Whitehall Street to the entrance, an inexplicable bundle of nerves in his stomach.

As he neared the entrance he spied a lumbering bear of a man standing outside, making notes in a small notebook. Then he caught a glimpse of the red hair under the flat cap.

"Collins," Leo called out. Collins looked up and a wry familiar smile curved his mouth. "Just the man I was looking for."

"Well if it isn't Leo the Lion," Collins commented holding out his hand for Leo to shake.

"Still here then?" Leo grasped his enormous hand firmly and slapped his shoulder.

"Still here for now, been thinking about following you out the door." His brown eyes flicked over Leo's clothing and Leo knew he had noticed the difference. It would be impossible to miss for a seasoned investigator like Collins. "Is this a social visit?"

"Not exactly."

"I haven't seen you around for a bit, what brings you to The Yard?"

"There's a delicate bit of business and I need some eyes on it. Eyes I can trust."

"Alright."

"Well look who it is," a snarling drawl came from over Leo's shoulder, and he turned to see Locke. A dark haired and dark hearted idiot who had somehow ended up a police officer. The two men had never seen eye to eye on anything. Leo had never appreciated Locke's tendency to cut corners, and Locke had never respected Leo's thirst for answers and justice.

But this was too serious to allow past grudges to hamper him. "Locke."

"I'm surprised you came here yourself Kingston, seeing as you're all high and mighty now, a peer of the bleedin realm." It was clear he was trying to engage in lighthearted banter, but the simmering envy in his eyes was twisting it into something more bitter.

"Are you?" Collins asked.

"Yeah he is look at that waist coat. Look at them boots. What are you now? An earl, a duke?"

"A baron," Leo replied tightly, resisting the urge to tug down on the blue-black brocade waistcoat. "Not that it matters."

"Isn't that interesting?" Collins commented, a glint of humor in his eyes.

"Don't start." He grumbled. "I need help. Do you remember Edward Harrison?"

Collins rolled his eyes. "Unfortunately, why?"

"He is in England, and he's been making threats to me. I believe that he is responsible for the murders of at least two of my cousins who were in line to inherit before me."

"He's a blustery kind, you can't handle that yourself?"

Before he could finish Leo was shaking his head in silent contradiction. "This isn't bluster Collins. He was nearly a baron, he was publicly accepted as the heir until my claim was discovered."

Collins blinked and tilted his head back slightly. "So now you are the only thing in his way."

"Yes."

"Already wielding your power eh?" Locke jeered. Christ, was he still here? Didn't he have something to do other than stick his nose where it wasn't needed?

"Back off Locke," Collins growled.

"Not even a fortnight and you're here to put your polished boot on the working man's neck. A veteran."

Leo turned to face him, his patience running dangerously thin. "He is not the only veteran here, Locke. I am not the one with an agenda."

"I believe you," Collins said resting a hand on Leo's shoulder.

"I don't."

Collins rolled his eyes and glared at his colleague. "Shut up Locke."

"Seems to me you could have killed them and all," Locke said folding his arms.

"I didn't even know I was in the running." Leo replied.

"A likely story."

Jesus Christ. "I don't have time for this," He grumbled turning back to Collins.

"Are you working with anyone on this?" Collins asked.

"Bielson, I'm meeting up with him after this."

Collins nodded. "He's good. Get me some hard evidence. I can't move on suspicion alone Leo, or word of mouth. I need witnesses."

"I know, I don't expect you to bring him in tomorrow, I more want you to keep an eye out for anything he might be up to."

Leo sighed and slapped his shoulder in appreciation as relief crept up at last. "I can do that."

Starkley House
St. James, London

HE WAS LATE. Already he was late, even to spend time with his friend, something as simple as an opera. She fastened two golden bangles around her wrists and rose to her feet, the purple and blue shot silk dress swirling over her shoes. She took one last look at herself in the mirror, mangal sutra and guttapusalu necklace with its matching earrings in place. Her hair was coiled at the base of her head and decorated with a rope of jasmine flowers. She looked every bit the baroness ready to engage with society. The only thing she was missing was her husband.

The man who had given his word that he would be here but for some reason was not. The door to the bedroom opened and she turned her head to look at her maid.

"The carriage is ready my lady,"

"Thank you Anna," she replied snatching her reticule off the vanity and striding from the room and down the hallway.

"You look lovely," Leo said. Her head snapped up to see him standing at the top of the stairs. Just like that the annoyance she'd felt disappeared.

"Thank you," she looked him over. "You're late, and you aren't dressed."

"Dressed for?"

And just like that the annoyance was back. "The opera, with Ada and Mr. Thompson,"

"You can call him Basil now Regina."

Her eyes narrowed. "Thank you for the permission, now why aren't you dressed?"

"Did I know about this?" he asked walking past her to his room.

Her head tilted to one side, wondering if he was being serious. "Yes, Leo you did."

"Ah."

She took a calming breath and counted to ten. "We will be late, but I can wait for you. I don't believe they will mind."

He paused and turned to her. "No go. I know you enjoy it."

"Now you don't enjoy the opera?" she asked.

"I didn't say that. But there's no reason for you to miss the opera because I am not ready." He shrugged. "Go and enjoy yourself."

"What are you going to do?" she asked. He couldn't just stay here alone while she went out to enjoy herself.

"I'll be alright." He called, walking into his room but leaving the door open.

"What if you miss me?" she asked, and he emerged from his room, a suggestive grin on his face.

"Then I shall use it as a lesson to never be parted from you again."

She gave him a speculative look. "I don't believe that for a moment, but I don't have time to debate it with you."

She had always known there would be an adjustment period for him. Her mother had warned her after all. But now that she was seeing it, she was annoyed. There was no way around it. The idea that he would give her such a ridiculous excuse as if she was a simpleton instead of being honest. She hadn't expected him to stray from the course so quickly.

She was nearly halfway down the stairs when she noticed the man standing in the foyer. He was tall and handsome enough, although his skin was a lighter shade of brown than Leo's. His posture reminded her of Leo and her father, which only meant one thing. Military. His gaze was as curious and assessing as Leo's which pointed to one profession. Investigation.

What on earth was he doing there? Did Leo know he was there? Had he arrived with him, or had he just entered?

"Hello," Regina greeted him, her eyes flicking up towards the third floor where her husband was. "Who are you?"

He bowed to her. "My name is Bielson, my lady. Mr. Llewellyn Bielson."

"Llewellyn… that is a very Welsh name, sir." His grey eyes were almost startling in his face, made even more so by the energy behind his gaze.

"Yes, it is. My mother was Welsh."

Had Leo only come home to change his clothes? "May I assume your business here is with my husband?"

"Aye Lady Starkley, it is."

"Did you come in with him and he left you here like a salesman?"

"No, he asked me—"

"Bielson, you are early," Leo came jogging down the stairs, his waistcoat half unbuttoned.

"On time is late."

"True enough," Leo replied shaking his hand. "Regina this is Mr. Bielson, he is a former colleague of mine."

She stared at him for a moment, annoyance now warring with confusion. It was clear he hadn't had any intention of joining her this evening. "Yes. I've met him already."

"Oh."

She let that word hang in the air uncomfortably while their apparent guest watched them both. She waited for him to explain his behavior, to explain why this man was here. Why he'd specifically arranged to meet him at this time believing she would be gone. But no answer was forthcoming.

"Well, I'll leave you two to catch up and carry on with my plans for the evening." She turned to Bielson who was watching the two of them with great interest. "Good evening Mr. Bielson."

"Good evening, Lady Starkley."

She nodded and left. She would deal with her husband later.

BIELSON LET OUT a low whistle as they watched Regina stride out the door in a cloud of jasmine and temper. Leo knew that he would have to pay the price later on that night. If the look on Regina's face was any indication she was likely to challenge him in a blood sport when she returned from the opera.

"She is a rare one." Bielson commented.

"In several ways." Leo agreed.

"And she didn't look very happy with you at all." He looked at Leo with comically wide eyes, as Leo guided him to the study.

"I was supposed to join her tonight. Part of her charm offensive to win over the ton."

He nodded slowly. "I take it she doesn't know about Harrison?"

"No and it's going to stay that way. She's been dreading him for too long, we need to neutralize him as quickly as possible so I can start playing the baron."

"It is bloody weird seeing you here," he commented looking around the room at the dark wood paneling and the richly upholstered furniture.

"How do you think it feels living here?

"Where is your mother?"

"I think if she never spends another day in London for the rest of her life it will be too soon. She's at the dower house on the Starkley Manor estate in Cheshire. I have multiple estates now apparently."

Bielson gave him a mocking look. "Mmm, I can't quite pity you. Especially not with a wife like that."

"Fair enough, what have you got?"

"For the death a year or so back it's hard to find anything concrete. But for the one earlier this year, I was able to find out that Harrison was at the same beach side resort where that poor idiot died. There were races, but the accident that led to the former baron's death wasn't due to a malfunction in the phaeton itself, but the beach. A wheel got stuck." Bielson's tone was dry as tinder.

"Stuck?" How did the wheel get stuck on sand?

"In a hole. Someone set it up for him to drive that vehicle over that exact spot and result in the accident that sent him flying and broke his neck."

Clever. "But you can't prove it was him?"

Bielson shook his head. "No. He's slippery and mostly careful. An accident at sea during a supposed storm, illness, an unfortunate hunting accident, an ill-advised phaeton race on the beach. There is nothing that links him to all of these at the moment. Just the one and it is tentative as hell. Essentially, we need an accomplice to turn, to catch him in the act, or for a police office to overhear him talking about it."

"I can't just wait for him to act." And he couldn't risk Regina finding out he was a threat either.

"Are you sure you don't want to mention it to your baroness?" Bielson asked. "I don't want to tell you your business, but if she is going to be attending public events she should be aware of the potential danger."

Leo shook his head. He couldn't dispel the image of her terrified face the night they made love the first time. The tears in her eyes, the way she had clung to him in desperation. He could only imagine the nightmares she'd had to drive her to beg him for something so unthinkable for a young lady of her breeding.

He didn't want her to have to spare another thought on that

man. He'd rather her be angry with him than terrified once again. "I don't want her to worry."

"Understood. There's a pub he supposedly frequents regularly; we can try there first. But we need an officer."

"I spoke to Collins."

Bielson nodded and approval. "He's a good one. Bring him next time. For now let's go and see what we find."

The Lyceum, London

ADA AND BASIL were already waiting for Regina when she arrived at the theatre. She pulled Ada into a tight hug the moment she was close enough and held on for a moment longer than usual. To Ada's credit she didn't let go, simply waited for Regina to release her. Then she took her arm as they made their way to The Starkley Box.

"Gigi, where is your baron? I thought he was coming tonight." Ada asked.

"I was under that impression as well," Regian replied, hoping her annoyance didn't show. "But he was unexpectedly detained. A friend of his came to visit, a Mr. Bielson."

"From the army?" Basil asked.

"I believe so." She turned to Basil as they all took their seats. "Do you know the man?"

"I'm familiar with the name, but frankly I don't know that I'd recognize him. He didn't go to school with us," he replied.

"Ah." That was annoying. She'd hoped he would have more information as to why Leo would be meeting with him so urgently. "Either way by the time I was ready for the carriage he was just getting back from wherever he had been."

"We could have waited for him," Ada said.

"I did mention that, but he insisted on staying behind. He assures me that he will attend the next event however." Regina gave her a smile she didn't feel.

"Oh, Basil," Ada turned to her husband and clutched his arm firmly, "do you think your mother would be willing to host a dinner to welcome the new Baron and Baroness Starkley?"

"You mean as she did for us?" he asked, taking her sudden grasp in his stride. He was much more accustomed to Ada's tendency to touch people at a moment's notice.

"Would she be willing to do that? I don't want to put her out." The Viscountess Sterling had certainly been kind in her son's absence, but meeting someone at a public venue wasn't hosting them for a formal dinner.

"She has been talking of little else other than Leo ever since she met him. It was becoming tiresome. I imagine she would be happy to do so."

"It would be wonderful honestly. But only if she is fully willing to do so."

He gave a decisive nod. "Understood."

"I think it's beginning," Ada said. "Are you alright?" she whispered to Regina.

"I believe so."

CHAPTER TWENTY-ONE

DAYS LATER LEO was in his study at Starkley House with Bielson, looking over their notes from the previous nights. Slowly a picture of Harrison's dealings and his network was beginning to come together. It wasn't enough to act on or bring to Collins, but it was certainly enough to have Leo's teeth on edge. He played the part with Regina as best he could in the meantime attending small events as needed, but twice lately he'd gone out with Regina and their friends only to leave early when he received a note from Bielson.

The floorboard creaked and Leo looked up from his desk to see Regina watching them closely. There was no smile, only civil judgment which she'd most likely learned from her mother.

"Good afternoon Mr. Bielson," Regina's voice echoed in the room.

She didn't say it, but he knew what she was thinking. The last few days when Bielson had come to the house she had gone to bed alone. But she had made plans for them tonight. In fairness to her she had informed him beforehand about the dinner, and he had made promises. But this was the first night Collins would be able to meet with them. He had told Bielson to meet up with him earlier.

At the sound of her voice Bielson stood instantly and bowed. "Good afternoon my lady."

"Regina." Leo straightened as if his own mother was giving

him a scolding.

Her dark eyes lingered on the desk and the papers strewn over it. "I do hope you are not going to take my husband all night again Mr. Bielson. He has a pressing engagement this evening."

"Oh?"

"For dinner," Leo said. Apparently Basil's mother had elected to invite them to one of her exclusive dinner parties. According to Regina it was the exact sort of thing they needed to cement their places in English society. Leo had agreed to attend with the unspoken caveat that nothing more important came up. Like Harrison.

"May I see you in the hallway for a moment my lord." Her voice was even enough but that wasn't a sure bet of anything. If she wasn't annoyed she would have joined them in the room not asked him to leave it. Whatever she was divining, she didn't like it.

"I'm—"

Regina's eyes went sharp. "Now," she snapped. "If you please."

He followed her, with the distinct impression he was about to get a sound scolding. She had been good-natured about his absences so far, but it was clear that run of luck was about to run out.

"Yes dear?"

She paused a few feet from the door and turned around, her hands clasped together at her waist. She didn't look at him at first, simply stood there with her mouth pursed collecting her thoughts. Then she took a deep breath and looked up at him. "Societal dinners are about more than just food Leo. It is how alliances are forged, how worlds are shaped."

He shouldn't have said it. But a part of him was beginning to chafe at her condescension. When she took that tone with him it was like she was schooling a backward country cousin instead of her husband. "I thought that happened in parliament."

"And it begins in the dining room." She snapped back. Then

she gestured towards his study. "What is this?"

"It is nothing to trouble you."

"You promised me." There was a tremor in her voice, but it wasn't fear. "You promised you would be there tonight."

He rested his hands on her shoulders and squeezed gently. "I haven't forgotten, and I will be there."

She shook her head, her mouth quaking. "Don't lie to me."

That struck a nerve. He was trying to console and encourage her, and this was all she had to say? "I am not a liar Regina."

She stared at him for a humming moment, her eyes already accusing. "Not yet," she replied before turning on her heel and retreating upstairs.

He watched her for a moment, his jaw flexing against a torrent of words he knew he'd regret. She would understand in the end. Once it was all finished she would be relieved.

SHE HAD BELIEVED him. No matter her words, she had believed that he would, in the end show up for her. Show up for them. So she dressed herself in a gown of hand woven royal blue paithani silk with a decorative border of copper and pink violet, a gold Kundan choker and earrings, and stuck white roses in her hair.

Then she waited.

And waited.

She waited until the last possible moment for him to come walking through the door. Then when the clock struck half past the hour, she stood and left for the carriage. How could he do this? How could he embarrass her like this? She didn't know how to merge the man she knew with the man he was turning into. She wished his mother was here. Naomi would have been able to make him see sense; she would have been able to make him understand how important this was.

She shouldn't have accepted the invitation. She should have

told Ada that she didn't need help. She should have noticed the clear signs that he didn't care about this sort of thing. She should have made sure no one expected him. Then she wouldn't be forced to endure this humiliating spectacle. As it was she couldn't very well cancel at the last minute. How would it look if Basil asked his mother to help them only for them to throw her courtesy back in her face?

The carriage came to a pause and Regina closed her eyes, bracing for the worst. The woman would be within her rights to send her away. Well within her rights to never put herself out for their benefit ever again. The door opened and the driver helped her down to the sidewalk. She braced herself for refusal and strode forward to the door, issuing three knocks.

A butler opened the door and ushered her inside. Standing near the doorway, was her hostess who smiled widely at her.

"Lady Starkley," she greeted.

"Lady Sterling," Regina replied sinking into a respectful curt-sy.

"I'm still getting used to calling you that," she said taking her arm.

"I'm getting used to hearing it," Regina replied with a nerv-ous smile. So far so good.

She paused and glanced at the now closed door. "Where is your delightful husband?"

"He… he has been," Lord what on earth was she meant to say? "He had a conflict this evening."

"A conflict?" she blinked, her smile dimming.

"Yes." She felt sick. This was humiliating. "We had some crossed lines of communication. He promised he would try to be here, however."

It took the viscountess a moment to process that information but eventually she nodded. "Ah, I suppose that is reasonable. There are so many new duties to contend with, it is a true adjustment and men after all have different priorities. Even the viscount still shows up late to certain events and I've been his wife for well over thirty years."

"We are so grateful for your efforts on our behalf."

"Not at all dear. Any friend of Basil's. Do you suppose we should wait upon the Baron?"

"No, I don't want to put you out any more than we likely already have."

She patted her arm gently with one gloved hand. "If you insist dear, now come let me introduce you to my guests this evening."

Her guests as she called them were no less than 4 sets of couples, all Barons or Viscounts not including her and the viscount. She and Leo were meant to be the sixth. It would have been a wonderful evening, and a very thoughtful arrangement provided her husband had actually elected to participate. Instead, he had left her there to the humiliating spectacle of picking up his slack and make lukewarm excuses on his behalf.

THE TAVERN WAS dark and hot. It smelt of old cheese, stale beer, and sweaty unwashed humans. Leo and Bielson had set themselves up against the far wall, allowing themselves to blend in with the crowds of factory and dock workers. All salt of the earth seeking a moment of levity after a hard day's work before heading home. The exact opposite of his prey.

Bielson and Collins were unknown to Harrison. The idea was for them to keep an eye on Harrison once he arrived at the one pub where he didn't owe money and wait for Collins to arrive. It wasn't the first time Leo had lain in wait for a suspect. But unlike before, he was growing more restless by the minute. Everything about this establishment was a far cry from Regina and her bed. Not that he'd ever have the privilege again. Marriage was until death and Regina was likely going to kill him.

Despite his best intentions he was late. Horribly late. He glanced at his pocket watch. Eight. If he left right now he would be able to salvage something. Possibly.

"Around what time does he normally come here?" Leo asked.

"Six usually. He's late."

That was an understatement. Leo put away his pocket watch and took a deep breath before picking up his warm beer.

"Do you have to leave?" Bielson asked him.

"I should have left an hour ago. Regina is going to have my head."

"You don't strictly speaking, have to be here Kingston."

Leo looked at him, wondering for the first time if perhaps he shouldn't have been there. He couldn't wrap his mind around not being the one to bring him in. He trusted Collins, and Bielson but after last year with Trent, Leo couldn't imagine leaving Harrison to anyone else. He had to be the one. He had to know that Harrison was delt with and behind bars. That he couldn't hurt Regina anymore. "I do. I need to do it myself."

Bielson nodded. "I'm sure she will understand once you've explained."

He had believed that more readily when he hadn't proven her correct. He couldn't stop thinking of the look in her eye when she'd called him a traitor. She hadn't said that exactly, of course. She'd simply *implied* that his choices would make him a liar. In the moment he'd believed himself within his rights to be offended by the assertion. But now… if he had left her to face those people alone only to return with nothing to show for it how would he be able to justify his absence? "You have more confidence in that than I do."

"He isn't a normal working-class person. He has too many resources and connections here for us to afford to lose him. If he goes to ground then it's going to be a wait and see."

"I understand that." Yet another reason he needed to succeed. This was about more than his ego. Once they moved tonight, once the trap had been sprung, there would be no way to regain the element of surprise and whatever mischief Harrison was planning for him and Regina would be escalated. It would be impossible to keep it from her and the danger would be intolerable. He couldn't allow that man to ruin anything more than he already had.

IT HAD TAKEN a full course for the snide comments to begin. Regina could only credit the restraint to her host and hostess who had been nothing but gracious all throughout the evening. The first one to break was Lady Small, a paradoxically tall woman with the face of a horse. "I'm sorry we couldn't meet your husband Baroness."

Lady Horton a fiery red head with a pinched face, shared a conspiratorial glance with Horse face. "Indeed your ascension into our ranks has been the talk of the ton for weeks."

"What a shock it gave us," Lady Small continued.

Regina summoned a smile as a plate of salmon poached in fennel and cream was laid before her. "You mean my husband, yes it gave me a shock and all."

"Oh, yes I can imagine," Lady Gosling trilled. She was a chubby matron with a head of bouncing golden curls. She seemed well meaning, however. One of the few among the group.

"I know how much he was looking forward to this evening," Regina lied, reaching for her fork.

"Mmm," there was a subtle glance to the left, and a silent response rippled around the table. *Not enough.*

She couldn't fault them. It would have been a shock if no one had noticed the fact that he was missing. All eyes were on them after all. For him to stand up such an established member of the nobility like Lady Sterling, who's invitation was sought by others must have seemed like the height of arrogance and bad manners.

"I suppose it is a difficult transition for him," Lord Sterling commented. "As a peer of the realm he will have so many affairs to keep in order, from properties to ledgers and personal, affairs of state."

Regina couldn't tell what his angle was. His words were innocent enough and certainly true. He might have been trying to help, but there were so many double meanings to what everyone said she found herself thinking the worst of all of them. "Indeed. He has always been a busy man, but the scope of his responsibilities has increased greatly."

"Mmm, there is more to being a Baron or Baroness than moving into a house and wearing pretty jewels," Lord Horton replied, a sly look in his eye.

Ah. There it was. "Indeed." Regina forced herself to eat a few bites of her portion before setting down her fork.

"Is the fish not to your liking?" Lady Gebling asked, her stone-grey eyes flicking down to Regina's plate. "I suppose you are used to more aggressive flavors in your homeland."

"Not at all," she looked to Lady Sterling, "it is delicious, truly."

"Then eat up." Lady Gebling insisted, "A half-starved Baroness cannot do her duty to her lord."

"Indeed. Your baron must be expecting a son soon," Lord Gebling said.

"Yes, two daughters will certainly not suffice," His wife added with smug smile.

Regina's hand tightened about her fork as her jaw clenched down against a biting reply. It was impossible to miss the reference to her mother, or the assertion that she had failed her father. The white husband who had clearly miscalculated and now had to scheme in order to foist his undeserving daughter onto the innocent pure nobility. She wanted to slap their faces.

If she lost her temper here, it would not only embarrass her hostess but vindicate their ignorant assumptions. They were no different than every bully at Miss Pollitt's but this wasn't school and there was no Elodia or Ada to support her.

"Children in general tend to be a bit of a shot in the dark as far as I've seen," Lord Sterling spoke again. "One can have three sons, and they can all be useless or die before their time."

"Very true," Lord Gosling replied, "Such workings gave us Queen Elizabeth the First, and our dear Queen Victoria,"

"Indeed. God save the Queen." Lord Gebling said raising his glass.

"God save the Queen," Regina mumbled the chorused reply along with everyone else and made the toast.

"I believe that rather proves your dear mama's point Lady Starkley." Lady Sterling said, with a cheeky sparkle in her eye.

She glanced at the woman. "Does it?"

"Mmmm, something about trusting in the wisdom of providence."

A shocked laugh escaped Regina's lips. "Yes, I suppose that is true."

She gave her a wink and then nodded towards the salmon, "Don't fill up on that dear, my cook does an absolutely exquisite roast goose with chestnuts and white wine."

For a moment Regina thought she could handle it, that maybe things wouldn't be so bad as all that. It wasn't school but that didn't mean there weren't ways to fight back. She needed to remember what she was above all else. A strategist. A fencer. A fighter. It didn't matter if they scored a few points so long as she kept her head and her feet under her.

Then, as the fish course was cleared, Lady Sterling directed the footman to remove Leo's place setting and Regina's heart sank in her chest. Her hostess was officially done waiting.

"Is THAT HIM?" Bielson asked.

Leo glanced back, "Yes."

Harrison entered and looked around. Clearly he was searching for someone here. This was it. All he needed was to start talking and they would be able to change positions to get the information they needed.

Then moments later Collins arrived. After one sweep he began moving towards Leo and Bielson greeting patrons as he went. He sat down beside them and nodded.

"Gentlemen."

"How long were you following him?" Leo asked.

"Two blocks."

"Did he notice you?" Bielson asked.

Collins gave him an annoyed look. "I don't mean to be disrespectful but fuck off."

In fairness, Collins was known for his stealth, second only to Leo. Leo didn't know if anyone had questioned his ability to tail a mark in recent years.

Bielson hid his grin behind his mug but said nothing further.

"Oi, here he comes," Collins said his eyes still on Leo. "He's coming over with two men who also look like they shouldn't be here either."

"Are they working with him?"

"They were waiting for him when he arrived, so I'd reckon, yes."

"I don't like not having my eyes on him." Leo grumbled.

Collins shook his head. "You were smart to sit where you did. He knows you and if those men are working with him you can be dead certain they know your face as well."

Bielson nodded towards Leo, "They're about to help you out," then his gaze flicked over Leo's shoulder. They were behind him. Leo closed his eyes trying to pick out Harrison's voice in the din.

"Can you hear them?"

'Ere, I heard he's a noble.

Barely. That was Harrison.

It don't matter, he's a Lord.

Leo nodded. Yes he could hear them.

He stole that from me, but he isn't going to be a Lord for much longer.

What if he's onto you?

He's neck deep in that bitch, he's not thinking of anything but pussy.

Leo smirked at that. Little did that jackass know he was a brilliant multitasker.

So what's the plan Ned? Are we gonna take him?

I have someone watching—

"Oi!" a voice drowned out Harrison and his accomplices. Leo's hand curled into a fist and frustration flooded his chest. What were they planning? Where were they watching? And who the fuck was being so loud for no reason?

His eyes opened as he searched for the source of his frustration.

"Who the fuck is this?" Bielson asked.

"Fucking Locke," Collins growled in annoyance. He was on his feet in a minute and Leo looked over in time to see Locke coming over with malicious glee. Collins intercepted him, pulling him into a rough hug and driving him backwards away from their booth.

"Who is that?" Bielson looked at Leo who shook his head and stayed where he was.

He couldn't panic. No one knew who Locke was speaking to as yet, which meant his cover wasn't blown just yet. The situation could still be salvaged. He closed his eyes again attempting to ignore Locke and refocus on Harrison and his partners.

"Well if it isn't Leo the Lord, what brings you around here eh?"

The anger and irritation that flooded his mind was almost overwhelming. He was going to kill him. He was going to put his hands around his throat and choke the life out of his stupid worthless body.

"Locke shut the fuck up." He heard Collins hiss.

"What's the problem? It's him ain't it?" He turned to Leo with a smug glint in his eye as he glanced over at the booth beside them. He knew. God fucking damn him, he knew what they were here for. He was doing it on purpose.

"That's not him and keep your fucking voice down."

All the talking on the other side of the partition had ended. Damnit.

Locke shoved Collins into a wall then slid onto the bench beside Leo, stinking of alcohol and grinning with real malice. "Are we having drinks?"

"What the hell are you doing?" Leo growled.

"Never thought I'd be able to drink with a real baron in this life, eh Collins?"

"Fuck," Bielson grumbled, and Leo turned to stare straight into the eyes of Harrison. There was shock there but also annoyance. As though he was irritated that Leo was quicker on the uptake than he'd expected. He sneered and headed for the door. Bielson cursed again and slid out of the booth following him out the door. Harrison's companions stood as well and followed Bielson out the door.

"Move," Leo snapped at Locke.

"Where are you going?" Locke jeered.

"Get out of my way or I will beat you to death." Even though he knew he would never waste that much time on that when Harrison was getting away and Bielson was about to be outnumbered. He wasn't about to get arrested for beating the shit out of a police officer in the wrong side of town.

"You think I was gonna let you get away with this?" he asked.

Leo looked at Collins who was staring at Locke in both embarrassment and outrage. "Get your man Collins, because if I do he'll be out of commission for a month."

Collins grabbed hold of his colleague and dragged his flailing body out of the booth pinning him to the wall. Leo wasted no time rushing out the door into the balmy night his heart racing in his chest as unease built steadily. Where the hell was Harrison? Did Bielson find him or were those men able to waylay him? He scanned the crowd of men milling around.

"Two men just left, which way did they go?"

"I didn't see nothing guv."

He turned and grabbed another who was walking past with a woman. "Did you see two men leaving?"

"That big black one?"

"Yes. Which way did he go?"

He pointed to the left and Leo took off in that direction. The further down the street he went the darker it became. He heard the sound of a scuffle and started forward until a shadow move across his path. There was a glint of metal and Leo jumped out of its way. He heard the rip of fabric. Shit. Where the fuck was this asshole?

Another rush of air and he stepped back but shoved his hands forward with all his strength hoping to knock his assailant off his footing. He heard a grunt and a crash to his left.

"You fucker," he heard Harrison grumble.

"Is that you Harrison?" he taunted. "You waited for me and all?"

"I'm going to kill you, you bastard."

Leo backed up to the right reaching out for the wall, waiting for his eyes to adjust. He heard Harrison walking towards him his arm swinging through the air. The minute he could make out his body Leo moved, first grabbing his wrist and twisting it until he heard something hit the ground. Good the knife was gone. Harrison slammed his head forward, in an attempt to stun him or break his nose, but Leo shifted his head to the side at the last minute, taking the blow on his shoulder. He twisted Harrison's arm behind his back and yanked up.

"You are coming with me."

Harrison began to laugh, and Leo's blood went cold. "You go on and take your time with me Kingston."

"You want me to beat the shit out of you?"

"I want you here. I have plans for you already, and that little wifey of yours goes first."

"What?" *Regina?* "You think you can kill a baroness, and no one will notice?"

"She is no different than the rest of them. And neither are you."

God if only Bielson and Collins were here to hear this. "Where are they? Where did you put them?" He only needed a clue as to how many were helping Harrison.

"You're going to wish you had stayed in the gutter where you belong."

A gun shot went off distracting Leo just long enough for Harrison to twist out of his grip. And he evaporated into the night like a phantom.

"Kingston."

He heard Collins calling his name. *Godfuckingdamnit.* Regina. He had to get back to her, he had to make sure she was safe.

"Leo," Collins called out again and he started towards his voice returning to the pub.

"I have to go."

"Did you get him?"

"No. I have to leave Collins, he sent people after her."

"What?" The man's eyes widened.

"My wife. I have to leave." He started walking, his stomach sick with fear.

"Where are they?" Collins called out.

"I don't fucking know." Were they at the house or waiting for her when she left the Sterling's? He glanced at his pocket watch. Ten. He had just enough time to catch her on the way out. If he ran.

CHAPTER TWENTY-TWO

Sterling House, London

"WHAT AN *INTERESTING* necklace you are wearing Baroness," Lady Gebling trilled as sweet as poison.

"Indeed but no wedding band," Lord Horton commented.

"How unusual."

"The necklace is my wedding band, Lord Horton. I wear it just as my mother does, as all women in my homeland do."

"Is that the only tradition you maintain from your homeland?" Lady Gosling asked.

"No, I make tea for my husband every evening."

"Is that not an English custom?" Lady Small asked with her usual air of condescension.

Regina had just about had it with her. "Not the way I make it."

"And what is different about the way *you* make it?"

"Well when I make it, it's potable," she replied with a sweet smile, allowing the answering silence to linger for a moment, until her hostess cleared her throat. "To my husband at least."

"Yes, I noticed he doesn't take tea," Lady Sterling commented.

"Yes, unless I'm making it, he drinks coffee. I also dance."

"Dance?" Lady Small's lip curled in disgust.

"Yes. India has several classical forms of dance. I practice three of them, outside of the European ballroom standards of course."

"How lovely," Lady Gosling commented.

"I've had the pleasure of witnessing it while in the Orient," Lord Horton commented.

"Have you indeed?" Lord Sterling asked, but his tone held a tinge of warning. As if he had an idea where the Baron was going and he didn't like it.

"Yes, it was in interesting affair but a bit too elemental for my liking,"

"I'm pleased to hear it," Lady Horton sniffed. "In England, Baroness, we do not make spectacles of ourselves for the voyeurism of others."

"I dance for myself Lady Horton. I do not require an audience."

"Well considering the energy spent on a quadrille I can only imagine it is very beneficial exercise," Lady Sterling commented.

"Oh yes, health is paramount."

"Your mother must have been quite relieved to have finally achieved her goal," Lord Small commented.

"Her goal?" Regina set down her cutlery and rested her hands in her lap. She didn't want to accidentally throw anything.

"Yes, marriage into the peerage." He was as presumptuous and insufferable as his wife.

Of course they would assume it was her mother who wanted Regina in the peerage. Any traits they found disagreeable must come from the Indian woman, never their countryman. "It was my father's goal, in actual fact. But I am gratified to fulfill the wishes of my parents as any dutiful daughter would be,"

"Quite right," Lord Horton said.

"I wish my Charlotte were half as obedient as you," Lord Gosling joked.

"I hope you continue to be a credit to your parents Lady Starkley, for your own sake as well as your unusually lucky husband." Lady Gosling gave her a beatific smile which Regina returned.

"We all learn on the job as it were," Lord Gosling said with a shrug. "Marriage is an adjustment in and of itself, is it not?"

"Not for me," Lord Sterling commented.

"You hardly count my lord," Lady Sterling responded waving him off, "It was for me certainly,"

"Oh Euphemia, be serious. You were born to the role of Viscountess," Lady Horton trilled, shaking her head in amusement.

Lady Sterling shook her head and wagged her fork. "No life is without its trials. I twisted that stubborn old man to my will in my own time—"

"—I beg to differ." It was hard to tell if Lord Sterling was amused or outraged by his wife's assertions.

"—and you will do the same with *your* baron my dear. In your good time."

Regina pressed her lips together against a laugh and nodded. "Thank you Lady Starkley."

With that, Lady Sterling rose to her feet and rest of the party followed her lead. "We will retire now, gentlemen, thank you for your company,"

Regina followed the women out the room, sliding her hands back into her gloves and fastening the tiny pearl buttons at the inside of her wrists. When she nearly ran into Lady Small she looked up to see the entire party had paused in the doorway. What were they all looking at?

At the sound of his voice her heart began to race. Leo was here? She found herself stuck between annoyance and sympathy. He had missed dinner entirely but perhaps he had a good reason. She discreetly pushed past the guests in front of her until she was able to see him. In that moment she decided, she was more than annoyed. She was angry.

There he was, unforgivably late and not even dressed for dinner. His chest was heaving as though he'd been running and there was an urgency in his face she couldn't attribute to anything but artifice. How dare he show up at the end of the evening and pretend as though he had rushed here? Was that supposed to placate her? Was she meant to care about how much he had struggled to fail her entirely? It made a mockery of everything she had asked him for, everything he had promised.

She didn't realize her hands had curled into fists until Lady Sterling's own closed over one of them. What the hell was he playing at?

"My lord," she said in as even a tone as she could manage.

"Regina, have I made it in time?"

"Oh, yes—" Lady Sterling began but Regina would have none of it.

"No. No you have not Lord Starkley, dinner is finished." She wouldn't allow him to embarrass her any further this evening. If he didn't care about Lady Sterling's generosity then he could maintain that even in her presence.

"Ah." He glanced between the two of them.

"Thank you Lord and Lady Sterling for your hospitality. If you are amenable I would like the opportunity to host you and return your kindness."

"Of course Lady Starkley," Lady Sterling replied with an awkward glance in Leo's direction.

She looked at the footman who had opened the door to her husband. "If you could have my carriage brought forward, I will leave now. Good evening everyone."

Regina curtsied and strode past him without a word. If she so much as looked in his direction she would scream. She took her wrap and walked out the door, standing on the steps in a mutinous silence. She would wait until they were in the carriage. She didn't trust herself to speak to him and maintain her composure. Lord only knew eyes would be on them and the last thing they needed after this last showing of his was for the Baroness Starkley to be seen with her hands around the Baron Starkley's throat.

Mercifully they only had to wait five minutes before she saw their carriage driver come forward with their vehicle. She tightened her silk wrap around her shoulders and strode forward, climbing in without his assistance and looking out the window instead of at him as she took her seat.

The minute they took off he spoke. "I take it you are upset with me."

What was his first clue? "You really are a detective aren't you?" She replied, her tone dry as dust.

"I'm sorry I was late," he began and she shook her head.

"You were not late."

"I wasn't?"

"No." She turned her head and met his anxious gaze. "If you had arrived during the fish course, you would have been late. You elected to miss the entire blasted evening altogether."

"Regina—"

"You didn't even have the decency to dress for the event." Despite her best efforts her temper was spiking dangerously.

"You make it sound as though I arrived in rags."

She shook her head, her eyes burning with the furious tears she hadn't allowed to fall earlier. "I feel so foolish. Do you know, when you came for me, I thought *'thank God he's here. I won't be alone anymore. I won't have to shoulder all of this by myself'*. I thought I finally had a partner, someone to help me bear the weight of all of this."

"You do,"

"Do I? You left me alone tonight and nights before. I told you where you were needed, you made promises, and you broke them without a second thought. Because you deemed them as unimportant to keep."

He shook his head. "That's not true."

"I was sitting there tonight at a dinner thrown in our honor and you were nowhere to be found. I was trying to make excuses for you, and I knew it didn't bloody well matter because Lady Sterling knew that if you wanted to be there you would have been. I have never been so mortified in my entire life. All those condescending old bitches shooting knowing looks at each other commenting on the adjustment for you and how *difficult* it must be for you to fill a role that you are utterly *unqualified* for. And I couldn't even say anything because it is the most basic concept of good bloody manners to simply *show up* to an event that you agreed to attend, and you couldn't even manage that."

"I never agreed to anything," he murmured.

She scoffed, the feeling rising in her was dangerously close to contempt. "Why did you even marry me? Why did you even come forward if you weren't even going to try for yourself let alone for me. We were meant to do this together and you keep leaving me behind."

"I am right here."

"You are wherever you feel like being,"

The carriage stopped and she moved to leave the carriage first. His hand closed around her wrist stopped her from leaving. She nearly commented on it, but he went out ahead of her, looking around, almost as if he expected to see something before turning to her and offering his hand.

She took it and descended, promising herself that no matter how long it took she would get to the bottom of this before the night was through. Two steps from the carriage she heard it. The sound of a gunshot and then a projectile hitting wood. She walked faster as he slid his arm around her, ushering her into the front door quickly, nearly picking her up off the ground for the last two steps through the door. A second later she heard it again only this time the bullet hit stone. Or at least she was reasonably certain it was a bullet. Gun shots. In St. James?! What on earth was happening? She glanced at Leo to ask but he didn't seem surprised. Instead his expression was grimly set.

"Was that gunfire?"

HE DIDN'T RESPOND to her question, he had too many of his own. Instead he helped her remove her cape and handed it to the footman along with his coat. It had to be a sharpshooter of some sort. Where the hell had Harrison found a sharpshooter willing to take up this job? How long had that man been there and who was he targeting? Was it him, or Regina? Or both?

The accusations she'd thrown in the carriage were eating at him like rust. He had never thought of leaving her to face the world alone. His entire focus was on ensuring that they spent a long happy life together. He thought she would be annoyed with his absence, not that she would take it as a betrayal or abandonment. And now, because of *fucking* Locke, he was not only a liar but an incompetent fool who couldn't protect her from anything, not bullets or hurtful words.

"Leo." She held onto his arm, and he paused turning his head in her direction. "Was that gunfire?"

"No." He couldn't look at her. He was too angry. Angry, ashamed and afraid. He had been so damn close to removing the danger Harrison presented but Locke had to show up. He had made him a failure once again and there was nothing he could do about it. Now Harrison was in the wind again and Leo didn't have enough to locate him again. How he would have to wait for him to move and hope to God that he was fast enough to counter anything he had in place. He was exposed and he didn't like it.

Now, as if he didn't have troubles enough, the man had some fucker shooting at him and Regina. Which meant his ability to keep the real horror of the truth from her was effectively null and void. There was no way she was mistaking that noise for anything else.

Her grip on his arm tightened. "Don't lie to me about something so stupid Leopold, I am familiar enough with the sound." She'd never called him by his full name before. Not outside of their wedding. He wasn't sure he enjoyed it at all. And he especially didn't enjoy that this was the second time she had called him a liar and he still couldn't argue against it.

"Then why are you asking?"

"I'm asking if that gunfire was meant for us or not." She clarified, every word curt and clipped.

He couldn't lie. Not again. But he didn't want to tell her the truth. "Then why not ask that question instead?"

"I'm asking it now."

His brain was going in every which direction, and she was staring at him with no patience left. This was the captain's daughter, and she was out of goodwill which meant he was out of time. "Yes it was."

That fear which their marriage had dispelled returned full force nearly displacing the ire in her eyes. "Someone is trying to kill you?"

"Yes."

"Who is it?"

Another question he didn't want to answer. "Harrison."

Her eyes grew wider. "Edward?"

"Yes."

"How long, how long have you known?"

He forced himself to meet her eyes. "Since before we married."

Her grip went slack, and her arm dropped to her side. "What?" She stared in shock. "This whole time? You've known he was out there gunning for you the whole time?"

"I knew he was angry and resentful, and more than capable of violence."

She shook her head slowly. "Leo."

Perhaps if he came out with everything there would be a way past this. "I've been looking into his record and whereabouts, to confirm my suspicions and establish a case to bring to Scotland Yard. He's been here awhile, or rather he's been out of the army for a while."

"What does that have to do with any—"

"Your former fiancés."

She froze, her big brown eyes flooding with horrified realization that made his heart ache. "What? He killed them? All of them?"

She had faced so much in her short life, he hated that she

would have to suffer this as well. "Only the last two. He's said some things that struck me as suspicious, so I've been looking into it."

"Your friend. That Bolston fellow."

"Bielson, yes. I've been handling it."

"If you were handling it then why is he attacking us in the street?"

"Because he got away from me tonight," he snapped. It was already galling to have to admit his own failure. She didn't need to twist the knife. "Apparently certain people at Scotland Yard don't think kindly of me especially now that I've taken this stupid fucking title. I had him but they blew my cover, and I lost him. I came from there to the dinner party because he told me he had someone watching you, but I didn't know where."

She stared at him in silence, the gears in her head turning. "So you came running to make sure I hadn't left?"

She had stopped shouting at least. Was that a sign that the worst had passed? Perhaps Bielson was right, all Leo had to do was tell her the truth.

"Yes." He reached out and ran his hand over her arm. "I was trying to protect you."

Her head tilted. "Keeping me ignorant of the danger we were both in was protecting me?"

Bielson was a bloody moron. "Devika."

"No! How could you keep this from me? How could you lie?" She swatted his hand away and he took a step back. She was a short thing, but she could do real damage if provoked enough and he had no intention of wrestling his wife.

"I never lied to you about this."

She squinted and he fought the urge to take a step backwards. "You let me believe all was well. If you knew he was in London we should never have returned here. But you agreed to all of it knowing I believed we were safe when you *knew* we weren't."

It was exactly what he had done but in his mind it didn't sound so damming and *stupid*. He wasn't used to feeling stupid.

He didn't like that either. "I wasn't trying to lie to you."

"I don't care about your intentions. I don't need you to coddle me as if I were a child." She turned on her heel and started for the staircase.

"I know that," he grumbled following after her.

"And what the devil do you mean you've been looking into it?" She rounded on him, and he fell back a step. "I hope you haven't been sleuthing about London with—" she cut herself off and scoffed. "Is that where you were tonight? What you've been doing all this time? Leaving me to manage everything else on my own?"

Perhaps a compliment? "You are better at all that other nonsense anyway." The answering silence put him on his guard. He reconsidered what he had just said. Damn. "I didn't mean—"

"All that other nonsense?" she repeated slowly.

"What I meant was that this is what I am good at. To each their own."

"Each to their own strength, is that it? Is that the sort of husband you mean to be? Without so much as a 'watch out for the rampaging murderer my dear'?"

"I didn't mean—"

She shook her head, her mouth curling in a sneer of contempt. "I cannot. I cannot do this now." She turned and walked away. Lifting her skirts with a delicate flick of her wrist as she started up the stairs.

He stood there watching her for a moment, his throat aching. She hated him. She thought he was beneath her and to be fair he hadn't put in a good showing so far as her husband, but it was beginning to wear on him that she wouldn't acknowledge what he was trying to do, or how important his objective was. He needed her to understand. He took a deep breath and followed her up the stairs.

"Rajani," he called out.

She continued without a backward glance having clearly decided that he was a villain who had only considered his own selfish interests. Which was the most infuriating thing. What right did she have to make him feel guilty about not attending a meal with the same pretentious people who had been sneering at her behind her back until now. Who didn't give a damn about her wellbeing. As if he hadn't been acting to protect them this whole time.

"Rajani."

Nothing.

Fuck. He followed behind her. "Don't walk away from me."

"I'm trying to protect you," she sneered over her shoulder and his hands curled into a fist. The utter audacity of this woman. To mock him about this as if she wanted to fucking die before her time. The anger felt better, better than the guilt and shame at any rate.

"Thank you, it is much appreciated."

"Oh I'm sorry, was that what I was meant to say?" she asked, as her lady's maid began unlacing the back of her dress, sending nervous glances their way as her nimble fingers hurried to complete her task.

"I'm trying to speak to you." He didn't like arguing with their servant within earshot, but he wasn't leaving either.

"Because you got caught?" she asked shrugging off her bodice and stepping out of her skirts.

"I—" His brain short circuited for a moment at the sight of her in her undergarments but she took that opportunity to light into him again.

"You know how terrified I've been about something happening to you. What it would mean for me to lose you so soon before—" she closed her eyes and shook her head.

"Before what? Before you secure your position with a baby?"

The maid snatched up her dress turned and scuttled out of the room, shutting the door firmly behind her. Regina glared at him silently before turning away a second time and walking over to the dresser. The next time he swore he would yank her right back.

"I don't know what I expected. I knew you wouldn't understand." She began pulling the golden hair clips out of her hair until the thick braid fell down her back in a sleek rope.

Was that what this was about? Was she truly more concerned about keeping her title than his wellbeing? His gut churned with acid as he stared at her. Lush, beautiful and as cold as the gold she had draped herself in. "I understand well enough. I thought that you actually gave a damn about me, but it turns out the thing you are worried about the most is the fucking title that put us here to begin with."

She removed her pearl necklace and earrings before meeting his gaze in the mirror. "Don't you dare. The title has always been a means to an end, and you bloody well know it. We are here because I am trying to protect my family. If you die before I have an heir what am I supposed to do?"

"It is truly galling that I've been running around London trying to protect your life and when you found out all you care about is your position in society instead of my safety. My death doesn't bother so much as my dying at the wrong time."

She scoffed and rolled her eyes. "Don't be ridiculous. Of course it is not the only issue at hand but your negligence in this could and would have far reaching effects."

"I'll be sure not to inconvenience you."

"It would be appreciated. You are a baron now Leo—"

"Don't remind me," he growled.

"You are not a private detective anymore. There are more people relying on you than just your mother."

The audacity of this girl condescending to him as if he were some mud lark she plucked out of the fucking Thames. "I am aware."

"Then act like it and conserve your interests to matters which are within your sphere."

"You are within my fucking sphere!"

"Not if you are dead you jackass!" she screamed, and he froze watching as the dam holding back her tears broke. "My whole life, my happiness, my position, my ability to protect my family all of it depends upon you staying alive. If you die then all of this is for nothing. I am left behind again with nothing all over again. Why don't you understand that?"

"Rajani I was doing this for you."

"Then why wouldn't you tell me? Why would you keep something like this from me. That madman wants your head and you all but made me his accomplice by allowing me to bring you here. How am I supposed to live with myself if you die because I wanted to return to London when we could have stayed well and safe elsewhere? You would put that on my head?" She swiped angrily at the tears streaming down her face. "You cannot die. You cannot make all this happen, make all these promises and then leave me alone."

"I never left you." He insisted, but it sounded weak, even to him.

"You say that, but if you saw me as a partner, as your equal you would never have left me out of your plans. You would never have made me party to your enemies' plans. You would never have treated me like this. You let me flounder in the dark like a dangerous, convenient idiot and said nothing. I don't know what you feel for me, but whatever it is, it is not love. It cannot be." She turned away from him again, defeat all over her face. "Will you go back to your rooms. I don't want you here tonight."

He would walk over hot coals for her, but he couldn't leave her any more than he could let her walk away again, not when she was doubting how he felt about her. If he left those thoughts would fester into something unsalvageable.

"I can't do that."

"You've been doing a wonderful job of it so far. What? No fun when it's actually what I'd like?" She started to walk away but he grabbed her arms to stop her, holding her in place.

"Let go of me," she hissed.

"I thought you wanted an heir as soon as possible."

Her elbow came back sharply into his ribs. He took the blow then pulled her closer wrapping his arms around her furiously wriggling body. "You're lucky I don't want your scalp."

"I never wanted to hurt you," he whispered against her hair, "and I don't want to spend a night away from you."

"If only I cared what you wanted." She threw the words over her shoulder but she wasn't wriggling half as much as before.

"What about what you want?" He breathed her in and saw the goose bumps flare up all over her skin pressing her half-dressed body between his and the bed.

"I want your absence," she replied but she had gone still. Did she even realize she had leaned her head against his chest?

He gripped her arms and turned her around keeping his hands on her waist. He wanted her close, and he would fight to keep her just here, in his arms. "Do you?"

She glared up at him mutinously, through angry tears. Her mouth trembled and she looked away shaking her head. She wasn't struggling but he couldn't tell why exactly. Was it because she refused to fight him? Did she want to stay there? Was she passively accepting it until he gave up? Was it really over so soon now that she believed him to be a liability to her ambitions?

His grip on her tightened without him realizing it. Her eyes returned to his for a moment of uncertainty. He felt when her body gave way, saw the frustration and desire in her eyes when they flicked down to his mouth. Then her mouth was on his and her hands were fisted in his hair so hard it hurt, her mouth clinging to his. If she meant her aggression to dissuade him it had the opposite effect. He was rock hard in seconds. If she was after a rough romp in the sheets he could deliver that and all.

It shouldn't have mattered to him. He should have pushed her away and asked the question he wanted to. Namely if his only value to her was as a boon to her cause. But she smelled so damn good, and her firm lush warm body was arching into him, begging for more of his touch, more of him. Before this night was over he'd make sure she understood that it was him she needed. Him and nothing else. He kissed her back gripping the back of her head pulling her up against him.

He should have known his Regina was never one to surrender anything by force or cede a point without a debate. She squirmed against him trying to get closer. When he lifted her up onto the mattress she jerked at his remaining clothes, ripping his shirt, scraping her nails against his skin. He ground his stiffening sex against hers and her strong shapely legs came up around his hips, pulling him closer, forcing a groan out of him. She held him in place rocking her hips against him moaning into his mouth.

He needed to get back control of the situation. He was trying to prove a point to her, that there was more to him than a title, that he meant more to her than security, but with every moan and sigh all he wanted to do was surrender to the heat between them. He hated arguing with her, hated how lonely it felt especially with those gunshots ringing in his head. He wanted to punish her for doubting him, for ignoring the importance of what he was doing for both of them. He wanted to sink into her and hold her close until there was nothing left between them, not even breath.

She was still wearing her stays. He couldn't hold onto her lush curves the way he wanted to, but it left her full breasts high and wonderfully accessible. He jerked her head back and fastened his mouth to the curve of her neck and the slopes of her shoulders before burying his face in the soft mounds of her breasts. She moaned again, arching into him and holding his face to her body as he slid his hands between them to cup her firmly between her legs. Through the slit his fingers found her soaking wet and eager. Her head fell back with a desperate cry and her dark eyes drifted shut. He kept waiting for her to fight him and instead she kept pulling him closer, gripping his shoulder weakly and her groin churning against his hand. He wanted her to beg him as she had made him want to beg. To ask.

"Tell me you need me," he whispered rubbing her clit, feeling her jerk against him with every pass, a rapturous frown on her beautiful face.

"Leo—" she broke off on a gasp, shivering as he curled his fingers inside her. She leaned up for his mouth and he pulled away. "What?"

"Tell me."

"Tell you what?"

"You need me."

"You already know."

He drove his fingers in deeper and she hissed, her back arching as her fingers tightened convulsively on his shoulders. "Please."

"Tell me and I'll give you what you want."

Something in her gaze shifted, as if she'd seen the hurt and fear he was trying to hide. Her hand slid up to rest on his cheek, "I need you Leo," she whispered. "Please."

He kissed her hard and deep, hating the sting of tears in his eyes, the feeling that he was somehow left begging her for something she should have given him already. When he finally slid inside her, one thrust sending him hip deep she gasped, her legs tightening around him as her sex clenched down pulling him deeper. Driven by need, by a desperate urge to claim the rest of her, he picked up his pace, thrusting deep and hard. She just held him closer, pressing her cheek to him claiming more of him with every moan, every gasp, every ripple of her hot wet sex around his until all he could think about was how incomparable she was.

All he could feel was the pleasure ripping up his spine, forcing the air out of his lungs. All he could hear was her moans, her breathless entreaties and praises telling him everything he'd wanted to hear until the telltale ripples of her pending climax began curling his toes into the rug in a desperate bid to hold out. Her nails bit into his skin as she came calling out his name. He buried his face in her damp shoulder and panted fighting the draw of her with every fiber of his being. When she finally went limp against him, he tightened his grip on her and climbed up onto the bed. She lay pliant under him, watching him with heavy lidded eyes as he unhooked her stays. She shivered as his hands moved over her soft stomach, cupping her breasts through her chemise, teasing her nipples.

When he lowered his body over hers she wrapped her arms around his neck, welcoming him again. Denying him nothing.

CHAPTER TWENTY-THREE

REGINA WAS CERTAIN she wouldn't be able to move for another century. She'd never realized an argument could lead to sex like that. Leo had been insatiable, and more forceful than ever before taking her over and over until her entire body felt numb. Sometime during the third round he'd stripped her bare of her clothes kissing every inch of her body. Now she lay in Leo's arms, replete, her mind blissfully blank, her head nestled against his chest, her arm flung across his stomach.

"Did you want me?" his voice suddenly came, startling her into awareness.

"You need more proof?" she drawled starching against him. She expected him to chuckle, to smile. He did neither of those.

"I know you wanted to protect your family; I respect that. We are already married and I made my choice. I won't be angry. I just need to know what you feel for me. How you see me."

"How I see you?"

"Yes." He took a deep breath. "If the crown came tomorrow and said it was a mistake to confirm me, that I wasn't the true Baron of Starkley, would you regret marrying me?"

She pushed herself up to look at his face. "You think I don't love you?"

"I think without the title you might love me a little less." There was a bleak resignation in his eyes that he was trying to hide. How had she managed to put that there?

"That's not true."

"You said you can't separate me from the title. To me that sounds like without it, you wouldn't want me because you wanted a title."

"*I* never wanted a title."

He closed his eyes and sighed warily. "I don't want to argue again, Regina. I just want to know."

"I never had the luxury of thinking of marriage without a title attached, so it is difficult now to separate the two now. But to answer your original question, if we found out that the title wasn't yours, my main concern would be whether or not I could stay your wife."

"Truly?" There was a damp sheen in his eyes. She brushed his cheek gently her heart flooding with tenderness.

"Most truly. I do love you. You will always be more than a title to me, you are my *husband*. You are *the* husband I never dared to allow myself to hope for, because I knew better than to hope for a man for your wit, intelligence, integrity and capability among the ton."

"They do exist you know." He teased.

"Not to me. I nearly made myself sick wanting you even before the title. I'm sorry I made you think otherwise. I would be afraid of losing you more than anything. It is still what I fear the most. It's why I am still so annoyed with you." She slapped his bare chest lightly and she finally got the grin she'd sought from earlier.

"Ah," he winced, "still?"

"Absolutely. I married you to stand by your side no matter what. If you only allow me to participate in certain things and leave me ignorant of others you aren't treating me as your wife. You are treating me like a child."

"What would you have done if you knew he was still a danger after our wedding?"

"Well I wouldn't have insisted on returning to London for one thing, but outside of that I certainly wouldn't have insisted on making such a show of us and a target of you."

He sighed and reached up to sweep a fall of hair back over her shoulder. "You've shouldered so much too early on. You were so afraid of him and what he could do. I just wanted to lift the burden for you."

"No, you wanted to take all of it on yourself."

"That is my privilege as your husband."

Her temper sparked. "The hell it is."

"Mmm." He rolled his eyes halfheartedly but didn't argue further.

She took his hand in her and kissed the back of it. "I want you to hold my hand, and I want to never let go of yours."

He regarded at her for a moment. "To stand beside me, not behind me."

"Yes."

He closed his eyes, and she felt his body relax under hers, as some unnamed tension flowed out of it. "I'm sorry."

"You are forgiven my love," she kissed his shoulders and neck, moving across his chest until she could feel his heartbeat under her lips, slow and steady.

The next time he spoke, there was more uncertainty in his voice than she'd ever heard before. "I don't know the first thing about being a baron. I don't know how to be that for you. Perhaps I was afraid of failing you in that way, and too ashamed to admit it."

She nuzzled his chest, cuddling him closer with a sigh. "You have your own nobility. You define the position not the other way around. It would serve nothing and no one for you to change who you are."

"But the position will inform my choices won't it? It has to."

Was that what he was afraid of? Losing himself within a life of luxury? "Leo, informing some of your choices and dictating who you will be, are two very different things. However you act, whatever you chose you are still and always the Baron Starkley, and you will always be you."

"But not a private investigator," he teased.

She rolled her eyes. "I want you to be all of what you are. This title only means you can exercise more power than most. Your character and your experiences have prepared you to wield it well. You don't need to hide your true self from anyone anymore."

"I don't agree that a title makes me more of anything. I am prouder of the life I made on my own before all of this."

She would have to tred carefully there. It was clear that he couldn't see the difference between the freedom of privilege versus privilege improving oneself. The first was an unshackling, the other was a delusion. "That makes sense. I don't see it as a matter of pride. I think that your nature would allow you to rise no matter where you were placed. So many people have tried to limit you through sabotage or pettiness, and you've found your way around and past it without losing yourself in bitterness or self-pity. That is your true self, and it would show up no matter where you were. This title only means that the jealousy of others is no longer a stumbling block. They cannot diminish you to save face for themselves. Avoiding your new position at this point is you reducing yourself on their behalf."

"I thought that was called humility."

"Humility is knowing your limits, not conforming to the mediocrity of others to avoid hypothetical trouble."

"What do we call that Lady Starkley?"

"Cowardice. And it doesn't suit you at all, Lord Starkley."

He smiled then chuckled. "Yes my lady. Do we have any other functions to attend?"

"No." She had been ignorant before but now she knew the truth, it would be madness to maintain the current course of action.

"Truly? I thought we had to cement our position in society quickly."

"There will be time enough for that once we sort out Mr. Harrison."

He smiled again, playing with her hair. "I have a meeting with Bielson at the Oriental Club in a couple days."

"Mr. Bielson again," she griped. "Where were you tonight exactly?"

"A pub. We were scouting the location to hear something about what Harrison was planning."

"Seeing as he shot at us I imagine that didn't go as planned."

"It did not. But that was a separate issue. An annoying officer blew our cover and Harrison got away. But not before telling me that he had someone marking you."

"That's why you came tonight?"

"Yes. I didn't know whether they were watching the house or you. So I went to you first."

She stroked his cheek again and then laid her head on his chest, squeezing him for a moment. He'd come to rescue her from danger. He'd been terrified that she would be hurt and she'd shouted at him and accused him of not caring about her. It was his fault entirely of course, but she still regretted it.

"He's dangerous."

"What do you want to do?" she asked, listening to his heartbeat in her ear.

"Part of me feels like you should stay inside lest we trigger another episode like last year when your friends were kidnapped."

"Yes but thanks to you it wasn't for very long."

"You don't need to share the experience. Besides which the situation is entirely different. Trent wanted money. Harrison wants to do more than take our place, he wants to erase every trace of us from the family line."

It was a good point to make. "I will keep close to the house then. Although if he has gone to ground, we cannot do the same if we wish to draw him out."

"Meaning?"

"Meaning I cannot become a recluse, especially after tonight."

"So some social engagements but on a very small scale?"

It was a necessary risk, but she didn't want to spend her time looking over her shoulder. "Perhaps Mr. Bielson has some contacts to keep an eye on me while I do small errands. Your aunt did invite me to tea."

"Which aunt?" he asked, an adorably puzzled frown on his face.

"Aunt Theo."

He sighed. "When did she become 'Aunt Theo'?"

She swatted at his chest. His rivalry with that woman was both entertaining and infuriating. It was so obvious how much they enjoyed each other. "She is a dear woman, and you are fond of her, admit it."

"I admit nothing," he replied. "When is that happening?"

"The day after tomorrow. She is hosting a formal tea to endorse me now that I am well and truly a Baroness."

"Am I needed?"

"No. She likes me better." She stuck out her tongue and he rolled his eyes and smiled. "In any event it's a short distance away, barely ten minutes. I can stick my head out but if he moves I will have witnesses. Either way I shall take my new pistol."

"You think he'll move that quickly?" Leo asked.

"I haven't the faintest. I only didn't want to miss tea."

CHAPTER TWENTY-FOUR

H**E THOUGHT HE** was so clever, Harrison groused in his squalid lodgings. So fucking clever to find him in the back end of nowhere and have him followed. His shoulder still ached from where Kingston had twisted it. So Kingston had friends at Scotland Yard did he? Friends who could stake out his mother's house and force him to take lodging in a rundown boarding house in London. He thought he could pin him down with a few constables and a loyal dog or two. He would never understand the true loyalty of the white sons of England.

Locke was an idiot, but he understood the true order of the world. The way things had to be and would always be. He understood why it would never do to hand over an English peerage to a black man. He'd been useful tonight. If not for him Harrison would never have known Kingston had found him. It had annoyed him at first, the idea that he'd lost the advantage of secrecy. The idea that Kingston had managed to get the edge on him. Knew that Harrison had more plans than to simply take back his title. But he didn't have nearly enough details to do anything about it but worry, whereas Harrison still had all the information he would need to act.

The balance of justice had to be shifted back decisively in his favor. His shooter had missed them tonight. It was annoying but not unfixable. There would be ample opportunities in the future if he waited, but then again, if Kingston knew this much then there was no real point in waiting. He was wily, which meant that more time would only give him time to plan a counter measure.

The best solution was to strike hard and fast. Get Kingston neutralized and his sweet bitch of a wife dead along with any hope of progeny. But first he would get rid of his meddlesome great aunt. That woman had ruined his plans for the last time.

CHAPTER TWENTY-FIVE

Oriental Club, London

HE WASN'T CERTAIN it was a good idea when he parted ways with Regina that afternoon. But he couldn't think of a reason to tell her not to attend tea with his aunt. She was only going to Mayfair after all, hardly an unsafe part of town. And if it was reasonable for him to keep his appointment with Bielson surely he had no grounds to deny Regina something she clearly wanted.

Unlike her friends, she was hardly defenseless, especially sporting that new pistol her father had given her after their wedding breakfast. Part of him was almost curious as to what would happen if Harrison tried to take her on himself. No, his concern was more around what would happen if it wasn't just Harrison. Although the night's endeavors could hardly be called victorious, it hadn't been a complete loss. He now knew for a fact that he was working with others. At least three based on the two at the pub and the one at the house. And two of them he could recognize.

That at least was information he didn't have previously.

But while his Regina could likely handle herself one on one, he doubted she could take on three grown men on her own. With any luck Bielson would have more information and they would be able to do something other than sit on their spines and wait.

Which was why he was here, at this club. Regina's father had been as good as his word, ensuring Leo's entry, and the title hadn't hurt anything either. That being said he wasn't sure how often he would be here. The concept of the club as it existed among the ton was strange to Leo. Even stranger was how easy it was to gain access when one had a title, a military record and a white member to vouch for him. It was almost insulting.

Three years ago for all the assurances that there was only one requirement to enter, they hadn't even been interested in his record. But now he was here, lounging in a leather armchair in another suit with yet another fancy waistcoat. It still felt wrong. The only part of this entire situation that felt right was Regina. Everything about her suited him down to the ground from her scent and her taste to her choice in fashion and temperament.

If fate allowed it they would have a family of as many children she and The Almighty deigned to give him. His mother would finally have the grandchildren she wanted. He would have her guidance, and she would have his devotion. One last hiccup and they would be free to live as they saw fit.

It took him a moment to notice the footman observing him. He was a pale skinny little thing, and Leo was almost positive he'd seen him before but he couldn't place where. He wasn't one of the men at the pub last night. Any other time Leo would have made the decision to ignore him. But this time… perhaps it was the silk waistcoat, or perhaps it was Regina's words form the night before, but he just wasn't in the mood to avoid much.

He leaned his temple against his fist and stared right back until the lad gave up and walked towards Leo with a nervous smile on his face.

"G…good afternoon my lord."

"Good afternoon," Leo replied evenly.

He grew paler and glanced around. "We were told to prepare a private room for you, as you are one of our most illustrious members." He was anxious about something.

"I doubt that very seriously. Who exactly gave you that instruction?"

"Captain M…. Mason."

Leo raised one incredulous eyebrow at that. The man was

fond of him, but he couldn't see the captain heaping that sort of nonsense on him. To what end? It's not as though he needed to be bought or persuaded to do anything. Regina's father was many things but not a sycophant. "Captain Mason said I was an *illustrious member?*"

"No, not exactly. He said you might feel uncomfortable with all the stares, so a private room might be more comfortable for you. But I thought you might be offended."

"So you opted for flattery instead, because surely I have a high opinion of myself being so above my natural station, is that it?"

The boy floundered, his mouth opening and closing like a dying fish, his eyes blinking rapidly. Leo had half a mind to leave him in that state, curious as to how long it would take for him to recover or pass out entirely. The presumption was galling but he was growing tired of him already. A private room would at the very least make situations like this less likely.

He rose to his feet and nodded at him. "Well, lead on."

The boy clapped his hand together and bowed, backing away from him, gesturing towards a hallway. Again his memory was pricked. Who was he? Why was he so familiar? Not the pub, not the theatre. He was a servant at the club, so it was unlikely that Leo had seen him at any balls or private society events he'd been roped into. The young man stopped at a room and gestured for Leo to enter with another half bow. As he stepped forward it came to him. Scotland Yard. He had been one of the officers watching him with Locke and Collins.

The first thing that hit Leo when he entered the room was the smell of ether. He froze in the doorway and turned to face him. This little shit was in league with Collins and by extension, Harrison. He saw the boy's eyes go wide in fear as he realized his game was up.

"Where is he?" he asked. Two arms grabbed him from behind and a rag soaked with ether was placed over his nose and mouth. He fought against the instinct to breathe in and rammed his elbow backwards into his assailants' ribs. He heard the cry of pain and spun around his fists up and ready to fight. Something hard cracked against his temple, the pain sudden and brilliant then everything went black.

Regina.

THE DAY HAD started off well for Regina. She had spent the morning lounging in bed with her husband and then the afternoon with Aunt Theo at her tea party. It had gone off without a fuss. Elodia and her father had been in attendance along with other members of the ton. She had smiled and laughed with all of them, relaxed and in her element. She'd finally allowed herself to enjoy the gardens as she'd always wanted to.

Now that the guests had left everything had become a good deal less formal. She sat with a book, sipping her tea and listening to Aunt Theo and Albert play a game of chess. From the sound of it Albert was putting his great aunt through her paces. It was unexpected. It was clear that he was close to the old woman, but the way he teased and scolded her was more reminiscent of Leo than she would have believed before today.

So the last thing she was expecting when footsteps sounded in the hall was to look up and see Edward Harrison standing there. Her fingers curled around the edges of her book and her heart began to thump in her chest. She had never seen such seething rage in a person. It was just like the nightmare. How ironic for the nightmares to stop only for him to appear in real life. He didn't appear manic, to the contrary his face was utterly composed save for the glittering fury in his eyes. For a moment she thought she was the only one who had noticed him, then she heard someone clear their throat.

"Edward," Aunt Theo drawled, "we weren't expecting you."

His eyes narrowed. "I'm sure you weren't, you deceptive old bitch."

Albert frowned and turned to him. "Edward there are ladies present."

Two things were clear from their nonchalance. Firstly, they were used to his disgusting language and behavior. Secondly, they had no idea how dangerous he actually was. What was she going to do? *Your pistol. Get your pistol.*

Slowly she started making her way over to her reticule which lay on the side table at the far end of the sofa. With her pistol inside.

"Where? This half-animated corpse or that mercenary savage." He glared at Regina and she swallowed past her dry throat.

"Only one of those descriptors are accurate I'm afraid," Aunt Theo let out a tired sigh. "What do you want boy?"

"I have creditors coming for me because of you."

Aunt Theo glanced up at the ceiling and shook her head in confusion. "Odd, I normally remember when I do that sort of thing,"

"Because you took my title—"

"—the law of England gave him that title boy."

"—And my money, and you threw it away to this bitch and her husband!" He jabbed a finger in Regina's direction.

"The lawyers would have discovered it even if Aunt Theo didn't." Albert tried to reason with him.

"The only thing I did was spare her and the estate from your ravages." Clearly Aunt Theo didn't care about reasoning with Harrison. She only saw a petulant child throwing a tantrum.

"No one would have known about him if it wasn't for you!" He pulled out a pistol and Regina's body went cold. So that was his intention. He wasn't only here to make threats; he wanted blood and he didn't care who's was shed.

Albert went pale as he finally realized the danger they were in. "Here now, Edward."

"Shut up you mewling little cunt!" he snapped. "All you know how to do is follow a senile old woman's orders. Where is your loyalty?"

"Loyalty to what?" Albert asked holding his hands up.

"To the social order! To family!" The gun in his hand was swinging back and forth between him and Aunt Theo.

"Whatever your debts are Mr. Harrison I'm certain we can come to some sort of agreement. We can call the lawyer and draw up a settlement for you," Regina said freezing where she was. She wasn't close enough to reach for her purse yet.

"You impudent little slut."

"I recognize that you perhaps made anticipatory decisions out of a mistaken belief, but it doesn't mean you have to suffer." Perhaps she could calm him long enough to reason with him.

"How kind of you to dispense *my* money to me. You and your husband rutting in my house, spending my money—"

"That is enough!" Albert started forward and Harrison back-handed him so hard he collapsed to the ground, knocking over an end table and sending a crystal vase careening to the ground. Regina winced but started moving again while his attention was elsewhere.

"Bertie," Aunt Theo started for him, concern registering on her face for the first time.

"Stay where you are bitch!" Harrison screamed.

Regina closed her eyes for a moment struggling to stay calm. She was just close enough now. She reached for her reticule inches away from her, her gaze fixed on Harrison. His eyes snapped to her without warning and she froze, snatching her arm back, folding her freezing hands in her lap. "You too *my lady*," he sneered. "Still as a statue or I paint your brain all over this room."

"What is it that you want Edward?" Aunt Theo asked, her eyes flicking anxiously to her nephew who was holding his head and groaning on the floor.

"I want justice," he said, "I am owed justice."

"And what does that look like for you, exactly?" This was oddly enough, the first time Regina had seen the old woman truly annoyed. The man was standing in her face with a gun, and she was *annoyed*.

"First I'm going to send you along Aunty Theo so you can't ruin anymore lives."

If he was expecting a reaction to that he would have been disappointed. "And then?"

He turned to Regina, "I originally planned to kill your husband and leave it there, but since you are here, parading around my jewels—"

How dare he try to claim her mangal sutra as his. "These are mine."

"—Presuming to have the right to speak for anyone, or make deals with me, I'm going to kill you Lady Starkley."

Her stomach dropped to her feet, but she refused to let him see it. If a ninety-year-old woman could stand her ground, then so could she. "And what do you imagine Leo will do to you when he finds out what you've done?"

He scoffed. "I can handle him."

Aunt Theo chuckled. "You imagine you can handle that man when you can barely handle your finances."

"That is your fault you bitch!" he screamed, charging forward with his gun in his hand.

Regina rose swiftly darting between the two of them, holding up one hand to halt him. Miraculously it worked.

"Don't," she said, her voice weak even as her spine stiffened. "Don't hurt her."

"I'm not afraid of that infant," Aunt Theo said waving him away.

"Aunt Theo, please," Regina hissed over her shoulder. What was that woman doing? There was bravery and then being foolhardy.

"I'm nearly one hundred years old and you think a quick death is frightening?" she argued.

He took another threatening step forward and Regina flinched but stayed put. "You—"

"—Make your threats, shake your little fist, brandish your firearm. Shoot if you can aim well enough to do the job well but make no mistake little boy, the only frightened person in this room is *you*."

Regina would have argued that point, if she could bring herself to speak.

His finger tightened on the trigger and for one horrible moment Regina wondered if she would witness a murder, but then Albert moved on the floor drawing Harrison's attention. In one unexpectedly swift motion he threw a handful of bloody broken crystal at Harrison's eyes.

Harrison cried out, his hands coming up to guard his face. When Albert scrambled to his feet, Regina moved forward. He slammed Harrison backwards into the door which flew open, sending them spilling into the corridor. Regina followed; her eyes trained on his firearm. The minute it went sliding across the tiled floor she moved snatching it up and checking the chamber for rounds. Three left. It was enough provided the blasted gun actually worked.

She turned to face the two men and saw Harrison holding a knife. She fired once up at the ceiling as a warning and as a test. *Good.*

Harrison jerked Albert back against him, holding his knife to the young man's throat. "Give me back my gun bitch."

"Absolutely not."

"I'll slice his throat wide open if you don't drop it."

Her mouth was dry as dirt, but for some reason even as her heart pounded away in her chest, her hands were steady. "You may well do that Mr. Harrison, but his life won't impede this bullet. The only way for you to have a future in this country or any other is to release him and agree to my terms of a settlement."

"You think I'm afraid of you?"

"I'm not really interested either way. I do not want to harm you, but if you kill Albert I will make certain he doesn't leave this earth alone." It was surprising how true those words were. She didn't realize it until after the last one had left her mouth. She was ready to kill him.

"There's only two bullets in that gun," he said his eyes flicking down to her hands.

"I'm aware, but at this range I only need one." She never imagined she would be using a gun for this. Up until now she's only shot clay pigeons, pheasants and the odd deer. This was deadly serious.

"You are nothing but a girl. I'm a killer. I've taken countless lives on the battlefield. I killed off those useless cunts, my supposed cousins to get my hands on this title. You don't have what it takes to kill a man."

"Perhaps, but I have what it takes to kill you."

They heard the unsteady clumping of Aunt Theo making her way to the door, genuine fear in her eyes for the life of her nephew.

"Bertie," she called out.

"Don't come here aunty, I'm alright," he said, terror on his face despite his brave words. The idea of his death was almost enough for Regina to drop the gun. Almost.

"Regina, my dear."

Regina shook her head. "Stay where you are Aunt Theo. I can manage this." She wasn't going to let this man's venom infect any more lives than she had to, and she wasn't going to live in fear of him any longer. Leo was planning to take him on, but he had come here. Now all she needed was clear shot.

"His blood will be on your hands," Harrison warned but there was an edge to his voice now. As if he was beginning to believe she would shoot. But clearly he didn't trust that she could hit her target. Namely his head.

"His blood will be avenged; this is your last warning Mr. Harrison. Do not make me kill you."

She let out the breath she was holding as his hand tightened on the hilt of the blade. At the bottom of the inhale she watched his arm shift to the left, she aimed for his forehead and squeezed the trigger.

He jerked his eyes wide with shock, but Regina saw the red dot on his head and knew she had managed it. Albert stared at her in shock and fear.

"Did you do it?" he asked, and she nodded. He moved Harrison's arm away from his neck and stepped away. With his body no longer there to support him Harrison collapsed to the ground in a bloody heap.

"Is he dead?" Aunt Theo asked.

Regina stumbled towards the staircase and sat heavily. It wasn't in keeping with decorum she knew, but it was hard to care. Firing that bullet had leeched all the strength from her body. Her hands were numb, and she was almost certain she would be ill all over the floor.

"He's not moving," Alberts tremulous voice came.

She could see it. It was disturbing how still Harrison's body was. He had to kill him didn't she? She'd *had* to do it. She would never know with any certainty whether or not he meant to carry out his threat to kill Albert. Only one thing was certain. She'd taken a man's life. An act she had believed herself to be prepared for, until his body crumbled to the ground. She closed her eyes and let out a breath. "Albert."

"He's dead aunt." Albert said in disbelief.

"Albert," she repeated with more urgency.

"Yes my lady?" He looked up at her with wide eyes and she dropped her gaze to the floor, where a pool of Harrison's blood was expanding. *Oh God she'd killed him.*

She couldn't look at him. Was Albert afraid of her, she wondered. Did he think she had taken a foolish risk with his life?

"Send someone to fetch a constable, Albert. Don't touch him." Should she have called for a servant? Would that have been better?

"Yes, at once."

She heard footsteps running across the floor, heard the door open and close. She couldn't stop staring at Harrison's body. She'd killed a man. She wanted Leo. She wanted him to take her hand in his and assure her that all would be well.

"Are you well my girl?" Aunt Theo asked, her wrinkled hand landing on her shoulder.

No. She wanted to scream it. "I'm sorry."

"About what in heaven's name?"

"I murdered your nephew." Was that her voice? Why did it sound so far away?

"He meant to kill all of us. If you did not stop him who knows what he would have done. You did well Baroness Starkley."

Done well. Had she?

CHAPTER TWENTY-SIX

The Oriental Club, London

BY THE TIME Leo awoke his right arm and leg were asleep. He was still in the same room however, which was something he supposed. His captors were murmuring in the corner, and he closed his eyes, feigning sleep to hear what they were saying while he took stock of his body. He was on his side, his hands mercifully shackled in front of him. That gave him one important piece of information. They were amateurs. If he moved fast and kept his wits he may have a chance to get out of here.

"He was meant to be back hours ago."

They were talking about Harrison.

"Let's give him some more time."

"I don't like this. Maybe he's already sorted out the old bat and scarpered. Kingston's an uppity black but he is a Baron. The crown confirmed it."

So he was going after Aunt Theo. Was Regina still with her? There was no way of knowing. She'd left home before Leo had. Would she have gone home immediately after or lingered? She did enjoy the old woman's company. Oh God. Was she safe? Was he going to lose both of them?

"This ain't no different than the other times we helped Eddie out."

So he was correct. Harrison was behind those murders and those men knew it. But they were losing their nerve. That was good. As long as he could keep them alive he would have the means to call on all the forces of Scotland Yard, instead of just

Collins.

"The hell it isn't. Eddie sorted out those without us, all we had to do was lie about where he was on the yacht and get rid of that phaeton the other time."

"You think we should kill him?"

"I'm not bloody killing anyone. If you want to hang with Harrison you can be my guest."

"We could just leave him and go. If Eddie's not coming back we don't have to hold him here. Someone else will come for him."

As if they would get away with any of this. He wouldn't stop until they were driven out of England.

The door crashed open, and Leo jerked up his eyes flying wide open. Bielson stood in the doorway with a thunderous expression on his face. He caught sight of Leo on the ground just as only one of the two men holding him decided to try his luck. Bielson was known for his ruthless efficiency of movement. It took one hit each to level the playing field.

"Starkley," he said before bending over to handcuff them both.

"Get me up." Leo said. Once the men were secure Bielson took him by the arm and pulled him up to his feet.

"Harrison left a few hours ago, I don't know where he went."

"I do. They mentioned my aunt. I think he means to harm her." And he needed to go to her at once.

"I'll take these to the yard. They'll confess easily I'm sure of it. If Harrison is free he won't be for long."

It was good news, but Leo couldn't care overly much about it. All he could see was Regina dead. His life with her cut horrifically short because he'd underestimated the impatience of his opponent. He felt ill at the idea. All that fire and drive silenced and extinguished so soon. It was impossible, it had to be.

He got to Harley House in record time, jumping up onto the cab of his carriage and driving the horses himself, much to his driver's chagrin. He didn't care.

The door to Harley house was wide open when he arrived. Leo didn't know what to make of it. Was it open because of Harrison? Was he still in there? Then he saw two constables walk out holding a stretcher with a body covered with a sheet. His throat went dry. *Oh God, Regina.*

He ran up the stairs and into the house. The first thing he smelt was the metallic tinge of blood. Was it the one person dead or had there been more casualties? His knees nearly buckled, and his gut roiled but he kept moving. He needed to know if she was alive or not. The further into the house he got the clearer the voices came. Aunt Theo and Cousin Bertie were arguing with someone.

"Is this entirely necessary?" Bertie said. "We already told you what happened,"

"We have to follow procedure, regardless of who it is." Was that Locke?

Two more steps and he was there. His aunt was in a chair, hunched over as if the weight of her bones was too much for her. Albert was near her with a split lip, and a black eye which did nothing to deter from the vexation on his face. The reason for his anxiety was standing in the corner in a dark green silk dress. Beautiful and fully alive. Thank Christ.

The relief nearly took him to his knees. Then he noticed her slumped posture, the way Regina rocked back and forth on her heels. Her eyes were downcast and glazed over. *Shock.* He'd seen that look a thousand times before. Then he saw the manacles clapped on her slender, dark wrists. Cuffs. Locke dared to put his wife in handcuffs? An entirely different emotion swept through him. White hot rage.

"What is the meaning of this?" he demanded.

"Just following procedure my lord." A younger constable replied. "This lady shot a bloke so we are taking her in for questioning."

Regina's head came up and her eyes met his. She was terrified.

"To the station?" he clarified walking up to them.

"Aye," Locke replied glibly.

His jaw tightened against a furious tirade. Regina didn't need him to beat this man into a pulp, no matter how much Locke clearly needed a thrashing. She needed him to handle this, and get those irons off her wrists. "Is there a reason you can't ask your questions here?"

"As he said, it's standard procedure, can't be making exceptions or else it'll all come down on our heads," Locke replied, turning towards him with his notebook in his hands.

"Since when is it standard procedure to drag a woman down to the station for questioning Locke?" he asked, knowing the answer. *Never.*

"She's a murderer," Locke replied as if it was all the reason he needed.

Leo glanced at Regina as she flinched at Locke's words. Who exactly had she killed?

"That is not true," Albert interrupted.

"She shot him point blank in the middle of his head," Locke continued to Leo.

"She had always been a good shot. Her father taught her," he replied.

"I'm sure her father did teach her, but here in England—"

"Her father is Captain Mason of the 39th foot," Leo interrupted, sick and tired of that ridiculous phrase. As if England was any less barbaric than anywhere else.

"You what?" Locke blinked in shock.

"That's right. He is a decorated veteran of Her Majesty's Armed forces. As white as you are. Not that it should matter." Leo walked over to Regina who was staring at her feet. "Rajani, look at me."

She lifted her head, with gentle encouragement from his hands.

"Tell me what happened," he said, stroking her damp cheeks.

"He... he came here, he was armed." Her voice was so soft

and unsure. It was breaking his heart. "He said he was going to kill us. I tried to reason with him but he wouldn't listen. He had Albert, he was going to kill him so I shot him."

"With your gun?" Leo asked.

She shook her head "No, his. I brought mine but I couldn't get to it. He was watching and I couldn't get to it."

He nodded and turned to Locke. "Does this account differ in any way from that was relayed to you earlier, Locke?"

"No," he replied, unapologetically.

So it was a power play. Leo's tenuous grasp on his temper slipped. "Then I reiterate, what the *fuck* are you playing at putting her in irons to march her down to the station when she hasn't even committed a crime."

"She killed the man didn't she?"

"She defended herself and the occupants of this house against a mad man that I warned you about previously. A madman that you helped escape no less than two nights ago. Although I can't really pretend to be shocked. Once again you couldn't be arsed to do your job so someone else had to manage it for you."

"Listen here Kingston—"

"No you listen. I came to you ready to deal with you as an equal, as a former comrade in arms and you turned your back, so you will suffer me as I am now." He was tired of making do. Tired of crawling to avoid being hit. He'd played nicely and where had it gotten him? Kidnapped and his wife with irons on her wrists. No more. He wasn't playing the humble layman anymore.

"Leo," Regina's voice came but he shook his head. He was done with this. Done. What the hell was the use of the title if he couldn't use it to protect her?

"I am the Baron Starkley, the woman you have in irons is the Baroness Starkley. You have already heard an account corroborated by no less than three people of what transpired in this room and how her bravery and skill saved at least two lives including her own. There is no policy that requires you to take a peer of the realm, and a woman at that, to the station for questioning especially when she is cooperating. Get those fucking irons off of her or I swear to God I will use every ounce of my power to have you not only driven from the police force but England for the rest of your miserable life."

He glanced at the young officer in the corner with a ring of keys in his hand. "Get these off her,"

"Don't move boy," Locke hissed.

Leo turned to the boy, "Get these off her or I come after you next. Australia is lovely this time of year."

That got it done. The officer didn't dare look at his superior, but shuffled over to Regina with shaking hands to do his bidding. There was a vicious satisfaction in seeing an order of his obeyed. Seeing how much terror he could strike in the heart of a man just because he was a peer of the realm. His threats held far more weight now.

He turned his attention to Locke who was watching his man break ranks with rancor. Leo couldn't help the urge to twist the knife.

"There's a present waiting for you at the station Locke. Collins has it for now. A present that is going to make this little turn of events very uncomfortable for you." He glanced at Regina to see her small wrists finally free of the rough iron. "Do you have further questions for the baroness?"

"No," Locke ground out.

"Then you can get out," Leo replied.

"Yes sir," he grumbled turning away.

"'My lord,'" Leo corrected. He wasn't in the mood to be gracious.

"You what?" Locke stared at him in shock.

"I am not a 'sir', I am a baron. Therefore, you will address me as 'Lord Starkley' or 'my lord'. Any questions?"

"No, my lord."

"Good boy."

Locke looked like he was about to explode but instead turned and strode from the room.

"I was only doing my duty my lord," the young constable murmured nervously.

Leo gave him a curt nod. "That's fine. Your duty is finished. Leave."

The moment they were out the door he turned to Regina and yanked her against him wrapping his arms around her as tightly as he could manage. She buried her face in his chest, trembling as her arms came around his waist. "It's alright devika."

"Leo," she whimpered.

"You're alright," he murmured rubbing his hands up and down her back.

"I killed him."

"You protected yourself, you protected them. You did nothing wrong."

"I thought he was going to take me to prison," she blurted.

"Like hell," he glanced at his aunt and cousin. "Alright Bertie?"

He nodded and shrugged. "I'll live."

"Are you well Aunt?"

"I think this bit of theatre has stimulated at least two more years of life out of me," she replied with a tired smile.

He shook his head in amusement. "Are you afraid of The Final Judgement or something?"

"Leo," Regina scolded, smacking his chest lightly before swiping at the tears on her face.

"She's fine."

Aunt Theo laughed. "Take your wife home Lord Starkley."

He nodded and leaned over to kiss her wrinkled forehead. "We'll come and see you tomorrow."

"Don't you have better things to do?" she grumbled.

"What, like making you yet another god child?" He asked.

She grinned again. "You think you can work that quickly?"

He glanced at Regina who was smiling but the shadow in her eyes was still there. "We'll see what I can do."

ONCE THEY WERE back in their carriage, Leo tucked Regina against his side, one arm wrapped tightly around her shoulders. An icy sensation had taken up residence in her body and refused to shift no matter how tightly she hugged herself. No matter how much she told herself she didn't have a choice but to pull the trigger. Regina pressed her face onto his firm chest and sighed. Somehow Leo seemed to understand that she needed him to hold her as tightly as possible. That she needed him to hold her together and warm her while her mind returned again and again to that scene.

That terrible calm, the surety she felt the split second before pulling the trigger and the horror that filled her when that red dot decorated his brow and she knew she had done what she deemed necessary. She had never imagined when she awoke that morning that she would have not only faced down a killer but become one herself.

It didn't feel real. Part of her wouldn't have believed it had happened, if not for the tremor that hadn't left her hands as yet, and the queasy sensation in her stomach. She couldn't get her mind past that moment. Couldn't help wondering if there was a way she could have avoided killing him.

"You are very quiet devika," he murmured rubbing her arm.

"I keep seeing him. I keep seeing myself killing him." She paused. "Do you think I'll ever be able to forget it?"

"No. You never forget your first. But you'll stop thinking about it so often."

"When?"

"When you make peace with it."

"Is it wicked to make peace with such a thing?"

"If it's kill or be killed then you had to choose yourself and the people with you. You chose me. He came there with the intention of causing harm, Rajani. He was going to kill Albert. He certainly meant to kill Aunt Theo and me."

"Do we know that?"

"Know what?"

"That he would have killed people. He could have been bluff-ing."

"He murdered his cousins devika. He killed them to get the title and the fortune. There was no reason to believe he wouldn't have killed me eventually. He made so many threats to me that he was more than capable of carrying out. He had me tied up and held at the Oriental Club to give him the time he needed to do his business. The only reason that didn't happen is you."

"But I didn't know you were kidnapped at the time. I…I wanted to kill him. I kept thinking of those nightmares I had. The things he'd said. I wanted him dead, I wanted to kill him. I can't help but think that a part of me pulled the trigger not because I had to but because I wanted to." It was a relief to say those words to him. They felt unnatural, as if she were a monster for thinking and feeling those things.

"Perhaps that is true, but I cannot blame you for it. I only wish I had been there to spare you that decision. I wanted him turned into Scotland Yard, I wanted him to be executed by the law. That would have been better. But in my opinion, consider-ing the situation, your choice to kill him was correct. He would never have stopped unless someone stopped him."

Her eyes were stinging with tears again. It was everything she needed to know, everything she needed to hear. That he wasn't ashamed of her, that he didn't think she was a monster. "Truly?"

He nodded and stroked her cheek, gazing down at her with so much love in his eyes it was almost unbearable. "I wouldn't lie to you about this, devika. And you are no less wonderful to me than you were this morning. You are still my devika, you are still the woman I love."

She smiled and nodded, pressing her face to his chest again because a sudden thought had her lifting her head. "What would you lie about?" she asked.

He rolled his eyes and kissed her forehead firmly. "Brat," he mumbled against her hair.

"Do you think that constable, Mr. Locke will cause trouble?" she asked. He hadn't been pleased with the outcome at all. Had been only too willing to drag her to a cell. Part of her had believed she deserved it.

"If he makes that impolitic choice he will have trouble with me, not I with him."

She believed that. She had never seen Leo like that before. She couldn't explain the thrill she'd felt when he stood up for her, making threats to preserve her dignity and her safety. There wasn't a doubt in her mind that he would absolutely destroy Locke if he even mentioned her name again. Her baron didn't play games when it came to her. And she wouldn't with him either. Both of them were willing to do what it took to ensure the other's best interests.

She didn't know if she would ever be able to pick up a pistol again, but one thing she did know was that anyone who attempted to harm them would do so at their peril. "Us," she corrected.

He looked down at her and smiled widely. "That's right. Us."

EPILOGUE

1852 November, London
The Palace of Westminster.

T ODAY WAS THE day.

She watched him from the viewing balcony as he sat beside the Viscount Melbroke in his formal parliamentary robes waiting for the queen to arrive. He had always been sinfully handsome but over the past months watching him grow into his title she could see there was an added air of regality to his perfect posture, his stillness regardless of the bustle around him. The way he tilted his head to catch a comment from the Viscount, his eyes taking in every corner of the room.

It was the first time he attended the opening of Parliament, and the first time in her life had been in London past the month of July. As Leo had asserted, he would not be an indolent member of the peerage, but seeing him here ready to take hold of the full extent of his powers moved something in her.

"What do they have that boy wearing?" Naomi asked and Regina laughed, hugging her arm. There were always horror stories about mothers-in-law but she had to admit she and Leo's mother had become fast friends. Regina had insisted on her being close by from the very beginning. As a result Regina had taught Naomi to shoot and fence, and Regina's mother and Naomi had bonded over the most amusing things like using spices in food and the correct way to make tea. Now she sat with her to watch her son take his seat in the halls of power. True political power. Her head had to be spinning.

"Those are his formal parliamentary robes. He won't have to wear them every day but he does today."

"They are a bit much are they not?"

"At least he doesn't have to wear a wig."

She hummed in agreement. "That is a mercy. Grown men wearing a sheep's ass on their heads, is that meant to inspire confidence?"

Regina choked back another laugh.

Naomi patted her hand and sighed. "I keep waiting for something to go wrong. For them to come and say he isn't supposed to be here."

Regina rubbed her arm again. "Mmm." That was a sentiment they could all agree on.

"You are sure everything is in order?"

"Yes. He received his writ of summons from the chancellor and that gives him the right to be here. All he needed to do was present it, take the oath and he is a member of the house of lords. There is nothing else to be done."

They were directed to stand and her Majesty, Queen Victoria entered. She was… tiny. Almost ridiculously so. Outside of that there was nothing particularly extraordinary about her appearance. There was however a singular energy around her. The speed with which she entered and took her chair. The cadence with which she spoke, pulled Regina's interest.

She couldn't say exactly what it was she expected from the figurehead of a country which was responsible for so much pain in her homeland. Perhaps she had expected a chill in the air, or a sternness. This diminutive woman was almost jolly. What did that mean? *Does it even matter?*

She turned her attention back to Leo as he glanced in her direction. When his eyes locked on hers, her heart began to race. He smiled and warmth flooded her body.

No it didn't. Whatever that woman's government had taken from Regina Leo had given back. Her name, her culture, her freedom. That was her husband. He had given her the room and the acceptance to come into her own and be more of herself than she had even been before. Her hand rested on her stomach, guarding the secret she would soon share with him. Now she would stand with him on this alien journey and ensure that he developed into the fullest version of himself. The warrior, the statesman, the father and the lord.

Et Fin.

Author's Note

In writing Leo and Regina's story there were two themes I wanted to draw on. One was the lure of the forbidden or the unknown, and the other was the challenge of committing to the unknown life and forcing it to suit you instead of the other way around. When I was deciding which opera for them to see together, *La Traviata* came to the forefront of my mind. Now while the opera is based on *'La Dame aux camélias'*, a play by Alexandre Dumas fils, which he adapted from his own 1848 novel, Verdi's opera *'La Traviata'* wasn't written until 1853 and wasn't performed in London until 1856. Four years after *Miss Mason's Secret Baron*.

I was aware of this when I included it in the book, but Violetta giving way to her feelings for Alfredo even though she knows the future there is more uncertain and could be potentially disastrous struck too close to Regina's feelings for Leo at the beginning for me to leave it out due to something so trivial as that. Both of heroines have established paths set before them that they have invested in but those pesky feelings show up and complicate everything. Violetta's story ends sadly, but our Regina gets a more successful end.

I ask you to look past this anachronism and go with the vibes.

Much love, *Addy*.